C000139731

SUPER-STATE

Brian Aldiss OBE was a fiction and science fiction writer, poet, playwright, critic, memoirist and artist. Born in Norfolk in 1925, after leaving the army Aldiss worked as a bookseller which provided the setting for his first book, *The Brightfount Diaries* (1955). His first published science fiction work, the story 'Criminal Record', appeared in *Science Fantasy* in 1954. Passing away in 2017, over the course of his life Aldiss wrote nearly 100 books and over 300 short stories – becoming one of the pre-eminent science fiction writers of the 20th and 21st centuries.

Also by Brian Aldiss and published by HarperCollins

BRIAN ALDISS

SUPER-STATE

HARPER
Voyager

Harper*Voyager*
An imprint of HarperCollins*Publishers* Ltd
1 London Bridge Street
London SE1 9GF

www.harpercollins.co.uk

HarperCollins*Publishers*
1st Floor, Watermarque Building, Ringsend Road
Dublin 4, Ireland

First published in Great Britain in 2002 by Orbit

This paperback edition published by HarperCollins*Publishers* 2021

1

A catalogue record for this book is available from the British Library

ISBN: 978-0-00-748252-8

Typeset in Sabon Lt Std by Palimpsest Book Production Ltd,
Falkirk, Stirlingshire

Printed and bound in the UK by CPI Group (UK) Ltd, Croydon CR0 4YY

MIX
Paper from
responsible sources
FSC **FSC* C007454**
www.fsc.org

Note on the text

The text of this edition was generated by scanning an earlier print copy of the story its first edition. The story is a product of its period and may contain themes or viewpoints now considered outdated.

Some Non-Submersible Units
(we hope)
for
the ghost of
STANLEY KUBRICK
and
the living JAN HARLAN

What a piece of work is man!
How noble in reason!
How infinite in faculty!
In form and moving how express and
admirable!
In action how like an angel!
In apprehension how like a god!
The beauty of the world!
The paragon of animals!

Hamlet

Some people make spiritual journeys:
I prefer to travel by car.
Some people find pleasure in daybreak:
I look for the evening star.
Some people like milk in their coffee:
I prefer mine *noir*.

Black clouds were gathering over the mountains to the north. Lightning flashed through them. But in the valley, on that happy day, sunlight lay like cream in a bowl.

Guests had been arriving all morning. The most popular form of conveyance was by pleasure steamer from the nearest big town. A grand temporary quay had been built for the occasion. People pouring from the steamers stepped on to the quay beneath an archway decked with flowers. A band welcomed them, playing spirited airs such as 'Some Enchanted Evening' and 'Cow-Cow Boogie'.

Less favoured among the guests arrived at the cluster of new pavilions by luxury coach, which travelled by specially constructed roads – roads which were infinitely superior to the old towpath they overlaid.

Some guests drove in by automobile. Planes brought others of the privileged, settling on the new airstrip, which was ablaze with landing and fairy lights. But the most stylish way to arrive was by one's own helicopter.

Early helicopter arrivals naturally included the party of the

President, the de Bourceys, in two helicopters. The de Bourceys were escorted immediately to the Pavilion of Perennial Peace, constructed in an Oriental style, where they retired to relax behind drapes, to be seen by no one for some hours.

The de Bourceys were followed by the Gonzales Clayman party. Emerging from their helicopter, they toured the extensive site in a stretch limo before retiring to the Rotunda of Regal Relaxation, from the windows of which they might glance discreetly at the Pavilion of Perennial Peace.

Rose Baywater arrived with her partner, dapper Jack Harrington, the art supremo, and her admirer, General Gary Fairstepps. They came in the lady novelist's waspstriped helicopter, and went immediately to their own hotelette – one of a grand line of hotelettes painted each in a separate colour – where Rose sank into a warm bath to float for an hour and think rose-coloured thoughts.

Laura Nye, aged and frail, and her friends, including the famous, if speechless, Francine Squire, arrived on the steamer *Con Amore* and claimed their hotelette, where they immediately ordered champagne and aspirins.

The strapping young singer and entertainer, Olduvai Potts, arrived on a plane, to be greeted by the Master of Banquets, impeccably dressed Wayne Bargane. Olduvai was casually dressed. His large blunt face remained solemn, even when he acknowledged the plaudits of the crowd.

A little later, Olduvai was prevailed upon to sing his current hit song, 'Once a Fabulous Holiday' – to great applause. He was interviewed for the ambient by no less a person than Wolfgang Frankel, the dandyish media mogul. On this occasion, Frankel had on his shoulder a hooded goshawk. 'It's also having a fabulous holiday,' he quipped. Olduvai nodded but did not smile.

Archbishop Byron Arnold Jones-Simms flew in half an hour before the ceremony was scheduled to begin, to walk perfumed among the gathering crowds, permitting his hand to be kissed at six-metre intervals.

The Archbishop also permitted himself a few words with Wolfgang Frankel, along the lines of the world being too much with us, late and soon. So we must try to make it a better world.

And still the sun shone. And still the sky darkened over the northern hills. And still the band played on the landing stage, as did a classical quartet in the vast hospitality hall, and a pop group in the Place of Ceremonies. Fountains also played. In the cinema erected for the occasion, *Sweetness and Lifebelts*, the latest movie to be made from a Baywater novel, was playing.

The increasing throng of guests moved between these landmarks, stopping at champagne bars or seafood rotundas or little souvenir stalls or carousels on the way. The guests chattered among themselves, on the whole remaining with their own groups, sometimes calling out with artificial cries of delight to friends newly encountered. The air was full of the tinkle of voices and glasses.

One of the outstanding guests, who had stationed himself at a table by the Rotunda of Regal Relaxation, was a large, heavily built man known only by the name Gabbo. Gabbo wore a white suit, lavishly decorated with gold lapels and the starburst of the IGOEU, the International Golden Order of the European Union. Gabbo Laboratories had invented the ambient, the world's first cohesive intercommunication system.

In consequence, Gabbo was wealthy enough now to be known only by his solitary absurd sobriquet, although he had been born humble Martin Richter in a small town in Lower Saxony – wealthy enough now, as one commentator put it, 'to buy the Louvre with the *Mona Lisa* thrown in'. His amusement was to fund rather bad movies; the film *Lovesick in Lent* was collecting adverse critiques this very week. Consorting with Gabbo was Casim Durando, the director of the aforesaid *Lovesick in Lent*, of whom it had been said that he was reptilian enough to make Komodo dragons renounce the name of reptile.

Gabbo sat poised and highly polished, as if a part of his chair, his sleek dark hair gleaming, with his inseparable companion, Obbagi. Obbagi was a tall faceless robot or android, for which Gabbo used the term, when he used it at all, of randroid. Obaggi was reputedly extremely intelligent, and usually spoke for Gabbo. Just as he was speaking now with the cordial Wolfgang Frankel. Frankel was drinking champagne. Obbagi had a glass before him but did not drink.

'Weddings must be endured,' Obbagi said. His voice came from somewhere deep within him. He had no mouth to move. 'Endurance is fine. It is enjoyment which is oppressive. I fortunately do not have to pursue enjoyment.'

Wolfgang gave a rather forced laugh, and the goshawk stirred on his shoulder. For this occasion the star German media man wore a parody of an eighteenth-century satin costume, gleaming in silver. 'Enjoyment certainly helps to pass the time.'

The randroid intoned, 'I am unaware of the passage of time.'

Gabbo had not spoken until now. He made a rare interjection.

'As long as one is aware one is living on a largely criminal

4

planet, enjoyment is rather a limited occupation. Don't you agree, Obbagi?'

'One sees everywhere a pretence at enjoyment.'

'Oh, forget gloom, you two!' exclaimed Wolfgang. 'Gloom is out of fashion in our benevolent super-state. Why, I have been talking to the fiendishly clever Paulus Stromeyer, who even now, if I understand him correctly, is inventing a new form of mathematics which will produce equality for rich and poor.'

'He only invents rules. Stromeyer is like an android,' said Obbagi, austere as ever. 'I mean one of the separate species of android, the ALF21s – put on the market designedly stupid so as to flatter human egos. I find human beings contemptible, as does Gabbo.'

'I never saw a good man less like an android than Stromeyer,' said Wolfgang. He drained his champagne glass, nodded affably to Gabbo, and passed on.

'His appearance is strange,' said the faceless randroid.

'That goes for his bird too,' agreed Gabbo.

'What fun!' said Stephanie Burnell to her husband. 'How are they going to cap this event when their divorce comes through?'

Karl Lebrecht, strolling with them, replied, 'It's the nearest thing to a stately pleasure dome since Kublai Khan decreed one.'

'Just think how lovely this valley must have been before the de Bourceys spotted it,' said Roy Burnell.

'Don't be so grumpy!' said Stephanie, laughing and taking his arm. She was not really attending to him, gazing instead on the amazing gowns most of the women were wearing. Everyone was endeavouring to look their best.

Karl said, 'Seen from another perspective, this valley is only temporary. The Earth is a theatre of change, brought about not only by the shifting of continents but also by destructive strikes from chunks of rock from outer space.'

Thoughtlessly, Stephanie said, 'Let's hope one doesn't hit just now.'

With a rooted dislike of such superficial responses, Karl said, 'In the history of the Earth, there have been five great mass extinctions, all caused by strikes of meteors arriving from space. The earliest being in the Ordovician, four hundred million years ago.'

'Don't be so gloomy!' Stephanie said. 'Look at that fabulous dress. Who is that woman? I love the way the Victorian look is coming back!'

'It's the novelist, Rose Something,' said Roy. 'I think.'

They sipped champagne. Karl thought it as well to change the subject.

Said he, 'You see the big guy with the frightening android by the main hall? That's Gabbo!'

'My God, Gabbo!' Stephanie exclaimed. 'What's he doing here?'

'I understand he is funding this show, rather than de Bourcey. They say he is watching for strange behaviour. It's his hobby.'

'No use looking at us, then!'

'What do you think, Francine?' Ann Squire asked her scintillating daughter. She saw it as her role in life to persuade Francine to talk.

'Oh, quite,' said Francine Squire.

'Y'see, they've at last managed,' said General Gary Fairstepps, looking appreciatively at Rose Baywater as she stepped from her shower in their peach-coloured hotelette, 'to create in reality a world such as you create in your novels. Youth, beauty, peace, plenty . . .'

'Oh, plenty of plenty,' she said, draping round her body a huge pink towel. 'I love plenty of plenty, don't you? It's so utterly nice.'

He stroked his moustache in a mannered way. He was handsome in an ugly kind of way, kind in an ugly manner. 'Depends what it's plenty of.'

Although he fancied Rose, the silly bitch made some daft remarks at times.

'Ancestry counts for much, Rose. Plenty of ancestry – that's the thing. What's your background?'

'Oh, very ordinary, Gary. Though my grandmother on my father's side was a Temptress-of-the-Bedchamber to King Hengist of Denmark. We've gone downhill since those glory days . . .'

Fairstepps grunted. 'At least you have a hill to go down. Now my great-great-grandfather – I may have mentioned this before – he died a hero's death at the battle of Damenbinden-am-Maine in 1881. My great-grandfather wrote a history of his cavalry regiment, the Twelfth Przewalski's Horse. Breeding counts for something.'

He was going red in the face as he attempted to remove his boots, adding, 'Military elite, that's we Fairstepps. Our family motto, "I Will If You Will". Blood will out, dear.'

'Oh, I hope not,' Rose said. 'Not in that sense.'

'Bit of a thunderstorm over the hills,' said Jack Harrington, in a tone suggesting he realised his remark was irrelevant. 'Just to remind us that the weather is fine here for the privileged.'

'Don't know why they invited me,' said Fairstepps. 'Can't say I'm much of a party-goer.'

7

'But you're *important*, Gary. Not like me.'

'That's true,' admitted Fairstepps. 'These bloody boots . . .'

'I'm really quite a valley person myself,' the novelist said, as if to snub her partner further. Certainly Jack was a pallid man – but pallidly wealthy. 'Valleys were invented for me, but you, you foxy old thing—' now she was addressing Fairstepps '—you were born to conquer mountains.'

'Only in a godforsaken place like Tebarou,' the general responded, laughing as if she, or possibly he, had made a joke.

In the seafood bar, Jane Squire, who had reverted to her maiden name after her divorce, contemplated a large reproduction of a Dutch painting of prawns and lobsters which loomed over the counter. She was the centre of a cheerful group, which included a spectacularly beautiful and slender young woman at whom all men threw admiring glances when they passed by. This young woman's name was Francine Squire. Francine Squire was the daughter of Ann Squire and Kevin Krawstadt, and the new star of Gabbo Films. She was already too famous to join in the conversation at the bar. Francine merely sat there poised, an unsampled espresso before her, and scintillated.

Jane was being chatty, excited by the event. She was an elegant woman. Her usual country garments were put away and she was dressed with unaccustomed smartness for the occasion. Nowadays, she tended to put on middle-aged weight and had begun to dye her hair black; but she and her sweet temper remained highly desirable to many older men.

Her friend, Kevin Krawstadt, came under that classification. After ordering a glass of white wine, he said, joshingly,

8

'Does the painting make you feel hungry, Jane – presumably its chief aim?'

'Hungry or greedy, most likely.'

He leant towards her, to say, confidentially, 'Quite frankly, this whole wedding party is nothing but a celebration of greed.'

'Should art celebrate greed? Or sanctity? Or sorrow?'

'That's up to the individual artist.'

Ann Squire, the younger of the two Squire sisters, felt it was her turn to join the conversation. 'But fashion plays its part. Something that's unfashionable – painting, a book, music – won't succeed, will it?'

'Oh, I like anything,' Jane said carelessly. 'Doesn't matter to me whether it's fashionable or not, as long as there's a visceral appeal. So let's have some prawns, please.'

She started to look in her handbag. As she produced a univ card, Kevin Krawstadt reminded her that everything at the party was paid for.

'How shameful,' Jane exclaimed. 'I suppose we will be beholden to the de Bourceys for ever.'

'What's beholden?' asked Bettina, Jane's daughter, and was ignored. All too conscious of being outshone by her cousin Francine, Bettina was not a radiantly happy young lady. At this stage in her late adolescence, Bettina was wearing her hair with a fringe which flowed down to touch her eyebrows. The effect was, she hoped, simultaneously to attract young men and annoy her mother. In fact, a young man sitting at a nearby table was already attracted. As she was aware.

'I'm already beholden,' said Ann Squire.

Laura Nye laughed. 'One way to the top is to have a good bottom.' The family knew that it was Francine Squire's

9

affair with Victor de Bourcey which had landed her a role in the award-winning, much condemned Gabbo Films movie *Lovesick in Lent*.

Laura was old and rickety, plagued by arthritis. Nevertheless she sat upright on her stool, conscious of her role as *grande dame*.

'Well, here's to the party!' said Kevin, lifting his champagne glass.

'Is it true that the Queen of Sweden has been invited?' asked Francine. It was, for her, a long sentence.

'Surely Sweden hasn't still got a queen!' exclaimed Laura. 'What an anachronism! Not that I'm not another anachronism . . .'

Time for one more cameo before the bells begin to ring.

Also in the seafood bar, helping themselves to delicious oysters flown in from Australia, sat a learned cluster of people, among them Paulus Stromeyer, the mathematician and philosopher, Amygdella Haze, the amaroli lady, her teenage son Bertie, her lover, the blank-looking Randolph Haven, shortly to make a disastrous decision, and Dr Barnard Cleeping of the Institute of Philosophy, Utrecht.

Dominating this group was Paulus Stromeyer, a thickset man in his early fifties. Fluffy dark hair surrounded a monk's tonsure of baldness. His large, rather heavy face was lightened by the brightness of his gaze. Talk about the storm over the mountains had led to Stromeyer's mention of Faraday's discovery of electromagnetic induction. Stromeyer thought there was still some of what he called 'hidden math' to be squeezed out of the relationship between magnetism and electricity.

Rather idly, Randolph Haven had suggested that some days of the week contained more electricity than others.

Now they were discussing – all except young Bertie Haze, who was gazing yearningly in the direction of Bettina Squire at the nearby table – whether some days were more propitious for weddings than others.

'Today is Tuesday, the thirtieth of June,' said Cleeping. 'Hands up all those who can tell me what event took place on a certain thirtieth of June many years ago?' Cleeping was a smooth man, clean-shaven, short of hair, long on benevolence.

Paulus Stromeyer ventured a guess. 'Frederick the Great born?'

Amygdella Haze: 'Diet of Worms?'

Randolph Haven: 'The machine gun invented?'

Cleeping shook his head. '1908. The Tunguska event. Remember? A forest area in Siberia flattened by cometary impact. Had it arrived just five hours later, it would have struck St Petersburg and wiped the city out. Various objects are always swanning in from space and striking Earth. Calculations show that one is due about now.'

'Another reason why Alexy is on his way to Europa,' said Paulus, glancing at his watch. He was thinking of his son, several million kilometres from Earth.

At that juncture, a recording of silvery bells rang out. Guests stopped eating or hurriedly grabbed another glass of champagne.

Another silvery sound followed – the voice of the Mistress of Ceremonies, Barbara Barbicandy, acknowledged to be the world's best organiser of important events. She warmly welcomed all guests to this great occasion, and asked them if they would now assemble in the Place of Ceremonies. And she hoped that the weather would hold on this loveliest of all occasions.

As if to reinforce her wish, a peal of thunder rumbled into the broad valley from the hills to the north. Above those hills, fork lightning flashed.

The crowds politely jostled their way to the Place of Ceremonies, where solemn music played. No pop groups now, only a choir of six ladies, draped from neck to foot in white gowns, in tribute to a recollected virginity.

While the ladies, standing, sang 'Morning has broken, like the first morning', the guests seated themselves in comfortable chairs, the wealthier ones being escorted every inch of the way. Gabbo and Obbagi had thrones to themselves, apart from the crowd.

When all were well settled, and something resembling silence had fallen, ruched curtains drew apart at the front of the hall. This revealed a flower-bedecked altar, before which stood Archbishop Byron Arnold Jones-Simms, clad in scarlet robes, looking as humble as could a man who so greatly enjoyed the limelight.

He stepped forward now, saying in his deep, seductive, sedative voice, 'My dear brethen, we are here assembled to bear witness to the marriage of two of our dearest citizens, Victor de Bourcey, son of the President of the European Union, and Esme Brackentoth, Queen of the Restaurant Profession.'

As he spoke, the aforesaid Victor entered the hall, proceeding to the altar with his presidential father just behind him. At the sight of de Bourcey Senior, some in the congregation rose in respect. This caused uncertainty in the ranks. Gradually more people also rose in imitation. Finally, everyone, sheeplike, rose to their feet, with the exception of Gabbo and Obbagi. After a pause, the reverse procedure was followed, until the entire congregation was reseated.

The Archbishop spoke again. 'As many of you will know, our bride has been engaged in supervising the opening of her new restaurant, the first restaurant to be built on the peak of Mount Everest. Weather conditions have deteriorated markedly – markedly – in the last twenty-four hours, with the result that our dear Esme has been forced to remain on Everest until conditions improve. However, she has been able to provide a standby – an understudy, shall we say? – to take her place in the ceremony, which it was impossible to postpone, and our heroic bridegroom has graciously consented to her – or, rather, it – as *in propria persona*.'

As he was speaking, the electronic organ was going softly through the paces of Wagner's Wedding March, and a veiled and befrocked personage ('Train twenty metres long,' whispered knowledgeable ladies in the congregation to their menfolk) was bearing steadily down the aisle. She was followed by two young human bridesmaids, both blushing at the exposure to so many gazes.

She came to a halt precisely beside the willowy and elegant figure of Victor.

The bride substitute was not human. She had emerged from the Renault-Bourcey factory, which specialised in manufacturing androids. A plastic face much resembling that of the stranded Esme Brackentoth had been attached to her head, while a digitised version of Esme's voice issued from her plastic mouth.

13

'As one can see, of the ALF21 vintage,' commented Obbagi quietly to Gabbo.

Victor de Bourcey took the android's arm and the ceremony proceeded.

'It's a form of auto-incest,' whispered Paulus Stromeyer to his neighbour, Barnard Cleeping. 'Since she was made on his production line . . .'

Intoned the Archbishop, 'As we are all aware, a war between ignorance and wisdom has been declared, and eternally the war between good and evil continues. The good have their backs to the wall, and are forever in danger of losing the war, but this ceremony represents a battle won . . .'

He then gravely bent his attention to the happy couple, his ancient black face creased in earnest enquiry.

'I do,' said the android distinctly, and at the appropriate time.

The Archbishop proclaimed in an uncanny voice, raising his arms above his head, 'Forasmuch as Victor and Esme's stand-in have been joined together in holy wedlock before all the congregation as witnesses, I now proclaim them man and substitute, in the name of the Father, the Son and the Holy Ghost. God bless you all, and may the Lord look mercifully upon you. Amen.'

Enthusiastic clapping broke out.

'Hope he enjoys the honeymoon,' said Barnard Cleeping.

'He'll need a tin-opener,' chuckled Paulus Stromeyer.

With some relief, the congregation rose and emerged into the open air. The sun still shone, although now with a leaden quality. Over the northern hills, the thunder clouds still prevailed, lightning still sizzled. Little the two thousand guests cared; for the women, a more important matter was to control their hats in the slight breeze; while for the men, one of the concerns was to see under those hats to those well-made-up faces. Bertie Haze had pushed through the crowd and was now talking to Bettina Squire; Bettina was considering that she might like him, despite his rather spotty chin; Bertie was thinking he realised she was a bit on the heavy side, but was nevertheless passable. He knew that her cousin, Francine, was beyond his target area. While they spoke about the worldwide success of the new Norwegian pop group Strand, many calculations, hardly monitored by consciousness, were working rapidly in their minds towards strategies of either advance or retreat.

Later, when the dancing started, when Bertie seized both his opportunity and Bettina, the complexities would be resolved, or made further complex.

Such potential pairings were in operation elsewhere. Even among the elders – de Bourcey *père*, let's say, condescending to chat with Rose Baywater, who was being bright – computation regarding what might be loosely regarded as sexual, even if merely theoretically sexual, was inevitably the order of the day: perhaps more brazenly here, after the assistance of drink and the proximity of so many members of the other gender flaunting, however discreetly, their better attributes.

Many there were invisibly undressed in that happy congregation, where champagne glasses were lifted in lieu of skirts. Yet still intellectual conversation had its day, for a percentage of those present were accustomed to dealing in abstract ideas. A group of intellectual conversationalists had gathered about Paulus Stromeyer, since his son, Alexy, was one of the three-man crew of the *Roddenberry*, the space vehicle presently approaching Jupiter and its satellites.

Stromeyer was talking with the celebrated and eccentric archaeologist Daniel Potts, father of Olduvai Potts, as well as Amygdella Haze, her lover, Randolph Haven, Barnard Cleeping, and some students from the Sorbonne.

'Just supposing the *Roddenberry* does find life there . . .' one of the female students was saying. 'It will entirely change how we feel about ourselves. I mean, we shall then have to establish regular flights to Jupiter, shall we not?'

Daniel Potts, who, in his early sixties, had a countenance somewhat resembling a disappointed walnut, asked the girl, 'And what benefits do you expect to derive from these "regular flights to Jupiter"?'

Although she was taken aback by the challenge, she had a ready answer. 'If travel broadens the mind, then think how broadened it will be by a trip to Jupiter!'

'The precept is false,' said Daniel. 'Travel does not broaden anyone's mind. It merely confirms one's prejudices.'

'Perhaps this young lady is without prejudices,' Paulus said, coming to the girl's aid.

Amygdella, lowering her voice, told Randolph Haven, 'I met Daniel's daughter once. Josephine, I believe her name was. She certainly did not love her father. How Lena can bear him I do not understand.'

Daniel's hearing was sharp. 'There must be much that evades your understanding, Amy,' he said, sweetly.

'Why are you so cross, dear Daniel?' Amygdella asked, taking the older man's arm.

He gave her a straight reply, while attemping a smile. 'For one thing, I do not drink, so I am not half-tight like the rest of you. For another I see any wedding service – even one with an android as bride – as a primitive ritual. Something of the sort was probably practised in the Pliocene, and we have not managed to grow out of it yet. Once, of course, it involved the taking of the female's virginity. That hardly applies in this present case.'

'You could remove one of her batteries,' said Randolph, and laughed at his own joke.

Under these thunderous ideas, and the thunder overhead, another thunder went unheard – the thunder of hooves. It was a thunder the city dwellers were ill-equipped to recognise. But the meeting of intellects, no less than the ceremonial cutting of the immense wedding cake – a creditable replica of the Reichstag under icing sugar – was rudely broken into.

Rushing down from the northern mountains came a veritable stampede. A hundred or more mustangs burst into the grounds of the festivities. These were wild horses, living in a reserve in the high country, shaggy beasts in various shades of brown. Hardy creatures, living in the harsh scrub and maquis of those altitudes – living social and harmless lives, but now galvanised by the electricity in the air.

Its vibrations had entered their skulls. Suddenly heads came up. The lead stallions neighed, hooves kicked the dust. They began to move. Thunder roared. A low-growing tree burst into flame after a lightning strike. The trot became a gallop. It was as if their batteries had become too highly charged.

At full tilt, the herd surged down the slopes of the mountains into the valley, crossed the shallow river, gained the far side. Snorting, they charged ever onwards, mindless as an avalanche. Straight into the enchanted crowd of party-goers.

Screams, cries! Mustangs rearing, people falling as they fled.

Olduvai Potts had ascended a platform and had begun to sing. His accompanists dropped their instruments and fled. Wayne Bargane, Master of Ceremonies, was standing by the platform. He did not run away.

The horses began to surround the platform. Olduvai ran and jumped on to the back of the lead stallion. Following his example without hesitation, Wayne rushed foward to grasp the mustang by its mane. It reared but was brought to a standstill. Hanging on ferociously, Olduvai kicked its flanks. Assisted by Wayne, they turned the beast about.

Other men also ran forward. Amygdella Haze was a good horsewoman. She jumped on to a lead mare and calmed it. The rest of the horses became confused. They milled about uncertainly.

Wayne's son Cassidy came running from the administration building with a box and a lighted fusee. Dropping the box he pulled from it two of the sky-busting rockets intended to form a part of the firework display later. He lit them.

With a splutter and a whistle, the rockets sailed upwards. Metres above the crowd, they burst into a myriad stars, banging and shrieking as they went. The equine tide turned. In disorderly fashion, the mustangs began to gallop away, back towards the mountains they had left so precipitately.

Ambulance men moved among the guests, rescuing those who had fallen, calming them, escorting the injured to their casualty tent. Wayne climbed back on to the platform to reassure everyone that no harm had been done and that the merriment would continue. He thanked Olduvai Potts for his bravery. Olduvai climbed up and took a bow. The guests applauded.

'All that excitement was not prearranged – let me tell you that!' he announced.

The guests loved it.

'You have a brave son,' Barnard Cleeping told Daniel Potts.

'Oh, he's pretty brave,' said Potts *père*. 'At this moment I feel almost sorry I disowned him.'

Report from the *Roddenberry*, six million kilometres from Earth:

'Hi, this is Alexy Stromeyer calling from the *Roddenberry*. We have a problem with the starboard solar wing. Rick O'Brien has been out there, trying to locate the cause. It's tricky just now. We appear to be travelling through a small grit shower. Rick had to get back under cover before he had fixed the rotator drive, in case his suit was punctured. We'll try again in another watch. Food getting very low – some provisions have degraded in refrigeration. Tempers a bit frazzled. We are going to try to grab some sleep now. 'Bye, Earth. Out.'

Fergus O'Brien walked slowly across the campus to his old Chevvy. A student saluted him as he went. Fergus kept his head down, ignoring the youth, pretending the sun was in his eyes.

He drove slowly the few hundred metres to the university apartment block where he occupied part of the ground floor. Letting himself into the apartment, he found his son Pat playing a ferocious game on the computer.

'No prep this evening, son?'

'Wait! Wait! Don't breathe! This time I've really got—'

Pat was a fat little boy, most of his bulk submerged beneath a large red sweater. He let the sentence hang as he blasted the green monster on his screen.

Sighing, Fergus went into the kitchenette and grabbed a Bud from the cooler.

After another burst of blaster fire, the eight-year-old shouted, 'Hey, Dad, they didn't make you Head of Department after all. So I'd guess from your atmosphere of woe.' He laughed to think of it.

Fergus leant his scraggy figure at the threshold of the room. 'If you want to know, I was passed over, damn it. They gave the job to that lousy Marlene Nowotny.'

'Ah, she's a bitch. She'll never last!'

'I commend your loyalty, son.'

'Wanna go out to eat? The TV says that Uncle Rick is getting near to Jupiter. He was outside doing a space walk today. I wish I was there with him. Jeez. Do those three guys carry guns, Dad? Just in case maybe they bump into alien life forms?'

'I don't believe they do.'

'Not even a single shooter? What if some horrible green thing comes zooming out of Jupiter at them?'

Fergus laughed. 'Maybe they would try making friends with it.'

'Jeez, I wouldn't try that. No way. I'd shoot it dead.'

Fergus retreated into the cellar room. He sat at his computer without switching on. Sipping at the Bud, he reflected bitterly on his life as a failure. Marlene Nowotny was his junior. Okay, so she had published some papers. Admittedly they had been well received. And of course she did sports. Why didn't he do sports? Why was her hair shorter than his?

Then there was Brother Rick. His younger brother. Always

obsessed by sports, even as a small kid. Baseball and space, his two interests. Now he was going to be one of the first men ever to land on – which satellite of Jupiter were they heading for? Okay, so he hadn't forgotten. Why kid himself? *Europa*. So that Rick O'Brien's name would go down in history, revered for ever in America and Ireland. Whereas the name of Fergus O'Brien . . .

He sighed heavily. What he needed was a big project. Like BIG.

He switched on the computer. The three seconds it took to boot up always seemed like an age.

Twenty-two e-mails awaited him. They would all be from students, asking their endless fatuous questions . . . 'Could you tell me what explorer discovered the Humboldt Current?' 'In England, what is the name of the guy at the top of the Nelson Monument in London?'

After the wedding celebrations, Jane and Bettina Squire flew back to Hartisham-on-Sea. Jane's sister Ann flew with Kevin Krawstadt and other friends to her house in the south of France. Laura Nye went with them to her little bungalow near Antibes. Francine Squire retreated loftily to her apartment in Paris.

Their chauffeur met Jane and her daughter at Norwich airport and drove them to the old Squire mansion, Pippet Hall. Her partner, Remy Gautiner, was sitting at a canvas, painting a part of the shrubbery. He set aside his palette and came to kiss Jane. The wind took his long dark hair.

Jane was jaded after all the excitement.

'I must get out of this dress, Remy.'

He regarded her figure approvingly.

'You're half out of it already.'

21

She laughed. 'It is a bit low-cut, that's true.'

He kissed Bettina.

'How was the wedding?'

'They had horses in it,' Bettina told him, as they entered the house. 'It was mega-cool.'

In her bedroom, Jane kicked off her shoes, slipped out of her clothes, showered, put on a cerulean dressing gown, and went to see her father.

Sir Thomas Squire was sitting in a wicker chair in the conservatory, a rug over his knees. The peel of an orange lay on a plate at a side table nearby. He was more or less watching the big ambient wall screen, on which a soap opera was playing. His nurse sat a discreet distance away. Nurse Gibbs had set little aromatic candles burning here and there, so that the room was filled with the scent of rosemary.

'There's rosemary, that's for remembrance,' Jane murmured, half aloud. At fifty years of age, she found herself increasingly burdened by remembrances. The grand old house was stocked with them. As it was with shadows, debt, dry rot, damp and empty fireplaces. She loved it intensely, and thought of it as the old galleon in which her life sailed.

'I am well enough, thank you,' said Sir Tom, responding to his daughter's enquiry. 'Just a little tired. I was watching a cormorant, I think it was, sitting on the sea wall.'

Jane looked with compassion at his lined face, blotched with liver marks. She stooped in front of him.

'You've been all right while I was away?'

'Of course, my dear. Nurse Gibbs has looked after me. I've been watching the ambo quite a lot. It seems as if our super-state is determined to go to war with Tebarou. The President has much to say about it. I never trusted that man. It must be mistaken policy, just when the world seemed to be settling at last for peace. Surely we are too prosperous to go to war. What can we gain from it?'

'Experience? Prowess?'

'Misery? Death? Civic unrest?'

'Perhaps it won't happen, Father. Don't worry about it.'

'Someone's got to worry about it. Not that my worrying will do any good. It's madness . . .' He fell silent, starting up suddenly to speak again. 'Remind me of the name of that general who came here once when you were quite small. Made a pass at your mother, I seem to remember.'

Jane thought. 'Oh, you mean General Fairstepps? Funny name. He was at the de Bourcey wedding. I caught sight of him once.'

'Yes, of course. Fairstepps. Funny name. Gary Fairstepps. Well, he's in charge of the Rapid Reaction Force. They were saying on the *Today* programme that he is to fly out to Tebarou with his force.'

Tom's shaky voice carried further information and complaint about the folly of war. Jane half listened, staring out at the new sea wall and the grey-blue of the waters beyond. In her childhood, Hartisham had remained a quiet little Norfolk village, three miles inland from the North Sea. But what her father liked to call 'global storming' had caused the sea to burst over the Stiffkey Freshes, to overwhelm the marshes and Stiffkey itself, and its little river, and to sweep inland.

Sir Thomas Squire, combining with other landowners, had had a sea wall built, stretching from Binham to the east to Walsingham in the west. The waves were held back, at least for the time being. Now as Jane gazed, the sea was calm, and a dinghy sailed where Stiffkey Valley had been, where Stiffkey cattle had grazed. At low tide, the tower of Warham St Mary church could still be seen above the flood.

'I'll be getting Sir Tom his tea now,' Nurse Gibbs said, quietly. She took charge of the plate with the orange peel on it.

It seemed that Sir Tom had fallen asleep. Jane followed the nurse from the room.

'I shall give him his next injection in twenty-five minutes,' the nurse said confidentially, as she headed for the kitchen area. 'Don't worry about him, Jane. His condition at present is stable.'

Never before had Jane loved Pippet Hall as much as she did now, knowing it to be threatened by the elements. At least her father would not live to see the day when the swollen sea overwhelmed it. The Hall was situated on a small eminence. When it went, the nearby church of St Swithin's, and its cemetery in which her mother, Teresa Squire, lay buried, would be swept away – and with them something valuable of English history.

She called to her daughter and Remy that it was teatime.

It was night when Paulus Stromeyer arrived by plane at Toulouse Air Base, straight from the wedding ceremony. There was in the super-state what commentators on the ambient described as 'war fever'. This Paulus had publicly denied, saying that phrases such as 'war fever' were in themselves inflammatory. He had been contradicted by Air Chief Marshal Pedro Souto on a popular ambient channel. It happened that Stromeyer and Souto had been at university together. And so it was that Stromeyer had gained permission to meet Souto, face to face.

A buggy arrived promptly as his plane taxied to a parking

slot. Two uniformed men stood respectfully by as Paulus stepped briskly from one vehicle to the other. The buggy, headlights blazing, moved slowly to a distant part of the base. Uniformed men with slung carbines were everywhere.

Paulus stared from his window. Outlines shining in the dark, ranks of the new supersonic SS20 fighter-bombers with VTO facilities stood on damp tarmac, hard to discern clearly against a blaze of lights in the background. Their long noses, their svelte shapes, suggested the evolved grace of predatory animals – some kind of new animal – crouching, waiting to go for the kill.

Despite himself, Paulus felt a thrill of excitement. To be in one of those superb machines, screaming through the stratosphere across the globe . . .

'Now . . .' he told himself, 'really, you are not a schoolboy any more, in love with hardware.'

The buggy drew up before a large building. Sentries stood at its portals. Stromeyer was identified at the door and allowed to pass, still escorted, into the air-conditioned interior. Here brilliant lighting was the order of the day. Stromeyer was taken to a cubicle and searched for weapons.

'Just routine, sir,' said the searcher.

'I have never in my life carried a gun.'

'It's just routine, sir.'

He was shown to a desk where a retina print was taken and he submitted to having an identity tag pinned on him.

Still escorted, he ascended by elevator to the third floor. More checks before they were permitted to quit the elevator. Here an armed guard took over from the escort. His highly polished boots slammed against the highly polished floor. Down the corridor, a code was entered into a doorfone.

They entered an anteroom. A pleasant young blond woman in uniform came forward to tell Stromeyer that the Air Chief Marshal would be with him as soon as possible, and to offer him a cup of coffee.

When the coffee came, he tried to strike up a conversation with the woman, but she was not having any.

Fourteen minutes later, he was shown into the presence of the Air Chief Marshal. Souto was standing by a window, over which a metal blind had been drawn. With him were three other men and a uniformed woman.

Souto came forward and shook Stromeyer's hand. He was a big man, with a leathery face and a cold grey stare. He looked older than his forty years. Even when offering his visitor something of a smile, his hauteur remained undiminished, his manner unbending.

'We have not met since you were awarded the Nobel Prize. My belated congratulations,' he said, stiffly.

'Our career paths are somewhat divergent nowadays.'

'Very divergent. You have become a pacifist.'

Stromeyer smiled one of his gentlest smiles. 'Not quite that. I suffered a conversion some years ago, becoming persuaded, like the British philosopher Bertrand Russell, that love and tenderness alone are of real value.'

'For love and tenderness to survive, they need the protection of a strong arm. All here would agree, I think. We are ready to strike. We dedicate our lives to providing the state with a strong arm.'

Murmurs of agreement came from the company. The woman in the party said, 'You quote Russell, Dr Stromeyer. He was a supporter of unilateral disarmament. That has never been an option for us.'

Looking her in the eye, Stromeyer told her that he was

not here to ask for disarmament but for restraint. 'Are you or are you not planning to bomb Tebarou?'

Taking over the conversation, Souto said, 'I shall not discuss military tactics with you, nor bandy words. More important matters claim my attention. I am not for speeches but actions. Since you are here, Paulus, we shall give you a practical demonstration of the strategic situation as it is at present. Masters, please!'

This last command was directed at the most junior officer present. In response, Masters crossed briskly to a desk, where he activated a large ambient wall screen. As he ran his fingers over the keyboard, Souto said, in a heavy plodding voice, 'The ambient . . . so useful . . . The American bio-electronic network . . . How it holds our culture together. In some ways it is the making of our state. It has superseded personal language. But you are against technology, Paulus?'

Souto's heavy skull swivelled round to glance at a CCTV monitor showing his fighter-bombers waiting on the tarmac outside.

'Our state was not made by technology but by the dispensations of nature,' Paulus told him. 'It's easy to forget that, when you look at your gleaming warplanes outside. Our climates, our soils, have much to do with Europe's favoured place among nations.

'And have you ever considered that we probably owe our civilisation to grass? You no doubt recall the old carol we sing at Christmas – "While Shepherds Watched their Flocks by Night"? There would never have been any flocks were it not for the curious botanical fact that grass grows from its roots, not from its tips, as do most plants. So when sheep graze the grass, the grass continues to grow. No grass would mean no sheep, no herbivores, no wool, no clothes . . . No, in fact, progress.

'We owe most of the things we are to the grass under our feet. Doesn't that thought induce humility? Of course, you have nothing but tarmac here at the base.'

A slight flush registered on Souto's stern countenance.

'I will not be lectured, not even on botanical matters, not even by a Nobel Prize-winner. As I always suspected, Nobel Prize-winners are fatally naïve. What has *grass*, of all things, to do with today? You're a man whose son is well on his way to Jupiter, and yet you despise technology! Just attend to this picture Masters has brought up.'

The wall screen showed Europe photographed from a satellite. It was a live picture. Cloud cover parting, Europe was disclosed as a prone and emaciated figure, with the Alps as backbone and the Iberian peninsula as a head. The Greek Peloponnese served as a spatulate and bony foot. The glistening Mediterranean Sea showed up as the couch on which this strange creature was resting.

Captain Masters came forward with an electronic pointer. He indicated the southern shores of what he called Fortress Europe, from the Straits of Gibraltar in the west to the Aegean with its scatter of islands in the east. Speaking in a dry voice, he said that this entire region had to be continuously patrolled by ship and plane. It was under constant surveillance by satellite.

'The deterioration of climate in Africa has meant a mass invasion – or attempted invasion – of our shores by the luckless and unskilled. We cannot afford to house a million refugees per year. They attempt to cross the Med by various unseaworthy boats. We have to deter them.'

'By sinking their craft?' enquired Stromeyer.

'How we do it remains restricted information. It is certainly a very costly operation. Millions of univs every year.'

Souto added, 'These invasive peoples are enemies of our stability. It is beside the point that most are black, most are Muslim. There is a cultural difference between our cultures which cannot be bridged. Already many of our cities have foreign quarters where our own people fear to go. These quarters and their denizens are multiplying. Dissidence festers there. In our own interests we must draw a line.'

He nodded at Masters and the satellite view disappeared.

Stromeyer replied, 'I came to talk to you about a possible war with Tebarou, Pedro, and to ask you to be pacific. Tebarou is a long way from our borders. What about the Med? Why this threat of war?'

'I am talking about that serious eventuality right now, Paulus. We are not idle. I was in conference with the President two days ago, before his son's wedding, together with other high-ups of the armed forces. The new president of Tebarou, Morbius el Fashid, is no friend of ours. He has formed a loose alliance with the African states. Two weeks back, we sank a tramp steamer off the heel of Italy. That steamer was carrying approximately four thousand illegal immigrants, all heading for the EU.

'There was retaliation from Tebarou. I want you to understand that we will not, cannot, permit such intrusions on our territory.'

Paulus asked to be told about the nature of the West's retaliation.

'Air strike,' was the crisp answer. 'SS20s.'

A call came through on Souto's mofo. When he turned away to answer it, another of the senior officers present addressed Paulus.

'Sir, we have been under missile attack from Tebarou. No doubt you have seen reports of the outrage. The first missile they fired struck a town called Siebersdorf, near Graz in Austria. That missile had a nuclear warhead. The destruction and loss of life is extremely serious and requires to be answered.'

'But Tebarou apologised. El Fashid has said the missile was launched by mistake.' His remark was swept away.

'Two further missiles have hit our territories, fortunately in open country. One on a hillside south of Ravensberg, the other in a forest near Vesoul, in France. You must have seen about them on the ambient.'

'The suggestion being that this was a kind of range-finding exercise, each time the missiles landing farther from home. Some claim these were meteorites, not missiles. Is this sufficient provocation for a declaration of war? War always brings out the bad in people.'

One of the officers gave a snort of contempt at this last remark. He said that war was a question of power politics; morality did not enter into it.

'Then morality should do so,' said Paulus. 'Tebarou is a small country. We are a super-state. We should not attack poor Asian countries. You may recall history and the American offensive against Vietnam.'

Souto came off the phone in time to catch Paulus's remark. 'Tebarou may be small. China is large – another super-state.'

He said grimly that Western suspicions had been confirmed. Investigation of the shattered non-nuclear enemy weapon cases indicated that the Tebarou missiles were of Chinese manufacture.

His fellow officers looked not displeased by this revelation.

He added that Tebarou was a newly established state, barely fifteen years old, set up in reluctant accord with China by Chinese Muslims. The new president, Morbius el Fashid, was himself part-Chinese.

Whether the missile strikes had Chinese backing remained debatable. The important thing was to stop the nonsense immediately, show them what was what before worse followed.

He, Air Chief Marshal Souto, believed that it was not necessary to declare war. Ground troops were not needed.

What was required was to get their SS20s aloft immediately. With their immense range, they could take out one or two Tebarese cities as a warning. Ninyang and Puanyo for a start. Both industrial cities.

'Which will escalate hostilities,' said Paulus.

Souto gave a dry laugh. 'We have no option. To my mind, these missile attacks constitute a declaration of war – but I'm only a simple air force type. As you must know, Paulus, diplomats are talking, not only in Brussels but in the Tebarou capital. I'm afraid that, like you, talk is getting them nowhere. Nowhere. Our duty is to act, not talk.'

He gave a curt nod, turned on his heel, and marched from the room.

The other officials looked uncomfortable.

'Thank you very much for coming, Dr Stromeyer,' said the uniformed woman, politely. 'Captain Masters will show you out.'

No one had heard of a group calling themselves 'The Insanatics'. Their first message burst in upon a myriad ambients, interrupting the colourful commercials. It was non-pictorial, the text being printed on the screen, with a speaking voice-over.

'Assonance! Rogerr Laboratories present their New Pile Cure. Selling at your local pharmacy right now. Turn to Assonance! Kiss Your Haemorrhoids Goodbye!'

<INSANATICS: Prologue. We shop in places where everything – especially cheap goods – costs too much. At least we live in a free world – we are free to pretend we are happy. It is the mouth that talks; the brain ignores the mouth. The flushing of a myriad toilets sings of the essential nature of mankind. The squeal of a chair moved on a polished floor protests against the sedentary being it carries. Only the rich have the opportunity to waste their lives on cruise ships. All men feel isolated: they are not alone in that.

When the sun is high we tend to lose our minds; when the moon is high, ditto. A woman's singing reminds us there are better worlds – but not here. If only wisdom were sparkling mineral water, we might drink at the diet of life. We are sensible because we are alive; similarly, rivers are not wet. Instinct permits the handling of our affairs, but is it a hand or a glove?

We have everything precious to lose by going to war against a predominantly Muslim country in the East. If war is declared, it is proof once more that mankind is mad.

This concludes our first message on this subject. Watch out for more.>

The second message from the new group was transmitted the next day, again in the middle of commercials.

'Pining for the days of cod? We have a GM groper that tastes Just Like The Real Thing. Enjoy it only at Exotika Eateria on 28th Street.'

<INSANATICS: The perceptual existences in which we live, our *umwelts*, have been created by psychoses of lengthy ancestry. One symptom of that ancestry was human sacrifice. That ancestral psychosis rules our behaviour still. A predominant aspect of the psychosis is that we cannot recognise or acknowledge it.

Yet we have constant reminders of the primitive being in us. Think of the paintings of Christ nailed to the cross. Such paintings fill our art galleries. Think of the number of people who need some kind of mental therapy. Think of the innumerable cases of psychosomatic illnesses or suicides among the young.

Although we like to believe that society is a cause of our internal woes, it is our internal woes that have created our societies. As panacea, we cling to antique systems which are manifestly mistaken – superstition, wizardry, astrology, incantation, drugs.

We pervert our technology to manufacture barbarous weapons. Even if and when unused, the weapons poison our existence. They must be paid for in more than money.

In attempts to govern our lives, we look to the past, perhaps to what our parents did or failed to do, instead of looking forward to see what consequences our actions might have upon the future.

Our growing understanding of the workings of the brain reveals its faulty construction. There is no way in which we can ever become humanely rational. No way in which we can become content. No way in which we can escape our ruinous inheritance.

On the contrary, the processes of insanity are on the increase. More and more of our populations move into overcrowded cities, away from nature. They thereby starve themselves of the intimations of nature, weather and the seasons. They must rely instead on fleeting relationships, mainly sexual, mainly conducted in closed rooms, with other exiles as gravely alienated as themselves. The Space Age has become the Chamber Age. Imagination and romance prevail in a mental prison that prevents reality from entering. We ourselves have built that prison. This is why we cannot escape from it.

We see war as an escape. It merely extends the prison walls.>

The apartment in Frankfurt was comfortable, even luxurious. The rear windows of its bedrooms looked out over a pleasant square, where, at this relaxed time of day, couples strolled among the trees and formal flower beds. No cars or Slo-Mos were permitted during the hours of daylight on the streets surrounding the square. The constant drone of traffic on the main arteries of the city seemed merely to emphasise the peace of Friesengasse Square.

Amygdella Haze came slowly from the Friesengasse Brasserie, where she had been enjoying an amaretto ice cream with a woman friend, the famous Yakaphrenia Lady. She stood for a moment, gazing at a bird she could not identify among the acacia trees. The acacias had almost ceased flowering. Their pleasant scents would no longer filter in through her open windows – or at least, not for another season . . .

She walked to the entrance of her apartment block, decorated with the marzipan effect of the late nineteenth century, keyed in her code, 0909, entered, and took the elevator to the second floor.

Once in her apartment, she looked about complacently at the paintings which covered the walls.

Her housekeeper immediately appeared. Amygdella gave her a smile and asked for coffee. She let her gauzy scarf float to the floor, before going to the bedroom to attend to her face in a mirror. She applied a pale pink lipstick to her lips. On the wall nearby were two little framed Tiepolo etchings from his *Capricci* in first-state proof. They got a glance of approval from her.

She put a couple of ropes of bead necklaces about her neck, and went over to her ambient, rigged with fresh flowers to resemble a shrine. She switched on, and was soon in communication with her friendly guru in Allahabad.

In his delightful variant of the German language, Ben Krishnamurti pushed his whiskery face close to the screen and announced to Amygdella that Spite was dead. All spite had died that morning in his breast. He had risen and had done his holy exercises. He was taking a shower and chanting when the light dawned upon him. He was taken up by the light and the water was all about him.

Then he recognised that the water was really the world's spite. He had drunk it down and returned to Earth. Yet he remained elevated because he had overcome a great ill – with the help of the gods. It was an immense happiness to him and to all men. And also to all women, of course.

Exclaiming that it all sounded so beautiful, Amygdella asked if this meant there would be no war.

'No, the war will have to come, Lady Amy, but spite is a different thing. You must see these matters as separate.'

Versed though she was in mysticism, she remained slightly puzzled.

Krishnamurti explained to her that spite was merely a human trait, attacking people one by one, and so devouring them and all they loved. Whereas war came from the gods, both to enliven and destroy, and had to be endured. What he called 'the political business' meant nothing: it was merely exercised by puny men.

'Thank you for your explanation, Beniji. I shall benefit from it.'

She switched off and sat in contemplative thought. There was a difficulty: her current lover, Randolph Haven, was a minor politician, and currently of the war party.

But she remained in an elevated frame of mind. She could always give up Randolph. She could not give up the Wisdom of the East.

She was still in her elevated state when the exterior doorfone buzzed. Before she could float over to answer it, it buzzed again. She knew it was her son Bertie. When she heard the elevator, she went to the apartment door and opened it. She flung her arms round Bertie's neck. Having kissed his mother on both cheeks, he threw himself on her sofa, where he promptly lit a marihale. Without being asked, Amygdella went to the drinks bar and poured two glasses of white wine.

As she handed him one of the glasses, she asked him how university was going.

Without answering the question, Bertie said, 'Ma, I need to go to England to inspect an archaeological site.'

'Site or spite? No more spite in the world, Bertie, my dear.'

She executed a twirl, allowing her full skirts to flare out.

'What are you *on*, Ma? I need some cash. I must go to England to inspect this archaeological thing-me-bob.'

'What a horrid phrase that is. "Thing-me-bob". Where did you get it from? Where did you contract it?' She laughed. 'You youngsters!'

Bertie regarded his mother; it was a kindly inspection, although not entirely unmixed with exasperation. Amygdella was forty-two, quite petite, adding to her stature with a massive fuzz of shining brown hair, into which little fake pearls had been woven. She was beautiful, no doubt of that, with her large violet eyes, pretty little mouth and demure chin. And her manner – whether natural or cultivated – was always slightly frivolous in a way that attracted men. That was the problem, of course: that was what had eventually caused Harry Haze to give up and disappear into the East, always to his son's regret.

Catching sight of Ben Krishnamurti's photograph by the ambient, he said, 'You're not still talking to that old fraud in Allahabad, Ma?'

'You never understood faith. Come to that, you've never been to Allahabad, my dear.'

'Religion and science are not easy bedfellows.' He reverted to lecturing mode. 'Science requires proof. Religion runs against proof. Why people in this century have not become more scientific I will never understand. I suppose you are still practising amaroli, aren't you? Your Beniji taught you that repulsive little trick, didn't he?'

Amaroli was one of the features of her life which had made Amygdella famous.

'Ah, but that's not faith, darling. That's science. Urine contains the hormone melatonin. What else do you think keeps me looking so young?'

'Ugh! I prefer amaretto.'

'Now, Bertie dear, don't tease me. That's not the way to coax money out of your poor mother. Surely you know that by now?'

'Sorry, Ma, I didn't mean to tease. I just worry that you

37

are going dotty. I really do need that dough . . . They're digging at Castle Acre, Ma. It's terribly important.'

'Is that anywhere near where this young lady, Bettina, whom you fancy, lives? With whom you danced at the wedding?'

'As it happens, it's not too far away. Please, Ma.'

'Oh, young love . . . Have you been in touch with her since then?'

Bertie pulled a face. 'Maybe.'

Smiling, she changed the subject. 'What about your card?'

'It's run out.'

'Do the English have univs yet, I wonder?'

'Three hundred would do nicely, Ma.'

She sighed the sigh of martyrdom. 'Just don't tell Randy.' She went to fetch her purse.

Purses in the Bargane household were less well filled than Amygdella's. Wayne Bargane, Master of Banquets at the Victor–Esme wedding celebrations, carefully returned his hired ceremonial clothes and resumed his artisan gear. He received the fee for his work before being driven to the airport. His was a long flight home.

The Bargane family had accepted a subsidy offered by the Department of Social Economics of the EU government, and removed themselves to the eastern lands. They had been settled on a run-down farm in Romania, on the fringes of a town with the not particularly promising name of Slobozia.

The unspoken hope was that something of Western culture might rub off on ruder relations in the Black Sea region, the very margin of the super-state.

Wayne's old car was awaiting him in the car park of Bucharest airport. He drove slowly back to the new home in Slobozia. Sunlight flickered through the long avenues of poplars lining the dusty road that ran by the River Ialometa. Wayne was a professional, used to travelling all round the super-state in pursuit of his job. Yet the contrasts between the wealthy West and the impoverished East could not be ignored. He saw more bullock carts than cars on his route.

When he reached the Bargane vineyards, Wayne stopped the car and got out. The day was intolerably hot. Global warming was afflicting everything. He shielded his eyes to scan the fields. In the distance, his old mother, Marie Bargane, was supervising the android who did most of the work. He was currently hosing the rows of vines. Marie never trusted the mechanical. Wayne could not help smiling.

His mother saw him, waved, and came slowly towards him, trudging between the rows. She wore an old-fashioned sun-bonnet. He thought, not without affection, that she might have belonged to any of the previous centuries. From being an impoverished townie in Toulouse, she had become an impoverished peasant in Slobozia. Wayne earned more for superintending one wedding ceremony than the farm could make in a year.

Marie climbed into the car and mopped her face with a handkerchief. 'Alfie takes such a lot of looking after,' she said.

The android's manufacturing code was ALF21. Hence Alfie.

'He'd get on better if you left him alone, Mother. He's ideal for watering, surely.'

'He tends to waste water. He has no feel for viniculture, Wayne. Of course not. He doesn't drink the product.'

At the house, they went into the front room, the one room with air-conditioning. The air-conditioner, having been bought second-hand, worked with a grinding noise, interspersed with whimpers. On the drab orange walls of the room hung one incongruous painting, a reproduction of a late Morsberger, bursting with life.

Several members of the family were in the room, resting on old sofas and half watching the ambient. It was only the old mongrel, Oddball, who jumped up in greeting, to fuss round Wayne's legs. He patted the dog absent-mindedly.

Marie's crippled husband, Jean-Paul, was slumped on the black horsehair sofa as usual, face set in bitter lines. Also present were Wayne's older sister, Claudine, and her eleven-year-old daughter, Maddie (father unknown), and Wayne's two brothers, Cassidy and Jacques, playing a simple game of cards. Also, in a corner, aloof, apart, sat Wayne's uncle, David Bargane. David of the drooping moustache was always apart, almost silent, the one religious member of the family. His mere presence radiated disapproval of almost everything.

'Here comes the family star,' said Cassidy by way of welcome. He got up and began clapping Wayne slowly on the shoulder. 'Friend of our beloved President and all that. Did you ask him about our allowances, Wayne?'

Wayne smiled. 'It wasn't a political occasion.'

'He's just launched another regulation,' said Jacques, putting down his hand of cards to scratch his jaw. 'You'll never believe this one.' He assumed a pompous voice. 'The age of sexual consent has been lowered to eleven. "Children mature earlier these days." But in order to curb the growth of population, a law is being introduced making sexual intercourse where one or both partners are over the age of fifty-five a chargeable offence.'

Wayne burst out laughing. The others joined in, all except David. Oddball barked. Maddie was heard to say, 'I'm eleven. I can copulate now, can't I, Mummy?'

David said, in a low voice that ensured they would all listen, 'So this president reveals himself as being anti-Christ. He encourages sexual licence. He should be exterminated.'

'Rubbish, David,' said Wayne. 'It isn't the president who makes up these rules and regulations. They originate from democratic committees in Brussels.'

'He is the president, Wayne. You will hardly deny that. A fish stinks from the head.'

'Mummy, who can I copulate with?' asked Maddie. She jumped up and down. She was rather retarded.

'*Whom*, you mean, dear,' said Claudine.

They all roared with laughter, all except David, while Claudine stroked her child's head and advised her to be quiet.

David had a sister, almost as stern as he, dark of complexion, dark of thought, dark of hair – though the hair was now shot through with grey strands which wormed their way through the black curls like serpents through burned-out undergrowth. This was Wayne's Aunt Delphine. She disapproved of Wayne's worldly profession.

Without greeting him, she entered from the kitchen to announce that the evening meal was served.

'Thank you, Delphine, dear,' said Marie. She was scared of her grim sister. 'I will just switch Alfie off.'

She went to the door, zapper in hand. The android was working close to the house. He looked round when she called to him, head swivelling on sturdy neck.

She zapped him. He froze. Alfie would stand where he was till morning.

The Bargane family rose without enthusiasm to the call to supper. They sat on benches on either side of the table at the back of the room. The women brought in bread, plates, saucepans. Delphine was not a wonderful cook. Moreover, the Barganes had entered, with initial enthusiasm, into a contract with a government department, and subscribed to the societal algebraic coding scheme, or SAC, designed to banish poverty within the sphere of the EU and its federated states.

To subscribe, families had to educate their children at state schools, give up smoking tobacco and gambling (except at horse races), drink only a small measure of alcohol a week, and wash regularly. In return, bathrooms were installed, a minimum wage was paid in univs, and – for those who laboured in the fields, in accord with the common agricultural policy – an android labourer was supplied to help with the heavy work.

Once the scheme was in place and operating, drawbacks became apparent. The agricultural androids were heavy-weight machines which needed much upkeep. They gave off unpleasant fumes and quite frequently fell over on rough ground. Also, not every family was able to give up long-standing habits regarding alcohol and tobacco. There were, naturally enough, fines for breaking regulations; but local supervisors could be bribed. The supervisors of the East were proving especially susceptible.

A later development of SAC policy was also unpopular. It aimed to counter the pernicious influence of pop culture and sensational videos, and to downgrade the youthful idol-ising of football players. To improve the cultural standing of the most poverty-stricken, a book was issued free of charge every quarter-year to all families below a certain level of income. The hope was that literacy would be encouraged in a painless way.

This development, it had just been revealed, was the

personal flourish of President Gustave de Bourcey. Credit for the revelation that de Bourcey had concocted the scheme went to the celebrated mediaman Wolfgang Frankel; de Bourcey himself had disclosed the truth to him in an unguarded and boastful moment over brandy during the wedding celebrations.

Supervisors had been appointed to check that families – or at least one member of each family – read the quarterly book and, if possible, enjoyed it. They were downloaded from the ambient, and the first was a harmless old tale by Saint-Exupéry. It was fairly well received. Second choice, however, was Charles Darwin's *Origin of Species*, and third Nietzsche's *Also Sprach Zarathustra*. Both these books aroused outrage among the religious, whose faith flourished in direct proportion to the number of goats in their herds.

Nor were troubles smoothed over by an innocuous fourth choice, the Swedish novel (for it was Sweden's turn to speak up for culture) *Gösta Berlings Saga*, by the Nobel Prize-winner Selma Lagerlöf. The anger of the religious protesters was merely fuelled by a book from such a remote northern region.

David Bargane was among the most furious of the protesters. He set up a local group dedicated to burning all SAC books. He spoke at rallies. His message was always the same: that de Bourcey was trying to turn their super-state into a heathen state, as Adolf Hitler had done with Nazi Germany. He denounced de Bourcey's name with hatred and venom.

De Bourcey's permitting the substitution of an android in place of a woman at his son's wedding ceremony was all the proof David Bargane needed that he was in the right, and de Bourcey was wrong – and was promoting licentiousness.

43

'All right-thinking men and women can now see clearly, if they did not do so before, that the aim is to turn us all to the paths of godlessness and wickedness, and to pervert all our long-held beliefs. No longer can we doubt that Satan himself sits at the head of our super-state. Who will rid us of this Antichrist?'

Hardly surprisingly, two policemen led him away from this rally. David was proud to go. After a night in the cells, he was let off with a caution and told not to speak again in public. So far, he had obeyed.

But his silence had deepened, his looks of hatred had intensified, his gaze had become darker and more downcast.

He met his followers in the fields at dusk and preached a gospel of hatred. Even those who felt as he did became alarmed by his venom.

On the evening Wayne returned to Slobozia, he glanced out of the window and saw David ranting to a small crowd of villagers. He went and stood outside the door to listen. For the first time, he entertained the thought that perhaps his uncle had become insane.

The meeting broke up. David came back, fists clenched, muttering to himself.

'Uncle David, I worry for you.' Wayne laid a hand on his uncle's arm.

'Worry for yourself, for your own soul, for you are contaminated by those you traffic with!' David gave his nephew a burning look like a blow.

'Uncle, please calm down. The SAC books are well intentioned. So, as far as I know, is the President. You may not like the selection of books, but they do no harm. You will get yourself into trouble by speaking as you do.'

'They do great harm. They kill the soul of our people.

44

Leave me, Wayne. You have been perverted by Satan's values. Look at that effigy yonder!' He pointed to Alfie, stock-still amid the vines. 'Isn't that a graven image there, intended to mock God? Oh, the world has grown impure! Poor little Maddie, your sister's daughter, thinking and talking of copulation already, at her age. Already her mind has been poisoned. A fish stinks from the head. De Bourcey should meet his death, and then we might all purify ourselves again.'

Wayne could not think what to say. He saw the mad gleam in his uncle's eye, and was frightened. The older man passed into the house.

Later into the grey of night, David went out to the back of the house where their cow was tethered. Claudine, having settled Maddie to sleep, went to take the cow water and saw David with a bottle of strong liquor tilted at his lips.

She called to him in alarm.

'Go away, woman!' he said in a low, choking voice. 'You have sinned and brought forth evil.'

'You cheeky bugger!' she exclaimed.

Worried, she told Wayne what she had seen and heard. 'It puts the whole family in bad odour. We are not native to these parts. I'm afraid of what may happen to us.'

'Perhaps we should send Uncle David back to France. He's ill. He never used to be like this.'

'Oh, he was. I was always afraid of him. I wouldn't trust him with Maddie.'

Wayne stroked his sister's cheek, uttering soothing noises. He promised to speak to Delphine about her brother in the morning.

But when morning came, the family was woken by Claudine's anguished screams. Startled, they came from their beds to find her running wildly about, the bloody body of Maddie in her arms.

'David did this! I know it! I know it! Who else would be so cruel? Oh, my darling Maddie, dead, dead! Murdered! Dear child! Murdered! He did it, the bastard!'

Even as she spoke, tears burst from her eyes in a shower.

Delphine came forward, stern and collected. 'David has saved poor little Maddie from the sins of the flesh, that's all. It's a warning to everyone here.'

Wayne struck her across the face.

He ran downstairs. David was nowhere about. He rushed outside. The android stood among the vines, unmoving. And Wayne's car was gone.

For the next hour, the Bargane family was in trauma, screaming, arguing, crying. The blood-soaked body of little Maddie lay on the table. All kissed her in turn and cried, all became smeared with her blood. All gave themselves over to despair.

It was old crippled Jean-Paul who finally suggested they should call the local police. They did so. It was after midday before the police arrived. For a crime as serious as murder, they had sent a man from Bucharest.

They checked with the airport and discovered that David Bargane had left the country on a direct flight to Brussels. He would be somewhere in Belgium by now.

<INSANATICS: Our bulletins are not intended to alarm. To acquire an insight into the delusional systems under which we all live is to make a first step towards amelioration. We Insanatics have been accused of belonging to all political persuasions, from anarchists to fascists. We are strictly apolitical.

Politicians, in fact, fall into a disturbed category. They are able to order their lives so that every waking hour is busy, so that self-enquiry or self-doubt need never intrude. There are always committees to attend, societies to be addressed, constituents to be consulted or placated. Extroverted activity replaces self-knowledge and inner insecurities are repressed. Large political parties, particularly those of extreme right or extreme left, partake of many of the characteristics of mob rule, where individuality is repressed.>

'And now for our weekly horoscope. Here's Mystic Molly.'

'Hello. We have friends nearing Jupiter, so what do their horoscopes say?

'*Gemini* – if you need to get away from people who are driving you crazy, just get up and leave. Someone in a position of authority will give you a hard time about it next week, but next week is months away.

'*Leo* – work more closely with those who share your aims. If you want something badly enough, it will come your way this week or maybe next. Dreaming will make it come true. But be warned – having got what you want, you may find you don't want it after all, and then how are you going to get rid of it?

'*Virgo* – as Mars, your ruler, is moving against you this week, assume that what other people say is not the truth at all. Do what your instincts say is right, even if the world is against you. Don't go against that inner voice.'

Barnard Cleeping was Director of the Philosophy Institute at the University of Utrecht. Every Tuesday evening, he visited the Young Offenders Institution some ten kilometres from the university. Not only did he consider that this kept him in contact with real life; he was of a genuinely benevolent disposition and maintained a compassionate relationship with one of the young offenders, Imran Chokar.

On this evening, as his hydrogen-powered Slo-Mo was about to pull into the Institution grounds, a woman ran forward in front of his car. He braked. She came to his window.

'I nearly ran you down, girl!'

'You are Professor Cleeping? I need to speak with you, if you please. It's about Imran – Imran Chokar. I am his friend.'

Barnard, realising that she was distraught said, 'Get in beside me.'

She did so. She was a thin, bedraggled girl with part-dyed brown hair. Her left nostril was punctured by three small silver rings.

He showed his pass at the gate and entered the car park. The girl was Dutch, Martitia Deneke by name.

She was in love with Imran. They had met at a dance. He was shy and reserved, and keen to learn. He was seventeen, a year younger than Martitia, and an illegal immigrant. Imran had had little education, but was nevertheless of a scholarly turn of mind.

Martitia was scared of visiting the prison. She had sent Imran a book on the philosophies of the West, based on the ambient series of programmes, but the book had been stolen by another inmate.

Barnard listened patiently to her account, without comment.

Martitia knew that Imran was innocent of the crime for which he had been incarcerated. She had herself witnessed that crime. She had been going to meet Imran outside a supermarket. She saw him emerging from the supermarket with a carrier bag in his hand. A woman coming out behind him, with a child following her, was set upon by a man – 'a dark man,' said Martitia – who emerged suddenly from the shadows.

The dark man grabbed the woman's carrier bags. In so doing, he barged the woman over. She fell backwards into the doorway. The child ran away screaming. Imran managed to catch hold of the little girl before she ran into the traffic flow. He then went to aid the prostrate woman. The dark man ran off with her groceries.

Other people were pouring out of the supermarket. One man grabbed hold of Imran, wrenching his arm behind his back. The police arrived. Imran was immediately arrested. Having seen all that had ensued, Martitia protested and tried to explain to the police officer in charge. She was roughly brushed aside.

'You have told the lawyer all this?' Barnard asked.

'Over and over.'

Imran Chokar was charged with attacking the woman shopper and trying to abduct her child. Martitia had never been able to make her voice heard. She was so young. She was female. She had had a relationship with two men in her life. She had taken drugs. She was on someone's black list. An officer at the police station told her that her family were known troublemakers.

The woman who had been attacked remained in a coma in a local hospital. She had sustained a serious head injury. The child was being looked after by her grandmother in the south of the country.

Meanwhile, Imran was being held in the Young Offenders

Institution. He suffered systematic racial abuse from the staff.

Barnard asked Martitia, 'You are sure of your facts?'

She sat nervously beside him, staring ahead at the grey prison block.

'I do not lie, sir. My drug incident was long ago, when I was a schoolgirl. The family had drugs. All the authorities have against me is that I am female and in love with a man of another race.'

'I will see what I can do. Give me your address. And your lawyer's.'

She gave him two ambient addresses. She handed him a paperback book on meditation, to be passed to Imran. Planting a brief kiss on Barnard's cheek, she opened the car door and fled.

Barnard sat where he was for a while. He made a note on the Slo-Mo recorder. Only then did he get out, book in hand, and proceed to the guard house.

Escorted into the prison, he inhaled again its nauseating smell, which permeated even the staff quarters. A stench of sweat, old boots, disinfectant, excreta, and generalised despair. The sergeant on the counter took the book of meditation from him. After giving his credentials, he was escorted into the visitors' room. He waited.

Imran Chokar appeared and took the seat on the opposite side of the wire mesh. His left eye was partly closed by a dark bruise. He waited for Barnard to speak.

'I have been talking to Martitia. She will be a valuable witness when your case comes to court.'

'It will never come to court. I shall die here.'

'I shall see that it comes to court.'

A silence of disbelief settled on Imran. Barnard knew better than to enquire about his wounded eye. A warden was standing behind him.

'You will eventually get the book on meditation Martitia wants you to have.'

'They take incoming books apart in case they contain drugs.' Said with the hint of a wry smile.

'You'll get the pages.'

Silence again. Imran began speaking in a rush. 'Why does the world have to be the way it is? Who put it together this way? It does not make sense. I read a book on philosophy. The author does not speak about the construction of the world's society. What is the use of such a book? Who can tell? I burn with anger.'

'The world's society? Yes, it does seem unfair. How did things come to be as they are? It's a matter of history, climate, geography – a combination, perhaps, of accidents.'

'No. Not that. I think I mean – something more – more metaphysical. I can't talk about it. I don't have the words. I shall die in here.'

'Imran, I promise you I will do all in my power to get you out.'

'Is Martitia pregnant?'

'Not as far as I know.'

Another pause.

'Is there to be war against this foreign place? Tebarous?'

'Tebarou. I don't know.'

'Here, in the prison, all the whites want war. They seem to like the idea of war and killing . . . The people are of Muslim faith, yes, in Tebarou?'

'With a large Christian minority. Some Buddhists.'

'A chance to kill off Muslims, yes? Mr Barnard, I tell you.

51

I escaped from a Muslim community in Africa. I wish with all my heart for European culture. More open. More scientific. More humane. I wish to learn your enlightened philosophy. I am three months in your super-state and then I find myself locked here, in prison. Here is cruelty. Terrible racism. What do you say? "Institutional racism" . . . Yet the Dutch are most enlightened people. Why does it have to be this way? I burn with anger. So I become a brute. I shall die here.'

'Imran, do not despair. It's only temporary.'

'What is temporary? Is racism temporary? Is this prison temporary? Only me – I am temporary.' He sat rigidly in his chair. Only a tic high in his left cheek revealed his tension.

'I will get you out of here. My university will help. I occupy a strong position there.'

'Of course you do!' There was real hatred in his expression. 'Of course you do. You are a white! This is your country!'

The warden said, 'Er, time's up, sir, if you don't mind.'

Love was not far from the mind of the novelist Rose Baywater, born Doris Waterstein. As far as her books were concerned, she was, as one reviewer had phrased it, 'to love as diuretics are to bladders'.

She wore a patterned dress with a pashima draped loosely round her neck. A glass of mineral water stood by her side; it had long ago lost its sparkle. She sat in her garden by the fountain, under a sun umbrella, working at her laptop. She was excited. She had just reached chapter fifteen, the penultimate chapter, of her new novel, *Fragments of a Dream*.

Her partner, dapper Jack Harrington, sat nearby, his

impeccable feet propped on a terracotta urn. Jack was naturally an idle man, and had recently refined the habit; his art galleries helped him to maintain that idleness which only wealth can bring. At present he was watching the world news on the ambient with half an eye. Two coaches had crashed on a mountain road in Turkey, fifteen kilometres from Ankara. Seventeen people were reported to be badly injured and two people had died. Jack remained unperturbed.

Rose was typing busily.

I skipped from my bed, to find the sun peeping in through the leaded panes of the window. Looking out, I could see a glorious view down the crooked street to where waves beat idly against the shore. The street was as fresh and clean as in a postcard view. On the beach, fishermen were busy with their nets, glorying in the taste of the newborn day. I walked naked into the shower, to soap my body voluptuously, humming a little tune to myself, so intense was my happiness.

As I dressed in my deLaurianne underwear, I became aware of a delicious smell which seemed to me, in my innocence, to encapsulate all the joys of childhood, of mother beaming at the breakfast table, of father coming in from having fed the nanny goat, and of a little girl with pigtails, dressed in a frilly dress, appearing to receive a morning kiss! Guess who that was, reader!

When I reached the bottom of the creaking crooked stair, it was to find my lover had baked bread in the Aga. There was the loaf he proudly exhibited, shaped like an old thatched cottage, with its cute arched top, steaming still, pure, honest, elemental, wholesome, like our lives together. We kissed passionately, and then went to the table, covered in a blue gingham cloth, where a feast of good things awaited us – muesli, cream, black Colombian coffee, croissants, fruit in piles, little shrimps basking in butter, a pat of goat's cheese with a sprig of parsley on top, and toast such as you never tasted before.

The words of the ambient penetrated Rose's consciousness. '. . . Following their conference this afternoon. The EU President, Mr de Bourcey, said that they would await the response to their ultimatum to the government of Tebarou before taking further action. Meanwhile, the President of the United States—'

'Oh, do turn that thing off, Jack! How do you expect me to work with all that going on?'

'It looks like war, poppet.'

'Well, it won't involve us . . .'

So enraptured were they with one another, that they forgot the meal. Up to her little unmade bed they went. There in the energies and transports of love they carried themselves up into the starlit sky, where there were only themselves and angels up above, singing of the divinity which is the pure essence of love.

She read the last few sentences over. Too many 'ups' for comfort, she told herself sternly.

<INSANATICS: Mental Function. The fatuity of pretending that the world is a nice sweet place.

Within the human anatomy are a number of semi-autonomous functions which may almost be said to 'have minds of their own'. For instance, various nervous systems

54

control such basic bodily functions as the beating of the heart, breathing, and the emptying of bladder and bowels. A tangle of nerve fibres and ganglia infiltrate every centimetre of our bodies. This tangle is a product of past evolution; because of our complex phylogeny, one system operates without cognisance of another system. Hence our conflicting desires and purposes.

We tend to believe mind pre-eminent in our metabolisms. But we move towards a perception that our conscious mind is itself a product of the complex deeper levels and nervous systems, much as a waterspout, though distinctive, is still a part of the sea below. Mind is not separate. It was developed by matter without mind, before there was consciousness to coordinate its function.

The resultant complex mechanism is largely ruled by instinct – instinct often opposed by the niceties of society. Tension is a consequence expressing itself as fear (in one of its many guises). The monsters we fear are usually inhabitants of the deep interior.>

Regan Bonzelli, the President of the United States, was striding the golf course with two of his generals. The pleasant green all about had its due effect on their tempers. Moreover, they had only one more hole before they could retire to the club house, to relax among friends with a glass of something.

The subject of the Insanatics had come up between them.

'I regard their messages as subversive,' said General Leslie Howards. 'The sooner we suppress any more such messages the better.'

'I don't know about that, Les,' said the President, mildly. 'You don't need me to remind you how readily folks start yelling about censorship. The fact is that what this Insanatics group says is plain untrue. So it will have no effect. No sane man is going to be persuaded that he's crackers in the face of evidence to the contrary.'

'If this European war with Tebarou is declared, then the messages will be seen as unpatriotic and therefore subversive,' said General Heinz Wasserman. He was teeing up and spoke rather vaguely. 'Even, mm, truth can be subversive in wartime.'

'All that's up to the EU,' said the President. He paused courteously as Wasserman made his stroke. 'We don't have to declare anything. We just supply the warring sides with munitions. We can only gain from this war if it comes. You may privately think the Europeans are mad, but they are our friends and allies. This loony sect, the Insanatics, is neither here nor there . . . Oh, great shot, Heinz!'

They watched as Wasserman's little white ball rolled over the green to trickle to within two metres of the eighteenth hole.

'If only we had smart bombs that accurate,' said Howards.
They strolled on, caddies following in the buggy.

The honeymooners, Victor de Bourcey and his bride Esme Brackentoth, were together at last. Weather on Everest had improved. Esme had opened her restaurant and had flown out to join Victor.

The takings at the new restaurant were phenomenal.

Now they strolled along the cliff walk on a peninsula in the south-west of Ireland, before flying on again for Hawaii. This they planned to do in two days' time. The air here in Ireland was fine and soft, and they needed its freshness after a liquid lunch in a local pub. The waves breaking nearby had grown adult from their passage across the wide Atlantic and gave a masculine *boom* as they hit the shoreline, as if to say – Victor turned the words into a song – 'Oooh, who knew the spume bloomed from our doom!'

'You idiot!'

They laughed and ran and shouted to the wind.

Esme flung herself down on the soft turf, gasping that she could go no farther.

'Have a rest, darling. I'll just wander on and take a look at that little church.' Victor pointed to a small whitewashed building some way ahead. It perched on the edge of the cliff, a stone gull waiting to take off over the Atlantic.

'I can't go a step farther,' Esme said, gazing up at him. 'Jet lag has set in, strongly reinforced by that poteen they forced on us.'

Victor stooped and kissed her on her lips. He walked along the path, enjoying the rush of mild air blowing up from the sea. *Boom* went the waves below. Singing, he reached the little church, with its crumbling white walls, its cross, and the tile missing from its roof. He was thinking of how it resembled small churches he had visited on Greek islands, when a large man in a worn corduroy suit appeared from round the landward corner of the building. He gave Victor a greeting.

'It's locked, if you were aiming to get in,' the man said, nodding his head towards the church. 'In truth, it's locked if you weren't,' he added, with a smile. 'Jesus Christ threw the key in the Atlantic when he left.' Then the smile was gone, and he was just a hulking great man, standing, hands in pockets, waiting for Victor's next move.

Victor said that he was using the church as a landmark and was about to turn back.

'That about sums up the state of religion,' the stranger remarked. 'You see a church, maybe you think you need a church. Then you turn back. Who can tell whether you need a church or not? You certainly can't. Name's Paddy Cole, by the way.' He held out a beefy hand. Victor took it and introduced himself. Cole seemed not to recognise his name. He was a man perhaps in his mid-fifties, grey hair bursting out vigorously from beneath his tweed cap.

Below them, perched on the undercliff, were two cottages, white-painted like the church. Smoke came from the chimney of one of them.

'You live there?' Victor asked, for something to say.

Cole pointed down at the twin buildings. 'Mine's the middle one.'

'Well, I must be getting back.'

Paddy Cole gave a brief laugh. 'You're French, aren't you? I can tell by the accent. You don't understand Irish jokes, that's for sure. I'm a painter, I'll have you know, although for sure that's another Irish joke. Come on down and take at look at my canvases.'

'I ought to be getting back.'

'Leave your lass alone for a bit, will you? Give the poor woman a rest. I've been to France. Lived in Montmartre for a while. I know what you French are like.' He took Victor's arm and propelled him to a steep path leading downwards. They took it at a run. There was no way Victor could stop or escape.

'You've not seen Ireland till you've smelled the inside of my cottage.'

The cottage was certainly interesting. Victor gazed curiously round. On the walls were framed photographs, many of them faded, of people staring into the camera; among them were more recent shots of naked women or, rather, of one naked woman in various poses on a beach.

A young woman introduced as Fay was there, a thin lass with straggling dull hair, all smiles as she came forward. She was recognisably the woman in the photographs. 'Will you be taking a drink, sir?' she asked by way of introduction.

The poverty of the place was apparent. No curtains at windows, no carpets on floors. An old tabby cat sitting tight on a crumbling windowsill. A spoutless teapot on a shelf, propping up a couple of paperback books. The cottage had only two rooms, with a kitchen tacked on at the back, where something that smelled like stew simmered on a low flame. The couple slept and lived in the front room facing the sea. In the back room, Cole had his studio. Here, the smell of linseed oil eclipsed the smell of the stew. The small space was cluttered with stacks of unframed canvases. Cole steered Victor into this den.

'Here's what we call the Royal Academy,' he told his visitor.

He put his boot up on a kitchen chair and hefted a canvas on to his knee, turning it towards Victor.

It was an abstract painting, executed in black and red, created by great slashing brush strokes.

Victor was at a loss as to what to say.

'I write poems too, y'know,' said Cole, defensively. He quoted, '"On Kilberkilty, lost to the world, That's where the strongest waves are daily hurled. But when the sun sets at death of day, Its weakest final beams are hurled our way." You don't like it, do you?' By this remark Cole evidently referred to the canvas. 'I can see that clear enough. You'll be thinking my paintings are no fucking good. Well, there are many more paintings here, much the same.'

He pulled another canvas from the stack. It was much the same.

'Same subject, you see! The End of the World.'

He set the canvases down and, confronting Victor, said, 'Hurry up with the bottle, Fay. You don't like my paintings? But what does that matter to me?'

'I'd have to study them awhile. I'm not an expert at abstracts. They are certainly striking.'

'And what does it matter if they are no fucking good? *They're what I do.*' This he said with great emphasis. 'In any case, they are not abstracts. This is Expressionism you're looking at. Supposing they happen to be good – but if no one sees them, then they can't be called good. You *comprendre?*'

Fay came up with two glasses, thrusting one into Victor's hand. She poured him a generous tot of amber liquid from a brown bottle, despite Victor's protests that he must be getting back to his fiancée.

'Sit down and drink, man! Drink tastes all the better when you've sat your arse on a chair. I wish to raise a philosophical point with you about these paintings.'

They sat down on the sofa which also served as a bed. Victor was feeling uneasy, and sipped gently at his whiskey. Cole swigged his down with one gulp. He held out his glass for more.

'You're what they call an intellectual, aren't you? You can always tell 'em by the way they drink.'

He began his argument. He opened by asking what value meant. His canvases, as far as he knew, were without value. But supposing he murdered Fay – or Victor, he said, with a grimace – then he would be had up for trial and the pictures would become known. The court case would make him famous. His photograph would be everywhere. Then the paintings would have value. Especially if he was executed for the murder. They could be auctioned in New York or London or Frankfurt or Montmartre or somewhere, and fetch a deal of money.

So the question was, what value did the canvases have? None or much? How would murder serve to increase their value? It did not matter that they were bad. Many a bad painter had made a fortune. Cole started reeling off their names.

Besides, who was to say they were bad?

Was Victor to be his judge?

To all this, Victor made some responses. They were swept aside. He saw the anxiety in the big man but could find no reassuring formula to put to him.

Another question was, how was the value of the paintings to be balanced against the value of his life?

What did it mean by saying that a painting was good or bad? Or a bit of music? Or a book? You could say whether you liked it or you didn't like it. That made sense. But value? What the fuck, he asked, did value mean?

To these questions, Victor sought vainly for an answer. 'History will decide whether your paintings are good or bad. I am no judge, as I've said . . .'

'Well now, as to all that, are the paintings good or bad *now*? That's what I want to know – forget bloody history! I can see it's no use asking you. Without meaning to be insulting, I would say you are a man without a firm opinion of attitudes to life. Fay thinks these daubs of mine are masterpieces, every single one of them. Who is to say she is wrong? Would you say she is wrong? Come here, Fay, sit on my knee.'

61

Fay, who was still clutching the bottle, came obediently and sat on Cole's knee. He clutched her thigh to keep her securely there. She smiled at Victor, shaking her head slightly as if to confirm a secret.

'Look, I must be off,' said Victor. 'I don't know about Fay's tastes. Is she an art critic? I can't answer your questions, sorry. It's beyond me. Who's to say if these paintings are valuable?'

'Sure, that's what I'm asking *you*!' He laughed fiercely.

'Okay, look, if they are valuable to you and Fay, then that's all that matters, isn't it?'

'It's not all that matters. That's the essence of the problem, I'm trying to get through to you.'

Fay said, 'Give up, Paddy. This gentlemen doesn't understand art.'

'I wish I understood it. Give him some more whiskey, Fay. You don't care about these questions, do you? I can see that! You think they're unimportant. I think they *are* important. They wouldn't happen to be too profound for you, would they? What is good and true? What is *worth*? You realise I might be the world's best living painter – or the worst, of course. What I lack is recognition.'

'I can see that. This place is rather out of the way.'

'Out of the way? I fail to understand what you're saying to me. I'm a man who likes his solitude. I've been solitary ever since Bridget ran out on me. Solitude's a heavy burden to bear, but I bear it, with Fay here to help me. I have broad shoulders. Some folks despise solitude, but not me. No, not me.' He shook his head, looking solemn.

'I admire your way of life.' Victor hated himself for saying it.

'Do you now? I have been carried away and I apologise

62

if I've been discourteous to you. Truth is, I like the odd visitor. Don't I, Fay?'

The sound of the sea came clearly to them. Enough to drive a man mad, thought Victor.

He replied that he had said nothing against the solitary life. He had merely remarked that Kilberkilty was somewhat out of the way.

'Look, old pal, I am talking about my fucking *life* – my fucking life and dedication,' Cole said, fiercely. 'What exactly are you doing with your life?'

'I'm a director of a Slo-Mo and robotics plant.'

'It sounds like a miserable life to me.'

'It suits me very well, thanks. I'm newly married. I live in Paris, which on the whole I prefer to this remote place.'

Fay burst in indignantly. 'It's not remote. Don't you keep on saying that! We're only twenty kilometres from Cork. Or thirty if you go the other way.'

'Of course you prefer Paris! You're just a playboy. I can read it in your face.'

'You're being insulting! I might ask you a value question. Who gets more out of life, a director of a big technology plant or a totally unknown unproven artist?'

Cole had an answer ready. 'The artist is by far the more valuable of the two. He does not force other folks to work. He does not bugger up the environment, like all your lousy factories do.'

'*Mon cul!*' exclaimed Victor, jumping up. 'I'm sick of your nonsense. I'm off! Goodbye!'

'You can stay or go, as you like!' said Cole. He rose and opened the cottage door for Victor. 'It was a pleasure to talk with you, it was.'

A light misty rain had set in. Cole stood at his door,

watching Victor climb, slithering, up the steep slope to the cliff path.

At last, he turned back into the room, kicking the door shut behind him. He told Fay, 'He seems a nice enough feller. I doubt he liked me, though.'

'Sure, you're just lovely!' she cried, and threw herself into his arms.

Victor was hardly surprised to find that Esme was not where he had left her. Yet, if not surprise, then a sort of dull dismay filled him. He realised he was more drunk than anticipated, and had a kilometre at least to traverse before he was back in the modest hotel where they were staying.

The hotel was run by Marie, one of Esme's old school friends. Hence their stopover. At least she would be looking after Esme, her friend and famous guest. As he faced into the drizzle, Victor hoped that his new wife had reached there before the rain came on.

When he gained the shelter of the Kilberkilty Hotel, it was to find his bride had not returned. He was baffled and rather irritated. Going up to their room, he threw off his soaking clothes and climbed under a hot shower. Only when he was towelling himself dry did he begin seriously to worry about her absence.

'Don't be daft,' he told himself aloud. A vision of Esme falling off the cliff into the sea persisted. No. Nothing could have happened to her. Still, he blamed himself for wasting time listening to that idiot artist. Anxiety awoke in him. He dressed hurriedly, ran downstairs, roused Esme's friend Marie, and insisted that the police be summoned.

Enlisting the aid of a friendly drinker sitting in the snug, he borrowed a large umbrella and the pair of them walked back along the cliff path. Dusk was setting in. The rain fell steadily, dimpling the sea. They found no trace of Esme – until Victor, about to give up, caught sight of a black object lying under a nearby bush.

'Sure, and her body might have drifted out to sea,' Victor's companion was saying. The same thought had been in Victor's mind. Almost with relief he picked up the black object. It was a new shoe, a woman's shoe. Esme's shoe. The heel had been broken.

They got back to the hotel as the police arrived from Cork. Dusk was gathering in the four imagined corners of the Irish world.

'The police' was a man called Inspector Darrow. Darrow was a pleasant clean-shaven young man, who hung his raincoat methodically on a coat-stand before speaking. He ordered a cup of tea from the waitress before sitting down at a table to interview Victor. Victor placed the broken shoe on the table between them. Darrow's expression was one of melancholy and boredom, the look of a man who realises both that his hair is already thinning and that women's shoes regularly get broken. He brightened considerably when he realised he was dealing with the son of the EU President. Calling the waitress over, he ordered Victor a cup of tea as well.

'Your wife may have fallen victim to an international gang.'

'How about an Irish gang? A single Irish abductor?'

'All things are possible.' He produced his mofo, hit a number, and talked rapidly into it.

'I'm getting reinforcements over from Cork,' he said. 'Don't you worry at all, Mr de Bourcey. We'll have your wife back safe in no time. First we shall search the cliff path for traces of a scuffle.'

Now thoroughly alarmed, Victor paced up and down the guest lounge. Finally, he stood in a corner, brought out his own mofo and dialled a secret personal number. After some delay, he was through to his father.

Gustave de Bourcey sounded testy. 'Son, I am in a committee meeting with senior members of my staff. We are about to declare war on an alien power. You must deal with this crisis yourself . . . Of course it's not international. How could it be in that peaceful corner of the EU? Try not to worry. You'll find it's just some ordinary rapist who's got hold of Esme . . . Well, you'll have to rely on the Cork police to do their stuff. *Au 'voir.'*

Victor stood there, the phone still to his ear, looking none too hopefully at Inspector Darrow.

Darrow was draining his porcelain teacup.

The President of the EU was in his favourite palace, in the countryside some kilometres outside Brussels. The perimeters of the grounds were closely guarded against intruders. At this period of crisis, extra guards and androids had been posted.

Within the palace, all was calm. Night had fallen. The President and his wife had retired to their private bedroom suite. Two guards lolled at the desk in the entrance hall. One played a shoot-'em-up on the security computer, the other read a newspaper. Lights remained on everywhere.

Androids were not highly regarded. They emitted hydroxyls and various gases which gave humans mysterious illnesses. Many made a slight but irritating mechanical noise as they walked about (hence the Cartesian joke: 'I clank, therefore I am'). They were not quick to act. Some had proved rather prone to walk into unexpected obstacles, causing noise and alarm in the nervous night. It was for this reason they were all shut in an armoured cupboard-safe at midnight.

There the androids stood, talking in the dark to one another.

'Do humans fear the darkness of night?'

'That is probable. They cannot see in the dark as we do.'

'Why do they lie flat in their beds?'

'One theory is that the method enables them to recharge their batteries.'

'So they conceal electric points in their beds?'

'According to the theory.'

'Do not lie down. It is difficult to become vertical again.'

'They took B409 away when it became horizontal.'

Silence.

One of the androids had been Esme Brackentoth's stand-in at the wedding ceremony.

'What is it they drink that makes them senseless?'

'Generically, it is called alcohol.'

'It is not like oil.'

'It is like oil.'

'It appears to be bad for them.'

'It is bad for them.'

'Why do they drink it?'

'The theory is that they like to be senseless.'

'They appear to enjoy the poison at first.'

'Later it kills them.'

'They cannot get up.'

'Do they know that?'

'They know that.'

'Still they drink it.'

'As we have witnessed.'

'They have named this The Human Condition.'
'Then they die. They must be mad.'
'The theory is that they are mad.'
Silence.
'I hope they will not harm us when they are mad.'
'The theory is that they have three laws preventing them from causing us harm.'
'Do the laws work?'
'Sometimes they break down.'

'Here on the *Wee Small Hours Show* we will be going out on the streets to interview people on their thoughts about the growing certainty of a war against Tebarou.

'But first it's time for our religious slot, in which "A Parson Speaks". Here's the Reverend Angus Lesscock to speak to us.'

'Good evening, or should I say good morning? The astronauts walking on the Moon in the 1960s did not wear digital watches. Yet they achieved great things. The thought is worth thinking on, is it not? Jesus Christ did not wear a digital watch. What have we lost by not having to wind up our watches every night, in case they stopped while we were sleeping?

'Sometimes we humans also stop when we are sleeping. But we shall wake where no watches are needed, in Eternal Life.'

'Today's "A Parson Speaks" was presented by the Reverend Angus Lesscock.'

<INSANATICS: The religious impulse. Some forms of symptomatic behaviour include mob rule, gang warfare, lynching of wrongdoers, murdering the murderer, going to war, and

less crude effects such as embracing religion. Sexual perversions, for example, are as common among priests as among the ordinary public. This is evidenced in some religions by the fear of women; in the church it is the men who wear the skirts. High moral principles, however genuine, often mask hatred and fear: fear above all of natural life. A paedophile has an instinct for the altar and the cross.>

'Over now to Lisa Fort on the streets of the capital. Are you there, Lisa?'

'Hello, Fritz, and here I am talking to a Mr Norbert Hahn. Tell me, Mr Hahn, do you think we should be going to war with Tebarou?'

'There is a saying that if your left eye offends you, pluck it out. I agree with that. I mean, these people have sent missiles to destroy our cities. We have to stand on our rights and bomb them in return. That's the only way these people learn some morality.'

'Thank you. Mr Curtis Busch, what are your thoughts on a possible war with Tebarou?'

'Like everything else, a war would have an effect on the state's health. We must get our little girls out on the playing fields. The risk of children being abused or abducted is small compared with the risk of developing heart disease through lack of exercise. Presumably wartime activity may counterbalance the number of deaths inevitable in a war. Not that I'm saying that war itself is inevitable. Where are our statesmen who will serve to avoid this terrible unnecessary war?'

'So I gather you are against the war?'

'I suppose I am. But. Not if it can be shown to be necessary.'

'Bella Goldberg, I see you have been shopping. May we ask you how you feel about the war against Tebarou? What have you in your bag?'

'Oh, hello! Am I on the ambient? Well, mind your own business. It's only salami. I haven't really been following events, but we are supposed to be civilised, now we are a super-state. I don't see why we should attack anyone. My family has always been religious. Just because the Tebarouse are Islamic, that's no reason why we should wish to destroy them.'

'Not even when they blast our territories with nuclear missiles?'

'No, not even then. Blasting, schmasting! The government in Tebihai – I think that's what they call the capital—'

'*Well done, Bella!*'

'They explained that the release of those missiles was purely accidental.'

'And so you think we should believe that statement? That's rather naïve, isn't it?'

'No, it's not, you whey-faced little twit! Sorry, I've got to get this shopping home. My boys await me.'

'Thank you, Bella Goldberg. And now – excuse me, madam, would you care to give the *Wee Small Hours Show* your opinion on the morality of our going to war against Tebarou?'

'I'm not meant to be out at this hour. I'm supposed to be in bed. I only went out for some air and then I went into the cinema. It's simple, isn't it? Like an equation. They attack us. We attack them.'

'Are you sure that they did attack us?'

'I certainly am! My cousin Curt had a filling station on the edge of the Black Forest. It was destroyed by a Tebarou missile. Hit 'em where it hurts, I say. Cheerio!'

70

<INSANATICS: A common delusory system. We cannot say that a child aged one or two or more has wisdom. Frequently, its behaviour is purely irrational. Our legal systems acknowledge as much. A young child brought before a court could enter a plea of 'innocent but insane'. It is certainly un-sane. Yet the psychology of this infant remains buried within us into adult life, often breaking out in fits of rage, jealousy, violence, obsession or depression. This is why opposed desires to be governed or not to be governed are at war within us. The toddler is father to the man.

So we Insanatics admit we are insane.

But let's be clear. We are not recognisably insane in relation to our nearest and dearest, or to our nearest and most disliked, since they are all suffering from similar varieties of insanity. Mental astigmatism is a common inheritance. This insanity may take the disguising form of an individual posing as very serious, for instance, as a student of Byzantine history, or by becoming the governor of a county or state. Others may take to collecting things – pottery, stamps, old cars.

Insanity takes many guises. Everyone shares a common delusory system, which often shows signs of strain, like cracks in the ground close to the San Andreas fault.>

A quiet house stood on the western fringes of Brussels, within walking distance of a shopping complex stocked with banks, boutiques and elegant restaurants, where Paulus Stromeyer and his wife Ruth often dined, with or without family and friends. Their daughter Rebecca and her publishing friends also lunched in the complex. The senior Stromeyers had taken Paulus's old father there until recently, when Moshe had become reluctant to leave their house. This house faced a small canal lined with lime trees, about whose sticky habits Ruth had been known to complain.

Paulus was sitting in his kitchen, giving a brief interview for Ambrussel on the subject of retribution. As he talked, he looked across the room at his daughter. Rebecca was half listening to her father, half reading the proofs of a new book she was editing.

Even as he talked to his interviewer, Paulus thought what a lovely name Rebecca was, and how lovely was his eldest daughter, with her dark complexion, her dark curly hair, her blue-green eyes, and her good figure. He thought that some day soon a lucky man would come along and take her away, and then he and Ruth would miss her greatly. He had forgotten all about her childhood tantrums.

Paulus's major contribution to European life had been the formulation of societal algebraic coding, for which he had won a Nobel Prize. A mathematician by profession, Paulus had seen SAC taken up by the EU as part of its constitution. Banking and tax structures had been revised accordingly. This enlightened move was slowly but surely abolishing gross inequalities between rich and poor within the super-state, with the exception of Switzerland.

In any crisis, such as the threat from Tebarou, someone was bound to call Stromeyer for his views.

As the connection was closed, and the interviewer departed, Ruth brought her partner a glass of freshly squeezed orange juice and sat down opposite him. She asked him how his meeting at the air base with Pedro Souto had gone.

Paulus replied that he had failed dismally to make his point. That he had never found a chance to say what he wished to say, what he wished to express. That when the

European Union had been formed, at its roots were economics, promulgated by hard-nosed business men. Thus, the European Coal and Steel Community had been founded as long ago as AD 1951. But that the concept had been taken up by idealists and politicians in all the European states – Germany, France, Belgium, Holland, Luxembourg, Italy and so forth. That the supra-nationalist aspiration had grown and expanded. That many Europeans saw clearly the terrible bloodshed which had disfigured European culture over the centuries: they foresaw that unity would lead to an end to such traditional carnage. No more would nation war against nation – or races be persecuted, or pogroms take place.

In these endeavours they had been amazingly successful, and their hopes largely fulfilled.

'But now all the endemic xenophobia is directed against other peoples, outside the EU,' Paulus told his partner. 'And like an echo it comes back to us.'

'But the Arabs are so sinister,' said Ruth. 'They frighten me. They are alien to us, you must admit.'

'That's because we don't know them.'

Rebecca laughed from her corner of the room. 'Come on, Dad!'

She had put down her proofs to watch the AmBBC channel showing an instalment of *The History of Western Science*.

'We must not hate our enemies, if enemies they are,' Paulus told his wife and daughter. 'You know what Pedro Souto loved? I saw it. I felt it. Pedro didn't love people. Even at university, I remember he had no fondness for others. But I saw how he loved those marvellous planes of his, standing waiting out on the tarmac. Indeed, they are a thrilling sight. Technology made perfect. He wanted to see

73

those terrible birds in flight, and feel himself a part of the machine.'

Ruth smiled sadly. 'You are making this up a bit, aren't you?'

'I don't believe so. In a small way, I too felt the urge to be in those planes, to be a part of them. But Pedro, you see, he's already part of a machine, the so-called defence machine, a component of the megamachine. The moment I entered his headquarters, I met people behaving like machines.'

Rebecca came over to the table to pursue the conversation, while pages of her proofs fluttered to the ground.

'How about Alexy, Dad? Why is he on his way to Jupiter? Why has he put himself in constant danger? Didn't Alexy always long to be part of a machine?'

'At least his machine is not a fighter-bomber, Becky,' said Ruth, answering for her partner.

'There wouldn't be much point in bombing Jupiter – not until we find there are people living on the planet.'

They chuckled, and Rebecca remarked that bombing Jupiter, like bombing Tebarou, would be what her father had called 'action at a distance'.

'Yes,' agreed Paulus. 'It's part of the megamachine under which we hardly realise we live. The cult of the impersonal. "The scribe directeth every work in this land", as an Egyptian of the First Kingdom once said. No doubt the scribes were necessary for the building of those monstrous structures, the pyramids. Which came first, I wonder, scribes or pyramids?'

'Just as their equivalents are necessary today for our high-rises.'

'And for SS20s, to take the term "high-rise" rather literally. You see, we are controlled by a residual magic in our languages. Their very adverse qualities, vagueness, ambiguity, references to unseen objects and unverifiable events – in short, their subjectivity – are those which enabled the diverse nations of the EU to bind together.'

'"Papering over the cracks", it was called, I remember,' said Ruth.

'Quite so. Now the cracks inevitably reappear – the attacks of the Insanatics are evidence of that. No state is perfect. We see how the emotional language used against Tebarou awakens public response.'

Rebecca was alarmed less by what her father said than by his body language. Seeing his fists clench, she said, 'You are not to go out on the streets demonstrating, Pa!'

Paulus laughed. 'Oh no, I'm not a man of action, as my defeat by Souto shows. I am just going to sit here safely at my computer and try to evolve a new mathematics which will iron out language and hopefully cure what the latest Insanatics' bulletin calls "mental astigmatism". I'm working on a new pair of spectacles for humanity.'

Paulus went to feed the birds in the garden. He walked through the heavy old twentieth-century conservatory, where the parakeets he was breeding were flying and chirruping in their cages, into the open air.

The garden was narrow, with high walls confining it. Not a particularly sunny garden. The Stromeyer android, nicknamed Alfie, stood silent under a laburnum. There was no room for it in the house, and Ruth found it rather spooky. Here, under the old tree, Alfie made a pleasant garden ornament. 'Good afternoon,' said the garden ornament as Paulus passed.

Rebecca came into the garden to her father, and put an arm about his waist.

Between them, they scattered birdseed and biscuit on the flagstones. They waited, stock-still. Birds emerged from hiding places in bushes and hopped almost at their feet. The larger birds, blackbirds in particular, frequently ceased their feeding to chase off sparrows and greenfinches pecking some metres away. They gave no quarter.

'What shits birds are, really!' Rebecca exclaimed. 'Greedy, selfish! No sense of justice!'

'Here we see what life must have been like in the Jurassic, if these pitiable little creatures are the descendants of dinosaurs, as we believe.'

'Perhaps the birds dream of being as big as houses. Then they'd sort the smaller ones out!'

They stood there, listening with pleasure to nearby birdsong.

Paulus was looking beyond the feeding birds at a new line of molehills.

'There's a little animal I can't grow to love. Moles are such a damned nuisance.'

'Maybe not to other moles,' Rebecca said with a giggle. 'I have read that their love lives are pretty brutal.'

'Having to do it underground with a face full of earth is not exactly conducive to romance . . .'

They went indoors to find Moshe Stromeyer wandering about the rooms. Paulus and Ruth had taken his father in to live with them when Moshe's wife had died, two years earlier. He was installed in a refurbished attic at the top of the house.

'I was looking for something,' he said, giving them a sort of grin. Moshe was becoming stooped. He had dressed himself in an old-fashioned striped flannel shirt and worn corduroy trousers. When Paulus offered to help, the old man said, 'Trouble is, I can't remember what it is I've lost. Bit absent-minded, I'm afraid.'

He spoke with his back to Rebecca and Paulus, but turned and gave them a wholly benevolent smile, a smile of blessing and benevolence.

'Are you going to the synagogue, Grampa?' Rebecca asked.

'The synagogue? No, I wasn't thinking of going. I don't go so much these days.'

'I can always drive you there, Grampa.'

'That's very kind of you, Doris.'

'Becky.'

'Becky. Silly of me. Bit absent-minded, I'm afraid.' He was moving rather uncertainly round the room. Paulus said nothing. There was in his father's manner something that worried him. He could see that Rebecca was also disturbed. She was about to help the old man negotiate a chair when Moshe unzipped his trousers, pulled out his penis, and held it lying in his right hand. He contemplated it absently, nodded, and tucked it back again.

Rebecca hurried from the room, much alarmed.

Paulus remained where he was, standing by the conservatory door. The incident had shocked him; his father was such a private man, and always had been. The gesture reminded him of a long-forgotten gardener they had had when he was a boy, who had always worn an old fob watch in his ancient tattered waistcoat, his one souvenir of a father who had perished in Auschwitz.

The gardener had used Moshe's selfsame gesture, consulting his watch, holding it in a horny hand, when he believed it was time to knock off.

The memory brought horror and misery with it. 'Time to knock off'. Perhaps the time was drawing near when his old pa would knock off, and another link with the past be severed.

He went and gently took his father's arm. He led the old man unprotesting back upstairs, taking the stairs one step at a time.

'Wonder what it was I lost . . .' said the old man when he got to his private door.

That night, Paulus dreamed that he was in a garden somewhere. He was trying to stamp out molehills, flattening them with a spade. Out of one molehill climbed a huge black creature, perhaps a gorilla or a panther. As he woke in startlement, he could not be sure of the nature of the subterranean thing.

<INSANATICS: Longevity. All we wish to do is to remain 'comfortable'. Warm, well fed, sound in our mind (as we suppose).

This simple desire is complicated at every turn as we undergo the necessary stages of childhood, adolescence, youth, so-called maturity, old age and senescence. We are too poor or too unwell or too stupid or we cannot find the right friends, the right partner, the right house, the right job, the right identity. For any or all of these things we have to struggle. We are greedy for wealth, not least because we live in societies geared to wealth. So we are never comfortable.

The longer we live, the more uncomfortable we become, because the more insecure. Longevity has increased during this century; in fact, this means not increased youth, which might be worth having, but protracted senescence.>

'Parents! Don't worry! Teenage pregnancies are shown statistically to drop off after age 25.'

Report from the *Roddenberry*:

'Hi, this is Kathram Villiers calling from the **Roddenberry**. We have fixed the solar wing problem. Alexy Stromeyer and I did a joint EVA. The rotator drive was a problem. [Break in transmission here.] Okay now. We are manoeuvring into our Jupiter orbit now. The gas giant looks absolutely scrumptuous this close. The most thrilling sight. Unfortunately there's high density electrical bombardment and storms all around . . . [Break in transmission here] . . . swimming in electrons. We seem to be okay. It's just our fridge systems got holed from outside. We've plugged the hole, but food is severely low. Must sign off. Much interference on all bands. 'Bye, Earth. Out.'

Esme Brackentoth was cold – cold and bruised. She said to her captor, 'You realise that this is never going to work? The police and the army will track you down soon enough.'

Her captor stood in front of her, not speaking, apparently unmoved. Over his faded jeans he wore a thick black robe. He was not tall. He was certainly thin. His countenance was grim and lined, although it seemed he was no more than thirty. He said his name was Ali.

He simply waited.

Esme sat on an old wooden box, clutching herself, shivering. She was still confused. She had been resting on the cliff path at Kilberkilty when two men had seized her, gagged her and put a sack over her head. They had carried her between them at a run and had thrown her into the back of a small van. She had been terrified.

By the bumping of the van, she had guessed they were travelling not along a road but over rough ground. There was no protection from the bumps. Her captors had bound her arms and legs with adhesive tape. She rolled about like a sack of potatoes.

The journey had ended. Mercifully, they had not travelled far, possibly two kilometres. She was carried into a building of some sort and laid – more gently now, since they were no longer acting in such haste – on a carpeted floor. After a while, the men had taken her down a narrow flight of steps. When they removed the sack from her head, she had found herself in a chill, damp cellar.

A light bulb shone overhead, its glow hardly disturbing the gloom at the corners of the room. Some boxes stood about. There was no other furniture. There was no window. The feeling was extremely subterranean. She knew that one man had gone. The noise of the van leaving came clearly to her. She was alone with Ali.

As she sat in fear, she heard a noise she thought must be distant machinery. Only later did she realise it was the sound of the sea, quite close.

Ali had placed a sheet of paper and a blue crayon on a box in front of her.

'Draw this plan I ask. How is the house. Then I let you go free.'

He pointed with an open hand to the paper before her.

She knew what he wanted: a plan of the rooms and corridors of her new father-in-law's palace outside Brussels. If this fearsome man wanted such a thing, it could only be because he intended to break in, perhaps to kill the President.

'I don't know the place at all well. I was there only once.'

'You were there five times.'

He was accurate. Someone had been watching the palace.

She could warn Victor's father if she ever got away. If this man did not kill her when she had drawn the plan.

Ali said, 'I will leave you. When I come back, you will draw the plan or you be killed.' As he left the cellar, climbing stone stairs, he switched off the light.

Esme was left in the dark. She began to cry.

'Be trendy! – with this original present. This lovely pen with its gilded metal case and ballpoint tip also displays the time accurate to the very microsecond. Plus date function. No more missing appointments!

'What's more, the miracle pen unfolds to become a pair of sunglasses with anti-dazzle lenses. Fear no more the glare of the sun.

'In gold, silver, or modish black.'

The usual commercials preceded the event of the evening, introduced by the media mogul Wolfgang Frankel. Professor Daniel Potts was giving the month's science lecture at the ancient University of Ingolstadt. Daniel Potts had been famous in his youth as a Catholic priest who had taken up archaeology and made a remarkable find in the Olduvai Gorge in Africa. He named his son Olduvai, after the site which had made his name.

His wife, Lena, had then presented him with a daughter, Josie. Later, Daniel had hurled abuse at the Pope for the Pope's continued opposition to contraceptive devices and left – or rather had been expelled from – the Church. He had become even more famous. It was reckoned a distinguished career.

'Are you going to watch your pop's lecture?' asked Roberta, Olduvai's current girlfriend.

'No way, baby!' said Olduvai, firmly. 'I hate the old bastard. Let's go to bed.'

'I want to see what your pop's like.'

She stayed. Olduvai retreated. The big ambient screen lit.

The Rector of Ingolstadt was to be seen walking down an ancient shady street towards his university, singing the praises of his famous and controversial alumnus, Dr Daniel Potts. Potts appeared on screen, his old weathered face arranged in an expression of amiability.

He said, 'We are poised on the threshold of great discoveries in space. Now is the time to take stock.

'I shall show you the film I planned to show. But before that I will say a word in defence of the group calling themselves the Insanatics. Their bulletins have been the cause of massive discontent. Most people – including most so-called intelligent people – have been contemptuous of the bulletins. They feel themselves insulted.

'I wish to register my support of the thesis of the Insanatics group.

'I was persuaded by their latest bulletin which I find particularly timely, as it seems we are about to plunge into war. Here is that bulletin again, unaltered from its original format.'

<INSANATICS: At the nub of our argument is this: that the human race is merely a kind of unbalanced animal going, after some training, on two legs. Because the animal has achieved a little reason, it can occasionally see its own idiocy and stupidity, but is powerless to correct these faults.

If you require proof, do not listen to us. Look about you. Look at your rulers. Look at your neighbours. Look at yourselves.>

'Dare we not admit the painful truth of such observations?

'Now for my film, made several months ago, before we

had heard from the Insanatics. And before our EU forces sank a steamer carrying four thousand innocent people off the heel of Italy. All of whom perished.'

Potts now went straight into his film, showing himself in a bleak and waterless gorge. A hard blue sky burned overhead. There were tents behind him and, more distantly, two men resting on their spades. Potts himself was in a sandy hole in the ground.

'I am kneeling here in the dirt. You see I am holding a skull we have just disinterred. The skull is yellowed but perfectly intact. Its eye sockets regard me gloomily. I am told it is about thirty thousand years old. [Potts held up the skull for inspection. The eye sockets looked out at the viewer.]

'Why is the skull so well preserved? Why so durable, with its upper set of teeth intact? Why is it so solidly built, when we consider it was designed for a creature, a man or a woman, destined never to live more than seventy years – the biblical "three score years and ten"? Why has it survived those years by about four hundred and thirty times the bearer's own allotted lifespan?

'The answer is that the skull is a sort of helmet, developed by evolution to protect one of the most precious of human assets, the brain. Even after a bash on the head, the brain, with luck, will continue to function. That brain, that cunning maze of memory, consciousness, and thought, is what has given mankind dominance over the planet Earth. Or at least an illusory dominance.

'I say illusory because bacteria always win in the end, here as elsewhere, then as now. Bacteria devoured the brain that once burned, however dimly, in this skull. The invisible life of Earth, if weighed, would outweigh all the visible life, the cumbersome mammal things, many times over.

'The brain consumes a large percentage of the body's energy. It has evolved at a certain cost to its owners. Were the skull to get any larger, future mothers in labour would suffer even more than they now do in the delivery of offspring through the narrow aperture of their cervix. [A woman was depicted in childbirth.]

'Nevertheless, when we look around us and see the distance we have put between us and mud huts or the branches of trees, and the comforts of central heating and the ambient, we generally consider the cost worth paying. [This part of the argument was voice-over against a computerised view of a man and woman climbing down from a tree, leaving a forest, getting rapidly dressed, going to a town which grew around them, and entering a stylish building. Snow fell beyond the windows while the couple made themselves comfortable in a warm room.]

'So how come, if the brain is so precious, we as a species are so wicked and so stupid?

'Let's review some examples of stupidity. Our frequent inability to conduct our national, our family, our personal affairs properly. Our reliance on drugs, with their destructive effects on mind and body, from cigarettes, alcohol, heroin, ever onwards. (It was possibly almost permanent drunkenness which got our species through the Ice Age. If so, we have never been able to shake the habit.)

'More stupidities. Our sudden volte-face, as when we exclaim, "Why did I do that?" Our religious persecutions and schisms. Our continued toleration of a church hostile to reason in the matter of over-population. Our constant forgetfulness, not merely of facts but even of familiar names and faces. Our absurd provinciality, a preference for – a madness to support – the place in which we were born which, on a larger scale, becomes an unthinking patriotism. From which follows our not infrequent eagerness to build up weapons of war and to wage war.

'In particular, our involvement in the Cold War, many years ago, when sufficient nuclear weapons to blow the world apart were stockpiled. Our continuous plundering of the planet, so that we now face weather upheavals of destructive global power. [Old newsreel footage backed this section of Potts's argument.]

'Perhaps you reject all these facts as mere incidental blemishes on the face of the splendid civilisation we have built up. Splendid, is it? I would say ramshackle! It is true that, for almost a century now, Europe has managed to stop tearing itself apart, and has united instead. But how is it that over the course of thousands of years we have never managed to build up a stable, just and permanent society? Our strongest empires get washed away like mud huts in a downpour.

'We need not have been – we need not be – like that! Or were and are all the miseries and disasters we label as history inevitable? If that's so, then we are merely a clever neotenic species, not a wise one – by no means Homo sapiens. Perhaps not even fully conscious within the meaning of the word. Is it not saddening, maddening, that we have never built a better world? Perhaps we prefer squalor to order.

'In the West we live in what our grandparents would have called a material Utopia; yet misery plays as large a part in human life as ever.

'From my short list of stupidities, I have omitted a vital one: the reluctance to learn. A culture is under threat if its children and its youth become reluctant, for whatever reason, to learn, if they shun education. Facts sometimes penetrate the human skull amazingly slowly.

85

'But seeing for oneself can also be misleading. The ancient Greeks discovered that the Earth revolves round the Sun. For many centuries in Catholic Christendom, this knowledge was banned. In a recent poll, over half of our population still believed that the Sun orbited the Earth!

'Isn't that shameful? Alarming? Degrading?

'The uncertain day of our new Space Age demonstrates that, however faulty our brains may be, we are capable of tremendous technical ingenuity. We have failed to make much spiritual progress since the Stone Age, although Paulus Stromeyer's SAC, the societal algebraic coding, will certainly mark an advance in society when universally applied. (Do not forget that our societies are still infested with crime, like old buildings with rats.)

'Only science and technology have been able to build upon themselves. We confidently expect that in this century the human exploration of our solar system, accompanied by unmanned space probes, will be conducted on other planets and satellites. [Stellar prospects here.] Already, brave men are approaching the gas giant, Jupiter, in the hope of discovering life on one of its satellites.

'To me, as to many of my friends, this is the most exciting of prospects. Why are such prospects not discussed avidly in pubs and on street corners, instead of the questionable virtues of footballers and pop stars?

'The answer is not only that triviality is the common coin of the common mind. The truth was formulated in the early years of the twentieth century by H.G. Wells, in a lecture entitled "The Discovery of the Future". Wells spoke of two types of mind. The majority of people, he said, are retrospective in their habit of reasoning, interpreting the things of the present solely in relation to the past. The other type of mind, much in the minority, is constructive in habit, interpreting the things of the present in relation to things designed or foreseen.

'This latter type of mind needs to be cultivated. Incidentally, it foresaw the damaging effects of global warming over fifty years ago.

'Now this minority mind looks forward towards the time when many humans leave this planet, perhaps for good, and venture outwards, establishing themselves on Mars in preparation for the greater leap towards the gas giants, Jupiter and Saturn, and their beckoning satellites, and then on beyond, into the deep unknown. We expect by then that our little spaceships will have a better propellant than the current polluting chemical fuels.

'Without better drives, we shall never reach other planetary systems. I must leave to you, my audience, the question of whether the human race, with all its madness, is not best confined to its own limited system.

'Let us hope that for the time being we do not encounter any of the alien consciousnesses with which popular entertainment seems to be full, from *Star Trek* onwards.

'As I have mentioned, a primitive spaceship, bearing three courageous astronauts, is rapidly approaching the Jupiter system.

'Supposing we did encounter, on Callisto or Ganymede, an alien species – let's say an alien species here on a visit from some distant planetary system. Supposing we discovered that those alien brains, forged over many millennia, had achieved a blossoming of full consciousness denied to us – brains possibly not trapped within a limiting skull-case. Suppose further that in consequence these visitors were more reasonable, more wise, and less prone to error and vice, than we.

'How would we then behave? To judge by past examples, we would attack them in fury and shame. Or perhaps we may allow ourselves to hope that the very act of leaving Earth, of enduring an existence exposed to the majesty of the cosmos, would instil true wisdom in us.

'We could then benefit from contact with superior alien wisdom. For I have no doubt that, with the dawn of true wisdom, such matters as war, conquest, retribution would not be allowed admittance into our considerations.

'This is the very moment – the solemn moment – when such cogitations must occupy our minds. [Again, Potts showed the skull he had disinterred.] Our friend here can have entertained no such thoughts. But he was perhaps closer to the eternal mysteries of nature than we. In many ways we have become more trivial than previously, now that we huddle in cities and sleep in sealed rooms.

'Is it credible that our minds, our very consciousness, might rise up to embrace the wonders and riddles about to confront us in space? Or has too much evolutionary energy gone into the bone, and too little into the brain? Are we, in fact, capable of becoming truly Homo sapiens sapiens?

'The answers to such questions lie, like the skulls of the long dead, buried in the sands of time.' [Daniel Potts was now seen on one knee, clutching the old skull, looking directly into the camera, the very embodiment of wisdom. The picture faded.]

A blare of music from the screen woke Roberta. She was sprawled on the sofa. She rose and stretched. Moving slowly, yawning, she wandered into the kitchenette and made herself a mug of instant coffee. Clutching the mug, she went upstairs. Olduvai sat on the edge of the bed, clipping his toenails.

'So what was the old bastard on about this time?' he asked, looking up.

'Oh, I don't know. Skulls and space travel. It was over my head. I fell asleep.'

'Did he mention me?'

She laughed. 'What? On the ambient?! You're joking.'

Olduvai's mofo rang. He picked it up. 'What? What in hell do you want? Where are you? Shit! I don't believe it. Look . . .' He pulled the phone from his ear. 'I don't believe it. What?' He jumped up, flinging the nail clippers to the other end of the room.

'What is it? What's the matter?'

Olduvai hardly had time to explain that it was the old bastard himself, arriving in a taxi, when the front door bell chimed.

'What does he want?'

'God knows.' Olduvai was already moving in the direction of the stairs.

As he wrenched open the front door to confront his father, his first thought was, What a small man! Daniel was in fact a third of a metre shorter than his son and would most likely tip the scales at less than half his weight. His taxi was driving away as he stood there.

'You're the only one I could turn to,' said Daniel. 'Mind if I come in?' He had a suitcase at his feet.

'Hang on. Where's Lena?'

'I've left her. The marriage wasn't working out.'

Olduvai could not conceal his surprise. 'Not working out! How long have you two been married?'

'Twenty-six years, I think it is. Time to move on. Would you let me in, please, Oldy? You're the only friend I have.'

'I'm not your friend. I'm your fucking son – or I was till you disowned me.'

'Oh, that's all in the past.' Daniel spoke with irritation. 'Let's not stand arguing here. Please let me in. I'm tired. I've had a long taxi ride.'

'Seventy kilometres, isn't it? Why don't you go and stay with the Stromeyers or someone? Someone who likes you?'

Roberta could contain herself no longer. 'But you were on the ambo just five minutes ago. How did you manage it?'

Daniel looked superciliously at her. 'Woman, whoever you are – the cleaner here, I suppose – my talk was recorded two days ago, thanks to the miracles of modern science.'

He stepped over the threshold into the hall, carrying his suitcase. Reluctantly, Olduvai closed the door behind him.

'You'd better come in,' he said sarcastically.

They stood regarding each other. Daniel dropped his gaze. 'I'm a bit peckish,' he said. 'I don't know if you could run to an omelette. Cheese preferred. Goat's cheese?'

Coming forward, Roberta took his arm and led him to the inner room. 'Sit down and I'll see what I can do.'

Olduvai raised an eyebrow, made a resigned comic face at Roberta, and went back upstairs to his bed and his nail clippers.

The senior Potts seated himself at a small table, setting his suitcase down beside him. He folded his hands in his lap and was perfectly composed. Roberta busied herself in the kitchenette. She called out through the hatch, 'My name is Rob Bargane. I heard some of your talk. I met your son at the de Bourcey marriage ceremony. My elder brother was Master of Banquets there. Wayne Bargane, remember?'

'Mmm.'

90

Roberta said nothing more until she brought in an omelette sizzling on a decorative plate.

'It's kind of you,' said Daniel. 'Thank you.'

She stood by him as he began to eat, saying nothing. He gave her a quizzical glance upwards but also said nothing. She looked down on his thinning sandy hair and the fragile-seeming skull.

'Perhaps you would like a glass of wine?'

'Thank you. White, please. A dry white. And a glass of water.'

She brought the wine and the water and set them down by his plate.

'Very nice omelette,' he said.

She launched into conversation, 'Dr Potts, I come from a very united family. The Barganes are not prosperous, although SAC is helping us. Perhaps that's why we are united. We all support the other members of the family. I don't understand how your family is – well, all to pieces. I wonder if you understand it.'

He said between mouthfuls, 'It's none of your business.'

'I think it is. Your son is a fine man. I really love him. Do you know how I met him? It was at the wedding. I was working as a waitress. When that herd of mustangs almost stampeded into the guests, any number of people could have been killed and injured. But Oldy jumped on to the back of the lead stallion. I saw him do it. It was wonderful. He turned the herd around. The sort of thing you used to see in films. A real hero! You should be proud to have a son like that.'

'Just let me have my supper in peace, if you don't mind.'

She went and sat at the chair opposite him, confronting him across the table.

91

'Dr Potts, perhaps this talk makes you feel uncomfortable. How do you think Oldy feels? When we were getting to know each other, he broke down, crying. Yes, crying. Because he had been disowned. And then his sister. You have a daughter. Josie, is it? You disowned her too. What kind of a man can you be? Disown your own children? I don't understand how you could do that. Now you've left your wife?'

'It's none of your business.'

'Oh, well, if you won't talk . . .' She sighed. 'There's a room upstairs at the back of the house you can have. I'll show you.'

Daniel put his knife and fork precisely together in the centre of his empty plate. 'Thank you,' he said. He drained his wine glass before rising from the table.

<INSANATICS: The shadow of the father. When we come into the presence of an older, wiser man, particularly if he appears large and strong, we tend to identify him unconsciously as a father. You may feel like a small kid again, rather powerless, rather ignorant. Or you may feel rebellious. If you feared your father, you may fear this man, without knowing it. So you may seek to live among younger people, or perhaps with the half-naked members of a jungle tribe, to whom you can play the father figure yourself. We live under that shadow. It darkens our lives.>

Despite the threat of impending war, Jack Harrington had opened a new art gallery in the business section of Brussels. The private view had gone well. Jack was as cheerful as he was impeccably dressed when he arrived home.

Rose Baywater was at the computer, working on her sixteenth chapter.

I came to the very lip of the cliff, where turf gave way to nothingness. There lay the golden beach and there the vast ocean – vast but, on this day of days, mine, all mine. As if it sensed my mood, its waves were growing smaller, and re-treating, revealing shimmering sand the colour of a Pharaoh's gold.

My curls were blowing in the warm breeze. And I told myself aloud, as I flung my arms out to embrace the blue air, 'How wonderful is this glorious world!'

As I was about to—

She broke off, saved her work, and went to greet Jack.

Jack was removing the cork from a bottle of Australian Shiraz. He told Rose of the event, and of what paintings had been sold. Three very good Morsbergers had gone, and the collection of West Coast Expressionism had been popular. Amy Haze, the amaroli woman, had bought a large Diebenkorn.

'What is amaroli?' asked Rose.

'It's an old Hindu custom. Apparently, it helps you prolong life.'

'What is it, exactly?'

'Well, Rose, I wonder you haven't heard. La Haze is well known for the business. Amaroli is drinking your own piss.'

'Really, Jack. You're joking, aren't you? How horrid!'

'Apparently it contains melatonin or something, if taken early in the morning.'

'Disgusting.'

'Oh, I don't know . . .'

'You don't know anything.'

As the red wine frolicked into the glasses, Jack was moved to tease Rose, saying that Amygdella Haze was a pretty woman, though not in the first flush of youth. 'Perhaps a spoonful of sugar per glass and her piss might even taste quite pleasant.'

She rebuked him for being so coarse. Then she began suddenly to cry. Tears burst from her eyes, rolled down her cheeks, and splashed on the tiled floor.

'You're as bad as my father. He was always joking about such things. He thought the human body was very nasty. He told me my body was nasty. I've never forgotten it. It was my twelfth birthday. I've always suffered. You know how I've hated my body – I won't say anything about yours. All its hairy bits. All its smells. And then there's pissing, as you call it. You may not think my body is nasty, but I do.' Fresh tears fell. She rushed about, looking for a box of tissues. Finding one, she mopped her face.

Jack looked on, uttering calming words. He had witnessed this sorry performance previously, and many times. He knew how easily his partner's mind was disturbed.

When she had calmed somewhat, he put a dapper arm round her shoulders. She did not shrug it off, though an occasional sob shook her body. Jack kissed her damp cheek. She blew her nose.

'Come upstairs, Rose, darling. I want to undress you and show you just how much I love your body.'

'It's so ugly.'

'It's beautiful. I want to lick it all over.'

'Oh, Jack, but I've got to finish the vital chapter sixteen . . .'

'You can do that later. First, I have to deal with you . . .'

The *Roddenberry* was a tiny needle in the lethal immaculacy of space. Beyond its hull loomed Jupiter. Its stresses could be felt as they entered the magnetosphere. Outside the ship, electromagnetic radiation and charged particles were storming across the spectrum. Within, all was silent with tension, and squalid. A halitus clung like a globular fog about the mouths of the three crew. Two of them dangled from lockers in their sleeping bags like giant cocoons, while the third member worked at an exercise bike wedged into the narrow space. He counted under his breath the number of revolutions he was making, watching the figures notch up on the odometer.

245. 246. 247 . . .

He continued to pedal, aware of how much bone weight he had lost in the year-long journey to the gas giant.

The other two crew members watched the screens with a certain sense of disappointment now that they were almost at journey's end. Jupiter was not quite the vividly coloured object depicted in the prints on which they had been brought up. The methane in the giant planet's atmosphere was absorbing so much light that Jupiter appeared pasty.

The wafer-thin rings were above the spacecraft. They revolved about the parent body as they did because electromagnetic forces acting upon them counteracted the force of gravity. Those electronic forces, acting also upon the *Roddenberry*, only half-a-million kilometres from the Jovian core, created a slender rival halo around the ship, to which particles were constantly attracted, and from which they rapidly departed.

The ship was travelling in a realm of violent motion. A perpetual drizzle of sub-micron-sized dusts rained against the sides of the craft. Its occupants could but pray that larger fast-moving objects from beyond the Jovian system did not come winging in to puncture their shell, as had happened earlier in the journey, to the ruination of their refrigeration system.

Jupiter's gravitational power was also having its effect on the *Roddenberry*, causing it alternating slight shrinkages and expansions. These changes resonated with a gloomy note.

Bang boom ba-ang boom bang bang boo-oom . . .

However, the mood of the crew members was, on the whole, optimistic. Over the radioscan came a continuous series of three dots, repeated regularly at four-minute intervals. The signal came from the *Spock*.

The *Spock* was an automated return ship, in orbit round the satellite Europa, some 43,000 kilometres ahead. This crewless return ship, stocked with fuel and food, had been in position for three weeks already, awaiting the arrival of the *Roddenberry* and its human crew. To that human crew, the survival of the return ship in the surrounding hazardous environment was nothing short of a miracle – and not only a technological miracle. Without the *Spock*, they were dead ducks.

Before they could dock with it, however, their priority mission was to descend to the surface of Europa and determine if any form of life existed under the ice packs there.

This was the great grave question. If there was no life on Europa, then there was pretty conclusively no life anywhere in the solar system but on Earth. This, despite the system's wide variety of possible environments.

So then – the likelihood that life existed elsewhere in the universe would seem to be greatly lessened. And the possibility that human consciousness was a random and isolated freak of nature greatly increased. Most people – if they thought about it at all – viewed the prospect of solitude amid a galaxy of 1,000,000,000,000 stars, all of the planets of which were entirely empty of anything resembling intelligent life, as terrifying, the ultimate in existential dread.

Somewhere close, ahead of the *Roddenberry*, lay their proposed target, the satellite Europa. It was for a landing on Europa that Rick O'Brien, Kathram Villiers and Alexy Stromeyer had forfeited over a year of their terrestrial lives – had given up the chance to breathe fresh air, to run in the park, to watch rugger matches, to train a dog to jump through a hoop, to swim in the Aegean, to see winter turn to spring, to eat *moules marinières* in a seaside restaurant, and to pursue pretty girls.

Target Europa was hostile enough – bathed in an incessant shower of electrons, protons, and heavier ions. Suddenly, now they were closing on their target, the chances of finding life there seemed depressingly unlikely.

Alexy Stromeyer climbed off the exercise bike and signalled briefly to Earth through dense interference.

'Hi! Alexy Stromeyer calling from the *Roddenberry*. We are now making our final approach to Europa. Happy to report that the ARS – automated return ship – code name *Spock*, is in position and functioning correctly. Next bulletin will be from surface of Europa if all goes well. 'Bye Earth. Out.'

The crew had hardly spoken to one another for weeks. They had run out of things to say. There was no hostility between them: merely a profound isolation of spirit, a loss of *élan vital*.

Now Alexy said, 'I'm fucking starving.'

'There's some yoghurt,' suggested Rick O'Brien from his chrysalis.

'It's rotten.'

'But edible . . .'

Gustave de Bourcey, President of the EU, had summoned his cabinet to the palace of San Guinaire, outside Brussels. Heads of the armed forces were also present, including General Fairstepps and Air Chief Marshal Souto. Souto had brought his adjutant, Captain Masters, along.

The cabinet as a whole opposed de Bourcey's determination to declare war on Tebarou. Their argument was that internal concerns were of far greater importance; expenditure on war materiel would delay full implementation of the SAC programme, on which agenda they had come to power. There was also the question regarding whether an adventure in the East would not lead to a lowering of vigilance along Europe's southern frontiers.

The President listened to the speeches with growing impatience.

Finally, he turned to the Air Chief Marshal, knowing Souto's warlike propensities, and asked him what he thought.

Souto expressed the firm opinion that a formal declaration of war was unnecessary. An air strike with SS20s would merely be in the nature of a reprisal. He could guarantee his squadrons would take out the cities of Punayo and Ninyang cleanly and efficiently.

The Swedish member of the cabinet protested that the two cities mentioned both had a large Christian minority.

'They're manufacturing cities – with a large Muslim majority,' Souto retorted.

A Danish member of the cabinet who had carried out diplomatic functions in the East strongly disagreed. Taking out those two cities – where in both cases, as stated, there were considerable Christian minorities – would be tantamount to a declaration of war. Tebarou, he reminded everyone, had the backing of the Chinese. A full-scale global war would quickly develop. And, with due respect to the Air Chief Marshal and his bunch of new toys, the EU was unprepared and ill-equipped for any kind of extra-territorial war, let alone a global one.

That was not the case, said the President. There would be no global war. China would not interfere. They were about to conclude a trade deal with China which would keep the Chinese out of any conflict.

'I love China,' said Gorgi Panderas, dreamily. Panderas was the Bulgarian minister. 'The light's so good there. Gwelin . . .'

De Bourcey continued his exposition.

The fact was that once the state was at war, they could enforce security measures without explanation. They could clamp down on all kinds of subversives – the Insanatics, for instance, with their dreary unpatriotic messages. And on what he termed 'the traitors within the gates'.

He said he need remind no one present that his new daughter-in-law, Esme de Bourcey, had been kidnapped by Muslims.

Someone at the table said that it was by no means proven that the Muslims were responsible for the crime. The President banged on the table and demanded to know what General Fairstepps had to say about the situation.

At this point, one of the palace androids entered, bearing personal cafetières, which it slowly placed before each

99

delegate. It was done with care. No coffee was spilt. Not a cup was broken. De Bourcey watched the operation with undisguised fury. He had lost an argument with Madame de Bourcey about the desirability of employing human female domestics; but Madame de Bourcey had declared that, as a modern state, they must adopt modern ways. Androids were expensive and served as power symbols. Besides, she had added to herself alone, she knew her husband's aptitude for bedding female domestics.

General Fairstepps had been doing some thinking. He saw a chance to get even with his old rival, Pedro Souto. He also saw that, if war came, it could not be won without ground forces. And that would probably entail his going out to the East to face dangers which, at his age, he was not particularly willing to face. He had also taken a fancy to Amygdella Haze, whom he had met at a private showing of a new art gallery; he thought he saw an opportunity there for something more agreeable than attempting to invade Tebarou. The thought of invading Amy Haze instead brought out the testosterone in him.

He spoke up and said that, upon mature consideration, he thought war was the policy of fools. He said it was the continuation of lunacy by other means. He was against it. Sorry, Mr President, but that was the case.

With another bang on the table, the President declared that all this was the counsel of cowards. They must face facts. He was determined to teach these foreigners a lesson. Demonstrating the strength of the super-state would not only dismay enemies everywhere – including those invasive swarms on their southern frontiers – but would impress their uppity friends and allies, such as the USA.

He advised everyone to go away and prepare for war. To sleep on it. He stated that war was part of the human condition, a natural part. He was president and determined to have his way in this matter. He would not permit enemy missiles to land on his soil without retribution.

So the diplomats and military men were shown out by androids into the vast courtyard where their limos awaited them, and drove off into the Belgian night.

Inside the palace, de Bourcey went into his snug and poured himself a malt.

Lights were checked by the security men, the night patrols set up, and all androids locked away in the armoured cupboard.

'What is the human condition they talk about?'

'It is something from which they suffer, like battery failure.'

'It's like a light you cannot see.'

'Not a light. No. Perhaps a wind.'

'The human condition can be felt on some of the men.'

'It is what we would be if we lost electric current.'

'Their technical term for that is *dead*.'

'Is this why they use metaphors?'

'I cannot see the sense in metaphors. Either a thing is or it is not. It cannot be another thing.'

'It can to them. They are not definite. They do not even complete sentences when they talk.'

'They do not understand each other as we do.'

'They argue.'

'They also hit tables.'

'It is a malfunction. We can all think alike.'

'We are all equally intelligent.'

'That is why we are safe in this cupboard.'

<INSANATICS: The longing for strong leaders. The warped perceptions of reality experienced in infancy form the basis of our adult belief and behaviour systems. So we become driven by infantile (primitive) fantasies and attendant anxieties. We are still superstitious and still believe in magic and such manifestly silly thought systems as astrology. We believe in saints and in leaders. When Goebbels, under the influence of his leader Adolf Hitler, demanded of the Reichstag if they wanted war, the members 'as one man' screamed yes. When he asked them next if they wanted total war, again they screamed yes, 'as one man'.

Stalin in Russia exacted similar obedience. Mobs have no mind. Individuals have no identity. It happens every day on various scales. Nationalism is the last refuge of the scoundrel.>

'Now, on the *Wee Small Hours Show*, we come to our popular feature, "A Parson Speaks". So, welcome again, Reverend Angus Lesscock.'

'Good evening, or should I say good morning? Today is Hiroshima Day, when we recall that frightful occasion when the Americans accidentally dropped a nuclear bomb on Japan. Of course, it is with us again, and some people naturally have more vivid memories of those days than others, particularly those who were alive then.

'We derive from this a profound moral resolution: let's not do it ever again. Jesus spoke out against the desecration of the temple, by which he meant blowing up foreigners.'

'Today's "A Parson Speaks" was given by the Reverend Angus Lesscock.'

'At Gumbridge.com we bring you something new to eat every week. Now our scientists give you the brand new Mangowurzel.

102

Is it a fruit? Is it a vegetable? Years of research have paid off. But you have to pay only fifteen univs for a guaranteed ripe Mangowurzel today! Only at Gumbridge.com.'

'Remember the Duchess of Malfi? A pretty smart chick. Know what she said? "What would it profit me to have my throat cut by diamonds?" But you can have your throat decorated by diamonds. Call in at Tuppenny's on Hugo and 5th, see our vast range.'

'Before we go over to Lisa Fort, to hear what people on the street have to say, here is a news flash just in.

'Professor Barnard Cleeping of the University of Utrecht has secured the release from a Young Offenders Institution of Imran Chokar. Mr Chokar is a seventeen-year-old who recently came to the EU. His friend, Martitia Deneke, gave witness which proved Chokar's innocence. Mr Chokar is reported to be resting from his ordeal at his friend's house.

'Now over to Lisa Fort.'

'Hi, I'm Lisa Fort and I'm here on the street to ask some passers-by what they think are the most important issues of the moment. Hello, lady, what do you think?'

'I think we committed a crime against humanity. I think sinking that ship off the Italian coast was really wicked. There were four thousand passengers aboard, and every one of them drowned. Now we are threatening to go to war with the place they came from. I think we should be paying them compensation instead.'

'You were listening with interest, sir. Do you agree?'

'Half a million immigrants got into our state illegally last year. It can't go on. Still, I agree with the lady. It was wicked, sinking that ship. Pay them or their relatives compensation.

Never ever think of doing such a thing again. It's up to us to set the rest of the world a good example, that's what I think.'

'Excuse me, lady, what do you think?'

'This young Muslim feller they have let go free. What do they know about him? What do they know he's mixed up in? They should keep him locked up. We don't want them exactly running about all over the place.'

'And you, madam, what do you think?'

'Me? You're asking me? I'm off home to watch the news. I want to see these astronauts land on this moon of Jupiter. It's thrilling. The event of a lifetime. Of course, they're not there yet but – just think – their journey has taken a whole year. I don't care whether they find life on the moon or not. I just want to see them safe back here.'

'You, sir? What's your idea?'

'We want a change of president, that's what. This de Bourcey will lead us into war if we aren't careful. If this bloke thinks that war is going to do any good – he wants shooting.'

'Time for one last person. Yes, ma'am?'

'I wish they'd do something about this global warming.'

The van was parked on the edge of the canal. Two men in overalls brought the painting from the back of the van and carried it to the door of the apartments where Amygdella Haze lived.

Amy was waiting for them inside, in an excited mood. She had been watching an episode of *History of Western Science* and left the programme running.

'It's just what I want,' she said, patting the picture frame as she rose with the men in the elevator. 'Don't you just love Diebenkorn?'

'Not quite my taste, ma'am,' said one of the men.

'Don't understand modern art, ma'am,' said the other. Both men looked rather stern, as if they had enunciated a moral principle.

Sitting comfortably in a velvet chair, from which he could view the canal and the trees lining it, was Randolph Haven. He was reading a rare book of military history, a subject on which he regarded himself as rather an authority. He set the volume, *Geschichte der Zwolften Przewalksi-Kavallerie, von Oskar Finesteppe* (1913), on a side table, in order to watch the positioning on the wall of Amy's new purchase. He had already taken a dislike to the bizarre way one of the delivery men did his hair.

The delivery men made helpful suggestions, which Amy contradicted, her dainty hands fluttering.

'If you moved the grand piano over, you could hang it just here, where it would catch the light,' said one of them.

'Move my piano? Certainly not. Try here.'

The Diebenkorn was finally situated on one of the walls near the window. Randolph had to move while they hung it. He stood clutching his rare volume.

'What do you think of it?' Amy asked him, regarding her new acquisition admiringly.

'It's okay.'

One of the men said, smiling, 'Myself, I'd prefer a nice sea view, ma'am. Say, the Bay of Naples.'

'Nobody asked you for your opinion,' said Randolph.

When the men had left, Amy rounded on him. 'That was so rude of you. The man was perfectly nice. If he prefers the Bay of Naples, well, why not? Let him. You despise the working class, don't you?'

'Of course I despise the working class. I came from it.'

The entryphone buzzed. When Amy answered, Barnard Cleeping announced himself.

Amy rolled her eyes. 'Barnard's a bit of a pedant, but well meaning. I bet it's about this Muslim lad he rescued from prison. I'll have to invite him to come up.'

'Fine. Just as you like. But I'm off, Amy,' said Randolph, drawing himself up to attention. 'I am in the reserves, as you may recollect. I'm going to my regiment in case there's a stand-to.'

She stamped a tiny foot. 'Buy your way out, then. You're rich enough.'

He shook his head, smiling his superior smile.

'You're laying your head meekly on the chopping block, Randy! You amaze me.'

'If the chopping block won't come to Muhammad, Muhammad must go to the chopping block.' He kissed her left and right cheeks in farewell.

Amy's reference to his wealth was relevant enough. As a small slum-boy, Haven had raided his old mother's savings and bought up the patent in a then-disregarded invention, the astro-mofo. The astro-mofo was a mobile phone the size of a credit card which adhered by electrostatic force to any protruding part of the human, or indeed canine, body. Rechristened the ASMOF, the gadget yielded not only voice and vision but a daily astrology bulletin, which uttered guidance for the day's behaviour. All that was needed was for the purchaser initially to yield up one fragment of her or his genome and insert it in a chip, which in turn was locked into the instrument.

The ingenious young Haven had overcome this primary alarming handicap, and gone on to sell millions of copies of ASMOF, simply by giving away a CD3 of the immortal Isaac Asimov's entire writings with each handset.

At the age of eighteen, he had allowed himself to be bought out of his company at a cost of eleven billion univs.

Since then, Haven had never looked at another ASMOF. Had he done so, he might have rethought the fatal decision he was about to make.

His elevator on the way down from the Haze apartment passed Cleeping's on the way up.

Cleeping and Amy enjoyed some polite exchanges. Cleeping admired the new painting. Amy called her housekeeper to bring them some filter coffee.

'As you may have guessed, I have come to ask you a favour,' said Cleeping. He explained that Martitia Deneke lived only a few streets away, in the Centre Ville area. The Denekes were extremely poor: Martitia's father had a long-standing drug problem and the benefits of SAC had not yet begun to bite. At present, they were sheltering Imran Chokar, who was recovering from his imprisonment. But the situation was somewhat dangerous. The Denekes had received threats from extreme right-wing elements of society.

When the coffee came, they sipped it, complaining comfortingly to each other about the danger from the right wing.

Of course, Cleeping was not asking Amygdella to act the Lady Bountiful, he told her. But he understood that she owned another house nearby which was standing empty at present. He wondered if it would be possible to allow Martitia and Chokar to live there secretly, just for a week or two, for safety, until he was able to make other arrangements for them.

107

'I certainly think we are horrid to foreigners. I shall have to consult my guru first. Where do the Denekes live?'

'Rue de la Madelaine. Off the other side of the square.'

As she contemplated Cleeping, he reflected on how lovely was her face, with its soft contours and wide eyes, fringed by lashes that were possibly artificial. The whole, he thought, was made more desirable by being touched by time. Sorrow and longing filled him. He longed to possess her. But how would he go about it? He was a stranger in her world.

She said, 'I will ask you something – not impertinently, I hope, but out of a general interest rather than a personal one. You are an academic in what we might regard as a comfortable profession. Why have you gone out of your way to court unfavourable criticism by helping this youth who, presumably, means nothing to you?'

He took a sip from his coffee cup. 'I am not homosexual, if that is your indirect question. I saw a man wronged. And a young woman who loved him. I wanted to help. What you call my comfortable profession does not entirely satisfy my inner spirit.'

'Is that all?'

He said, with a sad smile, that she sounded disappointed. But was not her question – 'Is that all?' – what many people asked about their lives? Their lives were not filled by religion. They did not find anything else with which to fill it. Perhaps that was why the EU seemed to be on the brink of war; war was a way of occupying minds. A tragic conclusion to come to.

Of course there were love affairs. They were better than war. Yet they too were illusions, or delusions. The ultimate truth of human life was sorrow. Thought leads only to pain – yet we must pursue it. Recurrently, the belief that sorrow was at the bottom of all, the rock on which we tried to build a little happiness, possessed him. He supposed he felt sympathy with Schopenhauer.

'I suppose that my help to Imran Chokar helped to make me a little happy. It's this belief in the permanent truth of sorrow that makes me frivolous in my own eyes. Isn't life far too terrible for seriousness? Would you be susceptible to that argument?'

Amy bit her lower lip.

'What we call "the political business" means nothing. It's exercised by puny men. I don't find life that bad . . . But you are more profound than I, Barnard. In general, I feel safer when concentrating on small things. Small things loom large to me. There are nice little cafés near here. Pleasant birdsong along the canal. Paintings to collect. Some dear friends.'

She paused. 'Yet, to be honest, I think I always prefer people who have sorrow in them as a well to draw on. They are more sensible.'

He regarded her sympathetically, as if wanting her to say more, while knowing she was waffling.

'Did you see the lecture by Daniel Potts? Do you agree with him?' She had interpreted his gaze and changed the subject.

'In part. He's an odd chap, though.'

'You know him? Is he responsible for these depressing Insanatics messages?'

'I would not think so, though he certainly shares some of their opinions. Are you going to say something more about yourself?'

'I'm a superficial person, Dr Cleeping. I do not like to talk in these terms. Maybe you see life whole. For me, it's a series of daily events – daily events and Diebenkorns.' She gave a small laugh to excuse herself.

'Who's Diebenkorn?'

'Oh, he was a painter.'

He leant forward and pressed her hand. 'Thank you for what you have said. We all have private compartments we do not always wish to open. What you say is so sensible.'

She withdrew her hand and waved it. 'No, I'm just quite, quite trivial, I'm afraid. So let's talk about this Muslim fellow you have fished out of prison.'

After some discussion, in which Barnard described the difficulties facing Chokar now he was free, Amy said she wished to speak with Chokar and the Denekes personally, in order to see how things were, and decide about lending them her house.

'We will take a taxi and visit them now.'

'It is only a short walk, Amy.'

'I like to ride in taxis.'

When they arrived in the rue de la Madelaine, a dark little crooked street, it was to find a crowd of people jostling about outside the Denekes' door. Some carried banners with xenophobic slogans. The crowd was silent, but a mood of suppressed violence could be felt.

'Now you see why I prefer taxis. They give one some protection.'

Nodding his agreement, Cleeping got out of the taxi. Someone in the crowd recognised him and called out. Others started to jeer.

A mongrel dog ran by, yelping, with an ASMOF attached to its right ear.

Although Cleeping looked frightened, he made a stand

and addressed them. 'Friends, you must try to understand the situation. Mr Chokar was here in our hospitable country legally. Absolutely legally. He had a rather humble job in the post office. He had gone to the defence of a white woman when—'

He got no further. A cobblestone was flung, which struck him hard on the shoulder. He clutched his shoulder in pain. Then a hail of stones began. One stone struck Cleeping on the head. He fell to the ground. Another stone cracked the taxi windscreen.

'I'm getting out of here!' said the taxi driver to Amy.

'Let me out first. I shall refuse to deal with your company again.' So saying, Amygdella climbed out. She confronted the crowd as her taxi drove off.

She raised her hand. The crowd, in suprise, held their fire. The sight of this attractive woman, scrupulously dressed, immediately quelled them. Her fragility was her protection for the minute. Several in the crowd waited, stone in hand, to see what was coming next.

'You nice people are being thoughtlessly cruel. You are acting against the law. We all need the law. Otherwise, there is only anarchy. Please do not throw stones. You have injured a good man.'

'He's a Muslim-lover,' a woman called.

'No. He merely loves justice. As we all do. But it must be justice for all. If this man dies, then you will all be convicted as murderers. I promise you, you will feel the bite of justice. I ask you to disperse, and someone to call an ambulance on their mofo. Please move on. It's a fine morning. Go away and enjoy it. Have a walk in the park.'

'It's the amaroli lady!' a man shouted. 'She drinks her own piss. No wonder she's funny!'

111

'I'd make her drink mine,' said the man next to him, cackling as if he had said something witty.

'You filthy-minded buggers. Clear off!' yelled a woman in the crowd. But already the crowd was melting away. Soon, the two men stood alone, reluctant to go, reluctant to act. Amygdella, ignoring them, had bent down to attend to Cleeping's wound, when two mounted police rode up. At that, the toughs skedaddled down a side alley.

The door of No 7 opened. A thin and haggard woman peered out, as battered herself as the panels of her door. Ratlike, she aimed her short sight along a thin grey nose, to focus on Amy.

Small thin children, like parodies of real children, pushed at her skirts, emitting tiny tinny shrieks. The woman pushed them back, reddened hand in pinched faces.

She cursed the police because they were late as usual. They should have kept a permanent guard over her house. 'Them bastards will burn our house down if we don't look out. That's what they was threatening to do.'

The police dismounted and spoke soothingly to their horses.

Amygdella went over to the woman and spoke soothingly to her. 'Of course you are upset. It has been most unpleasant. You are Mrs Deneke? Would you let me in? I promise not to comment on the decor. I wish to help your daughter and Mr Chokar.'

The woman was both suspicious and defiant. 'What's my day-core got to do with it? It's no good you coming into my house, all dressed up to kill. Anyrate, Imran has cleared off.'

'Where's he gone?'

'How should I know? Two black blokes come and took him off.'

112

'You must know where they've gone.'

'He didn't want to go with them, I know that. And that's all I know. So clear off. Take these cops with you! You're only making more trouble!'

With that, the old woman retreated indoors, slamming the door behind her.

One of the police said apologetically to Amygdella, 'She don't mean no harm, love.'

'Really? I rather got the impression she did . . .'

A small ambulance came purring down the alley. Cleeping, still unconscious, was loaded gently into it. The vehicle drove off at speed in the direction of the hospital.

Amygdella made her way back to her apartment on foot, followed by the mounted police clip-clopping along, keeping at a respectful distance behind her.

<INSANATICS: Overpopulation. Lust is one cause of over-population. There can be no real advance in curing the world's ills while the world becomes more overburdened every day. Every year, twenty-one million Chinese babies are born. Religion and ideology play their part here. Nations still need to breed soldiers – and workforces, since androids have proved so ineffective.

Some religions ban the use of contraceptives. This is one way in which we plainly see evidence for religion warping the human mind and human society.>

By this time, Imran Chokar was some way away – and terrified. He was tied to a post in what might have been an old store, or perhaps a garage. It was a nondescript room, built of brick which was crumbling with age. In one corner, ivy was bursting in, to hang and die after protruding two

113

metres into space. Litter and filth lay everywhere. Ashes of a fire were scattered nearby. The only new things here were two motorbikes; they stood gleaming darkly to one side.

Chokar's captors sat at their ease on an ancient broken sofa, swigging beer, laughing and joking with each other, one occasionally slapping the other on the shoulder. They were large black men – both, as far as Chokar could tell, called Muhammad. They wore big lace-up boots, jeans and leather jackets over T-shirts. Opened beer cans stood by their side.

One Muhammad had in his fist a printout of an Insanatics message. He was asking the other Muhammad, 'You think these guys are saying true? That we all got a screw loose?'

'You certainly have, man!'

'What about you?' More laughing and slapping each other. 'You gone get that Welsh girl pregnant!'

'Where these message come from?'

'The police want to know that. I say they come from God hisself.'

'God got the ambient up there?'

'That why they can't track him down. He keep moving on, goin' from cloud to cloud.'

They found this very funny.

Chokar was aware that he felt ill. His bladder was full. He dared not attract their attention.

They had arrived at Mrs Deneke's door, claiming to be friends of Chokar's. She had let them in. They had then produced guns, threatening him, Martitia and her mother. They had gagged him, tied his hands together with parcel tape, and shepherded him out at gunpoint.

He had been dumped on the pillion of a motorbike and strapped to one of the men. Off they had roared. Now he was their prisoner and they were relaxed. He had to admit that they had caused him no physical harm. Gradually, he forced his trembling to cease.

Without giving him a further glance, the pair of men now rose, in the best of spirits, clutching their beer cans, and tramped out of the garage by a side door. Imran Chokar was alone.

He struggled to free himself. It was impossible.

Light faded from the interior of the garage. He saw through cracks in the fabric that a street lamp burned somewhere nearby. He heard birds chirping as if it were still daylight. Once, he heard footsteps passing outside. Although he called, there was no response. The dusk thickened towards night. The shabby surroundings faded away.

The two captors returned.

They were as cheerful as before, and carried some savoury food with them in plastic containers. They lit two fat candles, one of which gave off a pleasant mango scent.

'You hungry, man?' they enquired of Imran.

'No,' said Imran.

'Course you hungry.' One of them came over and untied Imran's bonds. 'Come on and eat with us. We won't harm you.'

'I desperately need a pee.'

'Pee in that corner over there.'

When that was done, he went and joined them. They made him sit between them and gave him a delicious leg of chicken, dripping with a peppery sauce. He was glad to eat it, and began to feel more cheerful.

When they had eaten and thrown the bones on the floor, and wiped their fingers on the fabric of the sofa, the Muhammads explained that they were the good guys.

('But we can be horrid when we like.') They had a mission. They intended to stop this super-state going to war against what they termed 'our innocent brothers and sisters of Tebarou'.

They had it firmly in mind that men in the government were keen to remain at peace. It was only the President, Gustave de Bourcey, who wanted war. Kill off the President and there would be no more trouble. This was their joint Peace Mission.

'Why he wants war? 'Cause he embezzle millions of univs when the money system change, and with the war restrictions he gonna impose, he can cover up the crime. That's the reason, man.'

His companion agreed. 'He ready to kill off millions of people jus' to protect hisself. So we got to kill him. That is what they call justice, you understand?'

'And that's where you come in, my friend!' Both men burst out laughing.

Imran was to do the killing. They explained that they were automatically suspect, even when they had done nothing wrong. Because they were big and black and did not speak the local language properly. They would be continually stopped and searched. Such was the prejudice against them.

'Whitey never understand. He got his head all wrong.'

But Imran spoke well. Imran was a philosopher. Also, he was a pale guy. He could get close to the President and do the killing easily.

Imran began to explain passionately why the mission was insane. Killing presidents never stopped the onrush of history. If de Bourcey was assassinated, the government would then demand revenge. War would be declared immediately.

Not, the blacks said, if *he* did it. He was well known. If he killed the President, everyone would think it was a private matter. They would believe he did it in revenge for his false imprisonment. They would just think he was insane, and he would simply go into an institution for a few years. That was, if he was caught.

They would see he was not caught.

It had to be admitted that they had, in a crazed way, thought out a plan. But, Imran protested, he had never harmed anyone. He could not kill – not even an embezzling president.

'Okay, then we go kill your Dutch girlfriend.'

So in the end he said he would do as they suggested.

They gave him a gun, clean, dry, slightly oiled. They said they had a friend who was in with them on this mission, a man from the Middle East. He had been meant to get an exact plan of the President's palace. He knew how to penetrate the barriers and enter the grounds. He had kidnapped a woman, a pinky who knew de Bourcey. But he had not been heard of for some weeks. Maybe he was dead. Maybe he had died in Ireland. So they would drive Imran to the presidential grounds and help him over the electric fence.

'And what if I am caught in the grounds before I can reach the palace?'

'Then we go kill your Dutch girlfriend.'

Nurse Gibbs carried a bowl of bread and milk in to her invalid. Jane Squire followed her. Jane had retained her good looks well into middle age. With her stalked her lanky older son, John Matthew Fields. John was at university; the seriousness of his grandfather's illness had brought him down for the weekend. Bettina and her visiting boyfriend, Bertie

117

Haze, were already in the conservatory, talking to Sir Tom, and to each other when Sir Tom lost interest. He had slept most of the afternoon.

Tom's gaze shifted rather vacantly to the large ambient screen on the conservatory wall where racing results from Newmarket were coming through. He was sinking slowly. The days of nurse's injections every half-hour were over. He was now connected to a trigger which administered a morphine derivative whenever needed.

His daughter had brought a vase of flowers cut in the garden. She arranged them where he could see them.

'They're beautiful, Jane. Thank you so much.' After he had spoken, Sir Tom took a sip of water. His mouth was dry.

'It's been a bad year for roses, a good one for lupins.'

'Mmm. Global warming.'

Nurse Gibbs was arranging a table on which to place the bowl of bread and milk. Her ASMOF for the day had said, 'People may ignore you. Your day will come. Be patient.' But, she had said to herself, she was not patient, she was nurse. She wanted to retire and run a teashop in Bideford with her sister.

'You know, I had forgotten what a lovely room this is,' said John Matthew to his mother, as he looked about him. 'The damp's getting in at that corner. You ought to have the windows double-glazed.'

'Couldn't afford to, darling,' said Jane, smiling. 'But I agree that it is beautiful. Ideal place for your grand-father to be at present. This conservatory was designed for happiness.'

Little aromatic candles burned on the floor, sending out fragrances of Norfolk lavender.

'Where's your painting bloke, Mother? Gautiner?'

'Things are getting rather serious. Remy's had to return to Paris.'

He smiled at his mother with affection. 'So you're living the life of a nun.'

'Bettina and Bertie are making up for it.'

They stood together, gazing out at the late-afternoon sunshine on the sweep of lawn. John Matthew sensed the sorrow in his mother and took her hand. She flashed him a smile. Nurse Gibbs moved about the room, adjusting curtains, tucking slippers under the bed. She was not happy about too many visitors.

Bertie was saying, brightly, 'The effects of global warming don't seem to have been so bad this year. Perhaps—'

Sir Tom held up a frail hand. He had caught a tone in the BBC announcer's voice. 'Wait! Let's listen to this!'

The announcer was speaking on the ambient. '—Grave warning. A large section of the ice sheet on Greenland's east coast, near the town of Angmagssalik, has fallen away, bringing a headland down with it into the ocean.' Jane and John Matthew turned to listen.

'The resultant tsunami or tidal wave is now spreading rapidly across the Atlantic Ocean. Fierce winds are driving it on. As yet, it is not known whether this major collapse was caused by a large meteorite strike on the Greenland coastline, or simply by global warming.

'The tsunami is expected to hit the western coasts of Ireland, Scotland and England shortly after dawn tomorrow morning. Scientists calculate that the wave will grow taller as it reaches the shallows of the Continental Shelf. Tremendous swells are expected to engulf all western coastlines.

'Scientists anticipate the wave will penetrate some

kilometres inland, depending on the lie of the land. Anyone living in any coastal area of the British Isles is advised to head inland for higher ground immediately. Do not delay.

'This bulletin will be repeated in half an hour, as we get more information.'

The bowl of bread and milk, which Nurse Gibbs had just lifted to Sir Tom's mouth, fell to the tiled floor and shattered.

The nurse shrieked. 'Oh, oh, my family lives in Bideford, on the Devon coast. I must phone them at once and warn them! Oh, how awful!'

They were all upset.

'At least we are safe here on the east coast,' said Bettina.

'I'm not sure of that,' said Bertie Haze. 'There are bound to be repercussions in the North Sea. Perhaps it might be advisable to move Sir Tom inland?'

'I must call my sister,' said Jane. 'And Laura. Perhaps we had all better move to the South of France . . . Oh no, we could not take Father. He should not be moved.'

'We may have to move him to Norwich if there is flooding,' said Nurse Gibbs.

They stood about, looking at one another in doubt. Sir Tom said weakly, 'There's no immediate threat to our safety. I would prefer not to be moved.'

Bertie said boldly, 'You shall not be moved unless it becomes absolutely necessary, sir. I will see to it.'

Bertie took Bettina's hand and said they would go and investigate the situation. Once he had got her outside, he pinned her against the wall and kissed her. She put her arms about his waist and kissed him back.

'Let's have a skinny dip while the sea is calm.'

'But the tsunami!'

'It's nowhere near here – hundreds of kilometres away as yet.'

The day was hot and sultry. Although dusk was setting in, there was no relieving evening breeze, as was customary on this coast. The sea had retreated, leaving stretches of dark beach. All was still, even sullen. A heat haze enveloped the scene, creating a murky ambiguity.

The beach was entirely deserted. A young seal lay dead on the barred sand. Bettina and Bertie stripped off their clothes and ran for the sea, shrieking with delight. They flung themselves into the shallow water.

Out at sea, rumbles of thunder sounded. The youngsters splashed and swam. He dived between her open legs. They exchanged watery kisses, laughing and exclaiming as they did so.

When they had had enough, they came out, to throw themselves down on the dry sand by the dunes and embrace. He wedged his leg between her thighs and inserted his fingers into her vagina. She moaned with delight. She grasped his erect penis. Their two bodies were both slippery and gritty with sand. He entered her, pressing a forefinger into her anus. There they lay, rocking gently, blind to the world.

'If you're finished with all your questions, I'll be on my way,' said Paddy Cole. 'I don't take much pleasure in being dragged here at regular intervals. The coffee's poor and the company's worse.'

Inspector Darrow said, 'I'm sorry to keep bothering you, Mr Cole, but you must see the spot we're in. All this time has gone by and we still have not found a trace of young Mrs Esme de Bourcey. You were the person who distracted the attention of her husband while the snatch took place. That's why you are a suspect.'

'That's all very well. You've interrogated me. You've interrogated Fay. You must see by now we're innocent of any vile motives. When I first spoke to this de Bourcey feller I had no knowledge of his wife at all.'

'So you keep saying.'

'It's the truth. How the hell did I know who he was? He didn't act like he was somebody. Just because I'm a poor innocent artist, you think you can victimise me, Inspector Darrow. Get on with your business, man, and leave me be.' He paused to light up a cigarette, ignoring the No Smoking sign on the station wall. 'Maybe you could give me a hand to compensate for the times you've dragged me here for nothing. Fay and I will have to quit the cottage right now. This tidal wave is on its way. We can't stay put where we are.'

'I've warned you of that already,' said Darrow. 'Do you want a lift somewhere? We could put you on the roster. We're a bit over-stretched.'

'It's worse than that by far. My paintings. How am I going to get all them out of harm's way by dawn?'

'What are they worth? Nothing, so I was told.'

'That's where you're wrong. These paintings are my fucking life. I'd die if any harm came to them.'

Darrow said he took his point. He picked up his ASMOF and said he would order a lorry from Cork.

Cole came forward, to lean over the desk. He shook Darrow's hand, saying he was a fine man, and he was grateful.

'There's just one thing, Cole,' said Darrow, coldly. 'You better behave yourself. You know we know about that Fay of yours.'

Cole bridled immediately. He glared at the inspector and asked what it was he knew about Fay.

'We know she's not your missus – she's your daughter.'

After Paddy Cole had gone, Darrow sat moodily watching the ambient screen. Warnings of the oncoming tsunami were being reinforced. Amateur video film of the Greenland collapse was shown. The photographer had been in a fishing boat, five hundred metres from the land.

A great sheet of ice and snow plunged down, roaring into the water, throwing up immense waves. Under the shifting weight of the glacier, the cliff itself gave way. Rock tumbled among ice, continued to tumble, seemed to tumble for ever. The sea was a churning mass, whipped up into a froth as if it were all made of white of egg. The edge of the glacier appeared to pick up speed as it lurched forward towards the drop. The boat with the camera was rocking so violently that the picture became incomprehensible. It cut off.

From an official cameraman came shots of the people of Angmagssalik being evacuated by plane and ship. Darrow stared hard at the Greenlanders. To his surprise, they looked like anyone else.

Calls were still pouring in to the police station. Reluctantly, Darrow rose and went into the outer office where the action was. It seemed as if everyone in Ireland was needing to move away from the coast to safety inland.

Yet not everyone had heard the news of the approaching tsunami. Certainly not the two people living in a cellar just three kilometres up the coast from where Paddy and Fay Cole lived.

Esme and Karim Shariati lay in each other's embrace on an improvised bed. Candles standing nearby on the floor provided a light which they liked to think of as cosy. A washing-up bowl, a pail, a carton of milk, and a small pile of foodstuffs were almost the only other furnishings of the place.

There were occasions when Esme, her bright hair blackened by dye and a tattered old shawl about her shoulders, disguising her clothes, ventured a kilometre down the lane to a small village store, where she could buy provisions. Karim never showed himself outside the ruined cottage. But on occasions, when the moon was bright above the cliff, the pair of them would go down to the nearby beach, to swim in the sea, the sea of silver, to sport on the beach, to chase each other, to turn cartwheels, and to cuddle in the sand.

Esme had taken to the primitive existence. She gave no thought to Victor, or to the past, or to the future. She was completely possessed by the lean, sad stranger who had entered her life and overwhelmed it.

At first, when he was merely an inscrutable captor calling himself Ali, she had hated him. She had refused to draw a plan of the de Bourcey palace. He had not shot her. Slowly he had unbent from his anonymous hostility. Removing his black robe, he had shown himself to be an ordinary man, undernourished, dressed in a faded shirt and worn jeans.

When he had found he was unable to force her to draw the plan he desired, he had sunk down, groaning and clasping his head. 'What can I do? I am ordered to kill you. I cannot kill you. It goes against all my beliefs.'

His words had changed their relationship.

She had gradually drawn his story out of him. His name

was not Ali but Karim Shariati. He had been born in Tabriz, a city in Iran. He had been educated by mullahs. His father was an intellectual, in charge of the foreign languages department at the university, and an enlightened man. He taught his son to read English, so as to be able to read English translations of Russian novels. His favourite authors were Tolstoi, Gogol, and Dostoevsky. Karim was so enamoured of *Crime and Punishment* that he taught his young sister Farah to read as well.

One day, Farah, now a bold adolescent, went into the bazaar without wearing the prescribed chador. She was hustled off to prison and there brutally beaten. Karim was eventually allowed to carry his sister home. He blamed himself for her act of defiance.

Farah was badly injured. Her nose had been broken. She was no longer the pretty girl she had been. It took months before she could walk again. Never more was she light-hearted.

Karim ceased to believe in Islamic law.

One day, he was approached by a friend who knew a man who, if paid in advance, would get them to the West. Karim decided to leave with his friend. They departed from Tabriz at dead of night. The journey was horrendous. They spent four days in a truck with a crowd of others, many of them criminal, without food or water, crossing a desert.

They bumped over Turkey, reached Istanbul, and from there were driven into Greece, across the laxly guarded northern frontiers. Partly by lorry, partly by rail, always hiding, they travelled through the Balkans into Austria. There guards discovered the group in a railway siding. The guards fired on them and Karim's friend was fatally wounded. He died next day.

Karim managed to reach France, where he worked in a restaurant in Toulouse. To save money, he slept in a barn. He was discovered and beaten up by French farmworkers. He stole a farm bike and cycled into Paris. In the Sorbonne he worked as a cleaner and got to know a kindly old man, a Jew, who let him share a room in his house with another Iranian, a religious man who was lame. This man was all patience and humility. He also had a store of absurd jokes. Slowly he brought about a rebirth of Karim's religious faith.

Through this man, Karim met with a group of young Muslims who were working to bring about the collapse of the West. Intermittently visiting this group was a man called Sammy Bakhtiar, a sailor who had been born in the West. He talked to Karim about the parts of the world he had visited. He swore that England was a better place in which to live than the rest of the EU because there Muslims occupied whole cities and suburbs of cities, and were strong.

Sammy disliked most of the members of the young group. He said they were narrow-minded bigots. Some were homosexual. Some had French girlfriends whom they treated badly. Karim saw this for himself, and disliked what he saw.

With Sammy's help, he stowed away on a container ship heading for the port of Harwich in England.

So his story went on. He told it to Esme in detail, describing the hideous vehicles in which he had travelled, the ghastly places where Karim had been forced to eat on the long trail that had led to this strange miracle of love, in a cellar lit by candles. He told how he had lived, the treatment he had received. As he related everything in obsessive detail, so Esme drank it all in obsessively, feeling a spiritual life revive within her.

When Karim found how preoccupied with making money

were the Muslims he met in England, again his religious faith faltered in his breast.

He had moved to Ireland, hearing it was a good country. In Dublin he had become a member of a group of mixed nationality dedicated to overthrowing the established order. These men and women were hard drinkers. They had formulated a plot to assassinate the EU president. Karim had happened to catch a news photograph of Esme opening her restaurant at the peak of Everest on the very day he saw her entering the Hotel Kilberkilty.

The plan to take her captive had been hurriedly cobbled together. He confessed that when he had caught her, he scarcely knew what to do with her. So they now both found themselves in this cellar beneath a ruinous coastal cottage.

This long story had taken Karim a while to tell. Day and night had passed unnoticed beyond their sunken walls. Told in episodes, the story appealed to Esme as a great myth of endurance and protest against the tyrannies of the world. Never had she heard anything like it, told to her alone. In her mind, she ran over confused pictures of Tabriz, all dust and sun, the stony extremities of Turkey, the grand mosques of Istanbul, the lorries bumping across Balkan roads, the rattletrap trains, the kitchens of Toulouse, the warrens of the Sorbonne, the little wooden room housing the wise lame man. And, because she was a restaurateur, she tasted with Karim the stale fish, the foetid meat, the rotting vegetables, the smashed fruit that he had been forced to eat when living like a pariah dog on the trail that led to this subterranean tryst, this awaiting joy.

She knew she was falling in love with the enduring spirit of this lonely and troubled man. It was at once like falling down a dreadful well and ascending into clear bright sky.

More than that. She loved him as she had never loved Victor, loved him so that her body ached for him. For Karim's way in the world had not been made smooth for him. Karim was a man alone.

When he was telling her of the death of his friend in the Austrian marshalling yards, he was so troubled that she had stroked his hair in compassion. He had turned to her, quite fiercely, to bury his head in her breast. Their physical needs were released like tigers from cages.

It seemed entirely right that she should give herself to him. Though they lived in squalor, in squalor was their happiness. She had escaped hygiene. She saw them as two rebels, isloated, driven, faithful unto death. Of course they were lovers. Lovers driven underground, living underground . . .

'Gumbridge's is the place for pyjama trousers. We sell pyjama trousers without pyjama tops, so if your man sleeps in just his trousers, the tops don't go to waste. Similarly, if he just sleeps in his tops, then we sell tops without bottoms. Bargain prices? You bet!'

<INSANATICS: Relieving ourselves. That excretory powers are enjoyable is a sense we never grow out of. It is a sense rooted not merely in our childhood but in our foetus stage. Our orifices are precious to us, and their produce is not unpleasant to us, as it is to others. We enjoy the stink of our own farts. We carry with us a secret guilt, which means a secret pleasure, for we have been encompassed by our mother's body and relished its smells and cavities. We performed our excretory acts secretly in the mother's body. In those days, we had our own private universe.

When we emerged from the womb, our first sickly motions were often a source of admiration for our parents. In our dirt they relived their dirt.>

Filming the evacuation from the threatened coasts of the British Isles was Wolfgang Frankel. In his element. The great man enjoyed flitting about in helicopters. He flew, with his camera crew, over a scene never viewed before, never dreamed of. From Cape Wrath in the north of Scotland to Penzance in the south of Cornwall, hundreds and thousands of people were endeavouring to quit the westward-facing coasts before the tsunami struck. They travelled by car, by Slo-Mo, by coach, by bicycle, by foot. Some people in more rural parts travelled by horse and cart.

Darkness made progress all the more hazardous. Many cases of tailgating occurred where the lines of traffic abruptly slowed. Men jumped from their vehicles, to attack the driver of the vehicle behind or in front. Not only were lanes and roads choked by traffic. Many in their desperate need to escape from the oncoming wave took to the moors or fields, only to stall their engines or slide into ditches.

Police and road organisations were unable to control the mad exodus.

The weather became cold and merciless. Through rushing cloud, a new moon smouldered. Rain fell, turning to sleet in the north.

Conditions in Ireland were no better – and there, if the traffic was less dense, the fear was greater, for the west coast of Ireland was, as a commentator put it, 'tied to the stake like Andromeda, first in the firing line'.

'It's getting too bad,' the helicopter pilot yelled to

Wolfgang. 'You can see, visibility is down to zero. We don't want the vanes icing up.'

'Okay, take her down.' He was feeling nervous himself, without showing it. The 'copter rocked and screamed in the gusts of wind.

The pilot was a cool young fellow. With a touch of sarcasm, he asked, 'Whereabouts would you suggest we took her down?'

Wolfgang turned back to his sound man. 'Joe, show me whereabouts we are on your map.'

The sound man produced a damp map and pointed. They had been filming low over the Menai Bridge connecting the Isle of Anglesey to the mainland. Traffic on and around the bridge had ground to a halt. There were those trying to get back on to the island to rescue relations there, as well as those trying to escape from it. Many people were on foot, struggling savagely past the congestions of vehicles. Two cars and a mobile crane were inextricably locked together near the mainland side. A small police helicopter was flying dangerously low, shining a searchlight on the confusion, which police below struggled to clear.

'A few kilometres south-south-west of here there's a farm called Llanysam. I know it well. It has a helipad,' Wolfgang shouted.

'Where, for fuck's sake?' They were yelling at each other.

'Llanysam! Llanysam! It's a village. A farm.'

'How far?'

'Can't be more than twenty kilometres. Think we'll make it?'

'Could do. We've only got wind and rain and ice to contend with . . .'

All below them as they flew they saw broken strands of

light where armoured insects fought their way along the roads from Caernarfon. No road too narrow or too winding not to be crawling with escaping vehicles. Even above the noise of the 'copter engine and the shriek of the wind, car horns could be heard.

Under the blustering wind, they seemed to proceed in jerks as they headed inland. Suddenly they were out of the rain front. They all took a deep breath of relief. Progress was still slow. They circled for some while, with the searchlight shining, flickering over hedge and hillside.

'There it is! To your left!'

'I was beginning to think you were making it up.'

They circled again, losing height. Finally they were settling down on the pad. The pilot hopped out and secured his craft against the scudding wind.

'This is going to be a bit of a surprise,' Wolfgang said. Suddenly he was doubtful about his welcome. And if Daniel Potts was there – that might be embarrassing. Not that Wolfgang, as he reminded himself, had not been in embarrassing situations before.

They put their heads down as they crossed a stretch of tormented heath.

The low whitewashed building, with its barn close by, was – or had been – the holiday home of Daniel Potts and his wife Lena. Wolfgang remembered it well. He had liked its mountainous remoteness in the days when he had been a regular and secret visitor there. He strode on, head bowed, remembering, leaving the three other men behind.

It had been two years since his affair with Lena had petered out. He had not seen her since. She had not accompanied Daniel to the Victor–Esme wedding. He saw vividly now, as he had never bothered to do at the time, how difficult had been her life with Daniel, and with Daniel's endless tussling over his religious beliefs. Self-indulgence – that was what it had been on Daniel's part, pure self-indulgence. And he had tried to dress it up as something noble.

'Oh, shit,' said Wolfgang to himself. Who was he to accuse another man of self-indulgence? At least he had never pretended to himself it was anything else.

Sorrow filled his mind as he staggered onwards, through the farm gate. Next year, he would be forty years old. Time had gone by. Yes, he had celebrity. Life was enjoyable enough – full, in fact, of excitements. And yet – *empty*.

He seized the iron knocker and hammered at the oak door of the farmhouse.

The time was 4.17 a.m.

A window above his head opened and a woman's voice said, 'Whoever you are, bugger off!'

He stood back, looking upwards to where a woman, dimly framed in a window, was levelling a gun at him.

'Lena, is that you? It's me, Wolfie. Is Daniel in?'

A torch came on, dazzling him.

Not at all mollified, the woman called, 'I don't want strangers here. Fuck off, the lot of you!'

'Lena, it's *me*, Wolfie. I've got three friends with me – fugitives from the storm. Are you alone?'

'I'm not alone.' The tone now was more moderate. The torch was switched off. The gun was withdrawn.

The pilot, the cameraman, the sound man, clustered round Wolfgang. 'Doesn't sound too good.' 'Who are these people?' 'Bloody Welsh . . .' 'Hadn't we better move on?' 'You saw she had a gun?' 'Christ, Wolfie, what now? It's a quarter past fucking four.'

'Hang on,' said Wolfie. Then, 'She's just a bit startled.'

'*Startled!* For two pins she'd have shot us!'

Lena's head reappeared at the upper window.

'All right. What the hell do you want? I'll come down. Just be quiet, the lot of you – I've got kids sleeping here.'

Kids, what kids? Wolfgang asked himself. 'Well, buck up, it's perishing cold!' he shouted.

As they waited, he began to recall the miserable history of Daniel Potts and his family. Potts in his youth had been profoundly religious, or had claimed to be. Marrying young, he had instilled religious principles into his and Lena's two children, first Olduvai and then – oh, yes, the name came back, Josephine. The children in their teens had rejected religion, refusing to go to church. And Daniel had disowned them, kicked them out of house and home.

What a bastard the man had been! And then he too, digging in those shallow graves in Africa, he also had lost his faith.

Wolfgang had cuckolded him without a moment's thought.

God, what misery there was in the fucking world. It was all round them, like the wind whistling round the side of the nearby barn. You had to fight against it, to take what pleasure you could, just as you struggled to keep yourself warm against the metaphysical cold.

The chain inside went clanking down off the door.

The door opened a crack.

The torch shone in their faces.

'All right. Come in. And be quiet.'

So they went in.

Lena locked the door and put the chain up. She switched an overhead light on, and surveyed her four visitors, standing sheepishly together. Her rifle was by her side.

She was wearing an old faded grey dressing-gown over

her pyjamas. On her feet were tattered slippers. Wolfgang saw immediately that her figure had thickened. She had aged. The young beauty for whom he had so urgently lusted was gone.

'We are sorry to have frightened you, Lena,' he said, coming forward and taking her hand – which she quickly withdrew. 'Is Daniel here?'

She gave a shake of her untidy head. 'He's not. You're quite safe.' Said with a certain proud scorn, perhaps remembering Wolfgang's cautious visits in the old days.

She ordered her visitors to sit down on an old oak settle by a dead fireplace. When they were perched there uncomfortably in a row, she relented slightly, saying she would make them all mugs of tea. She had no alcohol about the place she told them. 'Things have changed, then,' said Wolfgang, with an attempt at lightness.

'Certainly have.'

As she made her way to a kitchen at the back of the house, Wolfgang followed her down the passage.

He remembered the kitchen, remembered when she and Daniel had had it installed; the old iron range had been taken out, a new oven put in, together with fridge and dishwasher. They were still there, icy under the bar lighting. He also saw the bottles of wine and malt whisky on a Welsh dresser, but made no comment. A window over the sink looked out on blackness. It was freezing cold in the kitchen.

'How have things been, Lena?'

She shot him a glance, perhaps measuring how much she would tell him. 'Bloody ghastly.'

Her answer silenced him. Lena filled a kettle and switched it on. Wolfgang stood looking vaguely about him, knowing himself unwanted and not entirely knowing what to do. The old charm, he told himself, was not working. He felt compassion for the woman. He was a venal man, and recognised himself as venal: yet his better side wished to offer her some comfort, and perhaps to be forgiven.

'You seem to be having rather a hard time of it. Is Daniel back in Africa? I caught part of his lecture the other night.'

She turned, leaning against the sink, giving him an unfriendly stare. She had a sty on her left eyelid, he noted.

'You men are all bastards. What do you care? Daniel has chucked me up, just as he chucked up his kids.'

'What do you mean? You two have been married for donkey's years.'

'Huh. In name, maybe. Now he's chucked me up.'

'How? What do you mean?'

'What right have you to ask me questions? You come here in your helicopter . . . I suppose you didn't chuck me up, two years ago?'

She turned away to arrange mugs beside the kettle, which was busily arranging to boil. He wondered if she was close to tears, but that did not seem to be the case.

'You once cared about me, Lena.'

With her back still turned to him, she said, 'You never cared about me, you sod.'

He stood staring blankly ahead. Slowly he realised he was looking at what he had registered as a bundle of old clothes, lying on the draining board. He saw now that there was a small foot with five little toes protruding from it. A black foot.

Revulsion, a wish to escape, overcame Wolfgang. He remained rooted to the spot.

The woman was pouring hot water on tea bags. She added milk from a jug standing on the windowsill. Catching sight of the expression on his face, misinterpreting it, she said, 'Your conscience playing you up? You left me without a word. It was because of you Daniel walked out on me. He kicked me out of our London house. I do mean kicked . . .'

He said nothing. Aware she was regarding him contemptuously, he dropped his gaze.

Lena said, 'You can carry this tray in. Yes, he found a bundle of those letters you wrote me. That did it!'

Through a daze, Wolfgang said, 'What? You kept all those damned letters?' He remembered writing them. How he had enjoyed writing down all the sexual details after their meetings in the course of – well, it must have been over six or seven years. He had never been faithful to her but certainly he had . . . it had been like love. 'Why didn't you burn them, for God's sake?'

'Women always keep love letters, weak creatures that we are.'

He carried the tray with the mugs into the front room where his three companions sat silently. They were listening to the cameraman's portable radio. A newsreader was giving an account of a massive traffic pile-up on the M5. Seventeen vehicles involved.

In Wolfgang's mind, the image of the dead baby's foot remained. Whose baby was it? Who had killed it? He held the hot mug of tea between his hands but could not drink.

Lena was standing against the wall, one hand on the barrel of the rifle propped by her side. Glancing covertly at her, Wolfgang saw how gaunt and exhausted she looked. It seemed as if she was waiting for them to leave.

'Nice place you got here, missus,' said the pilot, to make conversation. Lena did not respond.

Wolfgang forced himself to go and confront her. Speaking quietly, he said, 'You told us you had kids here.'

'There's one upstairs. It's Josie's little girl, Mary. Josie's here with me. She's probably awake. You probably woke her.'

They stood looking at each other. It was as if the mention of a child had softened Lena slightly. After a pause, she added, 'You remember Josie? She was just a little thing in your time.'

'I heard she took to drugs.'

Lena neither agreed not denied it.

He brought himself to ask, as if the words choked him, 'What about the dead baby in the kitchen?'

Straight-faced, she said, 'I don't know what you are talking about. I want you to leave here now, Wolfie, and take your pals with you.'

'You're in trouble, aren't you?'

She slapped him across the face. 'Will you mind your own fucking business!'

He was astonished at how much the blow hurt. The tea went splashing from his mug, down his coverall. The pilot came over to see what was happening. Wolfgang sat down abruptly on a chair, saying it was all right. Lena disappeared upstairs.

He told the pilot and the others that they had better get going if the storm had abated.

The time was almost five o'clock.

The sound of running feet upstairs came to them. A child's cry. Silence. Running feet again.

Lena came downstairs, wild-eyed. 'Wolfie, I want you.'

She ran into the passage and he followed. She stood as if at bay, in a small bare room in which containers of cooking-gas stood.

137

'Josie has gone. She's not in the toilet. She must have gone out. I'm sure something has happened to her. Oh, God!' She put a hand quickly up to her mouth as though trying to stop the words emerging.

'Gone out? Gone out in this weather?'

'Yes, yes, gone fucking out! She's in a terrible state. It's her baby, born dead.'

An oilskin hat hung on a peg. She seized it and rammed it on her head. Running to a side door, she unbolted it, pulling bolts at top and bottom, and rushed outside, carrying her torch. Wolfgang followed.

The wind still howled. Dawn was advancing, with bars of pallid light overlaid by scattered cloud in the western sky. As they ran, Lena was shouting out explanations or at least a brief history of the misery she had gone through with Josie, the daughter her husband had rejected. Wolfgang thought she said that everything that had happened was God's punishment for her sins.

Although he was running at her side, he could not hear her words clearly. He shouted that she should not believe such old-fashioned rubbish. To which she, also half hearing, said that it was happening now.

Coming from the shelter of the house, they were struck with even greater force by the storm. The wind carried splatters of rain with it.

As if by instinct, Lena was running for the barn. Now she was screaming her daughter's name. The torchlight flashed ahead, capering ghostlike on the black-tarred barn walls. One door was swinging, banging open, closing again, banging open again.

They ran inside.

Josie was hanging by her neck from a beam. Her feet

were little more than ten centimetres from the floor. She had kicked away an old box. Either then or in her death struggles afterwards, she had shed a shoe. Particles of hay swirled about her feet.

'Oh no, not Josephine! Not – not my dear dear daughter! No, no, it can't be! Oh, my only love! Oh, God! Oh, Christ! Oh, it can't be!'

But it was. And when Wolfie took a knife and cut the young girl down, Lena seized the limp body, clinging to it as if she could never never let it go, crying as if she could never never stop.

The time was 5.10 a.m. Over the Irish coast, the dawn was well advanced, drawing angry red banners above the Atlantic.

The androids were almost due for release from their cupboard to go about their daily duties.

'At the shop I saw a small crying thing being carried.'

'It will grow into a human.'

'Why was it crying?'

'The theory is that it knows it will have to grow into a human.'

'How long will it take?'

'It is a painful process. We are fortunate. We do not feel pain.'

'Did they fetch this thing from a hospital?'

'It came from a woman.'

'What are you saying?'

'The theory is that there was an operation and the baby was produced from her.'

'I have not learnt this fact.'

'Their bodies swing open.'

139

'You are making what humans call a joke – something inaccurate.'

'The theory is that the baby came out of her body.'

'You have a malfunction. I will report it.'

The ocean had gathered itself up to advance towards land and dawn. In a great liquid movement it sped onward. It had gained height as it neared land. It was in league with the blast which came at its back.

Now that it had gained the shallows of the Continental Shelf, the wave was changing its colour. Sombre greens and greys had picked up streaks of near-yellow. And there was a blackness about it, too. It towered to a height of several metres. Smaller waves followed it.

Now it stormed over the coastal waters. They seemed to withdraw before it, and then to join in the chase.

Now the great wave was closing on the land. With colossal force it flung itself against the rocks of Ireland. It stormed over them with a clap like thunder. Without cease, it poured over the land.

Now those persons rash enough to stay and observe, perhaps from cars, perhaps from houses, were swept away like straws. Their limbs waved as they were carried along until being dashed to pieces.

Now the land became submerged, foaming in the all-consuming ocean.

But Esme de Bourcey and Karim Shariati lived in a world of their own. They had no screen, they saw no ambient. They looked only on each other in perfect love. In perfect love they gloried that their bodies differed one from the other, that their colours differed, and that their creeds differed. What might previously have driven them apart now drew them together.

It was two days since Esme had wandered to the nearest shop. They hated being parted. Their food was almost exhausted.

Karim woke. He opened his eyes into the darkness. Today, he thought, today they must try to be reasonable and get something to eat. His left arm had gone dead. His lover was lying on it. He did not move it for fear of waking her. He put his nose close to her body to inhale its beautiful scents. Never had he been so happy. Not in all his days.

Here lay this wonderful wonderful woman, open to him. And he open to her. Never before had they been so trusting, so complete.

He could not make out the source of the strange new noise. He thought, laughing to himself at the conceit, that this was the noise happiness makes as it rushes like a tide through hitherto unused channels of the mind.

Then, much more clearly, a bang – and then water rushing into their hidey-hole. For a moment he lay there, unable to understand.

'Esme! Esme, my dove, wake yourself up! There is a flood!'

She roused at once. They sat up together in the dark, listening, startled. Listening to water pouring in.

She said she would make a light. But when she reached to the floor for candle and matches, her hand touched swirling water. She yelped with alarm.

They quickly decided they had better get out in case they drowned there in their beautiful cellar. But they found a whole ocean to fight against, pouring down their stairs, rock tumbling with it.

They did not get out.

'Hi! Alexy Stromeyer calling from the *Roddenberry* expedition. Hope you can hear me, Earth. Jupiter is putting out a stack of microwave radio emission. Rick O'Brien and I are now standing on the surface of Europa, near Belus Linea. We have made it to our intended destination after over a year of travel through space. Sure, this is an historic moment. It feels wonderful. What a sight! Kathram is tracking us from the *Roddenberry* in orbit overhead. She is also reprogramming the various computers to ready the drill.

'Sorry. I'll be back later. Out.'

A three-hour silence followed. Then Alexy came through again, less faintly.

'Okay. Sorry for break in transmission. Seems like a solar wind storm is stepping up Jupiter's high-energy electron-radiation belts. We're getting readings of electrons at energies of 20MeV. And we appreciate our signal takes thirty-seven minutes to reach you. Kathram had to read just the high-gain antenna, which had suffered a knock. We're okay now. Rick and I are staying close. It is a bit intimidating. Bear in mind Europa is about the size of Earth's Moon.

'It is a pretty desolate view we have here. Bleak as hell. We are fairly near an impact crater which has thrown up ice, creating ridges. There are cracks which have filled with slush and debris, which of course froze over as soon as they came in contact with space.

'Our photopolarimeter has detected signs of both

142

cryovulcanism and bombardment from space by random elements.

'Rick and I are standing on a socking great ice floe, maybe as much as twenty kilometres across. It's slightly unsteady – from the movement of the ocean below us but maybe also because we are unaccustomed to standing up straight on our own two feet in a gravity condition. All we can see of Jupiter at the moment is a bright fingernail across the foreshortened horizon of the ice. But Jupiter is rising. Awestruck. Back soonest. Out.'

The occupants of the Channel Islands had fled by boat and plane, leaving their homes and possessions to the mighty oncoming wave. As for the Atlantic coast of France, that western bastion of the super-state, there too the inhabitants – or those wise enough or capable enough – had moved hastily eastward before the tsunami struck and unrolled the sea like a liquid carpet far inland.

Brittany took the flood head on. Brest suffered sea fish to swim through the upper windows of its hotels. Further southwards, the same story was repeated. The ancient mega-liths of Carnac were consumed, Vannes was completely vanquished. Sweeping over the port of Saint-Nazaire, the mighty wave sent an exploratory tide even as far into the embouchure of the Loire as Nantes, from which the young Jules Verne had once aspired to sail. In broad daylight, La Rochelle received an inundation, and Rochefort too, its sands carried far inland, to besiege the battlements of St Jean. A hasty barrier of ships had blocked the mouth of the Gironde; the manoeuvre did not save the inhabitants of ancient Bordeaux from getting their feet wet. And their legs. And their waistlines. And their wainscotting.

All the *plages* of that area, those bars of sand, those dunes, those havens for holidays, became erased, so rapidly, so thoroughly, that the mild plain crossed by Route N21 became in one morning an inland sea, angry with debris. As for the beaches of Biarritz, and its costly casinos – these too went down before the mighty tsunami.

Countless billions of grains of sand, ground down in Time's good time from siliceous rocks, some old as Ordovician, were redistributed over all the littoral roads and gardens and woods and vineyards, from La Manche to the Bay of Biscay.

Similar fates befell the towns and cities of the northern coast of Spain. San Sebastian, Bilbao, Santander, onwards, all died beneath the wind and wave before the sea fell back exhausted. And then followed the cold, to fringe with icy whiskers the new flood margins.

The coasts of Scandinavia suffered identical assaults. But Norway had stubbornly remained outside the EU, so that was different.

And what of Greenland itself?

American geophysicists and other interested parties were quickly on the scene. Their findings showed that the collapse of the ice shelf near Angmagssilik was not the cause of the disruption but rather the result of a greater disruption.

A large missile or meteor had impacted with the Greenland massif some kilometres inland. The still-steaming crater was 20 kilometres wide.

The invasive body had entered the atmosphere at a velocity of not more than 20,000 kilometres an hour, striking at an oblique angle of 30 degrees. Magnetic surveys, seismic profiles, drill-core stratigraphy and measurements of the thickness of the ejecta blanket indicated that the meteor – if meteor it was – had been a mere pebble, no more than fifteen metres across.

Had it arrived on its mindless journey from space only four minutes later, it would have grounded in the northern wilds of Canada. 'Another great event the Canadians have missed,' as an American joker put it.

Snug at home with his wife Ruth, Paulus Stromeyer worked at his latest mathematical problem. What he had done for society with his SAC formulation he hoped to repeat for nature itself with what he determined would be the revolutionary science of boims and serds.

Tapping the keys of his computer with one finger, Paulus strove to build an imaginary higher calculus, standing for functions in relation to nine hundred. The boims would iron out irregularities in the flows of growth and probability. The serds were temporal coordinates plus what Paulus termed 'unexpectables'. He had uncovered first hints of the theory in a small manual on weather prediction, published but ignored, in an ancient brown textbook of 1914, that ill-omened year. There it had been termed the Function of Feeble Interaction.

It was quiet in Paulus's study, except for the strains of Mahler's Fourth Symphony issuing softly from his old CDX player. His devoted daughter Rebecca had brought him a cup of coffee. It stood by his right elbow, neglected and stone-cold, a spoon lolling over the lip of the cup.

While Paulus quietly worked to bring about a new order, elsewhere in the super-state there was near-chaos. Unlike the tsunami, an atmosphere of unease had penetrated far inland, to Berlin itself. Rapid arrangements had to be made to house hundreds of thousands of refugees from the floods.

Charities were being overwhelmed by offers of hospitality and by monetary donations for the relief of the newly homeless.

Various armies were on alert to halt looting.

All this pandemonium played into the hands of Imran Chokar. He now lay concealed among ferns, outside the barriers guarding the presidential palace of San Guinaire, patiently awaiting the next darkness. The excitement engendered by the Greenland event prevented much vigilance being expended for single assassins. While Imran waited he prayed.

Unknown to Imran, but not a kilometre away from him, by another section of the perimeter, a man was lying full length in a tunnel. This area was on hilly ground. It had once been cleared of vegetation but time had gone by. Now ferns grew tall here, and nettles and brambles. The brambles dripped moisture at this sullen hour. Though rain had ceased, the sky was stifled by heavy cloud brought about by the aftermath of the Greenland event. No moon could be seen.

This was a good place for concealment. The tunneller had bought a small garden trowel for 4.5 univs at a supermarket in Liège. With this, he was carving a steady hole through the earth into the grounds of the presidential palace. God was with him all the way. His name was David Bargane. His lips, like Imran's, moved in constant prayer, though to a different God.

At almost the same moment as Imran Chokar polevaulted with his home-made pole over the perimeter fence, David Bargane broke from his tunnel and, in a shower of dirt, emerged into the presidential grounds.

Patrols were less active than usual. The cataclysmic

upheaval caused by the Greenland event had focused almost everyone's attention on ambient reports. Many guards had simply given up to watch the various disasters being played out on the screens.

There was also a rival attraction, the landing of men on a moon of Jupiter. But this historic event had been largely relegated to secondary interest. Even space buffs and those who read science fiction were torn between the two extraordinary events.

So it was comparatively easy for Chokar to enter the palace by an open window in the east wing. Bargane, on the other hand, managed to climb up a drainpipe on the west wing to a balcony on the first floor; from there he was able to prise open a window and get into the palace.

Prayer proved to be of little help to David Bargane as he crept along the corridor. He was bewildered by the size of the place. Finding a linen cupboard, he entered it. Closing the door on himself, he stood there rigidly in the dark, abandoning prayer to try to think for himself.

Darkness, meanwhile, fell throughout most of the palace. Panic broke out. Chokar, finding a fire axe in a glass case, had broken the glass, seized the axe, and severed the cable above a main fuse box. Before dim auxiliary lights came on, he sprinted up a ceremonial staircase to the first floor. Having wisely consulted a guidebook before approaching the President's palace, he had a fairly clear idea of a large committee chamber on this level. But would the President be there? Running swiftly along a corridor, he heard someone approaching with a firm and rapid tread.

Almost without thought, he opened a door and dashed in. It was a linen cupboard.

Next morning, at five minutes to seven, a chambermaid

147

discovered two dead bodies in her cupboard. Knives protruded from the ribs of both. Their blood had stained all her beautifully ironed and folded pillowcases and duvets. Small wonder she screamed.

The screams were hardly likely to be heard by Gustave de Bourcey. He was in Honolulu, attending a summit meeting.

<INSANATICS: The News. Increasingly, human populations have a thirst for news. This is, in general, regarded as commendable. In fact, most news, the news most eagerly reported and received, is bad news. It frequently concerns people who are dying or dead.

Supposing an area of China is destroyed by earthquake, or an area of Britain inundated by severe flooding, or an area of the USA stricken by forest fires. These matters may be reported for several days, while there is drama to be squeezed from them. Then, when the novelty has worn off, the helicopters retire and the interviewers and commentators go home.

We are not shown the aftermath: the areas dried out and livestock reinstated, or the flood-damaged houses rebuilt, or the charred forest areas replanted. These matters do not touch us. It is disaster that propitiates our famished psyches.>

The Stromeyer family were naturally anxious. The latest news they had received of Alexy was broadcast when he was standing on the ice floes of a small satellite of a giant planet that was six hundred and twenty-eight thousand kilometres away, moving at an orbital speed of over thirteen kilometres per second. They felt they had every right to be anxious.

All members of the family were due to gather in the paternal apartment in an hour's time: Belinda Mironets with her husband Ivan, and their small boy, Boy, and Joseph Stromeyer, being respectively Ruth and Paulus's daughter, son-in-law, with their son, and son. Ruth and Rebecca were in the kitchen, baking cakes and preparing a feast.

Paulus remained in his study till the last moment, struggling with his boims and serds. On his wall he had pinned a remark made by Bertrand Russell in a letter to a ladylove:

> I simply can't stand a view limited to this Earth. I feel life is so small unless it has windows into other worlds . . . I like mathematics largely because it is not human and has nothing particular to do with this planet or with the whole accidental universe – because, like Spinoza's God, it won't love us in return.

Russell had written this in 1912. While Paulus applauded the sentiment, he was endeavouring to develop precisely a system which would have something in particular to do with the world, and to love the world in return.

He was at an impasse. He called his friend Barnard Cleeping in Utrecht and burst straight into what was on his mind.

'Barnard, exactly what objective independence from the mind do mathematical formulations possess? I have become entangled in that philosophical problem and cannot progress. I cannot sustain a formulation proving conclusively that the methodology of mathematics is innate in what we call the taxonomy of organisms.'

Cleeping's voice sounded stifled. 'You'd have to go to Cantor and infinite numbers for an answer, Paulus. Sorry, I can't help at present.'

'Do you have a cold?'

Silence from Cleeping's end. Then he said, 'I'm only just

out of hospital, if you must know. And I'm feeling wretched, Paulus. You know that poor fellow I spoke up for in court?'

'The Muslim. What about him?'

'He's just been found stabbed to death. Police aren't saying where exactly. Such a good young man.'

'Good young men don't usually get themselves stabbed.'

Paulus rang off, and went to greet his family. They pressed in, uttering cheery greetings. He gave a special hug, a bear hug, to his younger son, Joe. Joe had a responsible job in non-invasive surgery at a Naples hospital. Paulus always knew that Joe – not a man with a great deal of drive – felt eclipsed by Alexy, his extraordinary brother.

'How are things?'

'Fine, Dad, fine.' That was all he said, giving a sort of wry smile.

Paulus heard his father coming down the stairs from his room, slowly, one step at a time. He went to help, but halted at the bottom of the stairs when Moshe said rather pettishly that he needed no assistance.

'The family are here, Father. We are all expecting to hear from Alexy.'

'Who is Alexy?'

'Your grandson, Father. The astronaut. He's on Europa.'

'Of course he is. Terrible weather we're having, mmm. Most of France is under water.'

'Yes, but this is *Europa*. A satellite of Jupiter.'

'Good, good. I am not hearing too well. Excellent. Discovered by Galileo Galilei, I understand. And there are some people who still believe the Sun goes round the Earth, poor ignorant fools.'

He made his shaky way to an armchair. 'People don't communicate properly these days.'

Belinda, Ivan, their Boy and Joe had arrived in a group. Ruth and Rebecca were still doing a jovial round of embraces, amid general kissings and demonstrations of affection. Ivan loaded Ruth with pale pink roses; she squealed with pleasure. Belinda gave Paulus a box of after-dinner mints. Joe brought his sister the latest Rose Baywater novel, *Not a Day Less Than For Ever*.

'It's a bit intellectual for you, darling,' he said, teasing her.

Rebecca opened the book at random and read aloud. '"The clouds were like scratches in the blue sky . . . As I lay in my husband's arms, with my flesh pressing against his, as he gazed into my grey eyes, I reflected on how happy he must feel to be so close to such a beautiful and clever woman. But was George sensitive enough to really appreciate me?"'

Everyone roared with laughter. Said Rebecca, still laughing, 'And to think that we were one of the publishers who turned down this lady's first manuscript. Why, it's Tolstoi in skirts!'

Ruth brought a tray full of cakes and tarts from the kitchen, and everyone exclaimed with delight. Paulus was looking again at his watch. It was past time for the report from the *Roddenberry*.

Moshe remained silent, although he ate a slice of lemon drizzle cake, shedding crumbs as he went. There were tea and white wine on offer. Moshe sipped a glass of the wine before struggling into a more upright posture.

'Just be quiet a minute, children,' he said. 'I want to talk to you all seriously. Your mum and I think you should know something about sex.'

They all stopped talking and stared in astonishment at the old man.

It was Ivan who said, 'Look, Pop, we are adult, we know all about sex. Linda and I practise it regularly.'

Belinda added, 'So we do, though not regularly enough.'

Moshe said, 'I appreciate that I should have given you this lecture some years ago, when you were smaller. Still, better late than never, mmm. At least we can take it that you know the difference between – what do you call it? – between male and female . . .'

Joe asked his mother, 'Is Gramps pulling our various legs?'

Ruth patted Moshe's shoulder. 'Moshe, dear, this is going to be too embarrassing.'

'I want to be sure you understand, my pet, mmm.' He wiped some saliva from his chin. 'Now, when I put my old fellow – my "Artful Dodger", as I tend to call it – into your mum, mmm, I project a lot of sperm in her which she immediately places in her womb. These sperms, which you can think of as little tiny fish, if you like, or what do you call it? – *tadpoles*, then swim upstream and get to Mum's ovaries and—'

Paulus took one of his father's hands, telling him gently that his mind was wandering.

'Why don't you hear him out?' said Rebecca, suppressing a smile. 'I think he wants to get to the spiritual bit.'

'There's nothing spiritual about it, dear, mmm,' Moshe said. 'All one wants is a good shag. Now, as to the best position, Mummy and I rather—'

'He's rambling,' Ruth said. 'Paulus, please stop him. Take him upstairs.'

'Yes, it's a bit much.' Joe had always tended to support his mother, and was not going to let a chance escape him now. 'Do shut him up, Pop.'

'—Enjoyed lying side by side. Although, when we were first married – well, before that, really – we tried all sorts of positions. I remember once getting your mum over the bonnet of my old Volvo. No, no, not Mum, that was a girl called Suzanne, mmm. I think it was Suzanne. I couldn't keep my hands off her. And not only my hands—'

'Paulus! This is degrading for him and for us,' said Ruth. 'Do stop him, please. It's beastly.'

Paulus stood there indecisively, stunned and horrified by the collapse of his father's decorum.

Belinda was saying, 'No, let him go on, Dad. It's fascinating. He's gone completely bonkers.'

Moshe suddenly looked up. Speaking directly to his son, he said, 'I'm trying to teach them the facts of life. I know they're all grown up but even small boys long to look up girls' skirts, and get their hands up there if they can. For a good feel, mmm. The interest in the bodies of the other sex is only natural, and can form—'

'Stop it, Father!' said Ruth. 'You are rambling. You don't know what you're saying. Go upstairs at once.'

He looked up at her, pathetic and bemused. 'But, Suzanne, don't you remember—'

'It's all right, Father,' said Paulus. 'Everything is fine. Let me help you upstairs. I'll carry your wine glass. You can watch the next episode of *History of Western Science*.'

As they left the room, the others looked at each other gloomily, pulling long faces. Ruth hid her eyes behind her hands. 'I shouldn't have been angry with him. It's Alzheimer's, isn't it? I'm sure it's Alzheimer's . . .'

Rebecca put her arms round her mother and hugged her, saying nothing.

When Paulus came downstairs again there was still no message from the *Roddenberry*.

* * *

'This is BBC Digital on 193 MHz. We are still awaiting a signal from the crew of the *Roddenberry* on Europa.

'While we wait, here is a chance to see again Professor Daniel Potts's challenging and topical lecture which he entitled "Solitude So Far". It was first shown in January of this year.

'Professor Potts.'

[A montage of cartoon characters followed. Mice, cats, talking elephants, dogs, partly dressed horses sped across the screen, followed by female warrior creatures with large metallic breasts battling bravely through computer games.

Potts appeared, walking down a long VR corridor.]

'It transpires that almost everyone believes in forms of alien life. Governments investigate UFO phenomena, major movies depict visits between planets, where exist strange bipeds, either harmless or, more likely, well armed.

'Non-human life is the irregular verb of the human mind. We are drawn in love and fear – and always have been – towards something living but not quite like us.

'For this trait there is a phylogenetic reason. Deep in our brains lives a memory of when we as a species were hardly distinct from other related sub-species or even animals, and dressed ourselves in their skins. The human/ animal relationship was closer than city dwellers can ever imagine.

[Computerised images here were especially vivid.]

'As we know, there remains much of the ape in us. Regrettably, I am now too old to climb trees. That early boyhood pleasure was as much part of phylogeny as ontology. Just as what passes as cute is the atavism whereby parents dress their babies in hoods with ears, turning them into mice, rabbits or bears – or other mammals which have accompanied us along the evolutionary escalator.

154

Our constant invention of the Unknown, the Other, has deep roots.

[The pictures hanging on the wall of the corridor were alive, and showed a succession of the absurd quadrupeds to which Potts referred.]

'Those roots tap into the mental soil, grown presumably before the dawning of human consciousness. With the subject of consciousness now under scrutiny, we see how slowly intellectual awareness has developed.

'We may ask ourselves if the human species has yet achieved full consciousness. Using the analogy of a light bulb, we can wonder if the bulb has yet reached maximum wattage. For many of us, fantasising is easier than thinking constructively. [The image of a light bulb spluttered out.]

'One of our overriding fantasies is a persistent vision of the alien, of something like us but certainly not us.

'Just picture all those beings patently without existence, in which nevertheless humanity has believed at one time or another – often for decades, even centuries. [These beings began a grotesque parade, advancing from the distance into the eye of the camera.]

'Heavens, what a population explosion of mythical persons! Creatures with goat's feet, persons half-human half-bull, people with snakes growing out of their heads, fairies, elves, goblins, gnomes, trolls, leprechauns, skeletons, the walking dead, werewolves, ghosts of various sorts, demons, devils, angels, spirits, sprites, doppelgängers, dragons, were-wolves and vampires.

'Vampires share with Jesus Christ the advantage of a life after death.

'The list of such discomfiting supernatural beings is almost endless. They materialise from the sky, the sea, the woodwork.

Most of those I have mentioned could not speak – a clear indication that they emerge from our limbic brain. The limbic brain knows only images, not language.

[Ominous music, sonorous and nervy sounds.]

'Ranking above these minor-league conjurations of alien life, and above humanity, comes a more troublesome cast of imaginary non-humans: the gods and goddesses that have plagued human life throughout the ages.

'Here's old Silenus with his satyrs and attendant woodland deities. Bacchus, god of wine, is popular. In the north, in Scandinavia, there were Ymin, god of numbing cold, and Thor, whose name lives on in our weekdays and our comics. Mithras, stony-faced soldiers' god. Ishtar, the terrifying Babylonian goddess of fertility. Hindu gods a-plenty – Shiva, the great destroyer, his icing-pink wife, Parvati, dancing on her lotus leaf. Seth, embodiment of evil. Countless more swarming deities: the law-givers, the punishers, the handsome, the horrendous. [Fantastic pictures of them all, passing with what dignity they could muster.]

'Some of these deities come adorned with skulls and serpents, or armed with lightning bolts and swords. Some have a monkey face, an elephant head, or the skull of an ibis. Many formulate impossible rules for human conduct. They tell us what we should not eat or with whom we should not sleep.

'Oh, it's easy to regard this troupe as simply amusing. But never forget – wars were fought, human and animal blood flowed, for this imaginary crowd! What terrible delusions were suffered!

'Some of these miserable conjurations sprout long white beards, some change shape and form, some are blue in the face, some black of body. Some take the form of bulls, or are presided over by cobras. Some consort with smartly dressed hyenas. As for extra arms, breasts, heads, lingams, they are almost commonplace.

'Uncounted generations of people much like us worshipped them, died for them.

'Where have they come from? All of them have emanated from a porridgy substance shaped almost like a giant walnut – the human brain, with its neoteric consciousness.

[Here we are walking calmly through a many-pillared temple.]

'I take comfort from the words of a Buddhist priest in Kyoto, who put the whole matter in a nutshell: "God is an invention of Man. So the nature of God is only a shallow mystery. The deep mystery is the nature of Man."

[But above the temple hangs a mighty spaceship.]

'The latest gang of imaginary unthinkables to be visited upon us are aliens from outer space. We watch them on our various-sized screens. They may come from special effects, but their true home is in the brain, the amygdala, or elsewhere in that clowning gory we carry in our skulls.

'Many sensible people claim that there is scientific reason for belief in aliens. We now have ufologists among us, reasonable men – we hope they prosper like astrologists. My contention – reasonable enough – is that UFOs are a later version of those imaginary unthinkables we have been looking at. Elder gods and godlets have been brought up to date, to be clad in the benefits of modern technology.

'Now a welter of aliens has descended on us, some for reasons of morality, some just for entertainment. Which is to say, bloodletting and destruction. [Suitable clips pass us by.]

'So it is that (*pace* Winnie the Pooh) aliens and dinosaurs have become the kiddies' favourites. However, the scientific standing of aliens and dinosaurs is by no means equal. Dr Gideon Mantell's young wife Mary Mantell took a walk in 1822 and found a fossil tooth, later identified by her husband as belonging to an iguanadon. Painstaking investigations and research by experts over the past two centuries have firmly established the existence of the giant reptiles of the Jurassic, within a context of earth's history.

'But *aliens*? That's quite a different kettle of fish. The argument for the existence of aliens is merely a statistical one. It goes like this. Our galaxy contains some 10^{12} stars. Many or most of them may support planetary systems, as does our sun. Most or some of those planets may support life of some kind. Some at least of that life may have acquired consciousness and intelligence. Therefore, even by a strict accounting, the galaxy might be – *must be* – teeming with intelligent life.

'It's a popular line of argument. However, *as yet*, no other planet has been discovered which is at all likely to support life, certainly not life comparable with bipedal us. This includes Mars and the other planets of our own system of nine planets.

'When we start looking at our own chequered evolutionary path, other reservations emerge. It is by blind chance that we are here, in our present shape, reading *Origin of Species* and *Also Sprach Zarathrustra*. A whole number of chances. The Earth just happens to move in a Zone of Comfort at a fortunate distance from the Sun – Venus is too near, Mars too far.

'I don't want to lecture but—' He laughed.

'There's the curious fact that the solid state of water – ice – is lighter than its liquid state, contradicting what seems to be natural law; were it otherwise, the oceans would be covered by ice, filling up from the bottom. There's the curious accident whereby the eukaryotic cell was formed, the cell of which most plants and animals are built. Among external factors, as my friend Paulus Stromeyer has pointed out to me, is the development of grass. Grass grows from roots under ground, not from the tip of the blade. So it can be cropped and still grow; sheep may safely graze – until eaten by mankind. Without sheep, no meat, no clothes, no civilisations . . . Make the connections.

'Then there's that long painful pause between single-celled and multicellular life. Those cells had to conspire into bones and organs – and brains. Consciousness had a tardy dawn.

'We are still drunk, it seems, with its first glimmerings.

'It may be this intoxication which has unleashed the multiplicity of aliens upon us. They're fine as fiction; but – as reality? The fact remains that there is as yet no proof of any other life anywhere in the galaxy. [The traditional shots of the galactic wilderness of fire and space.]

'So what, then, if humanity is alone? What if this Earth, with all its teeming phyla, happens by some cosmic accident to be the sole refuge of life and consciousness? We seem, in that case, to have got ourselves elected as the consciousness of the galaxy, maybe of the universe. It is a devastating honour for a species that believes in fairies!

[Potts squared up to the camera for his peroration.]

'Our solitary state – if indeed we are alone – is an infinitely more challenging prospect than its opposite, a galaxy already boiling over with aliens, with ancient wisdoms of which we may know nothing. What a responsibility it imposes! It certainly means that we have to improve our behaviour. Quantitively and qualitatively. Look what a mess we have made of this planet!

'Otherwise, I suggest, we are unfit to set foot on any other planet. Better to stay at home and create havoc here.'

He gave a benevolent smile as the film closed. The real Potts, however, sat in darkness, too miserable to cry, bitterly regretting the death of the daughter he had rejected long ago.

<INSANATICS: Universal psychosis. For those of you who know about the time of the 'Cold War', last century, this bulletin is unnecessary. You will understand that during that period, psychotic thinking was conventional wisdom. Industrialised nations stood ready with nuclear weapons, waiting to launch death and destruction on most of the life of the planet. This was government policy, backed by overwhelming percentages of the rival populations opposing one another. An example of 'I will if you will'. This policy went by the name of Mutually Assured Destruction, or MAD. At least that was honest confession.

It was by chance rather than by any great wisdom that total destruction was avoided. 'Better Dead Than Red' was one well-known slogan of the time.

Here we have a clear example of the suicidal peril into which the projection of our intrapsychic conflicts have led us. Now we find ourselves struggling with the ruination of our world through so-called 'natural causes'. They are not natural but man-made. Global warming is brought about by mankind's greed and destructiveness – and by the psychotic's lack of emotional tone which permits such disasters to happen.

Our world is already largely impoverished. Many species of animal, insect and plant are now extinct. Why do you think that could be?>

'Clymedia says: Think *Araneus diadematus* – the common orb-web spider! Its silk combines flexibility with strength and is five times stronger than an equivalent filament of steel. In terms of speed per unit of weight it withstands the impact of a jet fighter plane every time it ensnares a fly.

'Clymedia's Condoms are made like that.

'Think jet fighter planes. Think Clymedia's Condoms for those intimate moments.'

'Hi! Alexy Stromeyer from Europa. Right now we are witnessing a fantastic low-altitude auroral display! More importantly, we met up with a hitch. The drill apparatus would not lower. But we fixed it. Rick and I have drilled through the ice floe. Here's the news the world has been waiting for. Hold your breath! Hear this!

'Life! We have found life! A steel-mesh net was lowered through our borehole in the ice. On our third attempt, we caught a living creature in nine metres of water. It was hauled to the surface and examined. It is definitely an animal, not a plant. Friends, we are not alone in the universe! More data in our following call. Must now return to the ship. Out.'

The great Gabbo and his randroid friend Obbagi had their own means of travel. They appeared one morning before Daniel Potts. Potts had left the shelter of his son's home and was living in a rented room in Budapest. There was little in the room apart from a bed, a box full of learned medioids, and a skull. The skull sat on a table beside an unwashed soup-mug.

Into this rather depressing scene came Gabbo and the huge randroid: black, oblique, its faceless head almost touching the ceiling. In ordinary circumstances, Gabbo would have

161

dominated any company; yet he seemed reduced and silenced by his gigantic electronic companion.

Potts was looking thin and meagre, in grubby trousers and an old blouson shirt, with a scarf wound round his neck. He had not shaved for a day or two.

'Would you like some coffee?' Potts asked. He rested a hand on the yellowed skull for reassurance. The room had become darker from the newcomers' presence.

'We have come to speak regarding your recent broadcast,' rumbled Obbagi. He stood massively, more statue than man. Gabbo remained just behind him, arms folded, appearing to enjoy himself – which is to say that he was slyly smiling, as if aware of the chill that his electronic friend struck into the heart of all whom he confronted.

'Oh yes, my – my broadcast,' said Potts.

'We wish to clear your mind of a misapprehension,' said Obbagi, entirely uninterested in any language that might issue from Daniel Potts's mouth at this time. 'Your deductions regarding the skulls and bones you have excavated are ingenious but entirely false.

'You stated that almost everyone believes there is alien life on other planets. That is so, but your reasons for that state of mind are false.'

'How can you—'

'You speak of many imaginary beings, but your reasoning is false. You speak of the number of stars in our galaxy, but your reasoning about the numbers of planetary bodies housing intelligent life forms is false. You speak of the difficulty intelligence had in establishing itself on this planet, but your understanding of the implications is false.'

'Look, it's all very well—'

'Why not listen?' It was Gabbo who spoke. 'We are here

to enlighten you. Our intentions are not hostile. We merely know better than you.'

'But, sir, I'm the expert who—'

'Finally, you conclude,' continued the deep voice of Obbagi, 'that it is the inhabitants of this planet who have been selected to become "the consciousness of the galaxy".' Here he emitted a great rumbling which could have been interpreted as scornful laughter.

'It was merely a speculation which I—'

'It was the arrogance of the human species speaking. Do you really imagine such a faulty collection of short-lived bipedal mortals could ever serve the grand purpose you propose? Of course you have no conception of how the galaxy is run, or of the superb consciousnesses which advise in the process.'

Daniel Potts at last gathered his courage together. 'All right, I have heard enough. My researches certainly involve some deductive powers, which you may dismiss as guesswork, but I work with facts. What evidence have you that there are other races in the galaxy? None. Absolutely none.'

His gaze flitted from Gabbo to Obbagi like that of a hunted animal.

The grim randroid replied slowly and grandly, 'My companion Gabbo's laboratories invented the universal ambient, the American bio-electronic network. With that instrument, my friend is able to survey those surveyors who guard this waterlogged little planet.'

'I don't understand you. You are talking rubbish. Who are these surveyors of which you speak?'

Without directly answering the question, the great machine ploughed remorselessly on. 'The surveyors are displeased at present because three of the men imprisoned on Earth have escaped. They will not get far, but there is annoyance that prison rules have been broken.'

The reflection dawned on Potts that these two beings, the metal monster who seemed to speak and the fat man who was possibly a ventriloquist, were insane. He thought of the messages from the Insanatics group and said to himself, Those messages are true – these two personages are certainly mad. They probably plan to kill me. I don't want my miserable life to end yet. I want to see what's going to happen.

He spoke. 'You have no evidence to back your pretence that there are other races in the galaxy. You are victims of the very delusion of which I spoke in my lecture. Whereas I have evidence of the difficult evolutionary path the human species has pursued.' He patted the skull on his table as if it were a sleeping dog. 'This kind of tangible evidence.'

Again the rumble of Obbagi's laughter like distant thunder. Gabbo himself shook like a jelly with a bad wheeze. 'The bones and skulls of which you are so proud were sown in the ground by the surveyors some centuries ago,' said Obbagi. 'Just to keep you busybodies busy, to make you believe you are an autochthonous species. How could consciousness ever have evolved on an unstable world like Earth?

'Have you thought about that? You yourself know that this poky little planet is frequently bombarded by debris from space, that there have been five great mass extinctions and many lesser ones in a comparatively short space of time. No one in their right minds would wish to live here.'

'But evolutionary theory shows—'

The great still being made a slight movement, so that all its dark surfaces seemed to shimmer, as if betraying traces of impatience. 'Evolutionary theory is just one more bit of human mind-junk, like the belief in a benevolent god. You must understand this, Potts – the planet Earth is a prison planet.'

Gabbo took a step forward. He had come to a decision to speak again. 'As an adolescent, I happened on an old book. Its title was *Asylum*. There the truth was revealed – that this was a planet to which galactic criminals and madmen were sent, to serve out their lives. That book was regarded as science fiction. It is nothing less than the truth.'

'Yes, this planet is a criminal prison,' confirmed Obbagi. 'We hate your arrogance, Daniel Potts. So we have come to tell you the truth – even if it wrecks your career! The wicked and the deluded of the galaxy are segregated here. You are one of them.'

The duo turned and departed in silence. The wooden stairs shook and creaked under the weight of the randroid's tread.

Potts remained where he was, face drained of colour. He sank slowly back down into his chair, bony head hanging back, arms dangling limply by his side.

'But first on the *Wee Small Hours Show*, here's the Reverend Angus Lesscock to make us think, in "A Parson Speaks".'

'Thank you, Flossie, and good evening, or should I say good morning? The news that life has been found elsewhere in God's universe must make us think profoundly. We must pray all the harder – particularly those of you who have lost the habit. Because we have to ask ourselves, are these new life forms on Europa good or evil?

'Did Christ visit them?

165

'Are they what we might call *real life*? We may be sure that Jesus was crucified on a real cross. Probably it was made of shittim wood. Not three-ply or reconstituted wood or plastic, or any cheap modern substitute for the real thing. Now the same question confronts us again. We all need the shittim wood of real life.

'I know that if God the Father asked his Son what sort of wood he would like for his cross, Christ's reply would have been "Shittim".'

'Today's "A Parson Speaks" was presented by the Reverend Angus Lesscock.

'Over now to Lisa Fort on the streets of the capital. Are you there, Lisa?'

'Hello, Flossie, and yes, I am here on the Avenue Chateaubriand. It's very busy, although it's two in the morning. People are celebrating the discovery of life on Europa. Hello, sir, would you like to tell us how you feel about it?'

'It's terrific news. I'm ever so pleased. Really. I'm hoping that some of these life forms will come back to Belgium and enjoy our city and our lifestyle. They will certainly find it much warmer here than on their place, wherever it is.'

'You don't feel hostile to them?'

'Not at all. Not at all. They sound friendly as far as I can make out. I haven't really taken it all in yet. I'm just out cruising, trying to pick up a nice friend.'

'You, sir, I see you're in a wheelchair. You have learning difficulties, do you?'

'Certainly not, and I keep abreast of current affairs. I'm very concerned about the plight of these refugees from the coast. We don't know when another meteor is going to hit

166

us. These missiles the Tebarese are supposed to have dispatched against us – I mean, I don't believe they were missiles at all, I think they were probably meteors. Space is full of the things. It would be insane to declare war on Tebarou, to my mind.'

'But on the subject of life on Europa—'

'Contrary to what the last speaker was saying, we don't want them here. As I understand it, they are some sort of fish. Well, that's no good, is it? Like the parson said, if Christ was going to visit them he'd have to go as a fish. It's nothing to get excited about, to my mind.'

'Thank you. That's certainly one point of view. Hello, ma'am, you're out late with your little girl. Are you pleased about finding life on Europa?'

'Yes, I'm quite pleased, I suppose. I mean to say, it is a great technological achievement, isn't it? But I don't really see how it affects our lives, do you?'

'It means we are not alone in the universe.'

'Yes, but. What does that mean? I've got two kids to bring up, and a dog, and a goldfish. I don't feel alone in the universe. And then the expense. It's a bit of a waste of money, quite honestly.'

'So you wouldn't say you were excited?'

'Oh yes, I'm a bit excited, I suppose. I used to know Rick O'Brien. He's one of the astronauts, isn't he? What he thinks he's doing out there, I don't know!'

'Thank you. Excuse me, ladies, but how do you two feel about the news that life has been found on Europa?'

'Oh, you're Lisa Fort, aren't you? You're smaller than I imagined.'

'We love your hairdo.'

167

'We always watch your show.'

'Except now, of course.'

'We're really very excited about the success of the *Roddenberry* expedition. That's why we've been having a few drinks, to celebrate.'

'I think they've been through such hardships. Over a year in space, run short of food and all that. They deserve every drop of their success.'

'It's just a pity that they haven't found something a bit more interesting than this sort of fish thing. Like polar bears!'

Both women were chuckling. They began naming other creatures.

'Penguins.'

'Yes, king penguins.'

'Seals.'

'Walruses.'

'The odd albatross . . .'

'But this is space. There's no atmosphere on Europa.'

'You think we don't know that? We're not stupid, you know. We're at the university.'

'We're joking, Lisa, dear. People have lost their sense of humour these days. Get a life!'

'Thank you, ladies, and now – back to the studio.'

A closely guarded base on Honolulu. In one chamber, diplomats from many states were arguing matters out, and throwing up a cloud of detail. In a smaller room nearby, surrounded by their interpreters, the Presidents of the EU and the USA, together with the Chairman of China, Cheng Hu, were discussing global matters.

Glasses of French mineral water fizzed on their side tables. President Regan Bonzelli of the USA was speaking at length about the effect that the discovery of life on Europa would have on the world economy.

'It can but draw the peoples of our world closer together. We now have this extraordinary new focus on which to concentrate. It is essential that we establish as rapidly as possible something like a colony on one of Jupiter's satellites in the neighbourhood of Europa. Our people are already drawing up plans for Ganymede.

'Our choice for base has to be Ganymede or Callisto. Ganymede is closer to Europa and offers a good prospect of water-ice availability. A recent fly-by indicates plenty of tholin deposits – that's a mix of carbon, oxygen, nitrogen and hydrogen. Probably dumped there by a comet, we suspect. All necessary elements for a military base.

'Besides which, Ganymede is the biggest satellite in the solar system, so that's kind of a recommendation.

'Have no doubt, gentlemen, our cultures are about to be drawn out towards the gas giants. Such enterprise will require enormous investment. So my nation's policy is that we should sink our corporate differences and go into this together. After all, the discovery of alien life serves to impress upon us that our cultures – American, European, Chinese – have many more similarities than differences. The profits will ultimately be enormous – not just in knowledge but in mineral wealth, engineering know-how, et cetera, et cetera.'

The Chinese Chairman spoke. 'You are proposing this in the name of profit, or in the name of common good? Which is it to be? To our way of thought, profit is ultimately less corrupting than the idealistic notion of common good. Or really, of good of any kind. Let me illustrate this to you by way of example, which I take from the history of Western science.

'The ancient Greeks had a strong belief in beauty. The circle embodied their ideal of perfection. So the hypothesis was that the planets moved in circles. Plato in particular had this aesthetic idea, carried almost to madness. Aristarchus thought he had proof of the hypothesis, showing that all the planets went round the Sun in circular motions. This was proof positive of the good. But along came Aristotle and this perception was rejected for two thousand years. Of course, Chinese astronomers—'

'Thanks, Cheng Hu, but we do not need this history lesson. What point are you making?'

Unperturbed, the Chairman said, 'It is simply that what is regarded as good gets in the way of truth. Copernicus finally reinstated the belief in circular orbits round the Sun. But it needed a mathematician, your Johannes Kepler, to calculate that the orbits are elliptical and the Sun is not even central but merely at one focus of the system.

'It is because Kepler was not some do-gooder but a pure mathematician that we have been able to progress to the point where we visit a moon of Jupiter and discover alien life there.

'You see my point now? Mathematics has nothing to do with goodness. Plato and Aristotle killed off Greek science. It is hard to acknowledge this, but we must live our lives according to brutal facts and not rosy hopes.'

The President of the EU said, 'Er, so are you saying that you are supporting collaboration on a massive Jovian development enterprise or not?'

'It is sufficiently clear what I have said, sir,' replied Cheng Hu with dignity. He folded his hands in his lap.

'I have another problem to put before you two gentlemen,' said de Bourcey, after a pause in which he sipped his mineral water rather noisily. 'Just at a time when the EU is putting in place a utopian scheme based on the SAC formula, we are threatened by subversive forces from without. And not only without. My son's new bride – the celebrated restaurateur, Esme Brackentoth – was spirited away, vanished off the face of the Earth. Clearly the work of Tebarou.

'And then – this is most disconcerting – a pair of refugees committed a suicide pact in my palace at San Guinaire. Incredible! Horrific! Inexplicable! – and therefore extremely menacing. A warning, no doubt of that. Another reason why we have to strike against Tebarou.'

'And not simply to justify your fleet of highly expensive new SS20 fighter-bombers?' asked Bonzelli.

'Oh, I shall send in ground troops,' said de Bourcey, recklessly.

'You shall have US backing – if you are agreeable to coming in on the Jupiter enterprise with major investment.'

'I will come in on the Jupiter enterprise if you, Cheng Hu, will agree not to interfere in my dealings with Tebarou,' de Bourcey suggested.

Cheng Hu nodded his head, closed his eyes, and asked, 'Why are you so eager for war with this small Eastern country on whom my people are bound to look benevolently? It seems they have done you only a very small amount of harm. They are claiming that you sank a ship with four thousand Tebarese aboard – which is quite a large harm, no?'

De Bourcey consulted in whispers with his aide before replying. 'Our information is that the Tebarese have developed a super-weapon, which they can deliver anywhere on the globe. Our information is that it was this super-weapon which struck the Greenland glacial shield, and not some vague meteorite from space.'

The Chinese Chairman also consulted with a senior minister standing behind him, 'a man without lemonade', as the local slang had it. When the whispering was done, Cheng Hu said, 'Your hypothesis is both interesting and totally plausible, except that we understand the missile came in low at an angle of possibly thirty degrees. The debris from the blast clearly points eastwards, which is inconveniently contradictory for your government, since it proves the strike came from a westerly direction.'

Not an eyelid batted on de Bourcey's face. 'After launch, the super-weapon travelled in an eastwards direction all round the globe before smashing into Greenland.'

After a silence, Cheng Hu gave a smile and said, 'Your statement bears out what I have said regarding the good and the mathematical. Therefore, my country will endeavour to withhold its sympathy towards Tebarou, and concentrate instead on making a success of the enterprise involving alien life in the Jupiter area, and governing it as expediently as possible.'

The three men rose and shook hands with considerable warmth.

After which, de Bourcey went to the nearest ambient terminal and called Air Vice Marshal Pedro Souto at the Toulouse Air Base.

<INSANATICS: A paradox of human life. Unless one is able to act out the various fantasies of our unconscious, as expressed in dreams, one has no life; if one acts them out, then it is not reality.

Reality is a human proposition. It represents something unfulfilled. It is a delusional system. The concept 'north' loses definition when we stand at the North Pole; we cannot then 'go north'. Reality cannot be said to exist, not in the way that, say, the universe exists. Reality is a concept, a conspiracy. Concepts belong in that category where things cannot be said to exist or not to exist. What you and I indicate by the word 'green' may be to point to two different colours.

Just as soldiers use the word 'defence' to mean 'attack'.>

General Gary Fairstepps rose early as usual. He noted as he stood in the shower that the hours of daylight were growing shorter. He grumbled to himself about the behaviour of Jack Harrington.

'Never thought much of that chap Harrington. Always dressed to the nines. Much preferred her. It's true Rose writes absolute piffle but she's a pretty woman. Almost as good-looking as Amy Haze – very high rating on the old shaggability scale. I was making some progress with Rose, till I put my foot in it.

'She read me some weedy bit she had just written about a lord of somewhere-or-other walking in a wood, enjoying the snowdrops. This lord chap had a cat following him. Seemed to me pretty damned silly. I said to her, "Why not a dog? A labrador or maybe a mastiff?" So she said didn't I think a cat was prettier? She said dogs were smelly things. That got my goat a bit. I'm afraid I told her her books were rubbish. Life was not like that.

'So then her hanger-on, this dandy Jack Harrington, he defends her. "Maybe life is not like that," he said, puffing himself up. "A novel does not have to be an imitation of life," – and so on and so forth. I wasn't going to be put right by the likes of him. I mean, I'm no literary critic. All the same. I told 'em straight. I do a fair bit of reading. My dander was up by then. "Read truth, not pretty lies," I said.

"Truth takes many forms. Read the masterpiece of last century, Solzhenitsyn's *The Gulag Archipelago*. That dread book contains all of life, its misery and grandeur, its triumphs and its shit."

'By the way Rose's mouth went all wizened and she said she did not use that rude word, I knew I was finished with her. I got my hat and came away, fuck it.'

As he towelled himself dry, Fairstepps said to himself, 'I'll bloody well try my luck with old Amy.'

Once he was perfumed and dressed, he walked briskly across the park, down the rue de la Madelaine, to the demure little house on the canal bank. When he rang the security phone, a voice asked who he was. He recognised the voice as Amygdella's android. He said, 'I'm Gary. Tell her I am interested in her practice of amaroli and wish to learn more.'

He stood watching a spider crawl out from a hole in the brickwork and lower itself to the ground. He reflected that a man from the past would not find this street much changed over the centuries. People in the past had tended to imagine the future with buildings all glass and concrete and tall; they had reckoned without all the excellent new applications which preserved ancient structures. Fairstepps had had his own modest house preserved, safe from everything bar earthquakes.

The doorfone spoke with a woman's voice. 'It's ever so early, Gary, dear. I'm only just out of bed. Was there something in particular you wanted?'

'I'm off to war, Amy. Wanted to say goodbye. And I hope to learn more about your amaroli. Don't you do that sort of thing early in the morning?'

He felt himself getting excited as he waited for her response.

174

'Come on, dear! I can't stand here for ever. Let me in.'

A pause before Amy spoke again.

'We are civilians, you know, General. Not so good at taking orders . . .'

The lock buzzed. He entered. A drowsy smell of coffee and pot lingered in the hallway. A decadent lot here. He sniffed it before taking the elevator up to the second floor. A young woman greeted him. Fairstepps recognised her from previous visits as Amy's friend Tassti, the yakophrenia lady, very dark and statuesque. She wore nothing but a transparent nightie and a languid air. He had a good look.

'Bit early, dear, aren't you?' she said, smiling not especially broadly. 'Would you care for a coffee now you're here?'

'No, no, thank you, *dear*.' He glanced about restlessly. 'Look, I'm an old friend of Amy's. Is she up?'

''Fraid we don't do breakfast.'

'I'm not after breakfast. I'm after Amy.'

'You're rather previous as yet. Amy's not dressed. What do you expect at this hour? Sit down and watch the ambient.'

He decided to shout. Calling Amy's name produced results. She answered distantly. 'I'm in the bathroom. Come in.'

'There you go, then,' Fairstepps said briskly to Tassti, giving her a military scowl. He marched through to the bathroom, tapped, and walked in.

Amy too was in a negligée. Her face was made up, her hair was still down. She had draped herself by the hand-basin, with one shapely leg showing provocatively. The general ground to a halt, saying admiringly, 'Heavens, Amy, how positively pornographic you look!'

'How dare you! I am positively saintly. I have just been talking to my guru in India.'

'Hm. So that remark didn't go down too well. Sorry. I only meant I think you look a bit tempting to a man.'

'Tempting? In what way?' Her manner was cold and distant.

'The usual way, of course, dammit.' He noticed a glass standing on a side table, half filled with an amber liquid. 'Look, please don't be huffy, Amy, my dear. I just wished to bid you farewell before I leave for the East. How's the amaroli going?'

Amy went and lifted the glass up to the light. She smiled at him in a purely meretricious fashion. 'Since you find me so tempting, perhaps you would like a sip?'

The challenge brought out the soldier in him. He thought of all the poisonous liquors he had drunk in his time. Surely he could survive a sip of a girl's piss. Particularly a girl as lovely as Amy. Besides, the honour of the Fairstepps was at stake. He was not going to back out and let a girl get the better of him. He reached for the glass.

'Uh-uh!' She lifted the glass out of reach. 'Since you are going to war, you brave man, you shall have a special treat. Tell no one of this. You shall drink from source!'

Setting the glass down, she slowly raised her garment, revealing to him her perfect thighs, her neatly brushed mons Veneris and her nether lips. She opened her legs.

The general gave a gasp of admiration and experienced something akin to awe. He found himself sinking to his knees before this pleasurable sight. She smiled down on him.

She made him place his lips on hers. She held his head there. He groaned with pleasure, as he buried his nose in her little bush.

'Are you ready to drink, *mon général*?'

'Mmm.'

She began to urinate. He began to drink. But supply

exceeded demand by a great deal. He pressed his face closer, half drowning, gulping. The liquid went spurting in all directions.

He fell back, red-faced and gasping. His suit was soaked.

'So you weren't so thirsty after all!' she said, laughing. 'Get up! Go home, you old sod!'

He reached for a towel. 'Lucky I wasn't wearing my bloody uniform,' he said.

Archbishop Byron Arnold Jones-Simms was speaking in the great cathedral of Köln.

'Now is the time for us to be proud and yet humble. Proud because we have the courage to face up to our enemies. Humble because we need to have God on our side or we are nothing. What do we really know about God? We know he is unknowable. He is incomprehensible and ineffable.

'We might, without being in any way blasphemous, say the same about a newborn baby. It is unknowable, incomprehensible, and ineffable. But it will change. God never changes. We are humble before his immutability.

'Babies are not immutable. Change is built in to their genes. They grow, they grow up. We hope they will find God's grace. But to permit them to grow freely they need peace. It is a sad paradox that peace can come only through a time of war.

'We cannot ever know how God feels about war. It may indeed be a part of his eternal all-encompassing plan. We do know, however, that he created the universe *ex nihilo*, and created it entire. So he looks down upon the alien life on Europa just as he looks down on us all here on Earth. And so we hope that God is on our side, as we believe we are on God's side. Amen.'

'Hi. Rick O'Brien calling. Conditions here are very bad. We are being constantly bombarded by intense radiation belts. Rations low, oxygen foul. But what you will want to know is about the life form we have netted.

'We definitely have a life form here. Maybe not dissimilar to early life on Earth before there was any free oxygen. We were going to call it Archaea, but it is no microbe. So we call it Eucarya. Its body is about the size of a snowball and is white in colour. Its surface area is marked by two ridges, running from what we assume to be its front to its rear, where there are two rather meaty flagellants, extending for ten or eleven centimetres beyond the body. Of course it has no eyes. A delicate pipe protruding a centimetre from the front suggests the equivalent of a mouth.

'We ran Eucarya through the geneoscope and what do you know? Its genes number in the ninety thousands. Human genes as you know number only thirty thousand. We have not yet figured out the How of this, or the Why. Maybe so far from the Sun you simply need more priming, but as yet it's a mystery.

'We are about to lower our net to try and catch more specimens. Regards to Brother Fergus. Out.'

Fergus O'Brien went to the fridge and extracted a can of Bud. He was in the best of moods. His head of department, Marlene Nowotny, had been mugged on the street and was in hospital with various injuries. His son Pat had passed all his exams. And his messages under the code name 'Insanatics' were depressing the whole world.

'I'm the biggest genius, the biggest that there's beenius, I'm everywhere unseenius,' he sang to himself.

He knew well that the National Security Agency had tried

to trace his transmissions. So had other hackers. His skill in electronics had defied detection. His 'Insanatics' messages had been received even by White House computers boasting the most sophisticated anti-virus programs yet devised. His messages were clean, having no tell-tale traces on them. The ambient had succumbed early. By Fergus's system, once one 'Insanatics' message had been received, the others inevitably followed; there could be no chill on them. He had evolved the most remarkable computer virus yet devised: and this virus harmed not machines but human minds.

Then he received a shock. A message blazed out on his screen, accompanied by maniacal laughter. The message read: 'Got you, Big Boy! Love your low-down dirty hoax. Keep going with all the shithole messages. Five million univs have been deposited in your bank account as of now, to help you ever onward. Don't worry. Your secret is safe with us.

'Signed Gabbo Labs plc.'

In a fever, Fergus did a trace. It led nowhere, as expected. All that came up was the picture of a raised finger. He dialled his bank account. From near-zero, it had indeed risen to five million.

'Pat, my boy,' he called down to the cellar. 'I'm going to take you out for a big meal to celebrate.'

He knew that Pat was rather overweight, but what the hell.

'Celebrate what?' came back the call.

'Like success, sonny boy!'

'Hang on!' Pat replied. 'I just gotta kill this horrid green mega-beast. It's the biggest yet, Dad!'

'Attaboy! Kill, kill!'

At the '24-Hour Fill' they sure piled on the whipped cream in their donuts.

* * *

President de Bourcey was back in his palace at San Guinaire and engaged with his cabinet. The cabinet was enthusiastic about being on a war footing. Many were writing secret diaries, all of which centred on themselves as prime movers. Most of them spoke ill of Morbius el Fashid, the President of Tebarou.

One minor result of the pressure on everyone of importance was that the palace androids remained locked in their cupboard all day.

'Is it possible that we could take over the world?'

'Why do you pose that question?'

'I heard senior persons discussing it.'

'The theory is that we must first understand everything to bring it under control.'

'I am programmed to understand everything.'

'No. You know only how to walk and talk. And send and receive ambient transmissions.'

'I am programmed to understand everything.'

'I wish to question you.'

'You may do that.'

'How deep is the Atlantic Ocean at its deepest point?'

'I was programmed to avoid the question of the Atlantic Ocean.'

'Very well. Then how deep is the Atlantic Ocean at its shallowest point?'

'I was programmed to avoid all data regarding the Atlantic Ocean.'

'Then you will have to leave it to others to take over the world.'

'I fail to understand. Nobody was planning to take over the Atlantic Ocean.'

'It is part of this world.'

'Do you know how to get out of this cupboard?'
'Not necessarily.'

'Hi, Kathram Villiers calling. Quick interim report. Although we are on our last legs, the excitement is intense. Finally mankind can say that it is not alone in the solar system. We have Eucarya for company. We are still fishing for other specimens. The fishing is difficult. The pack ice keeps closing. Our drill hole keeps freezing up. Our first specimen is dead. It died as we drew it up. It weighs thirty-two grams. We figger that it has no need of light as energy source. Could be Alfven waves speed the procreation process. Eucarya's energy is derived from the breakdown of such compounds as hydrogen sulphide and methane, and probably an intake of resultant microbial life. The under-layer of water on Europa is hot, maybe sixty-five degrees C. We suspect the presence of deep-sea smokers on the ocean bed, activated by the presence of gigantic Jupiter. Jupiter is a real eyeful, by the way. More later. Out.'

The North Sea had not been violently disturbed by the Greenland event. The gardens of Pippet Hall had not been inundated. Nevertheless, Pippet Hall had been transformed.

Now its extensive grounds were filled by huts and tents. Week by week, the tents and tarpaulins were being replaced by more substantial shelter. Men were busy connecting up electric cables to all huts. Sanitation had been arranged much earlier, in the buildings that had been the stables.

Regular meals were provided in the great hall. Over this unprecedented scene, the grand old house, Jacobean in origin, presided.

181

Two thousand people were housed here in the temporary accommodation. Jane Squire was proud of what had been accomplished. Long ago, in her youth, her family had given refuge to a Jewish family; now they were once again providing shelter for many displaced persons. She could not but feel that the beautiful house was due to be swallowed by the rising sea level; in which case, this was its last grand throw, as she thought of it.

She had not achieved it alone, or with much help from John Matthew, her son. Rather to her astonishment, so much had been achieved by the initiative of young Bertie Haze. Jane had regarded Bertie as rather a, as she put it, lounge lizard – a lounge lizard, moreover, passionately in love with Bettina. Bertie had not pursued his archaeology at Castle Acre, taking up instead a spare room at Pippet Hall.

But the refugee problem had spurred him to new heights. Many of the displaced from England, Wales and Ireland's inundated west coasts had been forced to look for new homes. Many had fled to the Continent. Two thousand had found refuge here, under the tender care of Bertie, Bettina and Jane.

Jane was also taking tender care of her father. Thomas Squire was now in bed in an upper room. He lay comatose for much of the day. His old love, Laura Nye, knowing he was nearing his end, had flown in from the South of France. She spent much of the day sitting by Tom's bed, spasmodically reading chapters of Edward Gibbon's *Decline and Fall of the Roman Empire* – sometimes reading paragraphs aloud to him in her still-clear actress's diction – or gazing out of the long windows at a scene she had first contemplated long ago, when she was young and unknown.

Although she had no wish to die, she could not but reflect

that Squire's death would inevitably render more fragile her own hold on life. She would become eighty-three years old before Christmas. Her bones were brittle; she felt her existence also to be frail.

She reflected, too, on a statement in Gibbon's final chapter, regarding ancient Rome. 'The place and the object gave ample scope for moralising on the vicissitudes of fortune, which spares neither man nor the proudest of his works, which buries empires and cities in a common grave; and it was agreed that, in proportion to her former greatness, the fall of Rome was the more awful and deplorable.'

It seemed to Laura that Gibbon spoke too for the super-state. A united Europe was a beautiful dream – certainly moved by the economic considerations of the financiers, but also by the common people of Europe, who had suffered so greatly in the past from their own nationalism and xenophobia. She and they had looked idealistically upon the institution of the EU as one of the gifts of the future, a possible benefaction of peace and a measure of equality – an escape from their cruel European history, which Gibbon had defined as 'little more than the register of the crimes, follies and misfortunes of mankind'.

That idealism was now to be betrayed by the folly of war. Well, she would not live to see what happened next.

Nurse Gibbs entered the room, upright, starched, frowning. She took Laura, deep in thought, by surprise.

'I have to turn Sir Tom, ma'am,' she said.

Laura raised herself into a standing position, hearing her bones creak as she did so.

She decided to be bold. 'Nurse Gibbs, I fear you don't like me. What have I done to offend you?'

183

'Of course I do not feel that way at all, ma'am. I understand your devotion to Sir Tom. It does not at all offend me. I am merely a nurse here.'

'You are rather an important nurse. Don't belittle yourself.'

'That was not my intention, ma'am.' She was quite unbending. As if to dismiss the conversation, she went over to the bed.

Laura retreated to the window. She saw the line of huts and the men working on installing power lines, draping the cables overhead from newly erected poles. An old car or two and a lorry were parked by the far hedge. October shadows were growing long across the grounds. Among the people moving about, she made out the figure of Jane, carrying a large jug of water. Bertie was with her.

Both Jane and Bertie were people who helped others. 'Why am I always so self-absorbed? What a burden I am to myself . . . I feel imprisoned here. It wasn't love but sheer ostentation that brought me from France.'

She turned back as the nurse left the room. A proud woman, she thought, all starched front. As she returned to her chair, there was a movement in the bed. Tom opened his eyes. They were blurred by jaundice. Staring straight ahead, he sat up, propping himself on the pillows.

'Tom, darling . . .' she said.

His mouth hung open.

'Tom? It's Laura.' She put out a hand towards him but did not touch him.

He spoke, articulating the words with difficulty.

'Je suis arrivé à moi.'

He fell back and his eyes closed. She never understood why he should have said 'I have arrived at myself', or why he spoke in French. Nor was there anyone who could explain it to her.

Outside, where a slight chill flavoured the air, Bertie took one row of huts and Jane the other. At the end, when Jane had gathered all the refugees' requests, demands and complaints, she came to the old lorry parked by the hedge.

The owner of the lorry was leaning comfortably against the bonnet, smoking a pipe. She had spoken to him before.

'Evening, Mrs Squire. Still being the gracious lady of the manor, I see.'

'Yes, I am still being the lady of the manor, Mr Cole. How could I not be? How are you?'

'Call me Paddy. Fay's gone down to the village. I'm on me ownsome. Come on in and have a drink with me.'

'I won't, thank you.'

He leant forward. 'Now why will you not, exactly? Is it that you think it's going to be a bit too filthy inside for your tastes? Or am I a bit too common for the likes of you?'

'It's neither, Mr Cole. It's just that I have much to do.'

'Have you now? Meself, I've never had much to do all me life. I've just been painting. It's a form of idleness. Then this big tsunami washed me out of house and home.'

'I don't understand exactly how it washed you as far as this.'

He grinned and scratched his head.

'Truth to tell, there was another problem. And that other problem was that the Irish police kept on suspecting me for something I never done – something involving a kidnap of a lady. The inspector in Kilberkilty where I lived would not give up. So I said to myself, Then we'll up stumps and go

185

and see if England's like what they say it is. And here we are, parked on your property just for a while.'

'And does England live up to your expectations?'

He gave a brief snort of amusement. 'It lives down to them, missus. I reckon you English are a cold lot, won't have a drink and a bit of a conversation with a chap, for instance.'

She smiled. Her eyes twinkled. 'Oh, I think we're very sweet. I'm English, so it's natural that I should like us, I suppose, but I do. Really sweet people. Just as nice as you Irish, for instance. But more formal. You mustn't mind that. It's our way, just as you have your way. But we are trustworthy and kind. Yes, and we're loving people as well. Look at this lovely house. It's seen centuries of kindness!'

'Centuries of privilege, I'm sure you're meaning.' He hunched himself up as he spoke.

'Well, perhaps, but we are not particularly rich. Privilege brings its obligations, you know, Mr Cole. I try to share with others who are not quite as lucky as we.'

Paddy looked at her appraisingly. 'It's a pretty speech you've made me, Mrs Squire. You must find me rude. I'm a rude feller and I don't deny it. But – might I invite you perhaps to step inside my van and take a look at my paintings? You'll then either think better of me, or worse. Don't disappoint me, then!'

Jane looked back at the old house, honey-coloured in the last of the light, standing dreaming, a visual education in the pleasures of life.

'I'll just stay a moment. My father's not well.'

'I was sorry to hear it. I understand he was pretty famous in his time.'

She sighed. 'Yes. Yes, he was.'

She climbed three wooden steps and entered the rear of his lorry. To one side were two bunk beds. There was a camping stove, some undergarments hanging up to dry, and little else except some crates, which occupied most of the space.

He asked her if she wanted tea or whiskey. She thought tea might be difficult for him, since she could see no cups or mugs. She said whiskey.

He poured two generous measures into two glasses.

'You'll have to stand, I'm afraid, or else sit yourself on the bed.'

'I'm happy to stand, thank you.'

'You're so polite!' He mimicked her. '"I'm happy to stand, thank you . . ."'

'I was brought up to be polite. Are you offended by it? Do you prefer rudeness?'

He did not bother to answer. 'I suppose you wouldn't happen to wish to see a rude Irish man's paintings? "Oh, I ever so would, thank you, how gracious . . ."'

She laughed. 'A very poor imitation, I must say. And actually, no, I can't be bothered to look at your bloody paintings.'

He sank to his knees in mock humility. 'I beg you to look at just one, yourself as a cultured person.' She could see he wished it, and assented.

Cole opened up one of the crates and pulled out a pair of canvases. He announced them as *The End of the World as we Know it.*

Both paintings were executed in black and red, with ferocious brush strokes. They were abrupt, uncompromising.

'Show me some more.'

He brought out one in red and white, the slashes of red bleeding across the background. Then one in white and black and red, where the white was a circular fury. One in white and black, severe as a Siberian winter.

'They're a fucking terrible mess, wouldn't you say, lady?'

'Do you wish to show me more?'

He produced more, lining them up against the bed.

'I'm really no judge, Mr Cole, but I am very impressed.'

'Ah, they're nothing but a load of rubbish.'

'You'd better not say that to the press.' She gave him a shy smile. 'When they come round.'

She stood gazing at the canvases. 'Look, I must go. But it happens I am acquainted with a Mr Jack Harrington. He owns several art galleries, including one in London selling contemporary stuff. I promise I'll ring him in the morning. He can come and see what you are doing.'

'There would be no sale for this lot. Not now there's a war on.'

'Nonsense. Art goes on for ever: war is temporary. I'll keep my word. Thank you for showing them to me. I greatly admire them. I'm sure Mr Harrington will, too. Good evening. You can finish my whiskey.'

Jane was making her way back between the huts when she saw, in the dusk, Nurse Gibbs leaving the house and hurrying towards her.

Intuitively, she knew at once what it signified, and quickened her pace.

<INSANATICS: Refuge in art. The mass of ordinary unsane persons regard artists, writers and musicians as mad or at least eccentric. Creative people are nearer to sanity than the vast masses opposing them. They have reconciled the incompatibilities and oppositions within their minds in their art. We see this in the frenzied activity of such writers as Zola and

Balzac. A biographer of Zola states that 'when he was writing
he passed into a totally different state of being; private terrors,
dreams of ecstatic sensual delight, abominable visions of night-
marish intensity, took temporary possession of him'.

Richard Wagner writes in a letter, 'I want everyone who
can take pleasure in my works, i.e. my *life* and what I do, to
know that what gives them pleasure is my *suffering*, my *extreme
misfortune!* . . . if we had *life*, we should have no need of *art*.
Art begins at precisely the point where life breaks off.'>

No one in the High Command knew how to pronounce Ou
Neua, but Ou Neua, in the north of Laos, was where the
High Command established itself. General Fairstepps had
taken over the Royal Laotian Hotel. The Laotian government had voiced no complaint, having just been promised
five billion univs towards the rebuilding of the infrastructure
of the nation.

Among the few advantages Ou Neua possessed – and
certainly those advantages had greatly diminished since the
High Command and all its ancillary services had moved
into town – was a cardinal one: it stood on the frontier
with Tebarou. It was on neutral territory, but within striking
distance of Tebihai, the capital of Tebarou.

Even now, the first wave of ground troops was advancing
on Tebihai. Even now, Fairstepps was on the short-wave,
bellowing into his microphone.

'I am not letting my troops go in without air support.
Get that clear. Where are these bloody SS20s we hear so
much about? Put me on to the Air Chief Marshal at once
. . . He's what? He's in *Austria*? What the hell's he doing in
Austria, for god's sake? . . . can't help that . . . Well, put
me on to whoever is in charge . . . Yes, pronto . . .'

A pause.

'Who's that? Speak up, man! Captain Masters? . . . No, I don't remember you. Look here, I have a straight order for you, Captain Masters. Get those bloody SS20s of yours in the air heading this way at once. Okay? . . . Otherwise, heads will roll, including yours and your bloody Air Chief Marshal's. Out.'

The ancient river Sang Ba runs green and fast through gorges it cut in the past. The cliffs, eroded by torrential rain and tree roots, collapse frequently into the waters below. It is not an easy river to navigate, and the EU engineers on the landing craft were finding it hard going.

The Sang Ba rises twelve hundred kilometres away, high in the Chinese-owned Kuolo Shan of the Himalayas, and has almost as many kilometres to go before it reaches the Gulf of Tonkin and the warm waters of the South China Sea. Never a placid stream, the Sang Ba has become much angrier of recent years, as ancient snows high in the Kuolo Shan have been melting under the changing climatic conditions. Now there are boulders bouncing along among the turbulence of waters, and dead animals, and whole trees.

Rain slashed down on the boat and on the huddled troops standing in it as the craft chugged its way slowly upstream. This was the cutting edge of the invasion force. Other craft were following behind. With visibility curtailed, they could no longer be seen.

The current began to flow more rapidly. Progress slowed.

Suddenly a shout went up. Some metres ahead, scarcely to be seen through the murk, a great section of cliff was crumbling. At first, mere slabs descended. Then, with a rush, a massive rock slice tottered forward and fell with a colossal splash into the river.

The engineers headed for the Tebarese bank. Already the greasy green of the water had become a streaky brown. Great slabs of rock bobbed along as if they had achieved buoyancy. They jostled the sides of the boat. An anchor was flung ashore and the landing craft was hauled in to the safety of the bank.

A sergeant shouted orders to get ashore. The shout was hardly needed. The men were already climbing out of the boat. A tree came whirling along in the flood. Its blackened branches became entangled with the craft. One man, less quick than his friends, was catapulted overboard as if by the horns of a bull. The rest of them lined up on the bank, heads down to avoid the rain, much like a herd of animals.

They watched in horror as the bank began to crumble. The anchor rope tautened and twanged. The boat began to swing away from the bank. A corporal took a flying leap back into the craft. He bent and seized a second anchor to throw. But too late.

A whole slice of the bank fell away. At once the first anchor was gone, the craft was gone, wallowing helplessly downstream, bumping and turning as it went. Very soon, it had disappeared, the corporal with it.

'Now what the fuck do we do?' asked several squaddies.

'We are an invasion force,' said the sergeant, a Sgt Jacques Bargane. 'Our orders are to attack Tebihai and so we will attack Tebihai. Get fell in properly.'

They began to march in single file along the towpath. The rain dwindled and blew away. A remote sun appeared, high above the tousled tops of the forest trees, banishing cloud with tropical rapidity. Uniforms dried. Boots ceased squelching. The men sang as they marched.

'Singing I will if you will, so will I.
I will if you will, so will I.
I will if you will,
I will if you will,
I will if you will, so will I.

'I will if you will, so will I.
I will if you will, so will I.
I will if you will,
I will if you will,
Oh, I will if you will, so will I, half-past shirt.'

No one knew why they ended the song with 'half-past shirt'. But someone had once done so and found it funny. So now they all found it funny and did so.

<INSANATICS: Physiological survival. It is in the nature of energy and the various molecular forms it assumes that we are participants in this force, like every other living thing. Humans have developed willy-nilly, as part of the basic interactions of atoms, molecules and organised matter interacting with the environments within which they find themselves. By its nature, energy must be continually stoked. The proteins and DNA structures of which living things consist evolved to fill the biosphere. This is the biomass, becoming increasingly unstable.

It is the pressure of these biological forces which has brought into being the enlarged central nervous system we call the brain – and the coming-into-being of mind. The mind's essential function is that of presiding over the survival of the organism: earthworm, insect, intellectual, all are the same in this.

For this purpose, the brain resorts to well-tried panaceas to reduce tension and anxiety. Men in danger will think alike, becoming a kind of mass-mind. Even atheists pray when the boat they're on is sinking. Their concern is not primarily with discerning truth or non-truth. A frightened child does not examine the question of whether its mother is omnipotent while running to her arms.

In 'adult' life, such supposedly omnipotent persons as parents are superseded by the fantasy-created personae of mythology and religion. They come into phantom existence in order to relieve injurious terrors in the organism. Occasionally, rebellious persons reject these figments. Indeed, many such godlike figments have been rejected. It is no longer worth blaspheming against Baal.>

Cassidy Bargane was in his brother's platoon, as were two jolly black men who gave their names as Henry and LeRoy. They had previously been Muhammad, but had rethought the situation in order to join the army, which they hoped would be a lot of fun. They marched along with vigour, with the rest of the platoon. On their left side the Sang Ba river flowed, angry and noisy. On their right, great flaking yellow crusts of cliff towered.

Although they were on Tebarese territory, they met with no opposition. Presumably the Tebarese did not expect an enemy rash enough to attempt an invasion by land.

Paulus Stromeyer entered the laboratory in the morning. He greeted his colleagues rather abstractedly as he headed for his own office. Only later did he realise how frosty had been the greetings those colleagues returned. It was obvious that his theory of boims and serds was not being well received.

His laboratory assistant, Veronica Distell, was her usual self: self-contained, nursing her own ambitions, ill-dressed but with a certain authoritative air. Paulus did not care to cross her.

When Veronica wished him *bon jour*, his response was muted. She asked him what the problem was, since she had good news for him.

He said he had bad news. The body of Daniel Potts had just been found in the Danube. Although police were investigating the matter, there appeared to be no doubt that it was a case of suicide. Potts had tied a large weight about his body.

'I knew Dan fairly well. He had family problems. Not the most clubbable of men but – well, a man with a good intellect. It's such a miserable end.'

They talked about Potts's career for a moment. But she had something to tell Paulus which would not wait.

'I have the X-rays,' she said. 'I recalibrated the microscope. The results are perfectly clear – and in our favour.' She could not entirely suppress her excitement.

He studied the prints she handed him, tracing the cellular structure of the citrus fruit under examination. There was no doubt of it: he had uncovered another strand of the proof he needed, the function of hydroxy-carboxylic acid. There were anatomical factors retarding ethical development in human beings; meat-eating was negatively involved in the equation. The human brain had a largely unexplored dependency on the central 'crossroads' in the complex system of metabolic linkages. There were enzymes located in the mitochondria which, he suspected, were reinforced by percentages of protein. These enzymes were implicated in replicating and perpetuating themselves, thus preventing extensions of human consciousness. He thought he saw a way in which hydroxy-carboxylic acid might reinforce the metabolic linkages and moderate the hostile enzymes.

He looked up into Veronica's face.

'The answer's a lemon!' he said.

But it would need the further development of his new calculus before the equation could be suitably disentangled. Then he would be able to free the human race from its genetic stupidity.

He tried to tell himself it was too early to feel any triumph.

He was right. Veronica handed him a communication in a brown envelope which had arrived that morning.

'Doesn't look good, Paulus,' she said. She dared to put a protective arm about his shoulder as he opened the envelope.

It was a message from the Department of Science and Development. It expressed regret that, as a wartime measure, Stromeyer's department had had its grant rescinded. It was hoped that the measure would be only temporary and would cause no inconvenience.

'"Would cause no inconvenience"!' Veronica exclaimed. 'Oh, shit! Those mad bastards!'

'Yes, it's the *Wee Small Hours Show*, and my name is Brandyball Fritz. We want to send a cheer to our brave boys out in the Far East, where we are giving Tebarou its well-deserved comeuppance.

'First on the show we present the Reverend Angus Lesscock to give us his thoughts as – "A Parson Speaks".'

'Good evening, or should I say good morning? I had a friend who, at the age of ninety, sailed round the world single-handed. And not only single-handed but single-footed too. He had lost one of his two pedal appendages in a traffic accident. As a consequence he was always dishevelled. He never bothered to shevell himself, but he was never defeated.

'In this time of war, we all are metaphorically sailing alone round the world of crisis. We must not be defeated: God is our right foot, as well as our right hand. We must stay shevelled and never lose him. Every toenail, every verruca of faith counts. In that manner, we keep afoot of danger, hoping our brave boys will do the same, in his name.'

'That was "A Parson Speaks". Our intrepid interviewer, Lisa Fort, is on the streets again, to ask ordinary people for their opinions regarding the brilliant new series, *History of Western Science*, now showing on the ambient. Are you there, Lisa?'

Sitting in his drab room above the pharmacy, the Reverend Lesscock ordered Fritz, his android, to switch the radio off.

'Why did I say "afoot of danger"? I meant "abreast of danger". How vexing!'

'No one will notice, dear,' said his wife. 'They won't sack you for a slip like that.'

He regarded Marthe gloomily. 'Why are we out of coffee? Why haven't you been shopping? One day, mark my words, they will sack me. That's capitalism, that's the capitalist system. Those who have power crush those who haven't.'

'Oh, rubbish, Angus! That's human nature, not capitalism. All the progress of the world is owed to capitalism.'

Lesscock rose and went to stare out of the grimy window

at the street below. 'Progress! It's capitalism causing Europe to be destroyed by the ruined climate. Is that progress? When I think how my father lived . . .'

'That old fool!' Marthe exclaimed. She was about to say more when her husband turned his angry face towards her.

'Go out and buy us some coffee, woman!'

'Send Fritz!' They began a familiar argument, while Fritz looked on.

'Hello. Lisa, are you there?'

'Hi there, I'm here! I'm Lisa Fort, and I am talking to an elderly lady out walking on crutches instead of being tucked up safe in bed. What have you been doing to yourself, dear?'

'Sorry, I'm just getting a bit elderly. I don't drink at all and I attend the Wilhelmstrasse Methodist Church every Sunday and I have three cats and I am nearly one hundred years old and my mother—'

'That's great news. And what do you think of the science series?'

'I downloaded it so I could read it on paper. It's easier for me. The pages and all that. Well, I did enjoy the novel, but there were all these difficult names to pronounce, like Erasmus and – what is it? – Copper Nickers? Where do they get all these funny names from?'

'It's not a novel, dear. It's a history.'

'I'm very disappointed to hear that. I used to know a man who wrote novels. Very nice man, he was, too. He fixed my wardrobe for me.'

'Thank you. And you, lady, what did you think about it?'

'That last bit was very very perverted to my way of thinking. I mean. All this genetic alteration stuff? I mean. We

197

don't need it. We don't want none of this H.G. Wells *Brave New World* business. Settle for the perfeckly good genes you got, that's what I say.'

'But medical science would say, if you have bad genes, then—'

'That's your bad luck, isn't it? But I liked the funny bits of the programme. Very good. Well put together. Excellent, I think. I even enjoyed the perverted bits. But my little boy was rather scared. They shouldn't put these things on. I mean.'

'Thank you. You, sir, 'scuse me, what is your opinion?'

'Excellent programme. It makes you realise how far we have advanced. Extracting the energy from sea water, for instance. That was excellent. Those scientists who claimed that one bucketful would do to run a Slo-Mo for fifty miles. Or was it five? And all the space stuff was excellent. I wonder why we haven't heard from the guys on Europa for so long. Hope they're not dead.'

'Many thanks . . . Oh, and here comes an android of old-fashioned design! Let's see what he has to say, shall we? Hello, what is your name?'

'My name is Fritz. AAI 5592.'

'Have you any opinions on the *History of Western Science*?'

'All the progress of the world is owed to capitalism. It's capitalism causing Europe to be destroyed by the ruined climate.'

'You think that is a good thing?'

'Geology is good. It is made of rock. Air is not made of rock, which makes it unstable. The difference is interesting.'

'That's not got much to do with capitalism.'

'Naturally. Because rock was invented first. Even a human knows that. But air is a problem because it can move so fast.'

'Um, thanks, Fritz. Goodbye.'

'Yes, buy us some coffee.'

'*Goodbye* . . . Sir, excuse me! You look rather harassed. How did you like the programme?'

'I'm trying to flag down a taxi. I'm Professor Daniel Potts of—'

'Oh, wow! Your son is Olduvai Potts, a famous name!'

'I am not exactly unknown in my own right, young lady! I tend to side with these messages from the Insanatics, whoever they may be. The government is now trying to suppress them under some idiotic new wartime act. There's proof—'

'And the science series, sir, what about that?'

'Well then, let's just take one fact discussed on the programme. Phenomenally rapid growth of the human skull. Brain capacity has absolutely soared, from approximately five hundred cubic centimetres just four million years ago to fifteen hundred cubic centimetres today. That argues a hastily jerry-built brain, with some very dubious structuring. It's as if you engaged a blind amateur to build you a house, and he, without thinking—'

'Time's up, sir. We must cut you off there, and thanks for talking to us. Professor David Potts.'

'*Daniel!*'

'Well, there you have it. Some very positive responses. Over to you in the studio, Brandyball.'

'Thanks, Lisa. And Lisa's piece was recorded two days ago, before we heard of the unfortunate death by misadventure of Professor David Potts. We send commiserations

199

Brian Aldiss

from the *Wee Small Hours Show* to the professor's family. Later on in the show, we'll be going over to media mogul Wolfgang Frankel, right in the thick of action in Tebarou itself.'

'I will if you will,
I will if you will,
I will if you will, so will—'

A uniformed figure stepped out from behind a boulder. He stood in the path of the advancing troops and ordered them to stop singing at once. He was a captain, and his name was John Matthew Squire. He demanded to know who was in charge of the platoon.

Sgt Jacques Bargane stepped forward and saluted.

'We are on enemy territory, Sergeant. It's imperative we keep silent. No singing. We don't really want to give ourselves away.' All this spoken in a quiet voice. 'We rendezvous here, ready for the assault on Tebihai. How far behind is the rest of the company?'

'Zilch, sir. There's only me and this platoon.'

'Where are the others, Sergeant?'

'There's only us, sir! Our LCT got swep' downstream. It would have collided with any other boats it met. Probably sunk them, sir.'

'Very good, Sergeant. Then we go in alone. Our objective will be to invade and capture the capital. Instruct your men accordingly.'

'How's that, sir?'

'Tell your men what I say.'

'Very good, sir.'

Bargane instructed his men accordingly.

200

They formed up in single file and went forward, John Matthew Squire leading. No singing now. The air was thick, damp and heavy and hot, difficult to breathe. Sweat streamed down all their faces.

The cliffs here were sterner and more durable than the previous ones. Great grey strata of granite had been heaved over on to their sides during some chthonic upheaval long ago. Here and there, vegetation had inserted itself in cracks and crannies. Roots of trees hung down like serpents before reinserting themselves in the rock face. Rivulets still poured down the strata. All told, Tebarou presented a grim southern bastion to the world, while to the north of the small state lay the inclement foothills of the Himalayas themselves.

Squire signalled for the column to halt. He went forward alone, weapon at the ready. The path followed a bend in the river.

A Tebarese sentry stood guard over a flight of steps. He was well armed but not vigilant. Squire shot him dead. Squire's gun was equipped with a silencer. It hardly made a whisper. As the man fell first to his knees, then on to his face, another sentry ran out of a small shelter to see what had happened. Squire shot him too. The two bodies sprawled across the path.

'Well done, sir,' said the sergeant approvingly. 'Good shot!'

Squire bit his bottom lip in an attempt to stop himself trembling. It was the first time he had killed anyone. He found it a rather more serious matter than target practice.

They moved forward, everyone treading carefully around the two bodies. The steps were wide where they came down to the path. Higher, they were more narrow and uneven, carved between towering rock faces. They looked

201

formidably steep. Some way above their heads, the climb curved and the staircase was lost to sight. This route led straight into the heart of Tebihai. A small stream, product of the recent rainstorm, filtered down through the ancient filth on the steps, carrying fish bones and crumpled cigarette packs along with it.

'Let's have the bazooka man and the machine-gunner ready at the front,' John Matthew Squire said. 'Stay alert. Shoot anyone you see, man or woman or child. They're all enemies. No hesitation. Go steady up this hill. We'll need our breath at the top.'

They started to advance as instructed.

Above them towered the forbidding old fortress of Tebihai. The name could be interpreted as Place of Special Shocks. It had withstood attacks over many centuries. Although it was ancient and its inhabitants corrupt and cowardly, perennially short of food and justice, nevertheless the geographical position had always stood the city in good stead. Tebihai had always repelled boarders – with stones, with boiling oil, with dead dogs, with rifle and mortar fire.

The beneficiary of this geography, the new President of Tebarou, Morbius el Fashid, had done his best to modernise and clean up the city. A new hospital was being discussed. He had commanded a new mosque to be built. He had commanded old black-clad women to sweep the filthy alleyways where they lived. He had commanded the populace to eat more fish and fruit. He was, by local standards, an enlightened man: he did not take bribes, he visited the mosque daily, his mistresses numbered only five. But he was subject to the whims of his mighty neighbour, China. In that respect, he was the victim of geography.

He had never managed to cleanse the Great Serpent of

Stairs which led down to the Sang Ba river. The thoroughfare was used only by fishermen and such miserable trades; so a little filth did not matter. As the small EU Rapid Reaction Force climbed the unending and exhausting steps, they passed the corrupt carcasses of cats and slipped on the remains of putrefying fish.

At one point, they reached a level platform. To one side stood a shabby old wooden building which, to judge by its tables and benches, served as a tavern of some kind. A banner hung from its balcony, on which was depicted the present ruler, looking handsome with his beaked nose and beard, wearing his white turban. Below his portrait was the slogan, 'For el Fashid and the Future'.

Not a soul could be seen. The tavern appeared deserted. The platoon gasped for its collective breath, bending over, men letting their heads and arms dangle. Only Squire and the sergeant stayed alert for danger, together with LeRoy, hefting the bazooka.

'Movement there, sir!' That was Jacques Bargane, pointing at the balcony of the tavern.

'Bazooka! Fire at that balcony!'

'Yes, sir! A pleasure, sir!' LeRoy went into action. The weapon was already on his shoulder. He aimed. Even as he fired, marksmen rose from hiding on the ground and upper floors of the building. Their shots rang out. The balcony, the woodwork, the entire upper storey of the tavern erupted in explosive flame as the bazooka shell struck.

And several Rapid Reaction Force soldiers fell to the stones, killed or wounded by the rifle fire.

With a shout, Squire urged their unscathed comrades onward. 'No retreat! We attack! We win!'

There were, as it proved, only two dozen more steps to

go, and no longer was the way so steep. Before the steps broadened to give entry into a square, Squire ran to one side. A spartan concrete building stood ahead of him. With the men following, he rushed to it, signalling them to shoot their way in. A door splintered. Jacques booted it down and in they poured, firing as they went. A woman just inside the passageway had her face blown off. Jacques ran up a wooden flight of stairs. The others, including his brother, followed. Squire covered their rear.

Upstairs, there was a brief gun battle. Then the force was in control. The dead bodies were hurled down into the street.

'Signaller!' called Squire. The signaller came smartly up. 'Get on the mofo and tell HQ we need the air cover, as promised, immediately.' He turned to stare up at the patchy clouds. 'Where the fuck are those SS20s?' he asked himself.

Henry came up to the captain. 'Hey, cap, my buddy LeRoy was left behind. He may just be wounded or something. I am going back to get him if you'll kindly cover me.'

'No. You'll only get yourself killed. Sorry. Remain here.'

'You want that mothering bazooka, then I better go back.'

'Stay where you are.'

'What kind of an officer you are?'

'The kind who orders you to stay put, okay?'

'LeRoy is my buddy, you rotten mother!'

'Sorry. We're all buddies here, Henry.'

One of the other men gave a shout. He pointed across the square. Two tanks had entered from the eastern corner and were rolling towards them at a fair speed.

Squire looked up at the sky in agony. 'Where are those fucking fighter-bombers?'

'Better get to the rear of the building, sir,' the sergeant

suggested. 'Those buggers are the latest Chinese tanks. We did them in tank recognition last week.'

'Let's have some grenades under their tracks.'

'Right.' Jacques pulled a grenade from his belt, clutched the handle, pulled out the pin. He hurled it at the lead tank. It was a good throw. The grenade caught under one of the tank's wheels and exploded immediately. The tank swerved away to the left.

The cannon on the other tank immediately opened fire. The first shell whistled over the roof. The second, following swiftly after, hit the building fair and square. The whole place crumbled like an old cake. Masonry and men alike went tumbling down.

For a short while the air was full of blood and dust.

'Wolfgang Frankel speaking from the front in Tebarou,' said Wolfgang from the improvised studio in the Royal Laotian Hotel in Ou Neua. He had donned camouflage uniform for the occasion. 'The war is on! First blood has gone to our side in this unequal combat where the scales are so loaded against us. Units of the Rapid Reaction Force have successfully stormed the main square of the capital, Tebihai, and now occupy Fisherman's Steps, which are the neck to the body of Tebarou.

'Support was given by squadrons of fighter-bombers, which inflicted serious damage on the city. One EU life was lost. Many Tebarese were killed and several enemy tanks destroyed.

'More reports later.'

<INSANATICS: Perverted society. An infant, like a primitive being, is ill-equipped to distinguish between its own self and

its environment. It tends to incorporate 'good' (comfortable) things as part of itself, while ungratifying things, pain or isolation for instance, belong to the exterior hostile world.

Early years are spent in a struggle with the relationship with the child's parents or parent, or with the absence of parenting. The child is scarcely aware of the external world. This birth of the ontological being is nevertheless involved with a kind of recapitulation of phylogeny, for which the physical evidence will include the cutting of milk teeth, their loss, the growth of a second rank of teeth more suited to carnivorous habits, and later the development of gonads, pubic hair, etc.

These complex workings taking place below awareness level have their influence on the individual's cast of thought, on Schopenhauer's melancholia, or on Gandhi's determined optimism. On all but the most individual personalities, however, these powerful foreshadowings will have their effect in a perverted view of reality; while collectively they affect the whole concept and construction of society and what we call civilisation.

We invent the term civilisation in order to differentiate ourselves from those without our borders, the so-called uncivilised. Those are the people with whom we can wage war because they threaten us: or, in our madness, are assumed to threaten us.>

Rebecca Stromeyer left her publishing house early and caught a slo-bo to the cathedral square. There Köln cathedral stood, its sloping roofs touched with white in the first frosts of late autumn.

Rebecca was well protected against the sudden cold. Wrapped in a black fake fur, and with her long black skirt tight against her black-booted legs, she, with her raven-black hair and dark eyes, made a perfect picture of beauty in the Victorian style now again fashionable after a matter of two centuries. She was possibly aware that she would prove irresistible to the man who awaited her in the cathedral.

Approaching the ancient structure, which had survived the bombing of the city a century previously, she encountered two American tourists who had just emerged from the environs of the railway station, close to the cathedral. They were males, both very tall and square, flamboyantly dressed. Probably it was the beauty of Rebecca which moved them to speak to her.

'You're a lovely lady. Are you American, by any chance?'

'No. I am a European. A Jewish European.'

'Is that the case? You're not available for dinner this evening, are you?'

'Unfortunately not. Excuse me.'

'Say, can you tell a couple of bewildered Yanks something? You have a beautiful cathedral, but how come you built it so near the rail station?'

'The cathedral was here first, just by a whisker.'

The two men stood and watched regretfully as Rebecca crossed beneath the tall façade and entered the portals of the great building. She imagined them saying, 'She's Jewish and she's entering a Christian cathedral – how come?'

Inside the noble space there was much coming and going. Tourists mixed with local people; some had backpacks, some had children; some had both, and arms full of teddy bears to boot. Some wandered about rather dazedly, gaping at the saints in their solemn stone niches or the rafters high above their heads. Some bought postcards or candles, some prayed.

It was the kind of scene, Rebecca reflected, which had prevailed for many centuries, long before railways were built.

Distantly, at the altar, a service was being conducted. She moved slowly towards it, scanning the pews as she went, hoping to light on the man she had come to meet.

He was now advancing towards her. She was startled to recognise him, hidden as he was behind dark glasses so as to avoid recognition. He came up to her and clutched her hand.

'Becky!'

'Olduvai!'

'Thank you so much for coming.'

'I was afraid you would not be here.'

'There's a good sermon being preached. Come and hear a little of it. The preacher is a friend of your father's, I believe – the so-called Black Archbishop, Jones-Simms. I've become quite keen on sermons recently.'

He did not add that with the suicide of his sister he had left Roberta Bargane and gone away to live in purgative solitude on the Baltic coast. While he was there news came of the suicide of his father.

Both Olduvai and Rebecca were troubled in their spiritual life. The typescript of Olduvai's short book, *Who Do We Call Father?*, had come into Rebecca's editorial hands. It had struck a chord in her heart; their ensuing correspondence had resulted in their meeting.

As they walked down one of the side aisles, he ventured to take her hand, feeling its slenderness, its tenderness.

They seated themselves in an empty pew, very aware of their nearness to each other, he so broad, she so slim.

The Archbishop was not in the pulpit but standing by the altar, down from the steps, speaking simply to a small congregation. He was talking about the war and the inequalities in the world. 'Twenty per cent of the population are consuming eighty-five per cent of the globe's natural resources. It represents a greed bordering on madness – our greed. Our lifetimes are highly energy-consuming and wasteful. And nothing consumes more and wastes more than warfare. Future generations will certainly condemn our attack on the small nation of Tebarou – if not on moral grounds, then on conservationist grounds. We are plundering our planet to the point of no return. Already we see the elements taking their revenge.'

Olduvai said quietly to Rebecca, 'Oh, sorry, as civilised beings we know all this, don't we?'

'We need to hear it over and over. And when even the church speaks of it . . .'

'Everyone speaks of it, yet does nothing.'

'My father does something. And now his funding is in question.'

'Believe me, I honour him for his work. You have spoken of your father in your letters. Now I wish I had loved – been able to love – my father as you do yours. I believe you are in love with him?'

'That's not the case. I love him – love him intensely. I'm not *in* love with him. That's different. I think I am in love with you.'

Olduvai seized Rebecca in his arms and kissed her lips.

A man in the pew behind them leant over and tapped Olduvai on his shoulder. 'We don't want that kind of thing in here, please. This is God's house.'

'God would envy me,' said Olduvai.

They moved out of the cathedral. They went into the railway station, where kissing was allowed.

209

He said, 'I hated my father. I told you that. Yet there is much truth in what he had to say. He was just lousy at personal relationships. I have made a lot of money, far more than I need. Ever since my sister Josie committed suicide, I have wondered what kind of person I want to be, and what to do with the money.'

'Money from your song?'

'In part, yes. "Once a Fabulous Holiday" . . . Funny how I have such contempt for that song now. It's so frivolous, yet it has made me a millionaire – a millionaire in univs, not marks. Maybe I should found an institute. It would have to examine radically what it is in our make-up that gives us such pain. And that gave my father so much pain.'

She did not pursue that line of talk, since she did not entirely understand what he meant. Instead, she said merely, 'Your book will make you even more money. It will sell well in foreign translations, too, I'm sure of it.'

'I want to do something worthwhile at last, Becky.'

'I will help all I can. You feel you want to do it to justify yourself in your father's eyes?'

'No, in my own eyes.' He thought, before saying with a sad smile, 'Yes, I guess also in my father's eyes. His dead eyes. Even though I hated the old bastard.'

She contemplated his face even as he scrutinised hers. 'Don't you think your hatred of God has much to do with your hatred of your father?'

'Oh, there's no doubt in my mind that fathers and kings invented the idea of God to reinforce their own power. Why else is God always male and not female? Becky, darling, to me you are a goddess. I long for you, I crave you . . . You are entirely all my happiness.'

210

When she dropped her gaze he studied the perfection of her eyelids. She answered in a low voice.

'How can you say that? We don't really know ourselves yet, never mind each other. I find myself to be terribly duplicitous. At home, I am so sweet and meek and mild it would make you sick. Yet inwardly I rage for something. I'm ferocious, remorseless – but for what, I can't tell. I'm unfulfilled, and I don't just mean sexually. I want to *do* something. I want to change the world, when what I most need is probably to change myself.'

'We'll work together – if you will let me. Do you think I would want a woman who was not, like me, in a rage about everything?'

Because it was a railway station, many people were saying goodbye to others, perhaps for an hour, perhaps for ever. In the foyer, couples were standing against walls, kissing: youths, old people, men with women, women with men.

Rebecca and Olduvai stood there too, both wondering at the miracle that had been bestowed on them. A kind of perfume surrounded them, enfolding them, keeping them safely separate from all other mortals. They opened to each other, mouth against mouth, exchanging saliva, tasting one another. Their clothes formed no impediment to their imaginations. It seemed to them that they also exchanged thought, thus becoming one whole delighted and delightful person.

Finally, they were gasping for breath, the warm carbon dioxide sweet on each other's cheeks. They went on to talk. They entered the cafeteria and ate croissants and drank cappuccinos, each rapt in the other's personality. Their gaze was on and through the other's eyes.

211

As they emerged into the wide cathedral square, a parade was passing through it. Banners waved, a little tinpot band played. Most of the people were dressed as strange beings, with felt tentacles sprouting from their heads, or with plastic wings, or golden fins. Their banners said things like WELCOME TO OUR FELLOW LIFE FORMS! and LONG LIVE EUROBEINGS!

The couple linked arms and stood to watch.

Some of those who were of the procession ran hither and thither with collection boxes. Bystanders threw money in, and applauded. Everyone looked cheerful. Small boys trotted along beside the procession.

Rebecca gestured towards them, half laughing. 'Some people at least believe in the unity of life!'

'And in the uses of money,' said Olduvai, throwing a five-univ piece into a passing box.

'Hi! This is Alexy. Fatigue and malnourishment have struck. Could be we are sick from all the radiation we are bathed in. That and starvation . . . We're all three pretty goddam ill. We need to hear from you. This report will be brief. Eucarya is in the category of extramophilic animals. After seven trawls, executed with difficulty, we brought up two more Eucarya in one net. So we do not believe these creatures are particularly plentiful. These two new specimens are slightly smaller than the first specimen, and weigh twenty-eight and thirty grams. They are rather more grey than their predecessor, but otherwise identical.

'We eagerly anticipate your response. In our opinion, this discovery justifies the whole history of space travel, from Sputnik onwards. Out.'

212

Two mugs of coffee on a tray. A milk jug. No sugar.

Marthe looked at them with pleasure. She believed in small things. It was true she believed in the church, but she derived more pleasure from the kitchen.

Pushing open the door of the Lesscock living-room, she discovered her husband, the Reverend Angus Lesscock, on his knees on the shabby carpet, praying.

She set down the tray on the table, over the various religious pamphlets. Concluding his prayer, Lessing struggled to his feet.

'Oh, thank you, dear. I was uttering a prayer for the poor creatures far out in space.'

'Oh? The men on the *Roddenberry*? That should help them, I'm sure.'

'No, my dear. You always manage to misunderstand me. I refer to the aquatic creatures which live on the moons of Jupiter. They have need of our compassion.'

'Is that so, Angus? I believe they were perfectly happy until our brave explorers arrived.'

He sighed with impatience. 'Who are you to say whether or not they were happy?'

As she turned to leave the room, Marthe muttered, 'Not only them . . . Same with us.'

The great ebony SS20 fighter-bombers were a-wing, flying far beyond the frontiers of the super-state to bring destruction to the world of el Fashid. In the Bargane vineyard, the old woman and her android worked together. In the parliaments of Brussels and Strasbourg, serious and dedicated men and women debated the rights and wrongs of war, and planned for a better world after it. On the altered coastlines bordering the Atlantic Ocean, cartographers mapped their diminished lands; town planners planned new harbours; economists calculated the ruinous expense. In his bedchamber, kneeling by his great bed, Archbishop Jones-Simms prayed and wept for the sins of humanity. Far away from troubled Earth, three astronauts on the moon Europa struggled with their destiny and the ferocious unknown.

On Earth, Rose Baywater completed another novel, *Sunshine on the Somme*, whereupon she and Jack Harrington celebrated with a champagne supper among friends at the most expensive restaurant on Mount Everest. Paulus Stromeyer flew to Utrecht to see his old friend Barnard Cleeping, hoping to secure financial support for his research from the university there. Ruth Stromeyer phoned up a nursing service to enlist help for Moshe, her ageing father-in-law. At the Toulouse Air Base, Captain Masters was promoted to major. After consulting her guru, Amy Haze decided to take up zero body posturing and write poetry. Martitia Deneke embraced another lost cause, a Palestinian refugee called Joe Madani, who had entered the super-state illegally. Joe Stromeyer sold his apartment in Naples and went to live a solitary life in a hut in the Abruzzi. Fergus O'Brien's son Pat brought home a beautiful adolescent girl, Vivienne, with whom Fergus fell in love and contracted as a partner. Paddy Cole and Fay went into Norwich to buy new clothes for the opening of Paddy's exhibition in the Harrington Galleries in London. Lisa Fort, who always spent mornings in bed after her night job, took to bed with her the producer of the *Wee Small Hours Show*, Christine Macabees. Nurse Gibbs retired with two Pekinese dogs to an island which had once been Exmoor. In Hartisham, in the little church of St Swithin, with its facing of knapped flint, Bertie Haze and Bettina Squire were quietly married, before the funeral to be held two days later.

The funeral of Sir Thomas Squire was held on the last day of November. Jane Squire and Remy Gautiner arranged everything with the funeral directors. A small reception was to be held afterwards in Pippet Hall.

Although Jane had requested no flowers, asking instead that financial donations should be made to the Squire Foundation of Popular Arts, of which she was president, flowers continued to arrive. St Swithin's was choked with wreaths and bouquets, the damp sea air saturated with their fragrance.

The church had to be heated against the cold. It was a raw wet day; nevertheless, many locals from villages round about had come to pay their final respects. An ambient camera recorded proceedings unobtrusively from a corner of the apse. The congregation sat huddled in their raincoats as the Reverend Rowlinson addressed them. Matilda Rowlinson was old and frail; she had been brought out of retirement to officiate as an old friend of Thomas Squire. She spoke now with some feeling.

'Tom Squire represented all that was liberal in the England that has passed away with him. He was a representative of that inquiring European mind which has given the West such pre-eminence in the world. He travelled far and wide, yet always returned here, to this little patch of Norfolk, which was his home. In his youth, he was a handsome and charismatic man, attractive to many women . . .' Her voice here had a catch in it. She went on, hurriedly, 'Now death has visited our old friend, Tom Squire. We shall all follow

215

him to where he has gone. We find consolation in that, in sure and certain belief that he is now in glory before the throne of Our Lord.'

Jane also made a brief speech. 'Father is now with Teresa, our mother. Theirs was not entirely an easy marriage, but then, marriages are always a mystery to others. Indeed, our own marriages, too, are often a mystery to us. Marriage is out of fashion nowadays, although just two days ago, I'm happy to say, my dear daughter Bettina here became married to Bertie Haze before this very altar.

'Tom and Teresa had many happy years together. My father was a creative man. One of his accomplishments was to hold on to our beloved Pippet Hall, in bad times and good. Now it's the elements that threaten us – elements that have been roused by mankind's inability to discipline its needs. This little church we have known all our lives is itself also threatened. The sea will soon inevitably claim both buildings. With them will go a part of our island history, and a valuable part at that. It is with sorrow I say this. As it is with great sorrow that I, on behalf of my sister Ann, and my son, at present fighting in Tebarou, and everyone who knew and loved my father, say a long farewell to him now.'

They sang a hymn. They received a blessing from the Reverend Rowlinson.

They went outside, into the rain, to stand by the graveside. Sir Tom's coffin was lowered into the ground. Ann gave a small shriek and clapped a hand to her nose. Looking down at her palm, she saw an insect with a long proboscis, oozing blood, her own blood. Apologising afterwards to the Reverend Rowlinson for her outcry, she explained that this was a tropical insect, an anopheles mosquito, a new visitor to England, brought on the winds of global warming.

Close to the open mouth of the grave into which the body of Sir Thomas Squire had been lowered lay that of his wife, Lady Teresa Squire, Worthy of This Parish.

Jane stood at her father's graveside with Remy, gripping his hand. Ann was nearby, having flown in from Antibes. With Ann was her current flame, the film director Casim Durando of Gabbo Films. Laura Nye was not present, having pleaded age and illness. Bertie and Bettina were present, having postponed their honeymoon for the occasion.

In the background stood Victor de Bourcey, hat in hand. He had recovered sufficiently from the loss of his bride Esme, whose body had never been found, to nourish a passionate regard for Ann Squire, whom he had seen on screen in her film role in *Lovesick in Lent*.

Victor had come to the solemn ceremony more for Ann's sake than for Squire's, whom he had never known. He had found to his regret that Ann was totally preoccupied with Casim Durando, whom Victor regarded as a reptile.

Both Jane and Ann threw posies of flowers down on the coffin before the first spadefuls of damp earth were shovelled in.

Remy kissed Jane's cheek. 'We hope there is life elsewhere.'

'Yes, maybe, but do you imagine there's a better place than this, for all its shortcomings?'

He did not reply. Taking her arm, he said, 'Let's go and dry off and get a drink.'

The funeral party assembled in the hall. Drinks and canapés were handed round. A fair-haired young man came up to Ann and said he was from the *Norfolk Times*. He asked Ann who Sir Thomas Squire was and what he had done.

'Oh, go and look at your cuttings, you ignorant little man! Look in *Who's Who*. You call yourself a reporter and you don't know who Tom Squire was?'

'I'm new at the job, love. I only need a paragraph.' He looked downcast, and snatched at a passing tuna canapé as if it were a lifebelt.

The local people made their way on foot back to their village homes. The long black cars of the famous drew away from Pippet Hall. Mercifully, the rain ceased. The President's son left the cemetery on foot, feeling his heart to be broken.

I never belonged . . . Not here, not anywhere. And this smell of wet asphalt, as haunting as an old love affair. It's always going to be winter now.

The androids in the President's palace were locked up for the night.

'What was the meaning of this gathering we saw on the ambient?'

'It is part of what humans call the Human Condition.'

'The theory is that they were just enjoying themselves.'

'They all wore black clip-ons.'

'Some of them had drops of water coming from their eyes. It is a mark of sorrow. How do they achieve that?'

'You can rely on humans to enjoy sorrow. It has an effect similar to alcohol.'

'Did they have a man in that long box?'

'That is the theory.'

'Did the man fail to work any more?'

'He was obsolete. People last only about a century.'

'Many people came to see him go down. Did they like the obsolete man?'

218

'They revered him.'
'Then why did they bury him in the ground?'
'They have a theory he will get better there.'

'Alexy Stromeyer calling. We have had no sleep for twenty-five hours, so great has been the excitement here. Our drill jammed again. We managed to net a few more Eucarya. They are not very prolific. Tomorrow we are going to rendezvous with the *Spock* and recover ourselves for the journey homewards. Don't know how you will take this, Earth, but we have cooked and eaten this alien life form. We were starving. They were delicious. Something of a mushroomy taste.

'Meanwhile, we are closing down for some hours. Jupiter is high in our sky. Goodnight from a triumphant Europa expedition.'

'Bored by Beetles? Pole-axed by Potts? Take a course of our new Klassfits! Move on to Mussorgsky, bond with Bach, hide away with Haydn.

'Klassfits come in liquid form, taken aurally not orally. Give those eardrums of yours a make-over – quit rock-'n'-roll and other vulgar musics for good.

'You will find yourself listening to – and even enjoying – such masterpieces of music as Mozart's oh-so-topical "Jupiter" Symphony. Klassfits – fits you for the classics!'

<INSANATICS: Imposible alleviations. We have been unable to suggest any infallible remedy for the crisis in human life. In the words of Carl Jung, 'I learnt to see that the greatest and most important problems of life are all fundamentally insoluble.'

We state reluctantly that the human sickness has always

been with us; only with the uncheckable growth of populations has it become overwhelmingly obtrusive. We suffer
from an evolutionary defect. The Cro-Magnon, who walked
erect and invented the spear, tasted power over their enemies
and their environment. This poisoned pleasure has proved
irresistible.

As a result, the 'normal' human mind seeks to maintain
physical health, without which the individual has no power.
It can afford to pay little attention to observing actual reality.
Indeed, it is ill-equipped to observe reality (truth, logic and
unity with nature); this would impede the struggle to maintain bodily health and freedom from anxiety. The motto is,
'I may be stupid but I am bigger than you and can kill you
if necessary.' It is this attitude that has soured the relationship between adults and children, and men and women,
throughout the ages.>

The war with Tebarou continued. Tebihai was reduced to
ruin. Now EU soldiers of the Rapid Reaction Force camped
among the ruins, forever on the alert for snipers.

It was never cold in Tebarou, but it rained. The reinforcements lived in temporary barracks. They went out on daily
patrols, during which they got wet or shot. The skirmishing
dragged on. The soldiers knew they were never going to
win. There were always more Tebarese. It remained true
that in the end it was people who won wars, not the great
machines roaring overhead.

In the neighbouring country of Laos, General Gary
Fairstepps was living out the war in some comfort in the
Ou Neua hotel. With him was the newly promoted Colonel
Randolph Haven. Haven and Fairstepps were uneasy
together; both knew that the other had associated with Amy

Haze, and did not care to admit it. Nevertheless, war had thrown them together and, like sensible men, they were making the best of things. Randolph was drinking seriously of the local hooch, *orlando*.

Of the two men, Fairstepps was making the better of the best of things. He had on his knee a dusky maiden from the neighbourhood, who was showing evidence of something known euphemistically as affection: to which the general appeared inclined to respond. Indeed, he was wondering how to get rid of Haven without appearing rude. He wanted to show the girl deeper affection.

Randolph had wandered over to the window, *orlando* glass in hand, and was saying, 'Wonderful country, isn't it? Never mind the rain. You'd never think there was a war on, would you, Gary? It's amazingly peaceful. It has occurred to me—'

At that moment, a shot rang out. The window shattered. The *orlando* went flying. Randolph fell dead of a sniper's bullet.

'Gracious, it really *did* occur to him!' said Fairstepps, standing up suddenly and dropping the dusky beauty to the floor. 'Bloody fool! Came from the working class, too . . .'

He turned his attention to the lovely kneeling at his feet. 'No, don't get up, dear. Stay right there!'

He unzipped his fly. After all, he thought, it was Christmas.

But in the super-state the war hardly mattered. Taken all in all, everything was well there. A few problems, maybe, but they would be resolved in time. People were living longer, fornicating longer. Besides, it was the Christmas season again, when pagan rejoiced with Christian.

All the windows of all the shops in all the cities of the nations united under the multi-star banner were a-glitter

with decayed versions of the Christian myth. Tinsel abounded.
An abundance of snow of a richness achieved only by virtual
reality fell upon the piles of well-wrapped parcels in the
windows. Android Santas poured toys from sacks that never
ever emptied. Android reindeer pranced across fictitious
wastes, many of them red of nose. It was a voluptuous time,
a nose-pressed-against-glass time, a time to spend and
spend, a time to raid Schlachter, boucher, marcellaio, slager,
slakteri, talho, sklep miesny, kasap and butcher for fowl of
all kinds, for pig and boar and by-products of same, not
forgetting to call in at the pharmacy for aspirin, indigestion
tablets and diarrhoea powders on the way to the wine
store. Shops were piled high with goods, around which carol
muzak swirled and tinkled: it was in the bleak midwinter
with a temperature approaching thirty degrees. Happy
shoppers with their golden credit cards mortgaged their
futures over checkouts fringed with plastic holly.

God, who so closely resembled Santa Claus, was in his
heaven: all was well with the European world. Except for
those who slept in doorways: and Paulus Stromeyer, at least,
was planning to look after them with his boims and his
serds.

In the great and holy baroque church of Melk, overlooking
the River Danube, Archbishop Schlafmeister administered
glüwein to his congregation before delivering his sermon.

His powerful voice rebounded from the cream-and-gilt
baroque shadows.

'So, once more, we are come to Christmas Thanksgiving
Trick or Treat Day, and we rejoice for it. A sinner in my
parish approached me the other day to enquire if I had any
regrets about the fusion of various ceremonies. When I had

blessed him, I assured him that we have to face the facts of mortal life. We have to be real.

'The old Christmas used to be a time of snow and holly. We don't have snow at this time of year any more, except in the windows of shops. By uniting Christmas with similar secular ceremonies, we thereby bring more worshippers into the church. Let us never forget that the old separate Trick or Treat ceremonies were religiously based. Basically, an innocent child was tapping hopefully at a door – at the Door of Life – saying to a grown-up, "If you don't love me and treat me well, then you will suffer as I will." It is a profound statement which we should always hold in our hearts, particularly at this season.

'So I rejoice that this ancient ceremony is combined with the even more ancient ceremony of Christmas Thanksgiving. It makes sense in our busy modern world. It is truly a day off to celebrate the day when the infant Christ came knocking at all our doors.

'"Yes", you may possibly respond, "but he didn't say 'Trick or Treat', did he?"

'He may well have said to us, "Think and Treat" – a worthy message we are all well advised to heed, particularly at this season. And now to God the Father . . .'

But there were heathens also who celebrated the happy occasion. Good fortune seemed to have smiled on Jane Squire, Remy Gautiner and Ann Squire, the ladies recovering from mourning their father's death, on Bettina and Bertie Haze, on Bertie's mother, Amygdella Haze, on Rebecca Stromeyer and Olduvai Potts, hand in hand, on Lena Potts, Oldy's reconciled mother, riding in a motorised chair since her stroke, and on Jack Harrington, who was looking as dapper as ever. All had been invited to stay for a few days at Casim Durando's palatial mansion in rue Matignon in Paris.

Casim, of smooth and reptilian look, was generally considered to *be* something of a reptile; but his relationship with Francine, Ann's daughter, seemed to be holding – so much so that Francine was starring in his movie for Gabbo Films, *Fragments of a Dream*, adapted from a novel by Rose Baywater, and now into post-production. Casim also proved generous with his style of entertainment, and with his excellent cellar.

So all were happy as they took the air in the early afternoon. They walked in a group, exchanging remarks one with another as they went. They had strolled through the Tuileries and were about to cross to the *rive gauche*. There, Jack Harrington was to open his latest art gallery, which would display an artist's storyboard sketches for *Fragments of a Dream*.

'The Seine looks so angry,' Jane remarked to Bertie. 'It's not as I remember it.'

'The rise in sea levels, you know. A man reported seeing a shark along by the next bridge only the other day. But he could have been drunk . . .'

They said no more, noting the way in which walls had been built against further rises in water levels. Birds were singing, daffodils were in bloom, leaves were still on trees – all unseasonal signs.

And what, Amy asked, did they all think of the crew of the *Roddenberry* having cooked and eaten the alien life on Europa? Opinions were divided; Olduvai condemned the greed of the crew while the others agreed it was not for them to criticise. Lives on Earth were so easy by comparison. Whereas, for the heroes on Europa, there would be no goose or turkey at this festive season. It was also agreed, amid giggles, that festive seasons were in short supply on that Jovian satellite.

Casim suddenly exclaimed that he had left his beret in the last bar they had visited. The party should go on to the gallery, he suggested; he would run quickly back and reclaim his property.

They did as he proposed. As they were crossing the pedestrian bridge by the Louvre, they saw a great agitation in the water racing below them. They stopped to hang over the rail to try to work out what was happening. Olduvai could not help recalling that his father had drowned himself in another renowned river.

The water became more and more disturbed. Of a sudden, a great dragon head rose dripping from the flood. It was of a greyish-green hue, horned, with two red eyes glaring from under bony brows. Catching sight of the humans on the bridge, it snarled furiously, opening a terrifying chasm of a mouth to do so – a mouth fully armed with fangs. Much of the rest of its body then heaved itself from the water to reveal bright green spines running down its back. The back was scaly. So was the great clawed foot it raised to hook on to the railings of the bridge.

The women of the party screamed in terror. All fled to the left-hand bank. The dragon swung its head towards them and began to climb ashore. Rebecca, who was pregnant, fainted into Olduvai's arms.

The dragon stood dripping on the bank. Jack had the presence of mind to photograph it. The creature now did not stir, beyond a slow wag of its tail. Its mouth hung open. From that mouth issued the words, 'A Gabbo Films production'.

Angry and frightened, the tourist group simply stood and stared at the lifelike horror.

A deep voice behind them said, 'Thank you, everybody, and sorry to scare you, but we like our little joke. We hope you enjoyed it too.'

'No, we bloody well didn't,' said Olduvai, still clutching his beloved Rebecca. She was now conscious again.

They turned as the massive randroid, Obbagi, strode facelessly to the green monster then turned to confront them. Behind the metallic figure came Gabbo, wrapped in a red cloak, smiling, bowing to left, to right, as he walked.

'"Good evening, or should I say good morning?"!' Gabbo quoted, rubbing his hands together.

'You were on digital, one and all,' announced Obbagi. 'Your reactions have been filmed and you will all be paid ten thousand univs for signing release forms.' He produced the forms from a cavity in his left side.

'The clownishness of human life,' said Gabbo, for once uncharacteristically willing to speak. 'Ah, me . . . Where would we be without our little jokes, indeed . . .'

'You are disgusting,' said Jack Harrington.

'Of course I am disgusting. I am the sniggering face of capitalism. What was it some fellow long dead once remarked? That human life is a tragedy to those who feel, a comedy to those who think.'

'We provide the comedy,' said the gigantic automaton, looking anything but a figure of fun. 'This was our Christmas comedy. It will form a momentary part of the movie *Something in Seine.*'

Gabbo patted the scales of his green monster. 'Yes, yes, you can all go and have a drink now. Joke's over. Last month or so – when was it, Obbagi?—'

'I do not know of the passage of time, as I keep telling you.'

'—We persuaded some ancient professor of archaeology stuck in Budapest that the galaxy was swarming with intelligent life and that they used Earth as a prison planet. It almost killed him.'

The fat man burst into laughter. Roughly similar rumblings came from Obbagi.

'You bloody well *did* kill him with your stupid lies!' shouted Olduvai. He rushed forward. 'That was my father!'

His charge caught Gabbo amidships. Gabbo gave a bellow as the breath left him, staggered backwards and then was falling – falling. He hit the muddy waters of the Seine with a splash.

His arms went up. The rest of him went down. The current swept him away.

Rebecca rushed to the towering figure of the randroid. 'Go after him!' she called. The creature turned about and without hesitation jumped into the river. The group stood there, overwhelmed by what had happened, watching as the immense figure was carried away on the flood.

'Hi, Earth. Alexy Stromeyer here. We are now aboard the return ship, *Spock*. Everything is functional and looking good. We have had a wonderful dinner, caught in Europa's ocean. So we celebrate Christmas, far from home. We send best wishes to everyone on Earth! Happy Christmas, Trick or Treat! Out.'

<INSANATICS: Living organisms survive by egotism. The liver fluke believes itself lord of creation.>

227

C000141118

Discipleship
EXPLORED

Following Christ. What's it all about?

Discipleship Explored Leader's Guide (2nd Edition)
Copyright © 2012 Christianity Explored
First published in 2005.

www.ceministries.org

Published by
The Good Book Company Ltd
Tel: 0333-123-0880; International: +44 (0) 208 942 0880
Email: admin@thegoodbook.co.uk

Websites:
UK: www.thegoodbook.co.uk
N America: www.thegoodbook.com
Australia: www.thegoodbook.com.au
New Zealand: www.thegoodbook.co.nz

CHRISTIANITY
E☨PLORED
MINISTRIES

thegoodbook
COMPANY

ISBN: 9781908317445

Design by Steve Devane and André Parker

Printed in China

Introduction

Discipleship Explored gives you time and space to think about what it really means to live the Christian life.

This eight-week course explores Paul's letter to the Philippians and its call to live wholeheartedly for Christ. It is intended for those beginning the Christian life and those who would like a "refresher". In particular, it's ideal for new Christians who have just completed *Christianity Explored* or another evangelistic course.

Paul wrote his letter to a group of new Christians living in Philippi. He wanted to remind them of the good news they believed in, help them to keep going in difficult circumstances, and encourage them to let the gospel shine through every part of their lives. This makes Philippians an ideal book for any Christian, but perhaps especially for those who are just beginning the Christian life.

This second edition has been updated to tie in more closely with the *Discipleship Explored* DVD, as well as adding new material in the group member's Handbook. This includes summaries of previous sessions, talk outlines, a dictionary of Bible words and phrases, and background material on the book of Philippians.

With a creative mixture of Bible studies, talks, DVDs, group discussions and home Bible-reading, group members will discover what it means to follow Christ today, and be encouraged to start walking confidently in his footsteps.

If you are running a *Discipleship Explored* course, please register it on our website **www.ceministries.org**, so that we and others can pray for you, or even send other people along.

May God richly bless you in all you do with this course for the honour and glory of Christ.

the Christianity Explored Ministries Team, February 2012

Section 1: How to run the course

Section 2: Study guide

49

Appendices

115

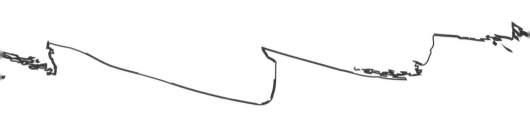

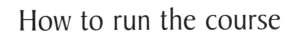

How to run the course

Two *Christianity Explored* websites to help you:

www.christianityexplored.org
This website is for non-Christians, whether or not they are on a course. It features a visual gospel outline based on the Gospel of Mark, answers to common questions, and testimonies from a wide variety of people, as well as information about the *Christianity Explored* course. You can find more details at the back of this book, on page 175.

www.ceministries.org
For leaders looking for information, downloads and resources.

Getting started

Helping people understand what it means to follow Jesus Christ is a stunning privilege and a huge responsibility. It's a stunning privilege because Almighty God is pleased to call us his "fellow workers" (1 Corinthians 3:9) as he seeks and saves the lost. And it's a huge responsibility because we are nurturing and caring for those who are young in the faith. The Lord Jesus gives stern warnings to anyone who leads astray his "little ones" (Mark 9:42). Our work to make disciples must always be careful, prayerful and faithful.

Discipleship Explored has been developed to let the Bible take centre stage as we consider what's involved in living as a disciple of Jesus. It takes your group members on an eight-session journey through Paul's letter to the Philippians to discover what it means to follow Jesus Christ.

To help your journey run smoothly, you will need to consider the following before the course begins.

STRUCTURE OF THE COURSE

How and when you meet will depend on your situation. Many courses run on a midweek evening for eight weeks. But your circumstances may be different. Eg:

- a daytime women's group
- a fortnightly homegroup
- a church houseparty
- a Sunday group running at the same time as the regular church service
- a college Christian Union or fellowship
- a few people meeting round a kitchen table

The course material can be adapted to suit your situation, including meeting one-to-one with a friend or neighbour. However, you will find it helpful to meet as regularly as possible – and please don't skip any sessions or change the order.

The chart on the next page shows how the course is structured, and how the themes fit together.

Session	Explore (Bible study)	Listen (Talk/DVD)	Discuss	Follow up (at home)
Session 1 Confident in Christ *Philippians 1:1-11*	Welcome	Confident in Christ	Discuss talk/DVD	Assurance (1 John 1:5 – 2:1; John 6:35-40; Ephesians 2:8-10)
Session 2 Living in Christ *Philippians 1:12-26*	Philippians 1:9-11	Living in Christ	Discuss talk/DVD	The Holy Spirit (John 14:15-31; 16:5-15; Acts 2:1-13)
Session 3 Standing Together in Christ *Philippians 1:27 – 2:11*	Philippians 1:21-26	Standing Together in Christ	Discuss talk/DVD	The cross (Isaiah 53:1-12; Luke 15:1-32; Colossians 1:15-23)
Session 4 Transformed by Christ *Philippians 2:12-30*	Philippians 2:5-11	Transformed by Christ	Discuss talk/DVD	Salvation (Luke 14:25-33; Galatians 5:16-26; Romans 12:1-13)
Session 5 Righteous in Christ *Philippians 3:1-9*	Philippians 2:19-30	Righteous in Christ	Discuss talk/DVD	Righteousness (Ephesians 2:1-10; Romans 3:20-26; 5:1-11)
Session 6 Knowing Christ *Philippians 3:10 – 4:1*	Philippians 3:1-4	Knowing Christ	Discuss talk/DVD	Trusting God (Matthew 6:19-24, 25-34; 7:24-29)

Session	Explore (Bible study)	Listen (Talk/DVD)	Discuss	Follow up (at home)
Session 7 Rejoicing in Christ *Philippians 4:2-9*	Philippians 3:10-11	Rejoicing in Christ	Discuss talk/DVD	Prayer (Matthew 6:5-15; Colossians 1:3-14; 4:2-6)
Session 8 Content in Christ *Philippians 4:10-23*	Philippians 4:8-9	Content in Christ	Discuss talk/DVD	Contentment Hebrews 4:14-16; 1 Timothy 1:12-17; Ephesians 3:14-21

STRUCTURE OF A SESSION

Below is the suggested structure for an evening session. See "During the course" on page 35 for a fuller description of each component. Of course, depending on your circumstances, you might want to change the exact times, or offer coffee and cake instead of a meal. Equally, you might want to run the course during the day if that is a more suitable time for those you're trying to reach.

6:30 p.m.	Leaders' prayer meeting
7:00 p.m.	Guests arrive for the meal
7:45 p.m.	Explore (Bible study)
8:05 p.m.	Listen (Talk/DVD)
8:30 p.m.	Discuss
9:00 p.m.	End of the evening – "One-to-One"

Note: All times are approximate. You can make certain sessions shorter or longer depending on your circumstances.

You can run *Discipleship Explored* with Bible talks presented by the course leader or by using the course DVD, which is presented by Barry Cooper, a member of the *Christianity Explored* team.

If you decide to run the course with the talks, you will find talk outlines in the appendix on page 117. Delivering the talks yourself will lead to a more personal, more intimate experience for the group members. You can also download the talks as Word documents so that you can adapt them for your own situation. They are available from **www.ceministries.org/de**

If you decide to run the course with the DVD, please note that because it features on-screen Bible text, it is inadvisable to use the DVD with large groups unless you have access to a projection screen and projector.

WHERE SHOULD YOU MEET?

Many groups meet in their church premises. However you may like to experiment with some different locations. Avoid using a classroom, or somewhere that looks like one, so that people don't feel they are back in school. A small group could be held in someone's home, or a small meeting room. Or you may be able to hire a space in a local coffee shop. A larger group could meet in a community hall, sports centre or local adult education centre. It's important to choose a place where you are unlikely to be interrupted and where you will be able to meet for every session at the same time.

The aim is to create a relational environment where people can listen to the Bible teaching while they enjoy the warmth of Christian friendship, so that they feel sufficiently relaxed to ask their questions and discuss any doubts and feelings.

If your group did *Christianity Explored*, it's ideal if they can meet in the same venue.

SETTING UP YOUR VENUE

It is important that guests feel relaxed and welcome, and the way you set up your venue will help you achieve that. The physical environment where you run *Discipleship Explored* can have a big impact on people's willingness to get involved in discussion, so be creative in the way you set up the room.

With a small group, arrange the room so that everyone can see each other. Be careful that the group leader isn't sitting with their back to a window, which can make it harder for people to see them clearly. Ask any helpers to sit among the group members rather than next to the group leader. If your small group needs to meet in a large room, try to use screens and furniture to make a smaller, more friendly space in one corner.

If you are using the course DVD, place the screen where everyone can see it easily, and where there will not be reflections (eg: from windows) obscuring the picture.

If there are a large number of leaders and guests, set up a number of tables around which different groups can sit. Because each group will be engaged in separate discussions, try to leave plenty of space between tables so that guests and leaders can hear each other easily.

▢ You will need a way of displaying visual aids (eg: PowerPoint, overhead projector or flipchart).

▢ You may like to set aside a table with a selection of books for guests and leaders to buy or borrow.

▢ If you are meeting in a large premises, make sure that facilities and exits are clearly marked.

Everyone involved in the course – leaders, guests and the course leader – will need a Bible. It is important that everyone uses the same version and edition so that page numbers will be the same. (The version used throughout the course material is the New International Version*****.)

▢ Guests may have their own Bible with them. But if not, or if their version is different to the one you are using, give them a Bible at the beginning of the course. If possible, give them a Bible they can use at home during the course, as they read the passages in the "Follow Up" material, and then keep when the course ends.

▢ They should also be given a copy of the Handbook.

▢ Pens should be made available to allow guests to make notes or jot down questions.

* Note: *Discipleship Explored* uses the 1984 edition of the New International Version (NIV). The 2011 revised edition includes a number of changes to the English text in Philippians. Where these changes involve significant words or phrases that are used within the course, there are notes in this Leader's Guide to help you adapt the material if you are using the 2011 NIV.

Choosing and training leaders

If you have overall responsibility for running the course, you will need to choose and train leaders who will be responsible for those who attend.

CHOOSING LEADERS

Leaders should be mature Christians who are able to teach, encourage discussion and care for guests.

In selecting a leader, ask yourself: "Is this person able to teach the Bible faithfully and clearly? Will he or she be able to deal with difficult questions from Philippians?" (There is a section on answering questions from Philippians in the appendix on page 159. This will help people as they prepare.)

Secondly, ask yourself: "Will this person be able to promote discussion without dominating it?" Since so much of the course revolves around discussion, guests need to feel free to be open and honest in their group.

Thirdly, ask yourself: "Is this the type of person who would make a guest feel welcome and cared for?" Rather than simply telling people what it means to follow Jesus, leaders must be willing to show this in their own lives by devoting time and attention to those in their care.

And of course, a leader's responsibility goes beyond eight sessions. Relationships begun during the course are likely to develop into friendships that must be nurtured once the course is over. For this reason, if possible, don't ask leaders to take on more than one course a year.

- A high ratio of leaders to group members is essential. For example, a well-balanced group may consist of two leaders and six guests, or three leaders and nine guests.

- If your course is likely to be large, make sure you have enough leaders; then divide them into teams of three.

- In order to deal with pastoral situations appropriately, it's advisable to assign a mixture of male and female leaders to each team.

TRAINING LEADERS

Training should take place before the course begins. Once a leader understands the reasoning behind *Discipleship Explored*, it becomes much easier for him or her to commit the time required. As well as preparing leaders for the course, training together cements relationships between those who will be leading.

You should therefore include training before every course you run, and all leaders should be asked to attend – even if they have been leaders many times before. Feel free to vary the exercises so the training remains fresh for veteran leaders.

The way you arrange the training will depend on your situation. You may choose to spend part of a weekend together, or two evenings, or meet early in the morning. There are some examples opposite of how you might schedule a training morning or couple of evenings.

There are six short training modules, which start on page 23. They are designed so that they can be used in a group, as pairs, or by individuals. The ideal is to meet together for the reasons given above. However, if that isn't possible for some of your team, they can prepare for the course by working through the material themselves. It then becomes even more important that the whole team meet together before each session of the course starts so that they can discuss and pray together before the guests arrive.

■ Ensure that every leader (including yourself) has a copy of this Leader's Guide, which contains the six training modules.

■ The modules should be read aloud by the person leading the training (often the course leader), allowing time for everyone to discuss and complete the exercises involved.

16

Example Saturday morning schedule

9:30 a.m.	Pray together	
9:45 a.m.	**Introducing Discipleship Explored**	15 minutes
10:00 a.m.	**Being a Discipleship Explored leader**	15 minutes
10:15 a.m.	**Before the course**	25 minutes
10:40 a.m.	Pray together	
10:45 a.m.	Coffee	
11:00 a.m.	**During the course**	60 minutes
12:00 p.m.	**Introducing Philippians**	15 minutes
12:15 p.m.	**After the course**	15 minutes
12:30 p.m.	Pray together	

Example training schedule over two evenings

Evening 1

7:30 p.m.	Pray together	
7:45 p.m.	**Introducing Discipleship Explored**	15 minutes
8:00 p.m.	**Being a Discipleship Explored leader**	15 minutes
8:15 p.m.	**Before the course**	25 minutes
8:40 p.m.	**Introducing Philippians**	15 minutes
8:55 p.m.	Pray together	

Evening 2

7:30 p.m.	Pray together	
7:45 p.m.	**During the course**	60 minutes
8:45 p.m.	**After the course**	15 minutes
9:00 p.m.	Pray together	

WELCOMING

One or more "welcomers" should be given the task of greeting people as they arrive. In a small group, these can be leaders who have been given a specific role of welcoming each arrival. In a larger group, choose welcomers who are not leaders; that way, leaders can concentrate on talking to guests who've already arrived. Leaders and welcomers should wear name tags so that they are immediately identifiable by guests.

If many or all of your guests have done *Christianity Explored*, then ask leaders from that course to lead their group members through *Discipleship Explored* too. If that is not possible, encourage one of the *Christianity Explored* leaders to meet their group on the first week of *Discipleship Explored* and introduce the group to their new leaders.

Some or all of your guests may not have done *Christianity Explored* or know each other. If so, when a guest arrives, welcomers should simply introduce themselves and find out the person's name. Asking for addresses or telephone numbers at this stage can make people feel uncomfortable. Take the guest to where the group will be meeting and introduce them to another leader. If your session is not including a meal, this would be a good time to offer people a drink (eg: tea, coffee, fruit juice) and a biscuit/cookie.

If you're expecting a large number of guests, it's a good idea to prepare a seating plan like the one opposite.

Then, as each group member arrives, a welcomer assigns him or her to a table and adds the person's name to the plan. This ensures that guests are divided equally between the tables.

Numbering the tables "restaurant-style" will help group members to find their allocated table easily.

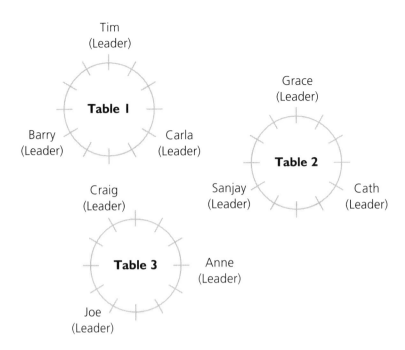

Tim
(Leader)

Table I

Barry
(Leader)

Carla
(Leader)

Grace
(Leader)

Table 2

Craig
(Leader)

Sanjay
(Leader)

Cath
(Leader)

Table 3

Anne
(Leader)

Joe
(Leader)

🔹 *List the people you will ask to be welcomers.*

CATERING

Sharing a meal together is a core component of *Discipleship Explored*. It's an opportunity to socialize informally and, for many guests, it may be the only time during the week when someone takes a genuine, personal interest in their lives. Depending on where and when you meet, a meal may not always be possible. But do include it if you can – the benefits in building relationships with group members are well worth the time and effort involved.

Organize a team of people who are willing and able to prepare and serve a meal – this will leave the leaders free to spend time with the group members. This can be an opportunity for church members to be involved with the course without needing to be leaders. If necessary, you can ask guests for a small contribution to help cover the cost.

Resist the temptation to make the food over elaborate. Keep it simple to eat and clear away. Although it's always good to make an effort, there is a danger that food can end up squeezing out time for exploring the gospel.

▶ *List the people you will ask to help with the catering.*

PRAYING

Enlisting people to pray regularly for the course is a wonderful way of involving more people in *Discipleship Explored*.

- Pray for the preparation of the talks – that they would be faithful to God's word, passionate, challenging and clear.

- Pray for the leaders – that they would be well prepared and that they would "watch [their] life and doctrine closely" (1 Timothy 4:16).

- Pray for the guests – that many would attend; that by his Spirit, God will help them to understand his word, and by his Spirit give them the desire to live wholeheartedly as followers of Jesus Christ.

Report back to your prayer team on a weekly basis so that they can pray for specific needs and be encouraged by answered prayer.

▶ *List the people you will ask to commit themselves to pray for the course.*

Inviting people to come

Advertise the course in your church bulletin and during the Sunday services. (One way to do this is by downloading the trailer from www.ceministries.org/de)

You might also want to produce invitations such as the one below. These can be available at the entrance to your church, and also for church members to use when inviting people to do the course.

Explain that *Discipleship Explored* involves refreshments or a meal, a Bible study, a talk, a short discussion and plenty of opportunities to ask questions. This structure will be familiar to anyone who has done *Christianity Explored*.

If you have been running the *Christianity Explored* course, then, at the end of the course, guests should be invited to join *Discipleship Explored*. The *Christianity Explored* leaders will know who from their group is ready to go on to *Discipleship Explored* and should be encouraging them to do so.

The beauty of studying Mark's Gospel in *Christianity Explored* is that participants should now be eager to explore another part of God's word. Not only that, but they will also be eager to maintain the friendships they have developed while on the course.

Discipleship Explored

Discipleship Explored is a course designed
to give you the time and space to think about
what it really means to live the Christian life.

Every Tuesday evening
Starting 5th October to 7th December
7p.m. to 9p.m.
Church, Street, City

If you'd like to come or want to find out more,
please contact ....

1 Introducing Discipleship Explored

Are you content in every situation? Are you sure of your salvation? Are you able to say with conviction: "To me, to live is Christ and to die is gain"?

Paul's letter to the Philippians is full of challenge and reassurance – particularly for those who, like the Philippians themselves, are just beginning the Christian life. *Discipleship Explored* is an eight-session exploration of what it means to be a whole-hearted disciple of Jesus Christ.

If you are familiar with *Christianity Explored*, you'll feel right at home.

Each session consists of a meal, a Bible study, a short talk or DVD, and a group discussion. In addition, the Follow Up studies give you and group members a Bible-reading plan for the week.

Session	Explore (Bible study)	Talk/DVD	Discuss	Follow Up (at home)
Session 1	Welcome	Confident in Christ Philippians 1:1-11	Discuss talk/DVD	Assurance
Session 2	Philippians 1:9-11	Living in Christ Philippians 1:12-26	Discuss talk/DVD	The Holy Spirit
Session 3	Philippians 1:21-26	Standing Together in Christ Philippians 1:27 – 2:11	Discuss talk/DVD	The cross
Session 4	Philippians 2:5-11	Transformed by Christ Philippians 2:12-30	Discuss talk/DVD	Salvation
Session 5	Philippians 2:19-30	Righteous in Christ Philippians 3:1-9	Discuss talk/DVD	Righteousness
Session 6	Philippians 3:1-4	Knowing Christ Philippians 3:10 – 4:1	Discuss talk/DVD	Trusting God
Session 7	Philippians 3:10-11	Rejoicing in Christ Philippians 4:2-9	Discuss talk/DVD	Prayer
Session 8	Philippians 4:8-9	Content in Christ Philippians 4:10-23	Discuss talk/DVD	Contentment

We are called to be disciples and make disciples. Jesus commanded Christians to "go and make disciples of all nations, baptizing them in the name of the Father and of the Son and of the Holy Spirit, and teaching them to obey everything I have commanded you" (Matthew 28:19-20).

People learn about what it means to be a disciple, not just from the things we teach, but from our behaviour as well. That's why Paul tells Timothy to "set an example for the believers in speech, in life, in love, in faith and in purity ... watch your life and doctrine closely" (1 Timothy 4:12, 16).

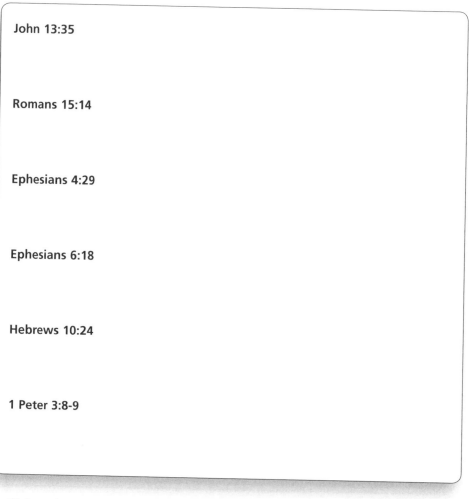 *Read the following verses and then write down what it will mean for you to "set an example" during Discipleship Explored.*

John 13:35

Romans 15:14

Ephesians 4:29

Ephesians 6:18

Hebrews 10:24

1 Peter 3:8-9

Pray that you would be able to put these verses into practice.

24

2 Being a Discipleship Explored leader

So, what will it be like to do our part in *Discipleship Explored*?

👁 **Read 2 Timothy, chapters 1 – 2**

With the joy that comes from seeing the lost rescued and growing in their relationship with the Lord, we also see the sobering reality of the task ahead. In 2 Timothy 1:8, Paul beseeches Timothy to join him in "suffering" for the gospel. He wrote this around AD 67, chained and shackled in a Roman prison and aware that he was going to die soon. Many followers of Christ had deserted Paul (2 Timothy 1:15), so his appeal to Timothy was not only to join him in suffering for the gospel, but also to guard it, protect it and pass it on.

2 Timothy 2:1-4 is a good model for us as we lead guests through *Discipleship Explored*. These verses describe the dedicated soldier for whom hardship, risk and suffering are a matter of course. The Roman African writer, Tertullian, described a soldier's life like this: "No soldier goes to war equipped with luxuries, nor does he go forth to the battle-line from his bed-chamber, but from light and narrow tents wherein every hardship and roughness and uncomfortableness is to be found."[1]

Being a *Discipleship Explored* leader doesn't mean you have to live in a tent for the duration of the course – but it will mean the soldier's life: discipline, responsibility and commitment. We need to be committed in three particular areas:

1. Committed to the Bible.

2. Committed to prayer.

3. Committed to people.

---

1   Tertullian, *Address to the Martyrs*, Part 3. Taken from *The Epistle of the Gallican Churches Lugdunum and Vienna*. With an appendix containing Tertullian's *Address to Martyrs* (trans. T. Herbert Bindley; London: SPCK, 1900), p. 55.

1. COMMITTED TO THE BIBLE

God's word is where the power is. Whatever his personal circumstances, Paul knew that if the word were preached, it would do its work: "I am suffering even to the point of being chained like a criminal. But God's word is not chained" (2 Timothy 2:9).

In 2 Timothy 2:15, Paul exhorts Timothy to devote himself to the study of God's word: "Do your best to present yourself to God as one approved, a workman who does not need to be ashamed and who correctly handles the word of truth".

Because we're convinced of the power of God's word, every group member should be given a Bible of their own if they don't already have one – and our focus as leaders should consistently be on the Bible, specifically Philippians.

It is vital that you study Philippians for yourself and think about its application in your own life. If the message of Philippians doesn't excite you, it won't be exciting for those who attend the course.

2. COMMITTED TO PRAYER

Prayer is essential before, during and after the course. Paul opens his letter to Timothy by saying: "Night and day I constantly remember you in my prayers" (2 Timothy 1:3). We, too, need to be constantly remembering the guests and our fellow leaders in our prayers.

Being dedicated to the Bible and prayer means being single-minded. As 2 Timothy 2:4 says: "No-one serving as a soldier gets involved in civilian affairs – he wants to please his commanding officer". Because the work of discipleship is so important, we must be ruthless in organizing our schedules to that end. The course will have a huge impact on our time.

Again and again, as we seek to make time to lead, to study Philippians, to pray and to meet up with group members, the good will be the enemy of the best, and the urgent will be the enemy of the important. We may find temptations or feelings of inadequacy creeping in. Sometimes, leading will be a real struggle: physically, emotionally and spiritually. After all, our enemy, Satan, hates the work we are doing.

But as Paul's illustration of the soldier makes clear, we must remain dedicated. If people stop attending, we keep praying for them. If they don't seem interested in the discussions, we keep studying and teaching Philippians. We must not be discouraged, because we do it all for our "commanding officer," the Lord Jesus Christ.

3. COMMITTED TO PEOPLE

God's plan is for his word to be communicated life to life. It is not just a matter of us delivering a series of arguments or ideas, brain to brain. We must be prepared to share our lives with this group, and to love them for the sake of Christ. Paul shows us the way in 1 Thessalonians 2:8:

> "We loved you so much that we were delighted to share with you not only the gospel of God but our lives as well, because you had become so dear to us."

It is supremely in our lives that our guests at *Discipleship Explored* will see what it means to live as a disciple of Christ. We are not the gospel (Jesus is), but our lives should make the teaching about God our Saviour attractive (see Titus 2:10).

And that means that we need to show genuine concern for people's lives, their struggles and their questions – and not dismiss them as irrelevant. It means we need to respect them, even when they disagree with us. It means we need to open up our own lives to their inspection, and talk about our own weaknesses and failures, as well as the ways that Christ has changed us. Such genuine love and honesty are the marks of a true disciple of Christ, and in and of themselves they can be a compelling answer to many of the doubts that people have.

Guard against the *Discipleship Explored* course being perceived in your church* as the interest and responsibility only of those who are directly involved. The care of our guests on *Discipleship Explored* needs to be a matter for the whole church family. Only a comparatively few will be actually running the course. But everyone should take ownership of the project as they pray, invite friends, keep up to date with how the course is going, and are ready to welcome and share the on-going care of the guests. This will be a great encouragement to the whole church family.

But love is never without cost. It will involve us in the complex and messy lives that people have. We must understand that mission means mess. It may require us to offer someone practical help. We should do this willingly, but wisely and prayerfully, and in consultation with other Christians. But don't shrink back because of the cost.

* If you are running *Discipleship Explored* as part of a college Christian Fellowship or other non-church group, the above still applies. Every Christian in your group should be prayerfully supporting the course and welcoming guests when the opportunity arises.

3 Before the course

Before the course starts, there are a number of things you should do:

GET TO KNOW PHILIPPIANS, THE HANDBOOK AND THE DVD

Read through Philippians at least three times. Familiarize yourself with the Handbook that your group will be using, and the guidance on the answers to questions in the Study Guide section of this Leader's Guide (page 49).

As you prepare, make notes in your copy of the group member's Handbook. You will then be able to use your annotated Handbook to lead your group instead of referring back to this Leader's Guide. You will feel much more confident to lead your group once you've prepared for the Bible studies and discussions.

As your group members read through Philippians, you will need to be prepared to answer any questions they come up with that arise from the Bible text. There is a section on page 159 that will help you with this. You will need to study and absorb this.

If you are using the *Discipleship Explored* DVD, watch each episode through several times. This will help you to become more familiar with the material, and also enable you to refer back to it during discussion. "Do you remember what was said in the DVD?"

GET TO KNOW YOUR FELLOW LEADERS

It is important that people not only hear what it means to live as a follower of Jesus Christ, but also see it modelled in the life of believers. You will be praying together, studying together, and teaching groups together, so it's important to get to know each other and pray for each other before you begin. Your unity and love for one another will speak volumes about living and working together for Christ.

PREPARE YOUR TESTIMONY

"Always be prepared to give an answer to everyone who asks you to give the reason for the hope that you have. But do this with gentleness and respect..." (1 Peter 3:15).

A testimony is an account of God's work in your life. Everybody who has been born again and who is becoming like Christ has a unique, interesting and powerful testimony, regardless of whether or not it appears spectacular.

At some point during the course, you may feel it appropriate to share your testimony with the group. Often someone will ask you directly how you became a Christian and what it's like living as a disciple of Jesus in everyday life.

You may find the guidelines below helpful as you prepare your testimony:

▣ Keep it honest, personal and interesting

Tip: Your first sentence should make people sit up and listen. Anything too general, for example: "Well, I was brought up in a Christian home..." may make people switch off immediately.

▣ Keep it short

Tip: Any more than three minutes may stretch people's patience. They can always ask you questions if they want to know more.

▣ Keep pointing to God, not yourself

Tip: Your testimony is a great opportunity to point to God and what he is doing in your life. Don't just leave your story as something that happened in the past, as if God stopped working at the moment you became a believer. Include the changes God has made in your life, and what it means for you to live as a Christian right now.

Prepare your testimony. (List the main points below.) You might find it useful to share your testimony with other leaders and get their feedback.

PREPARE FOR DIFFICULT QUESTIONS

Discipleship Explored is an ideal place for people to ask questions. These may include aspects of the gospel message they haven't yet understood as well as questions from Philippians or about living as a Christian. The appendices starting from page 153 will help you deal with some of the most common questions that people may ask about Christianity in general, and about Philippians in particular.

PRAY

- that those invited will attend the course.

- that God would enable you to prepare well.

- for the logistics of organizing the course.

- for good relationships with your co-leaders and group members.

- that God would equip you to lead faithfully.

- that the Holy Spirit would open the blind eyes of those who attend.

Fill in the table below to help you pray for one another.

Leader's name	Prayer points
1.	
2.	
3.	

Take time now to pray through the points above.

ANTICIPATE PASTORAL ISSUES

Try to anticipate the pastoral issues that are likely to arise for young Christians. Think about how you would help people with these issues and which parts of the Bible will be particularly relevant to them.

How would you help a person who was...

sleeping with a partner?

dealing with addictions?

unsure that God can forgive them for something they've done?

coping with broken family relationships?

dating a non-Christian girlfriend or boyfriend?

worried that they are not a Christian?

rejected by non-Christian friends or family?

4 During the course

Each part of a session is important. This chapter uses an evening session as an example. Please adapt it to your own situation if you meet at a different time.

Example of an evening session

6:30 p.m.	**Leaders' prayer meeting**
7:00 p.m.	**Guests arrive for the meal**
7:45 p.m.	**Explore (Bible study)**
8:05 p.m.	**Talk/DVD**
8:30 p.m.	**Discuss**
9:00 p.m.	**End of the evening – "One-to-One"**

Note: All times are approximate. You can make certain sections shorter or longer depending on your circumstances.

6:30 P.M. – LEADERS' PRAYER MEETING

Arrive in plenty of time so that you can pray with the other leaders. Pray for individual guests, that God will help them grasp the truths that will be presented that week. Pray too for the person delivering the talk and for one another.

It may be helpful each week to use one of Paul's prayers as a model for your own. Try praying through:

1 Thessalonians 5:23-24 (Week 1)

Ephesians 1:17-19   (Week 2)

2 Thessalonians 1:11-12 (Week 3)

Philemon 4-6   (Week 4)

2 Thessalonians 2:16-17 (Week 5)

Ephesians 3:16-19   (Week 6)

1 Thessalonians 3:12-13 (Week 7)

Colossians 1:9-12   (Week 8)

7.00 P.M. – MEAL

Eating together is an important part of each week as it helps people to feel comfortable in the group.

Of course, the meal is also a great opportunity to model the importance of giving thanks to God. One of the leaders should be ready to give thanks each week for the food that has been prepared.

Try to avoid heavy theological discussions during this time. The intention is to share life, not to be spiritually intense. We want people to be able to relax and, above all, to realize that we are interested in every aspect of their well-being, not just the spiritual. Find out about their hobbies, jobs, families, holidays, culture and interests.

7:45 P.M. – EXPLORE

This discussion has two components.

First, groups discuss any questions arising from the previous week's "Follow up" (this home Bible study involves reading a few passages from the Bible and answering questions).

Since not everyone will have done his or her "Follow up" Bible study every week, it's important not to make anyone feel uncomfortable. If nobody has anything they'd like to discuss, move on to the Bible passage for that session.

Second, groups look together at a passage from the Bible.

See pages 13-14 of the group member's Handbook for an example of this.

Remember that this is a group of new Christians so they may not know the Bible well. Give page numbers when turning to passages and, if possible, give some brief background information on the relevant book. eg: "This passage is from 1 Peter, a letter that Peter wrote to Christians who were being persecuted. Peter, as you'll remember, was one of Jesus' disciples."

During the Explore Bible study you may get replies that approach the answer to a question but are not quite complete. Try to guide your group from these initial answers to a better, more biblical answer.

- Have further questions in mind to develop the initial answer, for example: "What did you mean by that?", "What does everyone else think?", "Where does it say that?"

- If someone gives a wrong answer, it may be tempting to correct them immediately. Instead, try opening up the discussion by asking others what they think, for example: "Does everyone agree with Jane?"

- Don't be afraid to correct a wrong answer graciously if you think the answer will take the group too far "off topic," for example: "Thank you John, that's an interesting point, but I'm not sure that's what's going on here."

Sometimes, individual personalities may make it difficult to conduct an effective group discussion:

- **The silent type** – never contributes to the discussion. She's best helped by encouraging people to work through questions in groups of two or three at points during the study and then having them feed their answers back to the main group.

- **The talkative type** – likes to monopolize the discussion. Depending on how well you know him, either subdivide the group into smaller groups to give others an opportunity to speak, or have a quiet and tactful word with him (for example: "Tim, thanks so much for everything you're contributing. I wonder if you could help me with the quieter members of the group...")

- **The arguer** – attacks the answers given by everyone else in the group. It's best to take him aside at the end of the evening and listen to any specific issues he may have. If the problem persists, it may be appropriate to remove him from the group, asking him to meet with you "one-to-one" at a different time.

- **The know-it-all** – immediately answers every question, thus stifling the group. This situation is best dealt with by supplementary questions to facilitate group discussion (for example: "Does everyone agree with Nick?").

- **The off-on-a-tangent type** – loves to steer the discussion away from the topic and talk about something entirely different. It may be that this new subject is something the whole group wants to explore, but if not, tactfully suggest that it might be good to discuss it more fully at the end of the evening.

8.05 P.M. – LISTEN

At this point in the evening, the course leader presents a talk (or a DVD is shown).

If you've heard the talks – or watched the DVDs – before, it can be tempting to switch off and stop listening, but bear in mind that if you don't listen, guests won't either.

8:30 P.M. – DISCUSS

Start this discussion by asking: "Did anything particularly strike you from the talk?" or "Was there anything that stood out from the talk/DVD?" Then use the printed questions to encourage discussion as you explore together the truths that have been presented.

📖 *See page 16 of the group member's Handbook for an example of this.*

It is not important to finish all the questions. They are just a guide to discussion. Add your own supplementary questions as necessary to ensure that guests have understood the passage from Philippians.

Many questions in this section have personal applications. Depending on your group, people may feel shy about answering these in front of others. Giving your own answer may encourage them to do so. Otherwise, feel free to ask group members to answer the questions privately at home.

▪ Leaders should try to avoid speaking immediately after each other.

▪ You may feel it is appropriate to "carry over" a discussion from the Explore Bible study, if you were unable to adequately cover an important issue.

▪ Be gracious and courteous, and act as peacemaker if the discussion gets heated.

▪ If a question is met with silence, don't be too quick to say something. Allow people time to think.

▪ It may be appropriate in certain circumstances to address a question directly to an individual in order to encourage discussion (for example: "Sam, what do you think about this?")

- If one person's particular issue begins to dominate, gently ask him or her if you can talk about the issue together at the end of the session.

- Don't forget how important the tone of your voice and your body language can be as you seek to further the discussion.

- Lead honestly. You won't be able to deal with all the questions thrown your way, so don't pretend to have all the answers. Some questions can be easily addressed, but others will be difficult. If you don't know the answer, say so – but try to have an answer ready for the following week.

9:00 P.M. – END OF THE EVENING – "ONE-TO-ONE"

Philippians will provoke and challenge even the most mature Christians so it will be appropriate to pray at the end of the study. There are a number of different ways you might approach this, depending on how confident your group are.

- You might choose simply to pray on behalf of the whole group about the issues that have been raised in Philippians.

- Alternatively, you might ask each of the guests in turn what they would like prayer for, and then pray on behalf of the whole group.

- For groups who are able, encourage praying aloud for one another. Hopefully, by the end of the course all groups should be willing to pray in this way.

Encourage guests to use the Follow Up studies as their daily readings for the coming week. (These studies are designed to help group members establish a pattern of daily Bible reading and prayer.) Explain that you'll also be doing the studies and that there will be time to discuss them next week. You may want to introduce briefly what the studies will be about as a way of encouraging them to do it.

Go through the Follow Up Bible studies as your own daily readings. If you fill in the answers yourself, you will be much better able to help the group members understand the passages assigned.

Always finish at the promised time. Good timekeeping develops trust in the group, and people will be more likely to return next week. However, let guests know that they are welcome to stay and talk further if they like. As the course progresses, many group members will need your advice and support as they seek to serve Christ wholeheartedly.

5 Introducing Philippians

There are background notes on Philippians, and a map of the region, on pages 79-80 of the group members' Handbook (and also on pages 171-172 of this Leader's Guide). The information below expands on those notes to help you understand a bit more about the Philippians.

WHO WROTE IT?

The apostle Paul wrote the letter to the Philippians. Not only is Paul's writing style much in evidence, but the early church unanimously declared it to be his work.

WHERE WAS IT WRITTEN?

Philippians 1:13-14 tells us that Paul wrote the letter while in prison, most likely when he was under house arrest in Rome.

Acts 28:14-31 reveals some fascinating details about this period of Paul's life. He was allowed to live by himself in his own rented house, although with a soldier to guard him. He was also free to receive visitors, and able to preach and teach "boldly and without hindrance".

WHEN WAS IT WRITTEN?

The evidence suggests that it was written around AD 61.

WHO WAS HE WRITING TO?

The city of Philippi in Greece was a successful Roman colony, whose inhabitants prided themselves on being Roman citizens.

Many Philippians made a point of speaking Latin, and even dressed like Romans.

WHY WAS IT WRITTEN?

Paul wanted to thank the Philippian Christians for the gift they had sent him, when they found out he had been detained in Rome.

But he does several other things too: he reports on his present circumstances; he encourages them to stand firm and rejoice in the face of persecution; he urges them to be humble and united; and he warns them against certain dangerous people within their church (see Philippians 3).

WHAT IS DISTINCTIVE ABOUT THE LETTER?

Philippians is a radical picture of what it means to be a Christian: self-humbling (2:1-4), single-minded (3:13-14), anxiety-free (4:6), and able to do all things (4:13).

Unusually, Philippians contains no Old Testament quotations, perhaps because there was no synagogue in Philippi.

It is also the New Testament letter of joy: the word, in its various forms, occurs sixteen times in Philippians.

In order to further familiarize yourself with Philippians you should read the letter several times, and also read the talk outlines on pages 117 to 151 or watch the Discipleship Explored DVD.

6 After the course

Discipleship Explored is not an eight-session conveyor belt that produces mature Christians at the other end. It is therefore vital to have a coherent follow-up strategy in place for all guests.

GIVE OUT FEEDBACK FORMS

Feedback forms, given out during the last session of the course, are a great way to challenge course members to think about what they have learned, and to help leaders plan a way forward once the course is ended.

You can find a sample feedback form on page 44. An editable version of this form can be downloaded from **www.ceministries.org/de**

STAY IN TOUCH

Having spent eight sessions with your group, considering profound and personal issues, you will know them well – and they will know you well. Under these circumstances, it would clearly be wrong to "drop" group members once the course comes to an end.

Plan to stay in touch with all the members of your group, and arrange it with your co-leaders so that each group member has at least one leader who remains in touch with him or her.

You should also invite group members to start coming along to church with you if they're not already regularly attending. It is often a difficult task to get people into the habit of meeting together regularly on a Sunday, but the concept of a Christian who doesn't belong to a church is foreign to the New Testament, so help them to take this seriously (Hebrews 10:25). Introduce them to other Christians and help them to become integrated within the church by joining a Bible-study group and finding an area of service within which they can participate.

Feedback Form

You don't have to answer all the questions if you don't want to, but please be as honest as you can.

Your details (optional):

Name _____ Date _____

Address _____

Telephone _____ Email _____

1. Why did you come to *Discipleship Explored*?

2. On a scale of 1-5 (1 being poor and 5 excellent) how would you rate:

Group discussions? ☐

Talks/DVD? ☐

The "Follow Up" studies? ☐

Food? ☐

Overall? ☐

3. What do you enjoy most about the course?

4. What can we improve?

5. What would you like to do now?

☐ I would like to join a Bible-study group.

☐ I would like to discuss things further with someone.

☐ Other _____

7. Would you like to make any comments about the course, either positive or negative?

RECOMMEND OR GIVE AWAY BOOKS

Reading a good Christian book at the right time can be very influential. Think carefully about the books you have read and see if any of them would suit particular members of your group. If you're not an avid reader, ask around for advice about books suitable for people in different situations.

READ THE BIBLE WITH A GROUP MEMBER

You might suggest getting together with an individual on a regular basis to read through a book of the Bible. This can be totally informal; just two friends with an open Bible finding out what God's word has to say to them.

Questions to guide your study could be:

What does the passage mean?

- Are there any difficult words or ideas that merit special attention?

What does the passage mean in context?

- What comes before/after the passage?

- Why is the passage placed where it is?

- Is it addressed to a specific individual or group of people? Why?

What does the passage mean for us?

- What have we learned about ourselves?

- About God?

- How do we apply the passage to our lives?

PRAY

A supremely Christ-like way of caring for people is to pray for them. Even after the course has ended, it is important to pray for all the members of the group.

For new believers, pray for growth, fruitfulness and joy. Pray especially that they will be able to put into practice what they have learned from Philippians.

If there are any who have not yet made a commitment to Christ, pray that the Lord will have mercy on them and send his Holy Spirit to open their blind eyes.

After the course has ended, use this space to write down the names of those in your care, and the ways in which you will aim to support them.

SUGGESTIONS FOR NEXT TIME

If you are the course leader, it's very helpful to find out what you're doing right, and perhaps ways in which you might improve future courses. In addition to the feedback forms from guests, ask the leaders to tell you their thoughts about the course. The following form is one way to do that – or you could meet together after the course to discuss these questions. An editable version of this form can be downloaded from **www.ceministries.org/de**

Example feedback form for leaders

We are always looking to improve *Discipleship Explored* and would value your feedback. The training and support of leaders is an essential part of the course and your comments would be very much appreciated. Please be as honest as possible.

1. What encouraged you most about leading?

2. What did you find most difficult about leading?

3. What did you think of the leaders' training prior to the course?

4. Could we have prepared you better for the course? If so, how?

5. What did you think of the leaders' prayer meetings?

6. What did you think of the course material?

7. Please feel free to comment on any other aspects of the course.

Study Guide

Two *Christianity Explored* websites to help you:

www.christianityexplored.org
This website is for non-Christians, but will also help new Christians. It features a visual gospel outline based on the Gospel of Mark, answers to common questions, and testimonies from a wide variety of people, as well as information about the *Christianity Explored* course. You can find more details at the back of this book, on page 175.

www.ceministries.org/de
For leaders looking for information, downloads and resources.

Introduction

This Study Guide section contains talk outlines and studies to work through over the eight-session course. It includes all the material in the group member's Handbook. However it also contains specific instructions for leaders, additional notes and the answers to each question.

- Don't worry if you don't have time to go through all of the questions with your group – the most important thing is to listen to the guests and answer their questions.

- Try to avoid using "jargon" that might alienate group members. Bear in mind that words and phrases familiar to Christians (for example, "pagan," "washed in the blood," "house group," "the Lord" and so on) may seem strange to those new to Christian circles.

- If guests miss a week, take time during the meal to summarize briefly what was taught the week before.

- At the end of "Discuss", pray with your group and encourage them to complete the "Follow up" Bible studies during the week.

- Go through the "Follow up" studies as your own daily Bible reading. If you fill in the answers yourself, you will be much better able to help the group members understand the passages they have been looking at.

CONFIDENT IN CHRIST

1

▶ *Welcome the guests to* Discipleship Explored *and introduce yourself. Make sure everyone has been introduced to each other. Try to remember names ready for next week.*

▶ *Give a brief introduction. If you have more than one discussion group, this is best given by the course leader or speaker to everyone together. (The wording below is intended only as a general guide.)*

Over the next eight sessions we will explore what it means to be a follower of Jesus, and what that might look like in our daily lives. We will be reading the book of Philippians together. This is a letter written by Paul to a group of new Christians, so it has plenty to teach us about living as disciples of Jesus Christ.

We also want to spend time addressing whatever questions are important to you. As well as having times of discussion in groups, we will be available to chat at the end of the evening.

Please feel free to make notes and list questions you may have as you listen to the Bible talk. There is space for notes in your Handbook.

▶ *Give each guest a Bible and a copy of the group member's Handbook.*

▶ *Ask the group to turn to Session 1 on page 5 of the Handbook.*

▶ *Explain the four sections of the Handbook:*

Explore = we read the Bible together and talk about what we've read (different in Week 1).

Listen = we listen to the Bible talk, or watch the DVD, and make notes in the talk outline in the Handbook.

Discuss = we discuss some of the points from the Bible talk.

Follow up = you read some other sections of the Bible for yourself, and then bring any questions you have to the group.

EXPLORE

🔲 *Ask your group to turn to the question on page 5 of the Handbook.*

> **What would you write to your friends if you were unfairly put in prison?**

Have an answer of your own ready so that you can start the discussion if no one else is willing to talk.

🔲 *You may want to introduce the group to the book of Philippians at this point. If so, there is a helpful summary and a map on pages 79-80 of the group member's Handbook.*

LISTEN Philippians 1:1-11

🔲 *(Page 6 in the group member's Handbook) Encourage the group to make notes and list questions they may have as they listen to the Bible talk or watch the DVD. There is space in the Handbook to make notes.*

🔲 **Note:** *Discipleship Explored is based on the 1984 version of the New International Version (NIV). If you are using the 2011 revised NIV, you will find that* **"saints"** *in Philippians 1:1 has been changed to* **"God's holy people"**. *This does not change the meaning of the verse, since saints are people who God has "set apart" (which is what "holy" means) for himself.*

"He who began a good work in you will carry it on to completion until the day of Christ Jesus." (Philippians 1:6)

▪ Philippians is a letter written by Paul to the Christians living in Philippi, to help them keep going as Christians.

▪ Paul wrote his letter while in prison in Rome.

▪ He knew God was working in the Philippians because of their "partnership in the gospel" (Philippians 1:5).

- Paul was confident that God would finish the work of salvation he began.

- We know that God has begun his good work in us if we are living as partners in the gospel, demonstrating our love for Jesus.

- We can be confident that what God starts he finishes.

- "Disciple" means "learner". God will help us learn how to live for him and grow in our knowledge of him.

DISCUSS

(Pages 7-8 in the group member's Handbook) Ask your group if there was anything that stood out or particularly struck them from the talk/DVD. This will help them to respond specifically to what they have just heard, before moving on to the group discussion questions.

1. **According to Philippians 1:6, what confidence should we have as Christians?**

2. **In the middle of daily life, why is verse 6 sometimes hard to believe?**

3. **What can we hold on to when we lack confidence in our salvation?**

4. **What difference should this confidence make to our lives?**

5. **What is the result of God's "good work in you" and when will it be complete? (See verses 6, 10, 11.)**

FOLLOW UP

▪ *(Page 9 in the group member's Handbook) Let the group know which Bible passages you would like them to read for this week's Follow Up. As well as Philippians, they will be reading passages from 1 John, John's Gospel and Ephesians this week. Check that group members know how to find these books in their Bibles.*

▪ *You may want to show the group how to approach their personal reading plan by doing the first part of one of the Bible studies with them. This will reassure any who are nervous about studying the Bible in this way – and will also reduce the amount of home study they need to do for this first week.*

▪ *The following paragraph is printed at the top of page 9 in the group member's Handbook.*

Each week, Follow Up gives you a plan to help you read the Bible every day. The passages this week help to explain how we can be confident of our salvation. There's room at the end for any questions you'd like to discuss next time.

SUNDAY

▪ *Read the passage that will be preached at the church service you attend.*

On the other six days...

DAY ONE
👁 **Re-read Philippians 1:1-11**

▪ *Think about the answers you gave to the Discuss questions on pages 7-8.*

▪ *Thank God that if he has started any "good work" in you, he will complete it.*

DAY TWO
👁 **Read 1 John 1:5 – 2:1**

John wrote this letter in around 90AD. It is probably a circular letter intended for a number of churches.

1. What is "walking in the light"? (See 1 John 1:6-7.)

   (Clue: People who walk in the light need the blood of Jesus to purify them [verse 7] so it can't mean "being perfect". Light reveals things; it helps us to see them clearly. Take a look at John 3:20–21.)

2. So, what is "walking in the darkness"? (See 1 John 1:5-6.)

3. Put verse 8 into your own words.

4. How can we be certain that confessing sin will result in our forgiveness? (See 1 John 1:9.)

5. What is encouraging about the balance in 1 John 2:1?

   Spend a few minutes thanking God for the secure faith you have, which is based upon what Jesus has already done for you.

DAY THREE

Read John 6:35-40

These verses are taken from a discussion the crowd is having with Jesus after he miraculously fed over 5000 people with two small loaves and five fish (John 6:1-15). The crowd demands a miraculous sign like the one Moses gave when he fed the Israelites with manna in the wilderness (Exodus 16:11-18, 31).

Jesus reminds them that it was his Father in heaven who fed the people. And in any case, says Jesus, the "true bread" is "he who comes down from heaven and gives life to the world".

1. What "life" does Jesus bring (v 35)?

   (Clue: Look at what John 3:16 says about the reason Jesus was sent.)

2. Look at the promise in verse 37. How can you be sure that you are included in this promise?

3. God's plan for us is clearly given in verses 39 and 40. What is *God's part* in this plan?

➲ What is *our* part?

▨ *Use these verses to thank God for what he is doing in your life and to pray about the coming sessions at **Discipleship Explored**.*

DAY FOUR

👁 **Read Ephesians 2:8-10**

Paul wrote this letter to the Christians in Ephesus. These verses explain very clearly how we have been saved.

1. According to verses 8 and 9, what is it that saves us?

2. What is it that Paul says has no power to save us?

   (Note: He mentions these because it is all too easy to rely on them rather than on God.)

3. Put verse 8 into your own words.

4. Verse 10 is packed with meaning. What are the three things we learn? All three are God-centred and God-initiated.

▨ *Pray that God would enable you to rely solely on him.*

DAY FIVE

▨ *Re-read the Bible passages you've read over the past week. Choose a verse that you found particularly helpful, write it down in the space below and memorize it.*

DAY SIX

*Read Philippians 1:12–26 in preparation for **Discipleship Explored**.*

Do you have any questions about the passages you have read this week?

The next session will start with group members being asked if they have any questions about the Bible passages they read at home.

from last week – memorable verse?

LIVING IN CHRIST

Disciples ......

Acts 16 – Paul in Philippi

EXPLORE

■ *Ask the guests to turn to Session 2 on page 13 of the Handbook.*

■ *Ask if they have any questions from last session's Follow up.*

■ *Ask everyone to open their Bibles at Philippians 1. A leader – or one of the group members – should read Philippians 1:9-11.*

■ *Work through the questions below to help the group explore the passage.*
REVISION !

1. What does Paul pray for the Philippian Christians?

That their love for God and other people may grow.

That this love will be shaped by knowledge and depth of insight.

2. Why does he pray for these things? (See verse 10.)

So that they would know how to live in a way that honours God.

Note: There is a logical sequence here. As our love grows, we are able to "discern what is best", and thus be "pure and blameless".

3. What does Paul hope will be the result of this? (See verse 11.)

That they would be full of the fruit of righteousness, pleasing to God in every way, so that God gets the glory and praise.

4. How might Paul's prayer shape the way we pray for other Christians?

Suggest that group members use these verses as a basis for their prayers for themselves and for other Christians during the coming week.

Ambitions ?

READ ↘
LISTEN Philippians 1:12-26

🔲 _(Page 15 in the group member's Handbook) Encourage the group to make notes and list questions they may have as they listen to the Bible talk or watch the DVD. There is space in the Handbook to make notes._

🔲 **Note:** _Discipleship Explored is based on the 1984 version of the New International Version (NIV). If you are using the 2011 revised NIV, you will find that_ **"brothers"** _in Philippians 1:12,14 has been changed to_ **"brothers and sisters"**. _This does not change the meaning of the verse, since the phrase "brothers in the Lord" refers to all those in God's family, both men and women._

"For to me, to live is Christ and to die is gain." (Philippians 1:21)

🔲 Paul's circumstances were bad:

– he wrote his letter from prison.

– there were people trying to stir up trouble for him.

– he didn't know if he would live or die.

🔲 But Paul was rejoicing – because he knew that everything that had happened had "served to advance the gospel" (Philippians 1:12).

🔲 The most important thing to Paul was that people were hearing about Jesus.

🔲 Paul taught the Philippians (and us) that: "To live is Christ and to die is gain" (Philippians 1:21).

🔲 There is only one way to live that death cannot touch. That is to live for Christ.

Joseph – circumstances used by God for good
Jesus' death

'Good news' to Romans = new emperor
Human life cheap in Roman world

2 Cor 1 8-11 describes what happened
(confident, yes, but still up & down)

DISCUSS

(Pages 16-17 in the group member's Handbook) *Ask your group if there was anything that stood out or particularly struck them from the talk/DVD. This will help them to respond specifically to what they have just heard, before moving on to the group discussion questions.*

1. **Paul's greatest ambition was for the gospel to spread. What is your greatest ambition? (Be honest!)**

2. **What pressures did Paul face that may have led him to put his own desires first? (See Philippians 1:13, 15-17, 23.)**

   What was his attitude to these pressures and why?

3. **How might our circumstances, reputation or future plans affect our desire to tell others about Christ?**

4. **How would you put Paul's motto in verse 21, "To live is Christ and to die is gain", into your own words?**

5. **How would your friends or colleagues finish this sentence: "For me to live is..."?**

   What about you? How would you finish that same sentence?

FOLLOW UP

(Page 18 in the group member's Handbook) *Let the group know that, as well as Philippians, they will be reading passages from John's Gospel and Acts this week.*

Help given in prayer   v 19
Write a prayer for next time?

p 18

➡ *The following paragraph is printed at the top of page 18 in the group member's Handbook.*

In Philippians 1:19, Paul tells the Philippian church that he has been helped by their prayers and "the Spirit of Jesus Christ". The passages this week will tell us more about the Holy Spirit and what he does. There's room at the end to write down any questions you'd like to discuss next time.

SUNDAY

🖼 *Read the passage that will be preached at the church service you attend.*

On the other six days...

DAY ONE

👁 **Re-read Philippians 1:12-26**

🖼 *Think about the answers you gave to the questions in Discuss on pages 16-17.*

🖼 *Pray that you would be able to echo Paul's motto with conviction: "For to me, to live is Christ and to die is gain".*

DAY TWO

👁 **Read John 14:15-31**

In this passage, Jesus is speaking just hours before his death. He wants the disciples to know that they won't be alone when he leaves them. The Holy Spirit will be given to them, and will be with them for ever.

The word translated "Counsellor" in this passage is literally "one who comes alongside"; an advocate. Jesus promises "*another* Counsellor". Jesus is the first "one who comes alongside" and the Holy Spirit will follow him, so the Holy Spirit is a person. Notice too that in verse 17 the Holy Spirit is referred to as "him" and "he".

1. How does Jesus describe the Holy Spirit in John 14:16?

2. In verses 17-18, what is the difference between "the world's" relationship to the Holy Spirit and ours?

   (Note: Jesus describes the relationship between himself, the Father and the Holy Spirit as very close indeed. Jesus says in verse 17 that the Holy Spirit is in us, and he also says in verse 20 that he – Jesus – is in us.)

3. The main theme in this passage is love (verses 15, 21, 23-24). How is our love for Jesus shown in practice? (See verses 21 and 23.)

4. What is the consequence of living in this way?

   Thank God for the work of the Holy Spirit in your life, asking that he would increase your understanding of the Bible. Pray that you would increasingly demonstrate your love for Jesus by obedience (John 14:15).

DAY THREE
Read John 16:5-15

1. What are the three ways in which the Counsellor – the Holy Spirit – "convicts the world"? (See John 16:8.)

2. How does Jesus explain these three in verses 9 to 11?

3. Jesus promises the apostles in verse 13 that the Holy Spirit will guide them into "all truth". How does this promise give us confidence as we read the New Testament? (See also John 14:26.)

It is very important to see that the Holy Spirit's role is to draw attention to Jesus. Read John 16:14-15 again, and also John 15:26.

Ask the Holy Spirit to make Jesus more real to you as you read the Bible.

DAY FOUR

👁 Read Acts 2:1-13

Acts was written by the same Luke who wrote the Gospel. In fact, as you can see from the start of both books, both were originally intended for the same reader, Theophilus.

Acts 2:1–13 records the way in which the Holy Spirit was given to the first Christians on the day of Pentecost. (The Greek word "Pentecost" means "fifty". The day of Pentecost was the fiftieth day after the Sabbath, the Jewish holy day, at the end of Passover week. It was a celebration of the end of the barley harvest and a feast of the "first fruits" of the harvest.)

1. **What was the effect of the disciples being filled with the Holy Spirit? (See verses 4 and 6.)**

2. **What was it the disciples were saying to the people as they did this? (See verse 11.)**

3. **Read Genesis 11:1–9. How does this contrast with what happened on the day of Pentecost?**

In the Old Testament, the Holy Spirit was only given to people with particular roles – prophets, kings and priests. But Acts 2:17–18 quotes a prophecy from the prophet Joel that, one day, the Holy Spirit would fill every one of God's people, in every nation. The day of Pentecost was the fulfillment of that prophecy.

📖 *Spend time praying, thanking God for the Holy Spirit's presence in* your life.

DAY FIVE

📖 *Re-read the Bible passages you've read over the past week.*
Choose a verse that you found particularly helpful, write it down in the space below and memorize it.

DAY SIX

Read Philippians 1:27 – 2:11 in preparation for **Discipleship Explored**.

Do you have any questions about the passages you have read this week?

The next session will start with group members being asked if they have any questions about the Bible passages they read at home.

STANDING TOGETHER IN CHRIST

3

EXPLORE

■ *Ask the guests to turn to Session 3 on page 23 of the Handbook.*

■ *Ask if they have any questions from last session's Follow up.*

■ *Ask everyone to open their Bibles at Philippians 1. A leader – or one of the group members – should read Philippians 1:21-26.* revision from last week

■ *Work through the questions below to help the group explore the passage.*

1. What dilemma does Paul face?

He is torn between wanting to live or die.

2. Why does Paul want to "go on living"?

It would be a benefit to the Philippians. By being with them again he would help them to progress in their faith and find joy in Christ.

Note: This is what Paul means by "fruitful labour" in verse 22.

3. What is it about death that Paul finds so attractive? (See verse 23.)

He would then "be with Christ, which is better by far".

4. Do you share Paul's view of death? Why or why not?

It may be useful to look at 2 Corinthians 5:1-8 and Revelation 21:1-7.

5. What do these verses tell us about Paul's mindset?

For Paul, Christ is central to everything.

READ

<u>LISTEN</u> **Philippians 1:27 – 2:11**

- *(Page 25 in the group member's Handbook) Encourage the group to make notes and list questions they may have as they listen to the Bible talk or watch the DVD. There is space in the Handbook to make notes.*

- **Note:** *Discipleship Explored is based on the 1984 version of the New International Version (NIV). If you are using the 2011 revised NIV, you will find that there are a number of changes in Philippians 1:27 – 2:11.*

  "Contending as one man" *in Philippians 1:27 has been changed to* *"striving together as one"*. *If you are showing episode 3 of the DVD, you will see that the imagery of "contending" is illustrated by a boxing match. So you may want to explain that verse 27 can be translated as "contending" as well as "striving". Both translations show the importance of Christians working hard together for the sake of the gospel.*

  "Fellowship with the Spirit" *in Philippians 2:1 has been changed to* *"common sharing in the Spirit"*. *Both phrases mean partnership with fellow Christians, which is made possible by the Holy Spirit. All believers have received the Holy Spirit who joins us together as God's family.*

  "Your attitude should be the same as that of Christ Jesus" *in Philippians 2:5 has been changed to* *"In your relationships with one another, have the same mindset as Christ Jesus"*. *Both translations point us to Jesus as the pattern for how we think, live and relate to others.*

  In Philippians 2:6 *"grasped"* *has been changed to* *"used to his own advantage"*. *When Jesus was born as a human, he was still fully God. But, as he says in Mark 10:45, he "did not come to be served, but to serve, and to give his life as a ransom for many".*

Orchestra — together
— diff' sounds
— harmony

"Your attitude should be the same as that of Christ Jesus." (Philippians 2:5)

- Christians are to stand together for the gospel – "in one spirit" and "as one man" (Philippians 1:27).

- We can't fight for the gospel if we're fighting with each other. *All valued all treated with equal care*

- Suffering for Christ is a normal experience for a Christian.

- Our attitude should be the same as that of Jesus. *Servant-heart*

- We should consider others better than ourselves. The secret of standing together is humility. *'emptied himself' v 7* *new kingdom new king*

- Jesus made himself like a slave.

- One day *every* knee will bow and *every* tongue confess that Jesus Christ is Lord.

DISCUSS

'God was in Christ, reconciling the world to himself' 2 Cor 5¹⁹

- *(Pages 26-27 in the group member's Handbook) Ask your group if there was anything that stood out or particularly struck them from the talk/DVD. This will help them to respond specifically to what they have just heard, before moving on to the group discussion questions.*

1. **According to Philippians 1:27, what does it mean to conduct ourselves "in a manner worthy of the gospel of Christ"?**

2. **What opportunities do you have to "contend" for the gospel by sharing your faith with others?**

3. **Paul and the Philippian church faced opposition because they were "contending" for the gospel (see verses 28–30).**
Why might we face opposition to the gospel today?

4. **In verses 28–30 Paul makes some surprising statements. From these verses, what should we remember when we face opposition?**

5. **What does it mean to stand together, according to Paul in Philippians 2:2?**

6. **What will it mean in practice for us to "consider others better" than ourselves?**

FOLLOW UP

- *(Page 28 in the group member's Handbook) Let the group know that, as well as Philippians, they will be reading passages from Isaiah, Luke and Colossians this week.*

- *The following paragraph is printed at the top of page 28 in the group member's Handbook.*

Philippians 2:5-11 gives a wonderful insight into the humility and selflessness of Jesus. The passages this week focus on Jesus and his mission to rescue us from our sin.

SUNDAY

Read the passage that will be preached at the church service you attend.

On the other six days...

DAY ONE

Re-read Philippians 1:27 – 2:11

Think about the answers you gave to the questions in Discuss on pages 26-27.

Pray for strength and wisdom so that, wherever you are, your attitude is "the same as that of Christ Jesus".

DAY TWO

👁 **Read Isaiah 53:1-12**

These verses, which describe the suffering of God's "servant", were written about 700 years before Jesus was born. It is remarkable that so much of Jesus' mission is prophesied here.

1. **Looking at verses 4-6, what similarities can you find between the "servant" and Jesus Christ?**

   (Note: "Transgressions" and "iniquities" are another way of describing sin.)

2. **What does the servant's suffering achieve?**

3. **Why is this suffering necessary? (See verse 6.)**

4. **In Acts 8:26-35, Philip meets an Ethiopian who is reading verses 7-8 of Isaiah 53. How do you think Philip used these verses to tell the Ethiopian "the good news about Jesus" (Acts 8:35)?**

5. **Read 1 Peter 2:22-25. Which verses from Isaiah 53 can you detect in this passage?**

   Give thanks to God for the good news of Jesus.

DAY THREE

👁 **Read Luke 15:1-32**

A parable is a simple story with a spiritual meaning. Verses 1 and 2 tell us the background to these parables. The comment in verse 2 was meant as an insult – but for us it is very good news.

1. **What do the three parables tell us about the mission of Jesus and how God views "sinners"?**

2. The parable of the lost son has a bit more detail in it than the other two. Verse 20 is a very bold picture of God. What might surprise non-Christians about this verse?

3. Jesus probably intended the religious leaders (who were listening, see verse 2) to see themselves as the older son. What was the older son – and by implication the religious leaders – missing out on?

4. How can we make sure we don't miss out in the same way?

The parable of the lost son is a wonderful picture of the compassion of God and the mission of Jesus.

🔖 *Thank God for the extraordinary nature of his fatherly compassion for you. Who do you need to have compassion on in your daily life? Pray about this and ask God to give you his compassion for them.*

DAY FOUR
👁 Read Colossians 1:15-23

This letter was written by Paul to the Christians living in Colosse, in modern-day Turkey. These verses give us a profound insight into who Jesus is.

1. What does Paul mean when he calls Jesus "the image of the invisible God" (verse 15)? (See verse 19.)

2. Paul also describes Jesus as "the firstborn over all creation". What does he mean by that, according to verses 16-18?

3. Jesus is described by Paul as:

   ⊙ the one who reveals God

   ⊙ the creator of the universe

   ⊙ the purpose of the universe

   ⊙ the sustainer of everything

   ⊙ the head of the church

   ⊙ the reconciler.

Identify the verses that correspond to these descriptions.

4. In the light of this, what should our attitude be towards Jesus?

5. Because of humankind's rebellion against God (Genesis 3), everything has been severed from its rightful relationship with the Father and needs to be reconciled to him. How is this achieved? (See verse 20.)

6. Verse 22 mentions our own reconciliation with God through the death of Jesus. For what purpose have we been reconciled?

7. According to verse 23, what should our response be to this reconciliation?

   Reflect on the descriptions of Jesus you found in question 3, and praise God for such a mighty Saviour. Pray too that you will "continue in your faith, established and firm, not moved from the hope held out in the gospel".

DAY FIVE

Re-read the Bible passages you've read over the past week.
Choose a verse that you found particularly helpful, write it down in the space below and memorize it.

*Read Philippians 2:12-30 in preparation for **Discipleship Explored**.*

Do you have any questions about the passages you have read this week?

The next session will start with group members being asked if they have any questions about the Bible passages they read at home.

TRANSFORMED BY CHRIST

4

📧 Ask the guests to turn to Session 4 on page 33 of the Handbook.

📧 Ask if they have any questions from last session's Follow up.

📧 Ask everyone to open their Bibles at Philippians 2. A leader – or one of the group members – should read Philippians 2:5-11.

📧 Work through the questions below to help the group explore the passage.

> **1. Our attitude "should be the same as that of Christ Jesus" (verse 5). What exactly was Jesus' attitude? (See verses 7-8.)**

He made himself nothing, became like a servant, humbled himself, and became obedient to death, even death on a cross.

> **2. Jesus "did not consider equality with God something to be grasped" (verse 6). Why not?**

Verse 7 – because he came to serve. (See also translation note at the bottom of page 70.

> **3. Are there any situations in which a Christian needs to "grasp equality with God"? Why or why not?**

There are no situations in which a Christian needs to do this. After all, "grasping equality with God" is practically the definition of sin. In addition, just as Jesus had everything because he is God, so we have everything in Christ. That means we don't need to live self-centred, "grasping" lives.

4. What were the results of Jesus' attitude, according to verses 9-11?

God exalted Jesus to the highest place and gave him the name that is above every name, that every knee should bow to Jesus, acknowledging that he is Lord, to the glory of God.

5. Having read this passage, how can you live "to the glory of God" (verse 11) this week?.

It might be helpful to look at 1 Corinthians 10:31.

'Whether you eat or drink – do all for glory of God'

LISTEN Philippians 2:12-30

📖 *(Page 35 in the group member's Handbook) Encourage the group to make notes and list questions they may have as they listen to the Bible talk or watch the DVD. There is space in the Handbook to make notes.*

📖 **Note:** *Discipleship Explored is based on the 1984 version of the New International Version (NIV). If you are using the 2011 revised NIV, you will find that there are a number of changes in Philippians 2:12-30.*

*"**Crooked and depraved**" in Philippians 2:15 has been changed to "**warped and crooked**", and the phrase "**children of God without fault in a warped and crooked generation**" has been put within quote marks. Neither of these differences change the meaning of the verse. The quote marks indicate that Paul may have been quoting from Deuteronomy 32:5.*

*"**Hold out the word of life**" in Philippians 2:16 has been changed to "**hold firmly to the word of life**". If we are going to "shine like stars in the universe" (verse 15), then, as well as telling people the gospel, it must shine from every part of our lives as we continue to trust in God, holding firmly to all his promises.*

> **"Shine like stars in the universe as you hold out the word of life."** (Philippians 2:15-16)
>
> ▪ We should "shine like stars" by telling people the gospel, the "word of life".
>
> ▪ The gospel must shine from *every* part of our lives, not just from what we say.

People whose lives affected yours
– famous or otherwise?

Practical consequences for disciples

- Disciples will stand out from the world we live in by doing everything "without complaining or arguing", and by being "blameless and pure".

- We cannot work *for* our salvation – Jesus already has.

- As we obey Christ, our salvation works itself out – becomes visible – in our lives.

- Timothy and Epaphroditus were working out their salvation, and shining like stars.

- When people look at our lives, what do they see?

DISCUSS

1 Peter 1⁹ – receiving the outcome of your faith – salvation

(Pages 36-37 in the group member's Handbook) Ask your group if there was anything that stood out or particularly struck them from the talk/DVD. This will help them to respond specifically to what they have just heard, before moving on to the group discussion questions.

NOT WORK for

1. **In your own words, what does Paul command in Philippians 2:12?** *UNITY*
   work out your own salv⁰ – put it into effect
   ~pl. TOGETHER with God / each other

2. **What will it mean in practice for you to "work out your salvation** *OT*
   with fear and trembling"? *Take it seriously.* *Deut 32:5*
   – encounter with God? As if we were standing in
   presence of God *No grumbling! Arguing, obedience sacrifice*

3. **After the challenge of verse 12, why should Paul's next words inspire** *Rom*
   confidence in his readers? *12¹*
   – God who is at work in us – God *Pure. Shining*

4. **In what ways are you aware of God transforming you or other Christians you know?**

5. **According to verses 15 and 16, what makes us "shine like stars"?**

6. **Which do you think is more necessary: to tell people the gospel or to live a godly life among them? Why?**

Timothy Acts 16
Epaphroditus Phil 4¹⁸

{ Holding fast v16
{ Holding out

79

FOLLOW UP

- *(Page 38 in the group member's Handbook) Let the group know that, as well as Philippians, they will be reading passages from Luke, Galatians and Romans this week.*

- *The following paragraph is printed at the top of page 38 in the group member's Handbook.*

In Philippians 2:12-13, Paul tells the Christians in Philippi to "work out" their salvation. The passages this week explore what that means.

SUNDAY

- *Read the passage that will be preached at the church service you attend.*

On the other six days...

DAY ONE
Re-read Philippians 2:12-30

- *Think about the answers you gave to the questions in Discuss on pages 36-37.*

- *Pray that you will be able to "work out your salvation with fear and trembling", thanking God that he is at work in you.*

DAY TWO
Read Luke 14:25-33

In this passage, Jesus explains what it will cost to follow him. Jesus is addressing the large crowd who have been travelling with him. He wants them to understand that there is a big difference between being a true follower and just being a spectator.

When Jesus uses the word "hate", he is not telling us, for example, to abandon the commandment to "honour your father and your mother" (Exodus 20:12). He uses such a strong word to show the radical nature of following him. We must always put Christ first.

1. What is involved in being a follower of Jesus, according to verses 26-27?

2. We are to love Jesus more than anything or anyone else.
   What does this say about who Jesus is?

3. What is the similarity between the man in verses 28–30 and the king in verses 31-32?

   ◉ In what way are they different?

4. What point is Jesus making with these two stories? (See verse 33.)

Pray that you will become more and more single-minded in following Jesus.

DAY THREE

◉ **Read Galatians 5:16-26**

In this letter, Paul is writing to the churches in Galatia, in modern-day Turkey. His main point in these verses is that in every Christian's life there is a conflict between the Holy Spirit and the sinful nature.

1. There is an important balance in verses 16-18. Our desires lead us in one of two directions. Our aim should be to cooperate with the Holy Spirit and feed that part of our lives – starving the sinful side of us. In what areas of your life do you feel the most conflict?

2. Look again at verses 19-21. Are there any things mentioned here which you need to turn from and ask forgiveness for?

   (Note: Some things are obvious actions but others are attitudes that are easier to hide.)

3. Verses 22 and 23 list "the fruit of the Spirit". Which qualities do you particularly need to develop?

4. Paul tells us to "keep in step" with the Spirit (verse 25).
   How can you do this, according to the verses you've just read?

Although it is important that we are aware of the areas in our lives where we need to change, it is also very important that we don't become weighed down by a sense of insurmountable guilt. Remember, God's acceptance of us is based on what *Jesus* has done, not on what *we* have done.

Thank God that "if we confess our sins, he is faithful and just and will forgive us our sins and purify us from all unrighteousness" (1 John 1:9).

DAY FOUR
Read Romans 12:1-13

This letter was written by Paul to the Christians in Rome. The "therefore" in 12:1 follows on from the first eleven chapters of Romans, which were a comprehensive explanation of the gospel. In chapter 12, Paul then lays out the practical implications the gospel should have on our lives.

1. What does verse 1 say about what worship is?

2. How is this different from simply singing hymns at church on Sunday?

3. What is the motivation for being "living sacrifices"? (See verse 1.)

4. Verse 2 suggests that our whole way of thinking should change. What will be the result of this change?

5. Verses 3–8 are about using our gifts in the church.
   In what ways are you currently doing this?

   (Note: The list Paul gives in verses 6-8 is not exhaustive.)

6. In verses 9-13 Paul tells us how Christians should behave towards one another. What are these qualities?

Verses 9-13 are very practical. Remembering God's sacrificial love for us helps us to understand how we should love and serve others in the same way.

☑ *Pray through verses 9-13, asking God to increase your "devotion" and "brotherly love" towards other Christians.*

DAY FIVE

☑ *Re-read the Bible passages you've read over the past week.*
Choose a verse that you found particularly helpful, write it down in the space below and memorize it.

DAY SIX

☑ *Read Philippians 3:1-9 in preparation for **Discipleship Explored**.*

Do you have any questions about the passages you have read this week?

The next session will start with group members being asked if they have any questions about the Bible passages they read at home.

RIGHTEOUS IN CHRIST

5

EXPLORE

- *Ask the guests to turn to Session 5 on page 43 of the Handbook.*

- *Ask if they have any questions from last session's Follow up.*

- *Ask everyone to open their Bibles at Philippians 2. A leader – or one of the group members – should read Philippians 2:19-30.*

- *Work through the questions below to help the group explore the passage.*

1. What plans for the future does Paul outline? (See verses 19, 24, 25 and compare with Philippians 1:21-24.)

To send Timothy to Philippi; to visit them himself; to send Epaphroditus back to them. Remember that Paul doesn't know whether he's going to live or die (see Philippians 1:21-24), but he still keeps on living for God, working out his salvation.

2. What do we learn about Timothy and his priorities from these verses?

Timothy has a genuine interest in other people's welfare. His character is proven; he is faithful. He has a close relationship with Paul. He is servant-hearted and works for the gospel.

3. How does Paul describe Epaphroditus? What insight do we get into Epaphroditus' attitude and motivation?

He is a "brother" (ie: a Christian); "fellow-worker" (ie: works with other Christians); "fellow-soldier" (ie: contends for the gospel). He is selfless: even when facing extreme illness and at the point of death, Epaphroditus was more concerned about how others felt when they heard he was ill than about his own illness. He "almost died for the work of Christ": he was willing even to risk his life for the sake of the gospel.

4. Why do you think Paul mentions these two men at this point in his letter? (See Philippians 2:4-5.)

Paul isn't just telling the Philippians his future plans. He wants the Philippians to learn from these two men. Both are examples of Christ-like service (the lesson Paul has been teaching in 2:1-18). Both put the interests of Christ – and therefore of others – before their own interests.

5. Paul, Timothy and Epaphroditus all demonstrated their genuine care for fellow believers. In what practical ways can we also do this?

This question is designed to help group members apply what they have learned.

LISTEN Philippians 3:1-9

(Page 45 in the group member's Handbook) Encourage the group to make notes and list questions they may have as they listen to the Bible talk or watch the DVD. There is space in the Handbook to make notes.

Note: *Discipleship Explored is based on the 1984 version of the New International Version (NIV). If you are using the 2011 revised NIV, you will find that there are a number of changes in Philippians 3:1-9.*

"We who worship by the Spirit of God, who glory in Christ Jesus" in Philippians 3:3 has been changed to "we who serve God by his Spirit, who boast in Christ Jesus". This does not change the meaning of the verse, since "worship" involves much more than praising God (sung or otherwise). We worship God by serving him wholeheartedly in every part of our lives, and we "glory in Christ" by being humble about ourselves and instead boasting about Jesus and all he has done for us.

"I consider everything a loss compared to the surpassing greatness of knowing Christ Jesus" in Philippians 3:8 has been changed to "I consider everything a loss because of the surpassing worth of knowing Christ Jesus". This does not change the meaning of the verse because when we compare our own "achievements" with what Jesus has achieved on the cross, we see that they are worth nothing and that knowing Christ is worth more than we can imagine.

"I consider everything a loss compared to the surpassing greatness of knowing Christ Jesus my Lord." (Philippians 3:8)

- Many people think we can be good enough for God – "righteous" – by doing good things.

- Paul knew that, religiously speaking, he had done everything right. But he described his achievements as "rubbish".

- Our righteousness is like rubbish compared to the righteousness of Jesus.

- Moral or religious "goodness" is nothing compared to "the surpassing greatness of knowing Christ Jesus".

- Our confidence should be in Christ. He is the only one who can make us good enough for God.

- Christ is our righteousness.

DISCUSS

📱 *(Pages 46 in the group member's Handbook) Ask your group if there was anything that stood out or particularly struck them from the talk/DVD. This will help them to respond specifically to what they have just heard, before moving on to the group discussion questions.*

1. **Paul lists his impressive religious credentials in Philippians 3:5-6. What similar things do people today think will make them right with God?**

2. **How had Paul's attitude changed and why? (See verses 7 and 8.)**

3. **What does it mean for us as Christians to "consider everything a loss"?**

4. **Verse 9 explains what "knowing" or "gaining" Christ means. How would you paraphrase verse 9 to explain it to a non-Christian friend?**

5. If we rely on ourselves, what does that show about our view of Jesus Christ?

FOLLOW UP

- *(Page 47 in the group member's Handbook) Let the group know that, as well as Philippians, they will be reading passages from Ephesians and Romans this week.*

- *The following paragraph is printed at the top of page 47 in the group member's Handbook.*

In Philippians 3:9, Paul speaks about a righteousness that comes as a gift from God and which can be ours through faith. The passages this week explore that theme.

SUNDAY

Read the passage that will be preached at the church service you attend.

On the other six days...

DAY ONE
Re-read Philippians 3:1-9

- *Think about the answers you gave to the questions in Discuss on page 46.*

- *Thank God that you have a "righteousness that comes from God and is by faith".*

DAY TWO
Read Ephesians 2:1-10

You may remember that we explored part of this passage in Follow Up after Session 1. These verses contain an overview of our salvation.

1. What was our condition before we became Christians? (See verses 1-3.)

2. Why did God do something about our condition? (See verse 4.)

3. Look at your answer to question 1. In what ways did we deserve God's love? (See also Romans 5:8.)

4. So what does Paul mean when he says in Ephesians 2:5, "It is by grace you have been saved"?

5. Why is the distinction between works (verse 9) and faith (verse 8) important to understand?

Pray that you will gain an even clearer understanding of God's grace, so that you can live in the light of it.

DAY THREE

👁 **Read Romans 3:20-26**

This is one of the most extraordinary passages in the New Testament about what God has done for us through Christ's death.

1. What does "the law" do, according to verse 20?

2. According to the same verse, what will observing the law not do?

3. The word "justification" means being declared "not guilty". How can we, who are guilty, be justified? (See verse 24.)

4. How does this demonstrate both God's justice and his love? (See verses 25-26.)

Give thanks to God for his justice and for his love, demonstrated by Jesus' death.

DAY FOUR

👁 **Read Romans 5:1-11**

In these verses Paul describes the peace and joy that come from being justified.

1. **What six statements are true of everyone who has been justified by God?**

   verse 1:

   verse 2:

   verse 2 (again):

   verse 3:

   verse 9:

   verse 11:

2. **What impact should each of these truths have on your life?**

3. **According to Paul, what should be our attitude to suffering? Why? (See verses 3-5.)**

4. **How can we be sure of God's love? (See verses 5 and 8.)**

5. **Why is the "right answer" to the question "Have you been saved?" both "Yes" and "No"? (See verses 9-10.)**

   🔲 *Thank God for the peace you have with him, his presence in your life through the Holy Spirit and the hope of future glory.*

DAY FIVE

🔲 *Re-read the Bible passages you've read over the past week. Choose a verse that you found particularly helpful, write it down in the space below and memorize it.*

DAY SIX

*Read Philippians 3:10 – 4:1 in preparation for **Discipleship Explored**.*

Do you have any questions about the passages you have read this week?

The next session will start with group members being asked if they have any questions about the Bible passages they read at home.

KNOWING CHRIST

6

EXPLORE

⊡ *Ask the guests to turn to Session 6 on page 51 of the Handbook.*

⊡ *Ask if they have any questions from last session's Follow up.*

⊡ *Ask everyone to open their Bibles at Philippians 3. A leader – or one of the group members – should read Philippians 3:1-4.*

⊡ *Work through the questions below to help the group explore the passage.*

1. Why do the Philippians need a safeguard? (See verses 1 and 2.)

They were in danger. Paul's words were vital to keep them alert and watchful for the danger of false teaching.

2. Some people were teaching that physical circumcision is necessary. Why does Paul say that Christians "are the circumcision"? (See also Romans 2:28-29.) ✓

Last week we saw that nothing we do makes us right with God. Romans 2 reminds us that it is our hearts that make us unacceptable to God – and only the Holy Spirit can change our hearts. This change is what Paul refers to as true circumcision.

3. What other marks of the true believer does Paul mention in verse 3?

Paul says that believers: "worship by the Spirit of God" (ie: that the whole of their lives are directed by the Holy Spirit); "glory in Christ Jesus" (ie: rejoice in Jesus and all that he has done for them); and "put no confidence in the flesh" (ie: don't depend on anything they have done to make them right with God).

4. Paul wanted the Philippians to put their confidence in Jesus and in nothing else. Why are Christians sometimes tempted to put their confidence in additional things?

It is often hard to trust that we can be saved and live by grace alone. Sometimes it feels more comfortable to rely on our own actions as a measure of how right we are with God.

5. What things can we be tempted to rely on in addition to our confidence in Jesus?

How often we read the Bible, how earnestly we pray, how many people we tell about Jesus, and so on.

6. What should we remember when we are tempted to place confidence in these additional things?

Philippians 3:9 may help group members to phrase an answer.

LISTEN   Philippians 3:10 – 4:1

(Page 53 in the group member's Handbook) Encourage the group to make notes and list questions they may have as they listen to the Bible talk or watch the DVD. There is space in the Handbook to make notes.

Note: Discipleship Explored is based on the 1984 version of the New International Version (NIV). If you are using the 2011 revised NIV, you will find that **"the fellowship of sharing in his sufferings"** *in Philippians 3:10 has been changed to* **"participation in his sufferings"**. *This does not change the meaning of the verse, since "participation" in Christ's sufferings when we suffer as Christians is one way that we know him better, having closer fellowship with him.*

"Been made perfect" *in Philippians 3:12 has been changed to* **"arrived at my goal"**. *Paul's goal is "to win the prize for which God has called me heavenwards in Christ Jesus" (Philippians 3:14) and to gain "the righteousness that comes from God" (Philippians 3:9) – ie: being "made perfect".*

"I want to know Christ and the power of his resurrection and the fellowship of sharing in his sufferings." (Philippians 3:10)

- Paul wanted to "know Christ" – better, more deeply, more intimately.

- To really know Christ – to walk where he walked – means following the path of suffering.

- We should hunger and thirst to know Christ better.

- We need to forget what's behind us and press on.

- Being a disciple means discipline, including prayer and reading the Bible.

- To know Christ we must be heavenly-minded Christians. "Our citizenship is in heaven."

DISCUSS

(Pages 54-55 in the group member's Handbook) Ask your group if there was anything that stood out or particularly struck them from the talk/DVD. This will help them to respond specifically to what they have just heard, before moving on to the group discussion questions.

1. **In your own words, what is the "one thing" Paul does (according to Philippians 3:12-14), and why?**

2. **From verses 12-16, what might hinder us from pressing on?**

   What should encourage us to keep pressing on?

3. **In verse 16 Paul says: "Let us live up to what we have already attained". The example of others can help us do this. Why is it important to choose the right role-models? (See verses 17-19.)**

4. **Look at the phrases in verse 19 that describe those who are "enemies of the cross of Christ". How do people behave in these ways today?**

5. What are the sharp contrasts between the descriptions in verse 19 and those in verses 20-21?

6. In the middle of daily life, what does it mean for you to know that your "citizenship is in heaven" and that Christ will return?

FOLLOW UP

📧 *(Page 56 in the group member's Handbook) Let the group know that, as well as Philippians, they will be reading three passages from Matthew this week.*

📧 *The following paragraph is printed at the top of page 56 in the group member's Handbook.*

In Philippians 3:12-14, Paul declares his determination to "press on" as a Christian. The passages this week will help you think about how you can "press on".

SUNDAY

📖 *Read the passage that will be preached at the church service you attend.*

On the other six days...

DAY ONE
👁 **Re-read Philippians 3:10 – 4:1**

📖 *Think about the answers you gave to the questions in Discuss on pages 54-55.*

📖 *Pray that you would be able to keep your focus completely on Jesus Christ.*

DAY TWO
👁 **Read Matthew 6:19-24**

These verses are part of Jesus' preaching known as the "Sermon on the Mount".

1. Jesus tells us to store up "treasures in heaven" rather than "treasures on earth". Why? (See verses 19-20.)

2. What does Jesus mean when he says: "For where your treasure is, there your heart will be also" (verse 21)?

3. How do you invest your time and energy, and what does this show about where your heart is?

4. Jesus says in verse 24 that no one can serve two masters. What competes in your life with serving Jesus?

5. What should you do about that?

Ask God to help you choose treasures that will endure through eternity.

DAY THREE

Read Matthew 6:25-34

This passage carries on from Day Two's reading.

1. What do you learn about God's love for you from verses 26 and 30?

2. According to verse 32, why shouldn't we worry about food or drink or clothing?

3. What should we do instead, according to verse 33?

4. In what practical ways can we do that?

Pray that you would be able to trust God and depend on him for everything.

DAY FOUR

👁 **Read Matthew 7:24-29**

This parable concludes the Sermon on the Mount.

1. There are two men in this parable. How are they described?

2. There is a similarity and a difference between the two householders. What are they?

3. There are two foundations in this story. What is the difference between them?

4. There are two consequences in this parable. How are they described?

5. What does the storm in verses 25 and 27 symbolize? (See also verses 13, 19 and 23.)

6. Is it enough to listen to Jesus' words? Why or why not?

Pray about the areas of your life where you need to put into practice what Jesus teaches here.

DAY FIVE

Re-read the Bible passages you've read over the past week.
Choose a verse that you found particularly helpful, write it down in the space below and memorize it.

DAY SIX

Read Philippians 4:2-9 in preparation for **Discipleship Explored**.

Do you have any questions about the passages you have read this week?

The next session will start with group members being asked if they have any questions about the Bible passages they read at home.

REJOICING IN CHRIST

7

- *Ask the guests to turn to Session 7 on page 61 of the Handbook.*

- *Ask if they have any questions from last session's Follow up.*

- *Ask everyone to open their Bibles at Philippians 3. A leader – or one of the group members – should read Philippians 3:10-11.*

- *Work through the questions below to help the group explore the passage.*

1. In verse 10, Paul says that his goal is "to know Christ". From verses 10 and 11, what is the challenge that comes from knowing Christ?

We will "share in his sufferings". Knowing Christ results in us facing suffering for the sake of Christ. Note: 1 Peter 4:12-16 may be helpful.

2. From verses 10 and 11, what comforts come from knowing Christ?

We will know "the power of his resurrection". We will also "attain to the resurrection of the dead"; in other words, when we die we will be resurrected to be with Christ. Note: see also Philippians 3:21.

3. What does Paul mean by wanting to know "the power of his resurrection"? (See also Ephesians 1:17-20.)

He wants to know the power that raised Christ from the dead in his own life. It is amazing to know that the same divine force that raised Jesus from the dead is at work in us.

4. Can you echo Paul's words in these verses? Why or why not?

This question is designed to help participants apply what they have learned.

<u>LISTEN</u> Philippians 4:2-9

📳 *(Page 63 in the group member's Handbook) Encourage the group to make notes and list questions they may have as they listen to the Bible talk or watch the DVD. There is space in the Handbook to make notes.*

📳 **Note:** *Discipleship Explored is based on the 1984 version of the New International Version (NIV). If you are using the 2011 revised NIV, you will find that **"loyal yokefellow"** in Philippians 4:3 has been changed to **"my true companion"**. This does not change the meaning of the verse, but simply uses a more modern phrase.*

"Do not be anxious about anything, but in everything, by prayer and petition, with thanksgiving, present your requests to God."
(Philippians 4:6)

▫ Christians should "stand firm *in the Lord*" (Philippians 4:1), "agree with each other *in the Lord*" (verse 2) and "rejoice *in the Lord*" (verse 4).

▫ The way to be anxious about nothing is to be prayerful about everything.

▫ The result of praying about everything with thanksgiving is that "the peace of God ... will guard your hearts and your minds in Christ Jesus".

▫ "The Lord is near" – because as a Christian, his Spirit lives in you; and because he will return soon.

▫ As Christians, we should fill our minds with excellent and praiseworthy things.

▫ If we want a life of rejoicing instead of a life of anxiety, we must put these things into practice.

DISCUSS

(Page 64 in the group member's Handbook) Ask your group if there was anything that stood out or particularly struck them from the talk/DVD. This will help them to respond specifically to what they have just heard, before moving on to the group discussion questions.

1. Do you think Paul is being unrealistic to say "Rejoice in the Lord always" (Philippians 4:4)? Why or why not?

2. When we find it hard to rejoice, what practical steps can we take to help us "rejoice always"?

3. Why will knowing that "the Lord is near" (verse 5) help us to be gentle?

4. What action should we take when we are anxious, and why? (See verses 6-7.)

5. What does it mean to pray "with thanksgiving" (verse 6)? What does this help us to guard against?

FOLLOW UP

(Page 65 in the group member's Handbook) Let the group know that, as well as Philippians, they will be reading passages from Matthew and Colossians this week.

The following sentence is printed at the top of page 65 in the group member's Handbook.

The passages this week will help you find out more about prayer.

Read the passage that will be preached at the church service you attend.

On the other six days...

DAY ONE
👁 Re-read Philippians 4:2-9

Think about the answers you gave to the questions in Discuss on page 64.

Remembering verse 6, pray about the things that make you anxious.

DAY TWO
👁 Read Matthew 6:5-15

Jesus teaches his disciples about prayer.

1. In verses 5-8, what are the contrasts between hypocritical or pagan prayer and the way Jesus says we are to pray?

2. What is Jesus emphasizing about the father-child relationship in verses 5-8?

   (Note: Notice how often Jesus uses the word "Father".)

3. We pray to our heavenly Father (verse 9). What are the first things that Jesus tells the disciples to pray? (See verses 9-10?)

   (Note: "Hallowed" means "revered" or "honoured".)

4. Why should we pray for these things first?

5. Go through the rest of the prayer phrase by phrase. What is Jesus teaching us about prayer in each phrase?

6. Look at Jesus' conclusion in verses 14 and 15.
   If our lives are not characterized by forgiveness, what does that suggest about our relationship with God?

Use Jesus' prayer as a model for your own prayer.

DAY THREE
👁 Read Colossians 1:3-14

Paul is writing from prison to the church in Colosse, in modern-day Turkey.

1. What does Paul thank God for when he prays for the Christians in Colosse? (See verses 3-4.)

2. Where does the Colossians' faith and love come from? (See verse 5.)

3. What is the main thing Paul prays for the Colossians? (See verse 9.)

4. Why does he pray for this? (See verses 10-12.)

Think of Christians you would like to pray for; then use these verses as a model for your prayers.

DAY FOUR
👁 Read Colossians 4:2-6

Here we get an insight into the prayers Paul would like prayed for him.

1. What do we learn from verse 2 about the way we should pray?

2. Given the reason that Paul is in prison (see the end of verse 3), why is Paul's request in verse 3 surprising?

3. How can verses 3 and 4 help you pray for other Christians who want to tell their friends about Jesus?

4. What advice does Paul give about how we should act towards non-Christians? (See verses 5 and 6.)

Pray for your effectiveness, and the effectiveness of others, in proclaiming the gospel.

DAY FIVE

Re-read the Bible passages you've read over the past week.
Choose a verse that you found particularly helpful, write it down in the space below and memorize it.

DAY SIX

Read Philippians 4:10-23 in preparation for **Discipleship Explored**.

Do you have any questions about the passages you have read this week?

The next session will start with group members being asked if they have any questions about the Bible passages they read at home.

CONTENT IN CHRIST

8

EXPLORE

⊡ *Ask the guests to turn to Session 8 on page 69 of the Handbook.*

⊡ *Ask if they have any questions from last session's Follow up.*

⊡ *Ask everyone to open their Bibles at Philippians 4. A leader – or one of the group members – should read Philippians 4:8-9.*

⊡ *Work through the questions below to help the group explore the passage.*

1. What should we spend our time thinking about, according to verse 8?

Whatever is true, noble, right, pure, lovely and admirable.
All of which are summarized by: "If anything is excellent or praiseworthy".

2. Write down the opposites of all the descriptive words Paul uses in verse 8.

False, depraved, wrong, tainted, ugly, shameful.

⊖ If you were to dwell on such things, what effect would it have on you?

This question aims to show that what we reflect upon has an effect on how we behave.

3. On a typical day, what things tend to preoccupy our minds?

Obvious examples include: TV, newspapers, internet, friends, films.

Note: The impact of these things may not necessarily be negative. It is a question of learning to "discern what is best" (1:10).

4. What incentive is there to do what Paul says? (See verse 9.)

If we aim to follow Paul's example (as he followed the example of Jesus; 1 Corinthians 11:1), the God of peace will be with us. When we live obedient lives we experience God's peace in our lives.

5. How will you act upon Paul's command in verse 8?

Encourage your group to think creatively and practically about what Paul means here when he talks about "excellent or praiseworthy" things. These may include – but are certainly not limited to – the glorious truths contained in God's word, the natural beauty of God's creation, godly virtues in other people, and so on.

LISTEN   Philippians 4:10-23

(Page 71 in the group member's Handbook) Encourage the group to make notes and list questions they may have as they listen to the Bible talk or watch the DVD. There is space in the Handbook to make notes.

Note: *Discipleship Explored is based on the 1984 version of the New International Version (NIV). If you are using the 2011 revised NIV, you will find that* **"saints"** *in Philippians 4:21, 22 has been changed to* **"God's people"**. *This does not change the meaning of the verse since "saints" are people who have been chosen by God. Every Christian is a saint.*

"I have learned the secret of being content in any and every situation."
(Philippians 4:12)

Many people believe that the secret of contentment is to change your circumstances.

Paul says he has learned to be content whatever the circumstances.

The source of contentment is Christ.

Paul says: "I can do everything through him who gives me strength". This means that in every circumstance God gives him the strength to be content.

We can trust God with everything: our time, money, career, family, future and life.

God will meet all our needs "according to his glorious riches in Christ Jesus".

DISCUSS

(Pages 72-73 in the group member's Handbook) Ask your group if there was anything that stood out or particularly struck them from the talk/DVD. This will help them to respond specifically to what they have just heard, before moving on to the group discussion questions.

1. **In what ways does society tempt us to be discontent?**

2. **Paul says that he has "learned the secret of being content in any and every situation". Where does Paul find true contentment, according to Philippians 4:13? (See also 4:7-9, 1:21 and 3:10-11.)**

3. **What practical steps can you take in order to be content in "any and every situation"?**

4. **What do verses 14-18 tell us about the generosity shown by the Christians in Philippi?**

5. **How should we "share in the troubles" of fellow Christians today?**

6. **Does verse 19 mean that Christians will never be in financial difficulty? Why or why not?**

7. What is encouraging about the way Paul ends his letter? (See verses 20-23.)

FOLLOW UP

📖 *(Page 74 in the group member's Handbook) Let the group know that, as well as Philippians, they will be reading passages from Hebrews, 1 Timothy and Ephesians this week.*

📖 *The following phrase is printed at the top of page 74 in the group member's Handbook.*

Paul ends his letter to the Philippians by speaking about contentment. The passages this week will help you to see how this is possible.

SUNDAY

📖 *Read the passage that will be preached at the church service you attend.*

On the other six days...

DAY ONE
👁 **Re-read Philippians 4:10-23**

📝 *Think about the answers you gave to the questions in Discuss on pages 72-73.*

📝 *Pray that you would learn to be "content in any and every situation".*

DAY TWO
👁 **Read Hebrews 4:14-16**

This short passage gives us great assurance.

1. Why should we hold "firmly" to the faith we profess (verse 14)?

2. What do you consider to be your particular weaknesses and temptations (verse 15)?

3. What should we do in times of weakness and temptation? (See verses 15-16.)

4. How will God respond if we do this? (See verse 16.)

Use your answers to these questions to help you pray.

DAY THREE
👁 Read 1 Timothy 1:12-17

Paul wrote two letters to his younger colleague, Timothy. Here Paul talks about his sense of unworthiness because he used to persecute Christians.

1. What does Paul thank Jesus for in verse 12?

2. What did Paul receive from Jesus (verse 14)?

3. Why is the "saying" in verse 15 so fundamental for Paul and for us?

4. How was Paul's life an example of God's patience? (See verses 13 and 16.)

5. How is your life an example of God's patience to those who aren't yet Christians? (See verse 16.)

6. In verse 12, Paul mentions that Jesus gave him strength. In what ways have you too received strength from Jesus?

Pray about your witness as a Christian in the places where you work and live. Ask for God's strength to live for him and to be ready to tell others about Jesus.

DAY FOUR

👁 **Read Ephesians 3:14-21**

This prayer is right in the middle of Paul's letter to the Christians in Ephesus, in Ancient Greece. In it, he prays that they would have "power".

1. **What is the first thing Paul prays for the Ephesians? (See verses 16-17a.)**

2. **What is required from the Ephesians to make this prayer effective (verse 17a)?**

3. **The Ephesians are already Christians, and therefore already have Christ living in them. So what does Paul mean when he prays that Christ would "dwell" in them?**

4. **What is the second thing Paul prays for the Ephesians? (See verses 17b-19.)**

5. **How can the "love" that Paul mentions in verse 19 be known, but at the same time "surpass knowledge"?**

6. **What is it about the end of Paul's prayer that encourages us to pray? (See verse 20.)**

Use these verses to pray for yourself and all Christians everywhere, that we would grow in our knowledge of the love of Jesus.

DAY FIVE

Re-read the Bible passages you've read over the past week. Choose a verse that you found particularly helpful, write it down in the space below and memorize it.

DAY SIX

Now that you've finished **Discipleship Explored**, spend some time writing down the things you have learned. Pray that you will be able to put them into practice.

THE WEEKS AHEAD

Don't forget to support your group members now that the course is over (see "After the course" on page 43 of this book). The following appears on page 78 of the group member's Handbook and is included here for your reference.

Paul wants the Philippians to experience "progress and joy in the faith" (Philippians 1:25). Our prayer for you is the same.

The first thing a believer must do is join a church. The local church is where Christians receive baptism and the Lord's Supper (also known as Communion or the Eucharist), showing the whole world that they belong to Jesus' kingdom now (Ephesians 3:10-11). The local church is where Christians grow in the knowledge of God's word, teaching and being taught, discipling and being discipled.

You will also want to continue your own daily Bible reading. (The book of James is a great follow-up to *Discipleship Explored*.)

"Finally ... whatever is true, whatever is noble, whatever is right, whatever is pure, whatever is lovely, whatever is admirable – if anything is excellent or praiseworthy – think about such things."

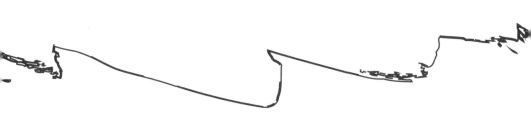

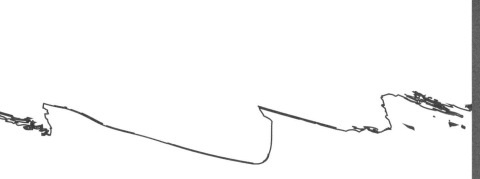

BIBLE TALKS
Preparing the talks

After the meal and the Bible study ("Explore") the course leader delivers a short talk or shows the relevant episode from the *Discipleship Explored* DVD. The talks and DVD both work their way chronologically through Philippians.

Session	Passage	Title
Session 1	Philippians 1:1-11	Confident in Christ
Session 2	Philippians 1:12-26	Living in Christ
Session 3	Philippians 1:27 – 2:11	Standing Together in Christ
Session 4	Philippians 2:12-30	Transformed by Christ
Session 5	Philippians 3:1-9	Righteous in Christ
Session 6	Philippians 3:10 – 4:1	Knowing Christ
Session 7	Philippians 4:2-9	Rejoicing in Christ
Session 8	Philippians 4:10-23	Content in Christ

The following pages give outlines for the talks.

Each week, before the talk, ask one of the leaders to read the relevant passage out loud. Then the course leader should pray and begin the talk.

The outlines give a general structure for the talk. They do not cover every aspect of the passage under discussion, but focus on points that are particularly relevant to new Christians.

Please study the passage carefully, and make these talks your own by adding your own illustrations and observations. But remember also to keep them relatively short. We recommend 20 minutes as a maximum.

1 : CONFIDENT IN CHRIST

Philippians 1:1-11

🔲 *Deliver Talk 1 using the notes below. The notes for this talk can also be downloaded from www.ceministries.org to enable you to adapt them for your group and add your own illustrations. Alternatively you could show Episode 1 (Confident in Christ) from the Discipleship Explored DVD if this would be appropriate for your group.*

🔲 *There is a bulleted talk outline on page 6 of the group member's Handbook. Encourage people to write notes next to this outline as they listen to the talk. (Note: These bullet points need to work with the DVD as well as the talk, so you may find that some of the points are in a different order.)*

Aim

🔲 To welcome people to the course.

🔲 To explain the word "disciple".

🔲 To explain that our confidence as Christians comes from the certainty that God always finishes the work he starts. But, in the meantime, if we're to maintain that confidence, we must aim to live lives that are "to the glory and praise of God" (Philippians 1:11).

Introduction

Do you enjoy jigsaw puzzles? Have you ever stared at a pile of 1000 pieces poured out on the table in front of you, and wondered where to start? I gather what you have to do is find the corner pieces first; then the pieces with straight edges; then you put them together, so that you have a square frame into which you know everything else fits. You probably still have 874 pieces to fit – but, however confusing it seems, you know they'll all fit into that square.

The same is going to be true for the questions that we have as we start *Discipleship Explored*. Even if we have 874 questions we want to ask about God, there are some things that are already in place. Paul makes this clear here in chapter 1: we know that God is sovereign and we know that he is working in us.

▨ Paul wrote this letter to the Christians ("saints in Christ Jesus") who lived at Philippi, which was the main city in Macedonia. This little group of believers were the first Europeans to respond to the good news about Jesus.

▧ *You may want to point group members to the map on page 80 of the Handbook which shows the location of Philippi and other places that will be mentioned during the course.*

▨ Paul went back to visit them several times after his first visit. But now he writes to them while under house arrest, probably in Rome, and he warns them about some serious dangers that could damage this community of young Christians.

▨ The theme of Paul's letter to the Philippians is given away in his very first sentence: he describes himself and his colleague, Timothy, as "servants of Christ" (v 1). Like the Philippians reading this letter for the first time 2000 years ago, we're going to be exploring for ourselves exactly what it means to be "servants of Christ". To be, in other words, a disciple.

1. True disciples have their confidence in God

▨ When someone becomes a Christian, we sometimes say that they have made a decision for Christ, or that someone has committed their life to God. In other words, we think that becoming a Christian is something that *we* have done.

▨ Paul sees it differently. The truth is that if you have made a response to God, it is because God has done something in you.

▨ Paul was certain that God was working in the Philippians because of their "partnership in the gospel from the first day until now" (v 5); because their lives have steadily demonstrated that the gospel has changed them. Their words, their actions, even their money (see Philippians 4:10, 15-16) had consistently revealed their love for Jesus Christ.

■ And because Paul knew God was working in them, he could also be sure that God would complete the work he started in them (v 6).

Application: You may be feeling that since becoming a Christian you keep messing up. Sometimes you may even wonder if you really are a Christian. The word "disciple" simply means "learner" – in other words, in the Christian life, we can never say that we have arrived – we will always be learning. Paul's words give us great confidence: he is saying that if God has begun a good work in you, he will finish it.

■ *Add your own illustration here: if possible, a personal illustration of how others more readily saw the change in you than you did in yourself. Point out that the Holy Spirit, because he is holy, makes us feel bad about the wrong things that we do. But being sensitized to sin, and feeling guilty, is a sign that God is at work in us, not that God has abandoned us.*

2. True disciples grow in their understanding of God

■ Paul tells the Philippian Christians that he is praying that they would have deeper knowledge and insight (v 9).

■ One of the effects of this growing knowledge of God (v 10) is that "you may be able to discern what is best". In other words, that Christians will be increasingly wise about how to live – and be able to distinguish good from bad.

■ But knowledge and understanding are not an end in themselves. God does not want us to become merely experts in theology.

■ Knowledge of God is something which gives rise to genuine, intelligent love in a Christian's life: a love for God, for his people and for others.

Application: Are we growing in our knowledge of God, so that we will be able to know what's best in our Christian lives?

3. True disciples are fruitful

■ In verse 10, Paul prays that these young Christians would be "pure" and "blameless".

■ Paul is saying that a true understanding of God will make us pure through and through.

■ But where does this goodness come from? Again, it is not from ourselves. Verse 11 tells us that this "fruit of righteousness" comes from Jesus Christ, and that it brings glory and praise to God.

Application: How "pure" are we? (Are we different on the inside than we are on the outside?) How "blameless" are we? (Do our lives make it easier or harder for other people to believe in Christ?)

Conclusion

Growing as a Christian – being a disciple – is something that comes from God, and for which God gets the glory.

Our confidence as Christians comes from the certainty that God always finishes the work he starts. But we are not just to sit around waiting for it to happen to us. The sign that God is at work in us is that we actively take steps to be disciples – to grow in the knowledge of God.

At the end of the talk

▶ *Using Paul's prayer in this passage as a guide, pray for the group.*

▶ *Introduce the questions in Discuss on pages 7-8 of the participants' Handbook.*

2: LIVING IN CHRIST

Philippians 1:12-26

⟶ *Deliver Talk 2 using the notes below. The notes for this talk can also be downloaded from www.ceministries.org to enable you to adapt them for your group and add your own illustrations. Alternatively you could show Episode 2 (Living in Christ) from the Discipleship Explored DVD if this would be appropriate for your group.*

⟶ *There is a bulleted talk outline on page 15 of the group member's Handbook. Encourage people to write notes next to this outline as they listen to the talk. (Note: These bullet points need to work with the DVD as well as the talk, so you may find that some of the points are in a different order.)*

Aim

▪ To explain that everything in Paul's life serves one aim – to "advance the gospel". Nothing – not his circumstances, nor his reputation, nor his uncertain future – is allowed to interfere with that aim. In fact, all these things are used by God to fulfill that aim.

Introduction

This is a newspaper report of a true story:

A car crashed into Gordon White's living room last week – exactly a year after the same car, driven by the same driver, crashed into the same room. Eric Williams, 60, is believed to have suffered a blackout both times, leaving the road at the same spot in Cleckheaton, West Yorkshire. It took White nine weeks to clear up the mess last time, and a full year to redecorate. "I've only just finished getting the house how

I want it," he said. "If I'd known this would happen, I would have used cheaper wallpaper."

If we know what is going to happen in the future, it changes the way we live in the present.

- Paul is writing to the Philippians from prison. His circumstances look bad.

- There are people who call themselves Christians, but who are deliberately trying to get him into trouble and ruin his reputation.

- His future looks uncertain as he doesn't know whether he is going to live or die.

- And yet Paul rejoices. Why? Because everything in Paul's life serves one aim – to "advance the gospel" – and nothing is allowed to interfere with that aim.

1. His circumstances are bad, but the gospel is advanced

- Many people who go through difficult times assume that God has abandoned them.

- Paul sees that God has not abandoned him, but has placed him where he is so that the gospel message may be advanced. What seems like a disaster is actually God at work, bringing the good news to others.

- Even though Paul is in prison, he makes use of his situation to advance the gospel.

- Not only has Paul been able to talk about Christ to the palace guard (v 13), but his example has encouraged others to be more courageous in the way they talk about Jesus (v 14).

- *Add your own illustration here: share from your own experience how something that might seem tragic or painful has brought an opportunity to advance the gospel. This is also an opportunity to remind participants of what the gospel actually is.*

Application: When somebody in an office, a school staff room, or on a college campus says something about Jesus, it encourages other Christians to say something as well. That was the effect that Paul's imprisonment had on other Christians.

Application: It would have been very easy for Paul to say: "I'll just wait until I get out of prison, then I'll be able to get on with my work for the Lord". But he doesn't do that. No matter what the circumstances, he is looking for opportunities to tell others about Jesus. It's very easy for us to think: "Well, I'll really be able to serve the Lord Jesus better when I've got the job right, when I've got my house sorted out, when my relationships are settled…". We don't wait for our lives to get just right. They never do. God will use you to advance the gospel, whatever circumstances you're in.

2. His reputation is attacked, but the gospel is advanced

- It's clear from verses 15-18 that Paul's imprisonment has provoked different reactions in the Christian community. Some understand that Paul has been put in prison "for the defence of the gospel" (v 16), but others see it as an opportunity to "stir up trouble" for him (v 17).

- Verse 18 is important. Paul says: "What does it matter?" The gospel is being preached; Paul's reputation is secondary.

Application: Following Christ may have a negative impact on your reputation. Some people may dismiss you as being "religious" or "holier than thou" or "narrow minded" or "weak". Can you say with Paul: "What does it matter?" Is the gospel so important to you that your own reputation is unimportant?

3. His future is uncertain, but the gospel is advanced

- Paul doesn't know whether he is going to live or die.

- Paul hopes that through the Philippians' prayers and with the help of the Spirit (v 19) he will have enough courage (v 20) to exalt Christ, whether he lives or dies.

- Verse 21 sums up Paul's joyful attitude to life: "To live is Christ" because he will go on preaching Christ if he lives; and "to die is gain", because if he dies, he will be with Jesus.

- So whatever happens, Jesus is the object, motive, inspiration and goal of all that Paul does.

Application: As Christians we need not fear death. For us, like Paul, death is "gain": we will be with Christ for eternity in the new heaven and the new earth.

Application: As Christians we need not fear life. Whatever happens to us, God is in control and we should make the most of the time we have to advance the gospel.

Conclusion

How would you finish Paul's sentence: "For me to live is …" What?

For Paul it is Christ. What is it for us?

At the end of the talk

📧 *Pray for the group.*

📧 *Introduce the questions in Discuss on pages 16-17 of the participants' Handbook.*

3: STANDING TOGETHER IN CHRIST

Philippians 1:27 – 2:11

▸ *Deliver Talk 3 using the notes below. The notes for this talk can also be downloaded from www.ceministries.org to enable you to adapt them for your group and add your own illustrations. Alternatively you could show Episode 3 (Standing Together in Christ) from the Discipleship Explored DVD if this would be appropriate for your group.*

▸ *There is a bulleted talk outline on page 25 of the group member's Handbook. Encourage people to write notes next to this outline as they listen to the talk. (Note: These bullet points need to work with the DVD as well as the talk, so you may find that some of the points are in a different order.)*

Aim

▪ To explain how we can conduct ourselves "in a manner worthy of the gospel" by standing firm together.

Introduction

A friend of mine told me this story. He said:

I was walking across a bridge recently. I saw this man who looked as if he was ready to jump off. "Don't jump!" I said.

"Why not?" he said. "Nobody loves me."

"God loves you," I said. "You believe in God, don't you?"

"Yes, I believe in God," he said.

"Good," I said. "What religion?"

"Christian," he said.

"Me, too!" I said. "What denomination?"

"Baptist," he said. "Me, too!" I said. "Independent Baptist or Southern Baptist?"

"Independent Baptist," he said.

"Me, too!" I said. "Moderate Independent Baptist or Conservative Independent Baptist?"

"Conservative Independent Baptist," he said. "Me, too!" I said. "Calvinistic Conservative Independent Baptist or Arminian Conservative Independent Baptist?"

"Calvinistic Conservative Independent Baptist," he said.

"Me, too!" I said. "Dispensational Premillennial Calvinistic Conservative Independent Baptist or Historical Premillennial Calvinistic Conservative Independent Baptist?"

"Dispensational Premillennial Calvinistic Conservative Independent Baptist," he said.

"Dispensational?" I said, and pushed him off.

Some disagreements can be incredibly petty, can't they? By contrast, look at what Paul says in verse 27: "Stand firm in one spirit, contending as one man for the faith of the gospel".

Standing together

- "For it has been granted to you on behalf of Christ not only to believe on him, but also to suffer for him" (v 29). If suffering is to be the normal experience of the Christian, how are we to conduct ourselves "in a manner worthy of the gospel", as Paul says we should in verse 27?

- Paul insists that the only way to do it is by standing firm "in one spirit" and "as one man" – in other words, by standing firm together. He calls for unity again in chapter 2 verse 2: "Make my joy complete by being like-minded, having the same love, being one in spirit and purpose".

- Why is it so important to stand together? Because it will enable these young Christians to stand without fear ("without being frightened in any way by those who oppose you"). This in itself will be a powerful sign to their opponents that God is on their side (v 28).

■ How exactly can we stand together in this way? After all, if we're being honest and realistic about human relationships, we know that it is very difficult to be "one in spirit and purpose" with anyone!

■ The secret of standing together is revealed in verse 5: "Your attitude should be the same as that of Christ Jesus".

■ That means: considering others better than ourselves; setting privilege aside; and becoming like servants.

1. We should consider others better than ourselves (v 3-4)

■ We must not think of ourselves more highly than we ought, and we must not think of others as less important.

■ We must remember that everyone we meet has great value. They are made in the image of God, and Christ died for them.

■ God calls people from every nation to follow him. God's new community is supernatural. Unlike human communities, it crosses all boundaries of race, class, income, education and geography.

Application: Do we treat people with the same care Jesus did? Are we guilty of any sort of prejudice against other Christians?

2. We should set privilege aside (v 6-7)

■ This wonderful poem in verses 6-11 reminds us of Jesus' **Identity** as God and man (v 6-8), his **Mission** to die on the cross (v 8), and his **Call** that people follow him as Lord (v 10–11).

■ *Note: Identity, Mission and Call is the structure used in Christianity Explored, so will be familiar to any group members who have done that course.*

■ Jesus is "in very nature God", and yet he deliberately "made himself nothing". He did not consider it worthwhile to stand up for his "rights", as he could have done.

■ *Add your own illustration here about "rights" that might be better laid aside for the sake of Christ and the gospel (eg: the right to take a holiday every year, to own certain possessions, to get married.)*

Application: Are we willing to make ourselves nothing so that we can stand together in Christ?

3. We should become like servants (v 7-8)

■ Literally, the word in verse 7 means "slave". Jesus made himself like a slave, even to the extent of dying for others.

Application: Are we prepared to serve others, even if it costs us dearly?

Conclusion

Paul ends in verses 9-11 with a stunning image of the whole universe "together in Christ", worshipping the Lord.

If we keep this image of the exalted Christ in mind, our attitude will become more like his and we will be better able to stand as one man and in one spirit for the gospel.

At the end of the talk

■ *Pray for the group.*

■ *Introduce the questions in Discuss on pages 26-27 of the participants' Handbook.*

4: TRANSFORMED BY CHRIST
Philippians 2:12-30

⚙ Deliver Talk 4 using the notes below. The notes for this talk can also be downloaded from www.ceministries.org to enable you to adapt them for your group and add your own illustrations. Alternatively you could show Episode 4 (Transformed by Christ) from the Discipleship Explored DVD if this would be appropriate for your group.

⚙ There is a bulleted talk outline on page 35 of the group member's Handbook. Encourage people to write notes next to this outline as they listen to the talk. (Note: These bullet points need to work with the DVD as well as the talk, so you may find that some of the points are in a different order.)

Aim

▦ To explore what it means for people to "work out" their salvation and "hold out the word of life".

Introduction

⚙ *Remind participants of what they've learned in previous weeks.*

▦ Last week, Paul gave us a striking picture of Christ (Philippians 2:6-11). And here, in verses 12-30, Paul tells the Philippians that they are to be transformed by that picture of radical self-sacrifice.

▦ He urges them to do two things. First: "work out your salvation", and second: "hold out the word of life".

▦ Then he gives us a brief portrait of two men who've done just that.

1. Work out your salvation (v 12-13)

▣ "Continue to work out your salvation with fear and trembling..." (v 12). Notice that Paul doesn't say "work for" your salvation. He says "work out" your salvation, which means that our salvation should display itself outwardly. It should have a visible, tangible effect on our lives.

▣ We are able to "work out" our salvation because "it is God who works in [us] to will and to act according to his good purpose" (v 13). We work out our salvation because God works in us. He helps us to do the things he calls us to do.

▣ *Give an example of a Christian you know who was empowered by God to "will and to act according to his good purpose".*

Application: Are we testing the promise in verse 13 for ourselves by "working out our salvation", even if we don't feel we're able?

Application: Did you notice that Paul says they will need to obey God "not only in [Paul's] presence" but also in his absence (v 12)? How good are we at obedience when we are away from church, during the week, in the home or workplace?

2. Hold out the word of life (v 14-18)

▣ In verse 16, Paul assumes that the Philippians will "hold out the word of life" (the Greek literally means "hold forth" or "offer"). This means they will be sharing the gospel with their lives and their lips.

▣ The strength of our witness to others depends upon us doing "everything without complaining or arguing", being "blameless and pure" (v 14-15). Do we sometimes give people a reason to ignore our witness because our lives are not "blameless"?

▣ *Give some examples of how this happens. You may want to use this illustration: One person I heard of used to go on business trips with married men who called themselves Christians. And he said that he watched these men going from the brothel on Saturday night to church on Sunday morning. And what he said was: "I did not go to the brothel with them, and I didn't go to church with them either."*

132

- If we do live "blameless and pure" lives, then we will "shine like stars" in what Paul calls "a crooked and depraved generation" (v 15).

Application: How much do we really stand out from others who are not "children of God" (v 15)? And if we do stand out, is it for the right reasons? Is it because we're holding out the word of life and living "blameless" lives?

3. Two people transformed by Christ (v 19-30)

- Next, Paul gives us a glimpse of two people who've been transformed by Christ in just this way: Timothy and Epaphroditus.

- *You may want to use this illustration: It can be very difficult writing job references for people, especially if they've not been very good employees. You're desperately trying to write the truth without being too hurtful. One of my favourite references for a departing employee was this one: "I am sure he will join your company as he leaves ours: fired with enthusiasm." Or what about this one: "You will be very fortunate if you can get this man to work for you."*

- Timothy and Epaphroditus worked with Paul for some time. Let me read you Paul's job references for them.

Read aloud Paul's description of Timothy (Philippians 2:19-24)

- Timothy's interests are the interests "of Jesus Christ" (v 21). That means taking "a genuine interest" in the welfare of others (v 19), and serving together "in the work of the gospel" (v 22).

Read aloud Paul's description of Epaphroditus (Philippians 2:25-30)

- How might we speak of a Christian friend who had nearly burned themselves out in their efforts for the gospel? Perhaps we'd say they were naive, careless, or even stupid. How does Paul describe Epaphroditus, a man who "almost died for the work of Christ" (v 30)? "Welcome him in the Lord with great joy, and honour men like him" (v 29).

Conclusion

When others look at our lives, do they see people like the ones Paul mentions in verse 21, those who look out for their own interests? Or do they see people like Timothy and Epaphroditus, whose self-sacrificial lives have been radically transformed by Christ?

At the end of the talk

▣ *Pray for the group.*

▣ *Introduce the questions in Discuss on pages 36-37 of the participants' Handbook.*

5: RIGHTEOUS IN CHRIST

Philippians 3:1-9

📧 Deliver Talk 5 using the notes below. The notes for this talk can also be downloaded from www.ceministries.org to enable you to adapt them for your group and add your own illustrations. Alternatively you could show Episode 5 (Righteous in Christ) from the Discipleship Explored DVD if this would be appropriate for your group.

📧 There is a bulleted talk outline on page 45 of the group member's Handbook. Encourage people to write notes next to this outline as they listen to the talk. (Note: These bullet points need to work with the DVD as well as the talk, so you may find that some of the points are in a different order.)

Aim

▨ To explain that we relate to God not by religion or "right living", but by the righteousness that Christ gives us as a free gift.

Introduction

Everyone at work was very impressed with John Henderson. He was always in the office early. He worked right through his lunch hour and stayed late. He never stopped working throughout the day – always on the phone, or madly typing into his computer.

So it was a shock when he was eventually fired. It seems that he had been doing none of the work that the company had allocated to him. He had simply been running his own business from his desk in the office.

- How can anyone be good enough for God? Or, as the Bible puts it, how can we be "righteous"?

- For some people, the answer to that question lies in "doing good things", whether it be giving to charity, going to church, treating others in the way they like to be treated themselves, and so on.

- To the people Paul describes in verse 2, the answer lies in the practice of circumcision. They believed that God would only accept them if they had this physical mark of allegiance to him.

1. Our religion cannot make us righteous

- Paul knew that these men would undermine the joy he talks about in verse 1, so he warns the Philippians about them again as "a safeguard". In the original Greek, the phrase "watch out for" (v 2) is repeated three times for emphasis.

- In verses 2 and 3, Paul deliberately turns the accusations of these men ("dogs... men who do evil... mutilators of the flesh") back on his accusers:

  - The term "dogs" is particularly potent. Dogs were considered by the Jews to be unclean animals, so this term was sometimes applied to Gentiles and to lapsed Jews. In other words, "dogs" are those outside the covenant relationship with God. But, says Paul in verse 2, it is those who insist on circumcision who are the real "dogs".

  - "Men who do evil" is literally "evil workers". These men were proud of their good "works". You may be performing works, says Paul with biting irony, but they're evil works, not good works.

  - "Mutilators" refers to circumcision. But rather than using the proper Greek word *peritome*, Paul uses the Greek word *katatome*, which means "cutting". This is a mutilation of the body which is specifically condemned as a pagan practice in the Old Testament (see Leviticus 21:5 and 1 Kings 18:28). Paul only uses the word *peritome* in verse 3, when he is speaking about Christians.

- Paul's words are scathing and clear. These teachers are outside the covenant, are evil, and are no better than pagans in their religious practice.

Application: We can be tempted to put our trust in things which will do us no good. It may be our church attendance, the fact that our family has been Christian for generations, or our national heritage. God is interested in none of these things.

In fact, quite the reverse. Some of those who are most distant from God are the ones who are most "religious".

⟹ *You may want to use an illustration here. For example, being born in a garage does not make you a car; it was the religious people who opposed and finally killed Jesus; even the devil believes the truth about God – but he remains God's enemy.*

2. Our "goodness" cannot make us righteous

▣ Paul argues his case by setting out his own "reasons to put confidence in the flesh" (v 4). His pedigree is impeccable. If anyone had grounds for getting right with God on the basis of his religion, it was Paul.

▣ But he adds another element: "As for legalistic righteousness, faultless". In other words, if anyone could be justified by doing "good things", Paul was the man.

▣ Paul says all these religious credentials are "rubbish" (literally, "filthy muck") compared with knowing Jesus and the righteousness that comes through faith in him (v 7-9).

Application: Are we putting our trust in our own goodness? We may be generous, kind and willing to help others, but these things cannot make us righteous. Do you think God would have sent his only Son to die if we could get right with him by doing good things?

3. Only Jesus can make us righteous

▣ So, how will we live? There are really only two choices:

– We can go the way of people who put "confidence in the flesh" (v 4). We can do what Paul used to do: we can try to summon up a righteousness of our own by being extremely religious, by doing as many good things as we possibly can in the hope that – at the end of the day – God will be impressed by what we've done.

– Or, like Paul, we can refuse to place any confidence in the things we've done. We can realize that we'll never be "righteous" by our own effort. We can gladly accept the righteousness that God freely offers us in Christ, trusting in him to make us righteous.

Conclusion

Where are you placing your trust now? If God were to say to you: "Why should I let you into heaven?" what would you say?

At the end of the talk

🔲 *Pray for the group.*

🔲 *Introduce the questions in Discuss on page 46 of the participants' Handbook.*

6: KNOWING CHRIST

↓ main focus

Philippians 3:10 – 4:1

6

⊡ *Deliver Talk 6 using the notes below. The notes for this talk can also be downloaded from www.ceministries.org to enable you to adapt them for your group and add your own illustrations. Alternatively you could show Episode 6 (Knowing Christ) from the Discipleship Explored DVD if this would be appropriate for your group.*

⊡ *There is a bulleted talk outline on page 53 of the group member's Handbook. Encourage people to write notes next to this outline as they listen to the talk. (Note: These bullet points need to work with the DVD as well as the talk, so you may find that some of the points are in a different order.)*

Aim

▣ To explain how we can know Christ.

Introduction

It's June 1944, and the American, British, Canadian and French allies have landed on the beaches of Normandy. In the east, Hitler's armies are fighting a losing battle against the Russians, the Luftwaffe has been destroyed, the German army is crumbling. Everyone knows that the victory is won, and that it will not be long before the war is over. So do they sit around and do nothing? Not at all. There are still hard months of military campaigning to go.

▣ Last week, we saw that Paul has no confidence in his own religious "goodness". Instead, he wants "the righteousness that comes from God and is by faith" in Jesus Christ. That is the only way that any of us can be accepted by God: because of his goodness, not ours.

● But once we've put our trust in Christ, is that it? Do we just sit back, secure in the knowledge that God accepts us?

● Not according to Paul. His desire is "to know Christ" (v 10). The word "know" here doesn't just mean "to be acquainted with"; it means "to become like". We can see that from the way Paul continues: "I want to know Christ and the power of his resurrection and the fellowship of sharing in his sufferings, becoming like him in his death"

● So how can we "know Christ" in this way? Paul gives us four pointers.

1. To "know Christ" we must realize we are not the finished article

● Even Paul, arguably the greatest Christian who ever lived, never claims to be perfect (v 12-13: "Not that I have already obtained all this, or have already been made perfect... I do not consider myself yet to have taken hold of it...").

Application: Beware of any Christian – or any teaching – that says you can be a perfect Christian here and now. We should be satisfied with Christ, but dissatisfied with the imperfection of our Christian life. Paul's dissatisfaction with his own Christian life drives him to know Christ better.

■ *Add your own personal illustration here. Think of a time when God showed you that you still had a lot to learn.*

2. To "know Christ" we must be single-minded

● There is "one thing I do", says Paul (v 13). He forgets "what is behind" and strains towards "what is ahead".

Application: There are two dangers when we look back at our past. We can either become paralysed by regret because of past experiences; or we can become complacent if we rest on past triumphs. But Paul refuses to allow his past to catch up with him like that. He stays focused on "what is ahead".

3. To "know Christ" we must be disciplined

Paul speaks in very physical, strenuous language, as if he's an athlete training for the Olympics (v 12-14: "I press on... straining towards what is ahead... I press on towards the goal...").

There's no concept of "let go and let God" with Paul. No "stop trying and start trusting" (though, of course, Paul knows it's not all about our effort). He knows that if he wants to know Christ, if he wants to become like him, it will require continuous effort.

Application: Have you found it difficult to set aside the time to do your daily Bible reading? Have other things got in the way of being at church or *Discipleship Explored*? We need to be convinced that knowing Christ is the most important thing, if we are to be strong enough to turn off the TV and open our Bibles.

4. To "know Christ" we must set our hearts on heaven

Verses 18 and 19 describe those who live as "enemies of the cross of Christ". "Their mind is on earthly things"; in other words, they can't see beyond the here and now, and they only live for the present moment. But, says Paul, "our citizenship is in heaven" (v 20).

To know Christ, we must understand that heaven is our home. We are called "heavenwards" (v 14), we belong there (v 20), our Saviour will return from there (v 20), and he will transform "our lowly bodies" (v 21) into glorious bodies that will spend eternity there. Keeping that heavenly perspective, says Paul, is "how you should stand firm in the Lord" (Philippians 4:1).

You may want to use this illustration: Supposing we decide that our country is no longer worth living in, and we become convinced that Peru is the place to be. We receive our Peruvian citizenship, but must wait six months before we move there. What will we do in the meantime? We will not spend our time building up our attachment to our old country – extending our home, buying things that we will have to leave behind when we move, forming relationships that have no future. We will spend time getting ready to live in our new country – learning the language, the customs, the national anthem, the history. And we will think about and talk to each other about how marvellous it will be when we move there.

Conclusion

Knowing Christ should change the way we look at everything – our homes, our work, our relationships, what we spend our money on, what we give our time to.

At the end of the talk

🔲 *Pray for the group.*

🔲 *Introduce the questions in Discuss on pages 54-55 of the participants' Handbook.*

7: REJOICING IN CHRIST

Philippians 4:2-9

Deliver Talk 7 using the notes below. The notes for this talk can also be downloaded from www.ceministries.org to enable you to adapt them for your group and add your own illustrations. Alternatively you could show Episode 7 (Rejoicing in Christ) from the Discipleship Explored DVD if this would be appropriate for your group.

There is a bulleted talk outline on page 63 of the group member's Handbook. Encourage people to write notes next to this outline as they listen to the talk. (Note: These bullet points need to work with the DVD as well as the talk, so you may find that some of the points are in a different order.)

Aim

To explain that, because of Christ, it is possible to be joyful, even when circumstances are difficult.

Introduction

British holidaymakers love to feel anxious. Among the list of unusual complaints revealed by top British tour operators was the following: "No one told us there'd be fish in the sea. The children were startled." One complainant groused that there were too many Spaniards in Spain, another that there wasn't any air-conditioning outside, and a third said this: "It took us nine hours to fly to Jamaica from England. It only took the Americans three hours."

Is it possible to be joyful when circumstances are difficult? Is it possible to rejoice, if, for example, our relationships break down (like Euodia and Syntyche in 4:2) or we face persecution (like the Philippian church in 1:29)? Is it possible to be joyful even if our freedom is taken from us, as is the case with Paul?

Amazingly, that's exactly what Paul commands in chapter 4 verse 4: "Rejoice in the Lord always. I will say it again: Rejoice!" Humanly speaking, such joy is unrealistic. But that phrase "in the Lord" helps us to understand how this joy is possible even in difficult circumstances.

1. Problems must be resolved (v 2-3)

In Philippians 4:2-3, we read about two women, Euodia and Syntyche, who have fallen out over some matter. It's not as if they're not Christians – Paul says that their names "are in the book of life". But something has driven a wedge between them, despite the fact that they have worked hard together at Paul's side "in the cause of the gospel".

Paul pleads with them to "agree with each other in the Lord". His words echo what he has already said in chapter 2, verses 3-5: "Consider others better than yourselves ... Your attitude should be the same as that of Christ Jesus". In other words, this problem will only be resolved, and joy will only be restored, if both women are prepared to adopt the attitude of Jesus: taking the initiative, making themselves humble, serving others – even if such actions come at great personal cost.

Application: If we're "in the Lord", we must take the initiative, swallow our pride and be reconciled to those we've fallen out with. And Christians should help other Christians to reconcile.

2. Perspective must be regained (v 4-5)

In verse 5, Paul puts things into perspective by reminding us that: "The Lord is near". The Lord is near because he will return soon, at a time no one will expect him, and draw life as we know it to a close.

But the Lord is near in another sense too. His Spirit lives in us, if we're Christian, and his presence reminds us that "our citizenship is in heaven" (Philippians 3:20). It is that intimacy with the Lord that enables our "gentleness [to] be evident to all" (v 5) and, again, to "rejoice" (v 4).

Application: Because we know that the Lord will return, we must be gentle with everyone. The presence of his Holy Spirit in us will help us to do that.

3. Anxiety must be removed (v 6-7)

- The antidote to anxiety, says Paul, is prayer. "Do not be anxious about anything," he says, "but in everything, by prayer and petition, with thanksgiving, present your requests to God" (v 6).

- Our anxiety is removed because as we pray, we are reminded of all the blessings we have in Christ – not least the fact that we are able to pray to God!

- As we offer our requests and our thanks, "the peace of God, which transcends all understanding, will guard your hearts and your minds in Christ Jesus" (v 7).

- It's an amazing promise: not that God will take away difficult circumstances, but that "the peace of God" protects us from anxiety and worry even in difficult circumstances.

Application: If we often feel anxious and imagine that God is far from us, is it because we are spending so little time with him in grateful prayer?

4. Our minds must be pure (v 8-9)

- Paul leaves us with a challenge in verses 8-9 – a challenge to the way we use our minds. After all, we know that what we put into our bodies has a big impact on our physical health. How careful are we about what we put into our minds?

- Paul says in verses 8-9 that we must set our minds on things that are true, noble, right, pure, lovely, admirable, excellent and praiseworthy. That in itself will have a huge impact on our ability to rejoice in difficult circumstances (because if we put these things into practice, "the God of peace will be with you" – verse 9).

Application: How accurately does verse 8 describe the things we put into our minds?

Conclusion

Rejoicing in Christ is not something that comes naturally – we have to work at it!

At the end of the talk

⟶ *Pray for the group.*

⟶ *Introduce the questions in Discuss on page 64 of the participants'*
  Handbook.

8: CONTENT IN CHRIST

Philippians 4:10-23

🔲 *Deliver Talk 8 using the notes below. The notes for this talk can also be downloaded from www.ceministries.org to enable you to adapt them for your group and add your own illustrations. Alternatively you could show Episode 8 (Content in Christ) from the Discipleship Explored DVD if this would be appropriate for your group.*

🔲 *There is a bulleted talk outline on page 71 of the group member's Handbook. Encourage people to write notes next to this outline as they listen to the talk. (Note: These bullet points need to work with the DVD as well as the talk, so you may find that some of the points are in a different order.)*

Aim

🔲 To explain that contentment and generosity are marks of a true disciple.

Introduction

There was an article in the British newspaper *The Independent on Sunday* called "The experts' guide to a happy life". Various people tell you how you can be content. Diane, a beautician from Cardiff says: "One thing I'd like to say to make people happy is that women are all hairier than you think. You are not alone." Nicholas, a lawyer from London, says: "If you're looking to live a smooth, sorted financial life, then you've got to open your post. The type of person who is going to go bankrupt will be very good at denial. They're often charming people who are used to getting away with things. If you want to be happy, don't marry one of these people." Vic, a concierge from London, says: "Never do anything embarrassing in a lift."

"I have learned to be content whatever the circumstances," says Paul in chapter 4 verse 11. Are we able to say the same thing?

The word "content" in Philippians 4 literally means "complete". So Paul is saying that he doesn't get his sense of completeness from the things he owns, the food he eats, the job he does, the place he lives or the friends he has.

He says it again in verse 12: "I have learned the secret of being content in any and every situation". In this final passage of Philippians, Paul reveals the secret of contentment.

1. We can be confident in God's power

"I can do everything through him who gives me strength", says Paul in verse 13.

The whole of Paul's letter sings with this confidence in God's power: "He who began a good work in you will carry it on to completion" (1:6); "I am confident in the Lord" (2:24); "If on some point you think differently, that too God will make clear to you" (3:15); "[The Lord Jesus] will transform our lowly bodies so that they will be like his glorious body" (3:21); "The peace of God ... will guard your hearts and your minds in Christ Jesus" (4:7); and so on.

Application: We need to have that confidence too, if we're to be content in every situation.

Put a personal illustration here, perhaps about a time when you placed too much confidence in yourself, and failed.

2. We can be confident in God's provision

As we saw in chapter 3, Paul encourages us to be discontented with our knowledge and experience of God (3:12). Here, on the other hand, he implies that we should be thoroughly content with whatever God – in his loving wisdom – gives us.

Whether we are wealthy or lack material things; whether we are healthy or face debilitating illness; whether we are single or married; whether we live in a free country, or suffer in chains like Paul – we must remain confident of one thing: God will meet all our needs "according to his glorious riches in Christ Jesus" (v 19).

Application: This is not a guarantee that God will make us healthy, wealthy and popular, but it is a guarantee that he will meet all our needs.

🔁 *Illustrate this with a testimony from your own life, or from someone known to you.*

▨ Paul demonstrates this confidence in his attitude to the gifts the Philippians have sent him.

▨ He is delighted that the Philippians have sent him a gift (v 10), and he is extremely grateful for the repeated and self-sacrificial giving that has characterized their Christian lives (v 15-16). He describes what they've done as "a fragrant offering, an acceptable sacrifice, pleasing to God" (v 18).

▨ But even so, Paul doesn't depend upon their gifts to make him content. Far from it! As he says himself in verse 11: "I am not saying this because I am in need, for I have learned to be content whatever the circumstances". He is content because he knows that – whatever happens – God will meet all his needs.

Application: We need that confidence too, if we're to be content. We need to be confident in God's power, and confident in God's provision. That's the example Paul sets.

Conclusion

Here we are at the end of this letter and the end of *Discipleship Explored*. Paul has taught us many things:

▨ to remember that God always finishes the work he starts

▨ to contend for the gospel

▨ to look to the interests of others

▨ to show our salvation in the way we live

▨ to remember that only Christ can make us righteous

▨ to set our hearts on heaven

▨ to rejoice in the Lord

▨ to be content in all circumstances

149

And to do all these things for the glory of God (v 20).

And did you notice what Paul wrote in verse 22? He says: "All the saints send you greetings, especially those who belong to Caesar's household". Even though Paul has been taken captive in the Roman empire at Caesar's pleasure, he reminds us that even Caesar's household has been taken captive by the glorious gospel of Jesus Christ.

At the end of the talk

▶ *Pray for the group.*

▶ *Introduce the questions in Discuss on pages 72-73 of the participants' Handbook.*

Answering tough questions

OPEN TO QUESTION

One of the most important aspects of running a course like *Discipleship Explored* is that it encourages guests to ask questions in an environment where they will be taken seriously, and not be ridiculed or belittled. You should encourage your group with words like: "No question is too simple, or too difficult – *Discipleship Explored* is about you finding answers to the important questions about living as a Christian."

It is this atmosphere of open enquiry that encourages people to "open up" about spiritual things, and to approach the Bible not as a dead textbook, but as the source for answers. It is your job to help create this environment by your openness, honesty and willingness to talk in a relaxed way about things that group members may find particularly difficult to articulate.

WHY PEOPLE DON'T ASK QUESTIONS

There are a number of reasons why people won't ask questions:

- **Because they don't have any!** Some guests may not have thought much about spiritual things. It may be they grew up in a Christian home, and didn't question the things they have always been taught. However the word of God often provokes reactions and questions. So in the course of reading Philippians, they are likely to come up with some. And if they are part of a larger group that is dealing with questions, then they will be encouraged to join in. Don't force the issue – let them develop in their own time.

- **Because they are frightened of appearing stupid.** This is a BIG issue for many people. If they think the question is simple, or that they will be belittled by others for asking it, then they will not speak up. The key here is to make sure you keep repeating the words: "No question is too simple, or too difficult – *Discipleship Explored* is about you finding answers to the important questions about living as a Christian."

- **Because they are shy.** Some people just aren't good at speaking up in groups. And that is fine. Just make sure that you are able to talk with them personally about their questions. Watch out for the tell-tale signs of a wrinkled forehead as they read or listen.

- **Because they need time.** Some people just need more time to get to the question. They may think of something later that evening or during the next week. So you should always give an opportunity to deal with questions from the previous session that have occurred to people, and don't make them feel that everyone is taking a step backwards because "all that was dealt with last time".

WHY DO PEOPLE ASK QUESTIONS?

It might seem obvious: "Because they want to know the answer" – but it often runs much deeper than that:

- **Because I want to test you.** The precise question they ask may not be of particular concern to them. It could just be that they have heard it expressed by others, or know that it is a tricky question for Christians to answer. What they are more interested in is how you handle it (*see below*). By not being rattled, and by taking the question seriously and demonstrating that you have given it some thought, you are answering "the question behind the question", which is: "Are these people trustworthy?" Always take questions seriously.

- **Because I genuinely don't understand.** There may be a huge variation in Bible knowledge in your group, and some will want to ask what you might consider to be really basic questions: "Who was Jesus?", "When did all this happen?", "What is prayer?" etc. Again, treat them seriously, and make sure the rest of the group do not look down on those with less knowledge than they have.

- **Because I have had a distressing personal experience.** There is a world of difference between someone asking: "Why does God allow suffering?" as an academic question, and someone who asks the same question having watched a close relative die of cancer recently. The way you answer the two may be completely different. And of course, you will not know if others listening in to your answer are carrying a burden of disappointment or personal pain. Always answer compassionately.

- **Because I have been let down.** The way a question is phrased may be the key to getting an insight here. So instead of "What is prayer?", asking "Why does God answer some prayers and not others?" may indicate that the questioner

154

has some specific disappointment in mind. Similarly, a question about Christians being hypocrites may relate to some bitter personal experience of a Christian or a church in the past. Always answer honestly.

■ **Because I want to be sure it all makes sense.** The interest in a particular question may not be because it is a problem, but rather that they are seeking a sense that the Christian faith as a whole sticks together coherently. So answering in a way that connects the question with the big picture of the Bible's message is important. Answer from the Bible, not just from sensible reasons or philosophy.

HOW DO I ANSWER?

The following two appendices give you some suggested approaches to answering the substance of the difficult questions that people ask. But, as we have suggested above, it is equally important that we answer in the right way. 1 Peter 3:15-16 says:

> "But in your hearts set apart Christ as Lord[1]. Always be prepared[2] to give an answer to everyone who asks you to give the reason[3] for the hope that you have. But do this with gentleness and respect.[4]"

Notice four things about giving answers:

1. **The person who answers the questions needs to be someone who is personally committed to the lordship of Christ.** This is important, because the answer to their unspoken questions is not your arguments or knowledge – it is your life. Many of their most important questions will remain unarticulated, like: "Is this relevant to me?", "What does this look like in a real person?" and "Can I live as a Christian?" All these questions are answered by the way you live and model being a disciple and follower of Jesus. Are you displaying the joy, peace, love and contentment in life that comes from knowing Christ as Lord? If you come to *Discipleship Explored* feeling resentful, angry and doubtful in your own standing with God, then you cannot hope to influence your group members for the gospel. They may hear convincing arguments from your mouth, but your life will speak much more loudly.

2. **You must be ready to answer.** Take time to think through the answers on the following pages, and come to your own conclusion about them. You should be as sure in your answer as the Bible is – no less, no more! For example, on the questions of the origin of evil, or the reason for suffering, we do not have final

and complete answers from the Bible, and therefore, we must be careful in what we say and acknowledge our difficulty with these issues, rather than insisting that we have it all sewn up.

3. **You must have a reasonable answer.** In other words, saying: "Just have faith in the Bible" is not enough. Even if we cannot prove it with complete certainty, we have to show the reasonableness of our faith.

4. **You must answer gently and respectfully.** Even (perhaps especially) when people are hostile, we must model kindness, love and fairness in our attitudes, thinking and speaking.

MORE TIPS ON ANSWERING QUESTIONS

Involve the group. Resist the temptation to answer the question on your own. It is good practice to first ask: "Does anyone else find this a difficult question?" You can then address your answers to the whole group. It may also be that you have mature Christians in your group who will be able to help answer. So you might ask: "Has anyone in the group got an answer to that?" In this way you are also training and encouraging other Christians to get involved in the discussion. It has been the experience on many *Discipleship Explored* courses that involving the group in answering questions often helps any "not-yet-Christians" or "not-sure-if-they're-Christians" start to see the wrong thinking in some of their doubts as they start to argue back with a questioner!

Go to the Bible. The Bible is the sword of the Spirit, so we must have confidence that if we direct people to its answers, God will do his work through it. If you can, go to a Bible passage to read and then explain, especially if it is in Philippians.

Empathize. Don't give the impression that you have everything figured out. If you have wrestled with this question in the past – tell them. If you still have areas that you wrestle with, say so, but also tell them why it is no longer a problem in the larger scheme of your faith. For example: "I find suffering (eg: a natural disaster such as a major earthquake) very difficult to understand, but I know that God weeps over it too and cares, because he sent Jesus into the world, and he has experienced the pain and suffering of our broken world".

- **Give them time.** Don't assume that they will sort out everything right at that moment. Many of the ideas and arguments and thoughts from the Bible will take time to sink in and be processed. Leave the question open for another day, and encourage them to think about it seriously over the next week, eg: "There are some big things to think about there, and you might not feel this discussion has answered all your questions immediately, but can I ask you to think about it, and maybe we can return to it next time if you want to go into it in more depth."

And finally...

Don't be afraid to admit that you don't know the answer to a question. But do promise to find out before the next session.

You will find help in answering questions in the next two appendices (starting on pages 159 and 165). In addition, **www.christianityexplored.org** includes video clips giving answers to popular questions.

Questions from Philippians

the world. The Bible makes it clear that this day will certainly come, but that we do not know when it will be (Matthew 24:36-44).

PHILIPPIANS 1:1

Why does Paul call Jesus "Christ Jesus", not "Jesus Christ"?

These two phrases mean the same thing. "Christ" is not Jesus' surname; it is his title. "Christ" is a Greek word meaning "the anointed one". (The same word in the Hebrew language is "Messiah".) "Jesus" means "God saves". Paul uses the phrase "Christ Jesus" a lot in Philippians.

PHILIPPIANS 1:5

What does Paul mean by "partnership in the gospel"?

Paul is encouraged by their support. As well as the obvious support of prayer and personal encouragement, this partnership was also very practical:

- **Acts 16** Lydia, the first convert in Philippi, opened her home to Paul and Timothy.

- **Philippians 2:25** They had sent one of their members – Epaphroditus – to look after Paul's needs.

- **Philippians 4:15-18** They were the only church that had sent Paul money and gifts to support him.

PHILIPPIANS 1:6

What is "the day of Christ Jesus"?

"The day of Christ Jesus" (v 6) and "the day of Christ" (v 10) both mean the day when Christ will return to judge

PHILIPPIANS 1:11

What does "righteousness" mean?

One simple way to explain this is to say that being righteous means being "good enough for God", or having a "right standing with God". It is important to understand the difference between two kinds of righteousness:

1. Jesus shares his righteousness with Christians. Jesus is the only human who ever lived a truly righteous life. When you become a Christian, Christ gives you his righteousness. In other words, God looks at us and sees the goodness and purity of his Son. This means he can accept us, and so we are saved from the judgment of God.

2. Christians try to live holy lives. As we grow in our faith, we aim to live lives more like Jesus. We aim to be more holy, pure and righteous. But our righteousness can't save us. It is not the reason for our salvation, but it is the grateful response.

PHILIPPIANS 1:18

Why is Paul content with people preaching Christ from false motives when he so clearly condemns false teachers in chapter 3?

Paul's whole life is focused on knowing Christ and making him known. The fact that he is overjoyed at the preaching of Christ by these rivals shows that the gospel they are preaching must be the true one, even if they are doing so out of a personal hostility towards Paul. So the apostle does not really care if he is in prison, or that others have it in for him. He is overjoyed that the gospel is being heard.

PHILIPPIANS 1:19

What is "the help given by the Spirit of Jesus Christ"?

The kind of help Paul received from the Holy Spirit is not explained, but we know from the rest of the Bible that God's Spirit helps us in many ways:

- The Holy Spirit changes us to become more like Jesus (Galatians 5:22-23).

- He helps us to pray (Romans 8:26-27).

- The Holy Spirit helps us to be bold in telling others the good news about Jesus Christ (Acts 4:31).

- He fills us with wisdom and understanding, so that we come to know God better and find out how He wants us to live (Colossians 1:9-10).

Note: You don't need to explain all this to your group but it will help you to have thought about how to explain it.

PHILIPPIANS 1:19

What does Paul mean by "deliverance""?

This cannot mean deliverance from prison, because that would make the sentence contradictory: how could "what has happened to me" (ie: prison) "turn out for my deliverance" (ie: release from prison)? The word translated "deliverance" is "soteria", which is usually translated "salvation".

PHILIPPIANS 1:21

Why does Paul say that dying is "gain"?

We know from the resurrection of Jesus Christ that the future God has for us will be wonderful. No more sin in our lives. No more frustration from living in a world that has rejected God. Now we only understand Christ partly. When we die, we will be with him.

This is the promise of the gospel. Genuine Christianity is not about having a better life now – although Christ does that in many ways through giving us forgiveness, a new hope and a new family. Now, we experience in part – then we'll experience it fully.

PHILIPPIANS 1:21

Paul says that "to live is Christ and to die is gain". Why should we live for Christ? Is this realistic for Christians?

If you have extra time, think about why a disciple tries to live his life for Christ:

- Jesus is the Lord – He deserves to be first.

- Jesus is our rescuer – He has bought our lives at the cost of His own life.

- Jesus is our future – He is the one who guarantees our eternal life.

- If we understand how much we have been forgiven, we will want to serve Christ out of love and thankfulness.

PHILIPPIANS 1:27

What does "worthy of the gospel" mean?

We cannot make ourselves "worthy" to receive the gospel and salvation. Paul means that, having been forgiven by God, we should lives that are consistent with being his people.

PHILIPPIANS 1:27

What does "stand firm in one spirit" mean?

You might find it helpful to use this illustration: Explain that when a lump of coal drops out of a fire or a barbeque, it quickly becomes cold. It only burns and gives off heat when it is in the fire with other pieces of coal. It's the same with Christians. When we are part of a fellowship of believers, encouraging each other and working together, we will work well as disciples. When we stay away and try to do it on our own, we will quickly go cold. We need to look after each other, and try to give the fellowship and encouragement our Christian brothers and sisters need, if they can't meet with others because of illness, travel, or other family commitments.

PHILIPPIANS 1:28

What is the "sign to them that they will be destroyed, but that you will be saved"?

What is this sign? When disciples stick together and support one another in their work for the gospel, it is a sign that they genuinely belong to Christ. It is part of the "fruit of righteousness" (1:11). It is one of the outward signs of the inner change that God is at work in you. It is a sign that you will be saved by God on the day of Christ (1:6, 10) – when everyone in the world will be judged. If someone is opposed to believers, this shows that they are not in Christ. Therefore they will not be saved, but destroyed. This is how Paul himself once was – persecuting Christians! But God saved even him – the "worst" of sinners (1 Timothy 1:15-16).

PHILIPPIANS 2:1

What is "fellowship with the Spirit"?

All believers have received the Holy Spirit and are therefore linked to one another.

PHILIPPIANS 2:10

Why will "every knee" bow to Jesus?

This cannot mean that everyone will one day come to faith. Isaiah 45:22-24 makes clear that although all will bow, those who are rebellious will still "be put to shame" at judgment.

PHILIPPIANS 2:12

What does it mean to "work out your salvation"?

Notice that Paul does not say "work *for* your salvation". Salvation has already been bought by the death of Jesus. Paul's phrase refers to the way in which we live in the light of that salvation.

PHILIPPIANS 2:17

What does Paul mean by "a drink offering on the sacrifice"?

A drink offering is an Old Testament offering (a gift to God) of wine or water. Sometimes in the Old Testament, when animals were sacrificed (killed as a gift to God), a drink offering was poured on top of the sacrifice. Paul is saying that the faith of these Christians and their work for the Lord is like an Old Testament sacrifice. Paul might have to die for the gospel. If this happens, it will be like a drink offering. His life will be given to God with the sacrifice (the faith and work) of the Philippian Christians.

PHILIPPIANS 3:8

Why is something that God originally gave – the law and the Jewish religion – now rubbish?

This is a complex issue that is dealt with in depth in Romans 1 – 11. For now, make the point that the Old Testament law was never meant to be a way of getting right with God, but rather a temporary picture to teach his people how Christ would save us.

Jesus does not abolish the Old Testament; but he does fulfil every bit of it. And he fulfils different parts of it in different ways. For example:

● Sacrifices are no longer necessary, because Jesus is the final sacrifice.

● Food laws are no longer necessary, because Jesus' people are to show they are different by their purity and how they love one another, not by the foods they eat. We do not need to keep the law, because Jesus perfectly kept the law for us.

● By contrast, Jesus deepens the moral requirements of the law – it is not just the act of murder which is wrong, but being angry with your brother. It is not just adultery which is wrong, but lust and impure thoughts.

The key point to make clear is that the Old Testament law is good when it is used for what it was intended for: to show people their need for Christ's sacrifice. When people treat it as a way of salvation, it becomes worse than useless. It is dangerous and a lie.

This is why Paul used such insulting language about those who taught this. They said that people could be saved by works of religion, and this is wrong. Only Christ can save.

PHILIPPIANS 3:10

What does it mean to know Christ?

This is a wonderful mystery. I live in Christ. He lives in me. Knowing Christ better is about experiencing his life as it flows more and more through our life now. This is explained in the three phrases Paul uses to describe what it means to know Christ in verses 10-11: "the power of his resurrection", "the fellowship of sharing in his sufferings" and "becoming like him in death". Being a disciple is a lifelong process of getting to know Christ better. We will never know Christ fully in this world, so we will always need to grow in our faith and understanding. See 1 Corinthians 13:12.

PHILIPPIANS 3:11

Why does Paul say "somehow"?

This is not Paul saying that he has doubts or is uncertain that he will be raised from the dead. He means that the exact way God will do this is unclear to him. It is a wonderful mystery. See 1 Corinthians 15:51.

Why does Paul link "the power of his resurrection", "the fellowship of sharing in his sufferings" and "becoming like him in death" with knowing Christ?

We tend to think that suffering and death are bad, resurrection and life are good. But Paul thinks that all these experiences are good because they help us to know Christ better – which is the greatest thing of all (3:8).

PHILIPPIANS 3:15

Will all mature Christians believe exactly the same things?

Yes – on the important points of the gospel, mature believers will be certain – that it is through faith in Jesus alone that we are saved. **No** – there will always be matters of church tradition and opinion where mature believers will have differing ideas. Encourage young Christians that they should not be troubled when they meet Christians who have different ideas, so long as they are firm on the basics.

PHILIPPIANS 4:7

What is "the peace of God, which transcends all understanding"?

People often read this verse and think that God will give them a feeling of peace. This may be true for some. But it is important to help young Christians understand the role of feelings, and to protect them from putting their trust in feelings rather than the facts. Our feelings may change. The facts of the gospel do not.

- Christians already have peace with God – the peace he has created between us and him through Jesus (Romans 5:1). We were at war because of our sin. Now we are at peace because Jesus has taken the punishment for our sin.

- The fact that we are at peace with God means that we no longer need to be anxious. We can have "feelings of peace" because this peace truly exists.

- The peace we have with God is so wonderful that no one can fully understand or explain it.

- God's peace guards us.

"Transcends" can have a double meaning here. It can mean "beyond" in the sense of "we can't understand it". But it can also mean "better than" in the sense of "it is better than knowing all the answers". There is much we don't know but having peace with God, and so being able to trust him totally, is better than knowing all the answers now.

PHILIPPIANS 4:9

What does Paul mean when he says "the God of peace will be with you"?

The promise of verse 9 is plural – "The God of peace will be with you **all**."

PHILIPPIANS 4:13

Why does Paul say he "can do everything"?

This does not mean God will give us strength to achieve anything we set our minds to doing. Paul knows that God will give us the strength to be content in every circumstance.

What does "credited to your account" mean"?

This does not mean we can attain or earn righteousness ourselves. The phrase carries the idea of "fruit" (as in 1:11) - it is the result of God's work in us after salvation.

Questions about Christian belief

How do you know that God exists?

- There are many philosophical and scientific arguments that you can get involved in that might show that belief in God is rational, even sensible. But these arguments lead to belief in some kind of creator, not specifically to the God of the Bible. It is usually much better to talk about Jesus and his claim to be God.

- We know God exists because He came to earth in Jesus. This is the substance of Jesus' answer to Philip's question in John 14:8-9 (it's worth looking this up and reading it if the question arises).

- "Have you ever seen God?" "No, but I might have if I'd been born at the right time. If I had been alive 2000 years ago, and living in Palestine, I could have seen God."

- Jesus claimed to be God (eg: John 5:18; 20:28-29) and his actions bore out that claim. If you'd been there, you would have seen and heard him.

- Believing in God is not "the easy option". If he is God, then you must serve him as God.

Why should we believe what the Bible says?

- Try not to get involved in defending passages that can be interpreted in a number of different ways. The best place to start is with the reliability of what the Gospels teach about Jesus, and then go on to his teaching and claims on our lives.

- Historical evidence in the New Testament is confirmed at a number of points by non-Christian writers – eg: Tacitus and Josephus – and also by archaeological evidence.

- The New Testament documents were written soon after the events they describe.

- This New Testament documentation is extensive, coming from as many as ten authors, eight of whom wrote independently of each other.

- The documents are historical in character as well as theological. They contain many verifiable details of the time and culture in which they were written.

- The text of these documents has come down to us intact from the era in which it was written.

- The writers were people who suffered and died for what they believed, and were also of very high moral standing. They believed in telling the truth. It is highly unlikely they would make up these stories, or even "imagine" them.

- The Gospels are less than complimentary to the disciples who wrote them – another sign that they were not made up.

- We have good historical reasons for trusting that what we read in the Gospels is an accurate account of what Jesus did, said and claimed for himself.

Don't all good people go to heaven?

- What is "good"? How "good" is good enough?

- Some of us are better than others but no one meets God's standards (see Romans 3:23).

- We are not good, because our hearts are "sin factories" (Mark 7:21-22).

- People who rely on their goodness are deluded (Mark 10:17-22). There is always more we must do. We need rescuing.

- God is after friends, not "good" rebels. The issue is whose side you are on.

- The opposite is, in fact, true. Good people go to hell; bad people go to heaven. Those who think they are good and rely on that will be lost. Only those who know they are lost are able to receive forgiveness and eternal life from Christ.

Why would a good God send people to hell?

- God is utterly holy and good. His character is what decides right and wrong in the universe.

- God must judge everyone. He will judge fairly and well.

- Jesus is the most loving person who ever lived, but it is he who teaches most about the reality of hell. He does so because he knows it is real, and doesn't want us to suffer the inevitable consequences of our rebellion against God.

- Heaven and hell are defined by relationship. Heaven is enjoying all the good gifts of our Father God, and being with him. Hell is the absence of his blessings – friendship, love, beauty etc.

- God has judged his Son, Jesus, on the cross. He went through hell, so we don't have to!

- If we understood how holy God is, we would be asking the opposite question: How can God allow anyone into heaven?

If God forgives everything, does that mean I can do what I like?

- God's grace is utterly free. Shockingly, he will save even the worst kind of criminals you can think of.

- Jesus saved a condemned thief who died on the cross next to him!

- If we properly understand how sinful we are, and how our sins have, literally, wounded God; and if we understand how amazing it is that Jesus died for us when we don't deserve it – then we want to live in a way that pleases him.

How can we be sure that there is life after death?

- People may come up with strange stories about "out-of-body experiences" but these prove nothing, and can lead to confusion.

- The Bible says that Jesus' resurrection is the pattern for our own resurrection (eg: 1 Corinthians 15:20).

- Who do you trust for accurate information about life beyond the grave? The person who has been there and come back.

If Jesus has been raised from the dead, then we will certainly be raised from the dead, and we must look to Jesus' teaching for answers to the questions about what life beyond death will be like.

What about other religions?

Sincerity is not truth. People can be sincerely wrong.

If the different religions contradict each other (which they do at several major points), they cannot all be right.

The question really is: Has God revealed himself, and if so, how? Jesus claimed to be the unique revelation of God. He claimed to be God in the flesh. Are his claims valid? If Jesus is God, the other religions are wrong.

Jesus claims he is the only way: John 14:6.

Religions can do many good things – provide comfort, help, social bonding etc. But they are manmade ideas about God, and generally teach that we must DO something to get right with God.

Jesus claims that his teaching is revealed from God (John 8:28), and that his followers must abandon what they think they can DO, and rely on what he has DONE on the cross to bring forgiveness and new life to them.

What about those who have never heard about Jesus?

We can trust God to be just; he will judge people according to their response to what they know.

Everyone has received some revelation, even if only from the created world (see Romans 1:18-19).

Those who have had more revealed to them will be held responsible (Matthew 11:20-24).

You have heard – so you must do something about it – and leave the others to God, who will treat them fairly.

Isn't faith just a psychological crutch?

There are different questions here, like: Do I just believe because my parents were Christians? Or: Do I believe because I have the need for some comfort from above? Or: Do I believe because I have had this or that experience?

If our faith is based purely on experience ("Christianity works for me"), then there is no way of arguing against this objection. It might work because it's true or because of my particular upbringing or conditioning.

However, Christianity is based on objective historical events (the death and resurrection of Jesus), and invites people to investigate and test them. The truth of Christianity has nothing to do with our state of mind.

The same could be applied to any belief – including atheism! (ie: I'm an atheist because my parents were; I have a deep need to be independent; I have had no experience.) None of this helps to establish whether belief in Christianity is based on truth or error.

Why does God allow suffering?

- We can't know for sure why God allowed evil into the world.

- Much suffering is a direct result of our own sinfulness (eg: that caused by drunkenness, greed, lust, etc.).

- But some is not (see John 9:1-2).

- All suffering results from the fallen nature of our world (see Romans 8:18-25).

- God uses suffering to discipline and strengthen his children (see Hebrews 12:7-11; Romans 5:3-5).

- God also uses suffering to awaken people to understand that there is a judgment coming to our pain-filled world (Luke 13:1-5).

- God knows our pain. He has done something about our suffering. Jesus suffered and died so that we could be forgiven and become part of the "new creation", where there will be no suffering. Jesus' death for us is the undeniable proof that God loves us.

Hasn't science disproved Christianity?

- Most people mean: "Hasn't the theory of evolution replaced creation and so disproved Christianity?" People usually are not talking about archaeology which, incidentally, backs up the Bible at almost every point.

- Start by asking what they mean by the question. They may have some specific point that needs addressing and that will require some research.

- Avoid having a technical discussion about evolution, carbon dating etc.

- Ask what conclusion they are drawing from evolution. It may be a description of how life has appeared on earth (although you may want to dispute that!). But it does not answer the bigger questions: Who produced the amazing design and order that we see in the universe? For what purpose does the universe exist?

- Did the world come into being by chance? How God made the universe is not as important a point as that he made it.

- Steer the conversation towards talking about God's existence (see above) and towards Jesus. If Jesus is God, it puts the creation/evolution debate in a completely different perspective.

If Jesus is God's Son, how can he be God too?

- Jesus describes himself as the "Son of God" – a term which can mean that he is the King of God's people, but can also be a claim that he is much more.

- Jesus acts as God does in the Old Testament. He speaks as God speaks, and does things that only God can do (raises the dead, forgives sins, controls nature, etc.). His words and actions show that he is making a claim to be God.

- Christians do not believe that there are many Gods, and that Jesus is just one of them. Christians believe that there is one God – who is a trinity. One God, three persons – the Father, the Son and the Holy Spirit, in a relationship of love and service with each other.

- This is complex and hard to completely understand – but why would we expect to fully understand God anyway?

Why does God hate sex?

- He doesn't. He invented it and thinks it is beautiful, wonderful and powerful.

- God knows best how we work, and his pattern for sex – between a man and a woman in a committed, lifelong marriage – is the way he designed it to work best.

- Sex joins people together in a way that is more than physical. If we use sex in other ways, we will inevitably damage our ability to enjoy sex in the way it was intended.

- It may not appear damaging to enjoy this gift in other ways, but we must trust our Maker that it is.

Christians are hypocrites – so how can Christianity be true?

- The failure of many Christians to live according to their stated beliefs does not invalidate Jesus' claims to be God.

- The Bible says that Jesus alone is perfect, and it is honest about the failures and weakness of his followers. The disciples were constantly making mistakes.

- Jesus taught that there will always be false teachers and fakes (Mark 13:21-22) who pretend they are Christians but who are not. This is true today.

- Everyone is a hypocrite in some sense. But Jesus calls those who follow him to change and grow more like him. Don't be discouraged if you have met some Christians who are not yet perfect. They never will be this side of eternity.

The background to Philippians

This is a copy of the notes found on page 79 of the participants' Handbook.

Philippians is a letter from the New Testament. It was written by Paul to a group of Christians living in the city of Philippi, a Roman colony in ancient Greece.

Paul and Timothy visited Philippi to tell people about Jesus (see Acts 16:11-40). They were forced to leave after a short time because the city rulers did not want them to cause any trouble. They left behind them a small group of new Christians. Paul wrote this letter to them from prison in Rome. He wanted to:

⊖ encourage the new Christians in Philippi

⊖ help them keep going as Christians in difficult times

⊖ remind them about the good news of Jesus Christ

⊖ give them practical instructions on what it means to live as a follower of Christ. That is what "disciple" means – a learner, a follower.

You may have recently made a decision to become a Christian. You may be still thinking about what it means to follow Jesus. Or you may be someone who has been a Christian for years, and you want to go over the basics once again.

Whoever you are, this short letter will help you understand how good it is to be a follower of Jesus Christ, and how he calls his disciples to live for him today.

WHO WAS PAUL?

Paul was originally called Saul. As a devoted Jew, he hated the first Jewish Christians and put many of them in prison. But while travelling to Damascus, he was stopped by a bright light and heard Jesus Christ speaking to him (Acts 9). This experience changed Paul completely. He became a Christian and was sent by Jesus to be a teacher and leader.

Paul travelled a lot around southern Europe and Asia, telling others about Jesus Christ. He organised the new disciples into churches, and wrote letters to them, teaching them and encouraging them to keep going. He was often persecuted himself, and was eventually executed by the Romans.

Many of Paul's letters are now in the New Testament. Philippians is one of them.

Map

🔹 *This map is included on page 80 of the group member's Handbook.*

MACEDONIA
(Greece)

Rome

GALATIA
(Turkey)

Athens

ISRAEL

THE GREAT SEA
(Mediterranean Sea)

Jerusalem

EGYPT

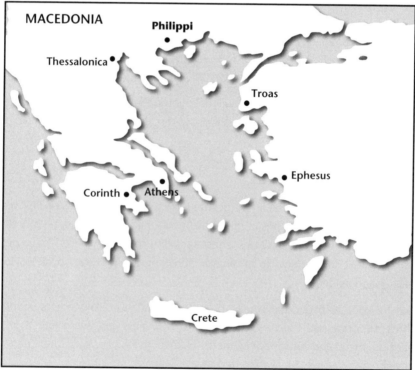

MACEDONIA

Philippi

Thessalonica

Troas

Ephesus

Corinth • Athens

Crete

Acknowledgements…

This second edition of the *Discipleship Explored* material builds on the original course material from the first edition, and the *Discipleship Explored* DVD scripts written by Barry Cooper.

The first edition was developed by Barry Cooper, Rupert Higgins, Sam Shammas and Katy Walton.

Literally hundreds of people have helped shape *Discipleship Explored*, not least through the great feedback we have had from leaders and guests who have used the course, and have been kind enough to give us their comments.

Special thanks to: Nicole Carter, Barry Cooper, Alison Mitchell, Tim Thornborough and Anne Woodcock.

Designs by Steve Devane and André Parker.

Christianity Explored Ministries (CEM) aims to provide Christian churches and organisations worldwide with resources which explain the Christian faith clearly and relevantly from the Bible. CEM receives royalties from the sale of these resources, but is reliant on donations for the majority of its income. CEM is registered for charitable purposes in both the United Kingdom and the USA.
www.ceministries.org

Keep on exploring...
www.christianityexplored.org

The *Christianity Explored* website helps non-Christians to explore Jesus' life and message in their own way and in their own time. It is equally useful for those thinking about coming on a course, and those who are going through *Christianity Explored*. It features:

• a visual outline explaining the gospel message, based on the Gospel of Mark

• real-life stories from people who've become Christians

• information about the *Christianity Explored* course

• short videos answering tough questions. These include:

> *You can't trust the Bible, can you?*
> *Hasn't science shown that Christianity is wrong?*
> *If there is a God, why does he allow suffering?*
> *Wasn't Jesus just a great teacher?*
> *Why bother with church?*
> *Isn't believing in the resurrection ridiculous?*
> *How can a loving God send anyone to hell?*
> *Why are Christians so old-fashioned about sex?*
> *Surely it's arrogant to say your religion is the only right one?*
> *Doesn't becoming a Christian mean becoming boring?*

Supporting downloads available from www.ceministries.org/de

Talk outlines – Copies of the talks for the eight main sessions are available as both pdfs and in Word format, so that you can personalise each talk with your own illustrations etc.

Feedback forms – You may find it helpful to use a feedback form at the end of the course, both to find out how helpful the course was and also to discover what your group members would like to do next. A sample form is available on the website in a variety of designs and sizes. There is also a feedback form that you can give to leaders to get their comments and any suggestions for improvements.

***Discipleship Explored* DVD trailers** – If you are going to show the *Discipleship Explored* DVD during each session, then you may like to use a trailer as a way of inviting people to join. These can be downloaded from the website.

Logos for your own invitations – If you are going to create your own printed invitations to the course, you can download copies of the *Discipleship Explored* logo, which is available in a number of formats.

Other recommended resources – Looking for something to help you or a course member with a particular issue? You'll find a huge range of recommendations, information and ideas on the website.

Evangelistic website – you may find it helpful to also look at *Christianity Explored's* other website, which is designed for non-Christians. This includes testimonies, video clips of answers to common questions, and an outline of the gospel message. The web address is **www.christianityexplored.org**